A FLIGHT OF CHARIOTS

*"The use of books for pleasure is the most
satisfactory recreation."*—VISCOUNT GREY

A FLIGHT OF CHARIOTS

*

JON CLEARY

THE COMPANION BOOK CLUB
LONDON

This edition is issued by arrangement with
William Collins, Sons & Co. Ltd., London.

Made and printed in Great Britain
for the Companion Book Club (Odhams Books Ltd.)
by Odhams (Watford) Limited,
Watford, Herts.
S.665.UC.

To Sam

WHO LAUNCHED THE IDEA

CHAPTER ONE

THEY closed the hatch and that was the beginning of the real loneliness. Solitude was a state of mind, one of the doctors had told him, and had quoted Byron: *In solitude, where we are least alone.* But neither the doctor nor Byron had ever known the loneliness of space, the solitude of the stars. He was neither poet nor psychologist, but perhaps by this time Thursday he would be able to add to the medium of each.

They had called him at one o'clock that morning, just over five hours ago. He had gone to bed at nine last night, weakly joking that he had "a long day ahead of me tomorrow." It had taken him at least half an hour to fall asleep and then he had woken again just after midnight. There had been no nightmare nor sudden panic bell in his sleep; he had come awake without fright and as naturally as if this were just another routine day. He had got up and gone to the window. The February night was cold and he wondered if they were burning the smudge-pots over in the citrus groves to keep the frost away. Down in Miami the vacationing Northerners would welcome the cold; their women would not now have to invent excuses for bringing their furs to Florida. He could not see them, but he knew there would be fires along Cocoa Beach, with early watchers huddled about them, putting up with the discomfort of the long cold wait so they could say they had seen yet another man shot into space. He knew there were regulars, people who had watched every launching since that of Alan Shepard, veterans who could tell whether a launching was good or bad almost as soon as the technicians at the control panels in the central blockhouse. They were out there now waiting for *him*, and it chilled him to wonder how many of them had been drawn there by a morbid urge for disaster.

He twisted his head, looking for the stars, but the glare of lights outside the hangar made it impossible to distinguish them. But he knew they were there, and they, too, were waiting for him.

He went back to bed, but sleep had gone for the night. He lay quietly on the cot, staring at the ocean-dark ceiling above him, surrounded by the noises outside in the hangar that brushed against his inattentive ear like the rumblings of prowling beasts.

He could feel the fear moving inside him, his own internal beast; he was not unconfident, but he knew he would be lying if he said he was unafraid. Poets could shout their welcome of death, but he did not feel that way. Life still had its hold on him and he on it. He had prayed last night for a safe return, but the desire for survival was something in the blood that went back long before the mind had invented prayer. This that he felt now was something he shared with the most primitive anthropoid in history. This morning he would be shooting for the stars, the human symbol of man's most advanced technological accomplishment, but some of the slime of creation still clung to him. Fear was the other side of the coin of imagination, the primeval heritage that no amount of intelligence could ever deny.

Then at one o'clock there was the tap on the door of his room. He lay for a moment before answering, not wanting them to think he had been waiting for them. *How we struggle to keep up appearances*, he thought, angry at himself for the deception; *what am I trying to prove?* When he did answer them, his voice was sharp, and he knew they would go away thinking to themselves: *He's on edge, he's feeling the strain.*

They left him alone while he shaved, showered and dressed. He had done the same thing for Rupert Meredith, when he had been the latter's back-up pilot. It was understood, without anyone's ever having mentioned it, that a man was entitled to some privacy at the beginning of what might be his last day on earth. Some men might want to pray; even the unbelievers must have something on which they wanted to meditate. He looked at himself closely in the mirror to see if any signs of strain showed in his face, saw none and wondered how he could be such a good actor. Then he pulled on a jacket and went out to have breakfast with his back-up pilot, George Raccoli, and the chief aeromedical adviser, Oliver Shor. He just hoped that his stomach would accept the food he was going to force into it.

"How's the weather?"

"Perfect all the way." Raccoli was ebullient even at half past one in the morning. It was hard to take, but you couldn't be sour about it. "The waiting's over, feller."

"I hope when it's your turn there's no delay. Ten days is too long to hang around."

"How do you feel?" Shor was an expert at the casually toned question. He was a big sleepy-looking man who, in his white coveralls, could pass for a collapsed parachute. Around the base he always wore coveralls, as if wearing a shirt and slacks was a

8

concession to the formality he hated; visitors were always mistaking him for a mechanic or wash-room orderly, a mistake he enjoyed. But he knew his job and the pilots had complete confidence in him.

"I'm okay. I'm glad the waiting's over, if that's what you mean. Who wouldn't be?" He was aware of Shor watching him carefully from beneath the thick shaggy eyebrows, but he made no attempt to overplay his unconcern. He sat down at the table and looked down at the plate of steak and eggs. "I must tell the Aussies when I pass over Muchea that I had their national dish for breakfast."

"Don't start any international incidents." Raccoli was a small man, the smallest in the team, and the most talkative. It was not nervousness that made him so garrulous; it was rumoured he had been born talking and had never got out of the habit. He knew his fault, but as he pointed out to the other pilots, they should meet his mother and father back in Philadelphia: they were *real* talkers, of Neapolitan championship class. "When I get up there I'm gonna be pals with everyone all the way along the route. I'm learning verbatim the national anthems of every one of those new African nations. You never know where you're gonna have to come down. What d'you say, doc?"

The small talk went on, the confetti of a carnival that was slowly but surely getting under way, and all the time he was aware of Shor and his dark sleepy eyes that missed nothing. He was glad when Bruce Blair, another of the pilots, and Joe Nebbia, one of the public affairs officers, came in, bringing with them some of the distraction from outside. The more people around him, the better he felt. It was some sort of camouflage.

"Do you want to call your wife?" Nebbia said. "I'll have them book the call."

He shook his head. "I called her last night. That will do till I get back."

Nobody pressed the point: they all understood how it was. Each man had his own way of saying farewell; good-byes were as personal as love-making. He had sent his love over the wire to her last night, and anything he said this morning would only be stale. He had learned long ago that nothing was as unsatisfying as the echo of love. He would call her Thursday, when he came back, and it would be the beginning of a new life for them.

An hour later it was time for his final medical examination. The doctors checked him and passed him. It was only a formality and they all knew it; if there had been anything physically wrong

9

with him they would have discovered it long before this. He lay on the table and once again he had the feeling of detachment from his body; it no longer belonged to him but to this team of doctors. They worked over it with the same impersonal thoroughness as the technicians would now be working over the rocket and capsule out on the pad. His body and the rocket and capsule had that similarity: each was a mechanism brought to as close a point of perfection as possible. His mind would be the one unknown quantity on the flight. The doctors had done their best to check that, too, but it would never completely divulge all its secrets.

Shor was still watching him and he began to feel uneasy. He wondered how the others had felt under Shor's searching gaze; then he remembered that Shor had been exactly like this with Rupe Meredith. So Shor didn't really suspect any weakness; he was just doing his usual thorough job. He suddenly smiled at the big doctor and felt a sudden warmth for Shor when the latter winked back. All these men were here working for *him*, and if they were over-attentive it was because they cared for his safety. He looked about the crowded, brightly-lit room and all at once felt the weight of responsibility that was his. He had thought about it and discussed it once or twice with the other pilots; but now suddenly it was a reality and he shrank under the weight of it. It was as if he were carrying the whole of the United States, all of America's prestige, on his back. Had Shepard and the others felt like this? And Gagarin and the other Russians— had they felt that they were carrying Russia on their backs? He smiled to himself, thinking how unfortunate were today's explorers who did their exploring in the glare of publicity, who were sent out as much for national prestige as for material or scientific gain. It went against the grain of his lifetime's teaching, but maybe the Russians had something in their secrecy. There was no propaganda value in failure. He wondered if Columbus would have set sail if there had been television cameras on the dock at Palos. But of course he would have: Columbus was a man who knew the value of propaganda.

Then they taped on the sensors, making the usual indecent jokes as they fitted the small pads to the various parts of his body, and at last he was struggling into his pressure suit. The bright lights of the room threw up a glare from the aluminised exterior of the suit, and he shut his eyes for a moment. "Okay?" he heard Shor ask, and he opened his eyes quickly and grinned, a little too brightly.

"This is a pretty sharp suit," he said. "I think I'll get me a couple."

"There's a nifty hat goes with it." Raccoli handed him his helmet. "Twenty-two-fifty the lot, and we throw in an extra pair of pants."

"Can I bring it back if I'm not satisfied?"

"Mister, the customer is always right in this joint."

None of the jokes was ever very good at a time like this. He remembered the corn that had sprayed the air before his first sortie of World War Two and again in the Korean War. Perhaps it was just as well that nothing really funny was being said; he was now too tightly wound up to let himself go with a real belly laugh. They handed him his portable air conditioner to cool the interior of his suit, plugged it in, and then he was ready to go. He stood up and was glad to feel that his legs were not weak. He knew now that he could make it.

Accompanied by Raccoli, Shor and Nebbia, he walked out of the room and out through the huge hangar to the waiting van outside. The cavern of the hangar echoed with the shouts of the men as they wished him good luck, a surf of prayer for his return. He was aware of their voices as one chorus, their faces as a blur of smiles; for months he had known many of them by name, but this morning they were as anonymous as the nebulae beyond the stars. For the first time he began to feel the loneliness closing in around him.

He got into the van and settled back in one of the chairs. He felt an unaccustomed awkwardness in his pressure suit, as if he had put on someone else's by mistake. Then he realized the fault lay with himself: his whole body was stiff. He made a conscious effort to relax, and once more saw Shor looking at him. He could feel himself growing warm within the suit and he flipped the switch on his air conditioner. All the men had now stopped talking, even Raccoli, and the van was a silent room speeding down the road to the launching pad.

Then the van came to a halt and a moment later he was clambering down the steps into the open. The chill of the morning air brushed his face, somehow comforting. He blinked in the glare of several photographers' flashes, then he smiled broadly at no one in particular. He felt like a film star at some premiere, and he found some small amusement in the thought; a measure of relaxation came back into his body and, still smiling, he walked towards the gantry elevator. He was committed now, it was too late to back out. Whatever was going to happen to him, nothing would be lost by putting on a good face. At the moment he slid into the capsule he would become an international figure, and face was everything on the international scene. He wore the face of America this morning, the land of the brave and the free. He felt neither brave nor free. He could back out, he knew; no one would force him to go if his nerve suddenly went even at the last moment. But with his volunteering, he had sacrificed his freedom, he had become a slave to national prestige. He felt pride in what he was about to do, but pride had never been a real antidote for fear.

As he rode up in the elevator he looked out at the Cape. The whole scene had the improbability of a dream, and he looked at it with a sort of desperate thoroughness, trying to stamp it indelibly on his memory. If he should die within the next few hours, this would be his last close look at the world; it was not what he would have wished for his last view, not a memory to take into eternity, but it was something. There was another Cape he would have wished to remember, but that was too far back in time now, lost in mists as thick as those rising from the vents where the liquid oxygen was escaping. This was the world he had known for the last three years and, for better or worse, this was the memory he must take with him.

"Do you have a sense of history, doc?"

Shor looked at him. "In what way? This is historic, if that's what you mean."

He shook his head, rising slowly in the elevator towards his own moment in history. "No, I don't mean it that way. No, out there——" He waved to the darkness beyond the glare of the base. Florida lay there, a state with two histories, that of the tabloid sheets and that of the history books. "I just wonder if Ponce de Leon had any vision of the future when he landed here."

Shor was a man of imagination: it was one of the reasons he had been chosen for this job. "I'm sure he knew that every day was a new beginning to history, even if there's no ending to the past. It's like new shoots on a tree."

"That's how I feel. Especially about there being no ending to the past. I could get a swelled head about all this——" He gestured at the suit and helmet, the uniform of his achievement. "Then it comes home to me that I'm only a link in a chain. And a pretty small link at that. Ten thousand people have worked to get this thing into space." He looked out at the shape of the rocket, still caged in the red framework of the gantry.

"How many other explorers had so many working for them?"

"That's what I've liked about all you guys in the team. You're all different, but you all brought with you one common quality—humility."

"It's not a quality that's difficult to cultivate, doc. Not if you have a sense of perspective."

"Sure. And how many of us have that?"

He turned away, knowing one man who had not had a sense of perspective, who, across at Muchea on the other side of the world, sat behind a mask of self-delusion. He knew that Shor was thinking of that man, but now was not the time to discuss him. He looked out of the elevator, concentrating again on the physical scene, narrowing his own sense of perspective. Below him he could see the vapour from the lox fuel lines, rising like witch mist out of the concrete apron. Workers, like toadstools in their helmets and white suits when viewed from above, stood by the foot of the gantry. Beyond the apron he could see the service towers lining ICBM Road, gleaming in the pre-dawn darkness like giant flowering trees of a mechanical world. Searchlights, as tentative in their searching as an old lady's fingers, swept the lower sky. Light was the keynote of the whole scene; it blazed and stabbed at him from every angle. There was a certain terrifying aspect to it all, as if all the lights were rising notes to the final crescendo that would be the explosion that would send him hurtling into space. There was sound to the scene: the shrieking of the pipes and tubing as they took liquid oxygen, the cold clang of metal against metal, the disembodied voices of the men hidden in the vapour, somewhere a siren wailing like a scream of despair. But it was the eye that held the terror, that could paralyse the mind. He turned away as the elevator slid gently to a halt.

"It's a wonderful sight, isn't it?" Shor spread a bear's paw towards the scene below. "I find it sort of comforting."

"How come?"

Shor shrugged, a movement that suggested he had broken a collarbone. "I don't know. I guess it sort of epitomizes all the preparation that has gone into this. Nothing has been over-looked—everything down there stands for a test of some sort, a check towards perfection. This isn't a pinch-penny operation, as some of our esteemed Congressmen would like to have made it at the start."

For the first time he laughed easily. Shor was not looking for flaws in him; indeed, he was trying, almost too hard, to reassure him. "That's an understatement, doc. One of your best. How many billions has this project cost so far?"

Shor grinned, showing his buck teeth. "Any figure that has more than five zeros in it is beyond me. I'm still a country G.P. at heart, just like my old man. But don't give me away. I like the money they pay me here."

"Your secret's safe," he said, and wondered how safe was his own secret. The beast of fear had begun to gnaw at him.

He stepped out of the elevator on to the platform that ran round the top of the gantry. It was crowded with technicians and for a moment he felt like an intruder. Then everyone turned towards him, and once more there was the feeling of committal, of not turning back: he was the guest of honour. He nodded and spoke to some of the men, walked round the capsule in its green plastic wrappings, then stood to one side, leaning against a window of the gantry penthouse. The men went back to their checking and re-checking, looking like surgeons in their white coveralls but for the NASA emblem on their backs. George Raccoli came and stood beside him.

"How do you feel?" Raccoli's voice was low, almost gentle; he was no longer the talkative joker. "Or should I shut my big mouth and not ask?"

"No, it's all right, George. I'm a bit fluttery, I'll admit. It's been a damned long wait."

"Yeah, sometimes I wish I'd been the first. Not for the glory, although that would've been okay. I'm a show-off and I can take any amount of cheering they want to give me." Part of Raccoli's charm was his frankness; who else in the team would confess to being a glory-chaser? "No, I'd liked to have been among the first to go because at least those guys have it behind them now. I'm not scared——" He stopped, then he went on: "Well, no, that's a lie. I *am* scared. But not so much that I don't want to go. But it's like everything else you've never done before—you just wish it was behind you. I felt like this 'way back when I did my first solo, back in '47. After it was all over I wondered what all the fuss has been about."

"I'll be telling you that same thing Thursday."

Raccoli grinned. "Yeah. But I'm gonna be the last to go. Who'm I gonna tell?"

"Your grandkids. You can tell them when you're going on vacation with them to the moon."

"Not me, boyo. I'm gonna spend my old age in comfort on Mother Earth. Who needs the moon?"

Then it was time for him to get into the capsule. They placed the steps beside the hatch and he mounted them; carefully he swung over the lip of the hatch and lowered himself into the capsule. There was no room to spare; the cabin of the capsule fitted him like an outer suit. He settled down into the contour seat.

Raccoli had already checked everything in the cockpit; he himself had done the same thing when he had been back-up man for Rupe Meredith. Nonetheless he went over everything again; he remembered that Meredith had done exactly the same. It was not that you distrusted your back-up man; it just gave you something to do. He went through the whole routine that he knew by heart; the complex panel before him was now no more than a simple alphabet to the success of his mission. He checked the small mirrors on his wrists and chest that would enable him to see anywhere within the cockpit with a minimum of movement; he flashed the tiny lights in the fingertips of his gloves that would help him in the periods of darkness during the flight. Then finally, as if to convince himself that it was only an afterthought, he checked the button set in the arm-rest of his couch. It was the button that would fire the escape rocket which would blast the capsule free if something went wrong on the launching pad. It was comforting, to a degree, to know it was there. That it had never been used, had never been tested on an actual launching, did not lessen the comfort it gave. When the final moment came, he might grasp at any straw of escape.

All his straps had been tightened, the last connections made into his suit. Now that he was in the capsule he felt more relaxed than at any time since he had risen this morning. He was constricted to a point where any normal man would have felt imprisoned. But over the past couple of years he had learned to live within the stifling confines of mock-up capsules; in a way this real thing was less confining because it gave a feeling of being alive around him. He looked up at the small clock and knew it was time.

"Good luck, boyo." Raccoli poked his head in through the hatch entry. "See you Thursday."

Then the hatch was closed and he was alone. For a moment he felt a chill of terror: he was the only man left alive in the whole universe. Then the feeling was gone, the training of the past three years asserted itself. He began going through the check-off lists again. He worked steadily and without haste; gradually the tension began to flow out of him. Men were still working on the gallery outside the capsule, but he ignored them; once or twice men stopped and looked in at him through the other end of the periscope viewer, but he didn't return their gaze. He had said his farewells and now all he wanted was to be on his way.

Twenty minutes after they had closed the hatch, the gantry rolled back and it seemed that the whole of the base then came into view in the periscope. He saw the crowd of workers now beginning to thin out below, moving away at a safe distance from the blast-off. Trucks were starting up and driving off, cars were pulling away from the blockhouse some three hundred yards away. He could recognize no one, everyone was a stranger at this distance, and again the sense of loneliness stabbed at him. Then the sun came up out of the sea right into the eye of the periscope, and the Cape and the world were gone in a blaze of red.

The countdown went on. He could hear the comments over his earphones of the men in the blockhouse; there were no queries, this was going to be a straight shoot. The inertial guidance system began to hum; there was a hiss as the pressurization gas was forced into the capsule. He sucked on the oxygen flowing into his helmet. He could feel his heart beginning to beat a little faster, and he knew that it would show on the medical panel in the control centre. His reaction was now being recorded: his pulse rate, his blood pressure, the quickening change of his whole basic metabolism. If a picture could be drawn of fear, it was being drawn now. He had no secret left.

"T minus 35 seconds—and counting!"

Through the periscope he saw the umbilical connection, his last link with the power and air feeders on the ground, fall away, writhing for a moment like limbs cut from a dying creature. The periscope came down, was covered, and his view of the outside was gone. He would see nothing more of the world till he was in space. He lay farther back in his seat, bracing himself and yet trying not to be too stiff and unyielding to the shock that was coming. One hand was on a stopwatch, ready to start it at the moment of lift-off, and the other was on the escape button. He said a quick prayer, then suddenly relaxed, not with a sense of faith but with a sense of hopelessness, of utter resignation. The suicide that was in every man took over for the moment: now he understood why the poets shouted their welcome of death: this was the real escape and he didn't need the button. Then in the final moment, in the last seconds of the countdown, the primitive in him came back: the urge to survive was too strong to be denied.

His hand went back to the button, but it was already too late: "Five-four-three-two-one-*zero*!"

16

CHAPTER TWO

THE summer was moving south, taking the green of the world with it, taking the visitors too. In another month Cape Cod would belong once more to its natives, they could take up the nine months of the year that belonged to them. The storekeepers and realty men would complain about the lean months ahead, but very few of them ever left the Cape in the wake of the visitors. If you were born on the Cape, your footprints were marked in its sands forever. That was what the old-timers said, but John Dalmead had never believed them.

He turned off the radio when he heard his mother coming up the stairs. Artie Shaw had been half-way through "Begin The Beguine." The big numbers that summer were things like "A Nightingale Sang In Berkeley Square," but he had never gone for schmaltzy pop numbers; if he had to listen to pop music he preferred to hear it played by real musicians like Shaw. He took up the melody at the point where he had left Shaw, whistling softly as he took his swimming trunks from the old cedar closet beside his bed. He felt nervous, but he knew he had to go through with it. Better now than later.

His mother knocked on the door. "You ready, John?"

"Come in, Mom."

She opened the door and came into the room, dressed in black as she always was on Sundays: going to Mass was a solemn occasion, not a dress parade as some people seemed to think. Julia Dalmead had once been a very pretty woman; traces of beauty still were smudged there in her features. She reminded John of a portrait that had been painted over by an artist whose talent had gone downhill as his confidence had decreased. Julia continually wore a frown, spoiling the eyes that had once been beautiful: she suspected the world, was afraid of it. Pessimism had become a drug with her. "Hurry, John, or we'll never get a seat. You know what it's like on summer Sundays——" For years, each summer Sunday, she had been saying the same thing. John had come to wonder if getting a seat in church meant more to her than actually attending Mass. "You're not even dressed!"

"No, Mom. I'm going swimming instead."

"Did you go to early Mass? No, of course you didn't. I'd have known, I've been up since seven. Come on, John, hurry. Your father is already getting the car out——"

"I'm not going, Mom."

The frown deepened, but there was no look of shock on her

17

face: she had been waiting years for the world to slap her in the face. "I don't understand. Is something wrong? All yesterday you were quiet——"

"Nothing's wrong, Mom. Or yes, maybe it is." He dropped the swimming trunks on his bed and turned to look at her squarely. "I've finished with church, Mom. I'm not going again, ever."

She stared at him, trying to comprehend what he had said, as if he had spoken in some foreign language she had never heard before. She had never fully understood him, but now suddenly he had become a stranger. She looked about the room, as if seeking some means of identifying him. But even the room did not help her much; it too had its strangeness. She stared at the photos pinned to the walls: men in baseball uniforms, with names that meant nothing to her, Jimmy Fox, Ted Williams; athletes in full stride, Jessie Owens, Harold Davis. Sport had never meant anything to her, not even when her husband had come home boasting quietly that they had a son who was a high school star at both baseball and track. She had been born here on the Cape, but she would never be an American; the regret her mother and father had felt at leaving Oporto had been passed on to her; she had never seen Portugal, but she would always be Portuguese. She looked back at her American son.

"You are talking foolish, John. You don't say things like that on the spur of the moment."

"This isn't something I'm saying on the spur of the moment, Mom. I've thought about it for months, years even." He moved about the room, restless with the pent-up disbelief of months, restless in his desire to avoid hurting her too much. He saw the saccharine picture of the Virgin and Child on the wall opposite the sports stars; he should have taken that down last night. To take it down now in front of his mother would only be an insult, like spitting at her. "I don't believe in God any more, Mom."

There was shock on her face now; even to his own ears it sounded melodramatic and profane. "You don't know what you're saying!"

"But I do, Mom! I know it's wrong by you. But it's not by me. I just don't believe in Him any more, that's all."

"*That's all?*" Her voice cracked. "John, what's got into you? Who've you been talking to? Have you met someone from outside?" She always referred to the rest of the United States as *outside*. In her forty years of living she had never been off the Cape, not even to Boston.

He shook his head. "Mom, that's why I'm telling you now

18

how I feel. I could have waited till I'd gone to college, written you from there, but I knew what you'd say—that I'd been talking to someone, that some outsider had influenced me. But they haven't! I've made up my own mind about this."

"Made up your own mind! You're only eighteen. How can you make up your mind about anything?"

Against his will, he lost his temper. "God damn it, you made up your mind about Pop when you were eighteen—you married him! Pete made up his mind at eighteen—he went off to be a priest. Did you question him?"

"Don't argue with me!"

He got his temper back under control. He could feel his lips quivering, almost as if he wanted to cry. "Mom, I don't want to argue with you. Believe me, that's the last thing I want. But I'm not going to church. I've been for the last time."

She stared at him for a moment, the frown deep enough now to be a wound across her brows. The hurt was spreading across her face now, like blood; he turned away, unable to bear watching it. She stood behind him, breathing heavily, then he heard her turn and go out of the room. He picked up the swimming trunks, looked at them, then flung them down on the bed again. He sat down on the bed and waited, his lips still quivering, his hands shaking, full of doubts now but committed, unable to turn back. Then he heard the screen door slam and a moment later his father's heavy tread coming up the stairs. The first of the arguments was about to begin: his father would be followed by the parish priest, by his own brother Pete: they would all be intent on saving him from self-destruction. Perhaps he should have waited till he had gone to college: there was no reward for the honesty of the unbeliever.

"There's some trouble, Duke?" It was the nickname he had had all through high school, ever since the day he had tried to claim descent from de Almeida, the Portuguese viceroy in sixteenth century India. It was his father who, in his gentle romancing, had encouraged him in the claim, pointing out that the name had been slowly Anglicized over the hundred years since the first de Almeida had landed on the Cape. Both he and his father liked the nickname: it would be a good name for a major league ball-player or a national track champion: Duke Dalmead. But his mother had never liked it and never called him anything but John.

"I guess there is, Pop." He looked up at his father, wondering how much he was going to hurt the old man. Phil Dalmead was fifteen years older than his wife; for forty years he had been a fisherman and the life had taken its price from him. He owned two boats, now, but he wore no mark of success. He was a dreamer who had the resignation of a philosophical man who knew his dreams would never be realized. His black eyes would sometimes become opaque with dreaming but never with disappointment. But that did not mean he was incapable of being hurt. "I'm not going to church any more, Pop."

"You're young, Duke, but I guess you got your reasons?" No reproach, just a gentle curiosity.

"I could tell them to you, Pop, but it would take too long. And anyhow, I don't know if Mom would understand even then. You know what she's like, Pop."

"I'm like her, too," his father said gently. "I'm a believer, Duke."

Duke got up and went to the window. The Dalmead house was an old two-storied clapboard that stood in an acre of its own grounds; it was his mother's pride, *her* mark of success. Every two years the outside of it was painted white, the trim and shutters dark green; every summer since he was ten years old Duke had earned his pocket money by mowing the lawns and keeping an eye on the oak trees against the depredations of the gypsy moth. The place had a safe look to it, undisturbed by fashions in architecture, uncluttered by the ornaments that are the extra symbols of an owner's success. Julia Dalmead had never wanted anything but a home of her own, one with dignity, and having achieved it she wanted no more than to preserve it. She stood now beside the car in the driveway staring up at him. Cars were a mark of success to some people but not to Julia: it was a seven-year-old De Soto and it could have been a twenty-year-old Model T. Cars were only for getting to places, church for instance. The destination was the important thing to Julia Dalmead, and heaven was her eventual destination.

"Pop, I'm not criticizing her. Nor you, either. You believe, I don't—that's all there is to it. This isn't something that's come over me all of a sudden. Two years I been thinking about it. Two years I been a hypocrite, going to Mass, getting down on my knees, never saying my prayers, just staring at the altar and wondering what the hell I was doing there. Learn science, you told me, Pop, remember, learn so's you can go to M.I.T. Well, I learned, Pop, and I'm going to M.I.T. If you wanted me to go on believing, Pop, you got me to read the wrong books—science and engineering books aren't the Bible."

20

"There's a place for both. The Lord ain't against progress, Duke."

He shook his head, turning back to his father. "It's not just all the logic I've learned, it's more than that. It's what I see and read happening in this world. If there was a God, I don't believe He'd let these things happen. You read what's been happening over in Europe. All those women and kids dying in the bombing of Rotterdam, Coventry, all those places. Innocent people being killed in Greece and Russia. Do you think a merciful God would let those things happen, Pop?"

"He never intended we should have a perfect world. He never promised us that. Maybe it's His mercy that's kept us Americans out of the war."

"You don't believe that, Pop." He tried not to be angry with his father. "He's not an American God, just looking after Americans. You sound like that archbishop down in New York."

The car horn tooted, impatiently, angrily. *She's going to miss her seat in church*, Duke thought bitterly. His father put his black hat carefully on his head. "If you don't believe in God any more, Duke, what are you gonna believe in?"

"I dunno, Pop. Myself, I guess. And you."

"Not me, Duke. Don't believe in me. Somewhere, I dunno where, I failed you. Don't believe in me." He stopped at the door, an old man crippled by almost half a century of storms at sea and now by this quiet storm of his son's rebellion. For some time now, in his inner heart, he had believed the world was coming to an end. This was part of the disintegration, another of the fuses that were being lit all over the earth. Already over in Europe men were hastening the end of themselves. "We'll talk about it later. In the meantime I'll say some prayers for you at Mass. Do you mind?"

Duke shook his head, suddenly wanting to weep, at the hurt he had inflicted, at the blind stupid faith of his father in someone who did not exist. "It'll do no good, Pop. But go ahead if you want to. And try and explain to Mom, will you?"

"How can I?" Phil Dalmead gestured helplessly with an arthritic hand: he had long ago begun to lose his grasp on things. "I don't even understand you myself."

Then he went out of the room and a minute later there was the sound of the car backing out into the street. Duke stood at the window watching it go. His younger brothers and sisters were leaning out of the car looking back at the house, the puzzlement on their faces apparent even at that distance. He could see his mother sitting up straight in the front seat, already smelling the fires of hell that would eventually consume him.

2

Matt Crispin pulled in the old Essex Challenger in before the Dalmeads' house and tooted the horn in the succession of notes that was his and Duke's signal. Then he sat back, one arm along the back of the seat, a man-about-the-Cape in his sporty runabout. He had bought the Essex from one of the summer visitors who had been about to abandon it; it had cost him fifty dollars, his life's savings, as he had told Duke, and it was his pride, his joy and the centre of his whole existence. He had worked on it for weeks last winter, and now the motor purred, the paintwork shone and even the upholstery decently contained its stuffing. The Essex didn't compare with the cars of some of the summer boys, but then he didn't have a rich father. You couldn't have everything, he had told Duke, but privately he sometimes would have swapped the Essex for a rich father.

There was a breeze blowing in from offshore and it might be cold in the water to-day. He did not like swimming when it was too cold, but Duke could go in and enjoy it when even the gulls looked miserable. He had experienced a lot of discomfort following Duke, he told himself: swimming, camping, sailing, digging for quahogs out on the Childs River when they had to break the ice on the mud. From now on he was going to lead a lonely life, but at least it would be comfortable. You couldn't have everything, he told himself.

Duke came running down the path, jumped on to the running board and swung over into the seat without opening the door.

"Watch the paintwork!" Matt cried. "Geez, you're the spectacular one. Always making like Errol Flynn. They're not gonna go for that at M.I.T. They're serious up there."

Duke slumped down in the seat. "How's your mom?"

"Still pregnant. Geez, why does a woman of her age want to have another baby? It makes a man embarrassed."

"How old is she?"

"I dunno. Thirty-eight or -nine, I guess. She's younger than dad, and he's forty. He's always telling everyone how life begins at forty. I'll probably be dead at forty. A flaming youth usually means a burnt-out old age."

"You've been reading the *Readers Digest* again. Don't you get tired of Picturesque Speech?"

"Did Oscar Wilde?"

"He was a fairy. They're always making Picturesque Speeches."

"Okay. I'm a normal red-blooded American youth. Epigrams are for decadent foreigners." They rode in silence till they were on the highway heading out towards Waquoit. Then Matt looked at Duke. "How did it go this morning?"

"Like I hit them with a baseball bat. It was tough on them, but I had to do it. What do you reckon?" He looked at Matt for support, wanting to be told he had done the right thing.

"It's your problem. I dunno why, but you Catholics always seem to make a much bigger thing of giving up your church than the rest of us do."

"I'm not just giving up church, for Pete's sake. I've given up God."

"Oh, I'm sorry, believe me, I'm sorry. I didn't mean to make out it wasn't a big deal."

"Okay, cut the lousy sarcasm. You've got about as much sensitivity as these summer visitors."

"It's my youth. Make allowances for it. I'm a normal dull red-blooded——"

"Okay. Cut it out, will you?"

They had known each other practically all their lives. They had had their fights, but never anything serious; they would be separated for a week or two, then gradually come back together like coagulating parts of a whole. Each knew that he needed the other; each was a sounding board for the other's ideas. They had no secrets from each other; Matt had known about Duke's problem for months. But, with the embarrassment of youth in the face of any show of affection, banter had always been their language. The more you abused your friend, the more you loved him. Until a certain point was reached, when the words suddenly became ugly and you knew the friendship was over. That point had never been reached between them and they were confident it never would be.

They went swimming and the water was as cold as Matt had expected. Duke swam around like a seal, and Matt made a pretence at enjoyment. Then they came out and lay in the sun in the lee of a rock. Along the beach they could see the wreck of the schooner that had been driven ashore in the hurricane of 1938. Most of its planking had been stolen and now its ribs showed like those of a decomposing animal. Three or four young boys played at Vikings discovering Vinland, their thin young voices mixing with the cries of the gulls.

"Remember when we used to play that game?" Matt said, feeling suddenly old at seventeen. "You always wanted to be Leif Ericsson and I used to say you were the wrong colouring, a Viking had to be blond like me."

Duke lay flat on his back, eyes shut against the thin dazzle of the sun. He was wishing now that he had stayed at home. With his rebellion this morning he had expected that the world would become a place of fireworks; why, he did not know, except that none of the rebellions he had read about had been as quiet and unsatisfying as this. The morning lay about him as an empty shell, and the world was outside. He was sorry he had hurt his parents, but he had wanted *someone* to salute his flag of rebellion. Matt was no help at all on this occasion.

"I always got to be him, though, didn't I?" He might as well play along with Matt. He suddenly felt a lot older than Matt, but he didn't want to sound patronizing. "What did you expect when all the rest of the gang was dark like me?"

"That's what I got for always playing around with Portuguese kids. I dunno why I never palled up with some Anglo-Saxons like me."

"You know why. Anglo-Saxons are dull and cold."

"Leif Ericsson wasn't dull and cold."

"He mightn't have been dull, but I bet he was cold. Did he ever sail south into any warm water? No, I bet he was a cold fish." A speedboat went by, its sound filling the shell of the morning. Duke opened his eyes and sat up, watching the boat head across the bay, bouncing gaily on the breeze-struck water. "That's what I'd like, my own speedboat!"

"Who wouldn't?" Matt pulled on his sweater. "I was over with my dad to Hyannis-Port last week. Boy, some of those houses there! All lit up like Christmas trees, practically every one of them having a party. I almost sneaked in, just to see how the other half enjoys itself."

"Just the same as us, only more so."

"How d'you mean, more so?"

"I dunno." Duke shrugged and lay back again on the sand. He tanned easily and now at the end of the summer he was a deep mahogany. He was not quite six feet and he was still filling out, but he had a physique that many young summer girls had admired. He was handsome and he knew it, but he never aired his conceit in front of other boys. He had thick black hair and

24

thick brows; he had his mother's eyes but they were not spoiled by her frown. He had his father's slightly hooked nose and also his chin, a profile for turning into the winds of the sea. His mouth was his own, wide and full-lipped and with a hint about it of a boy who liked his own way. That his mouth had never become petulant-looking was due to the fact that he had enough charm always to get his own way. "The girls, for instance. They aren't as cagey as the girls here on the Cape. Some of them around here, they are still playing at Puritans."

"You reckon the rich girls give it away more easily?"

"How else do they fill in their time? That's the disease of the rich. Boredom."

"You read that somewhere. I ain't impressed."

"Not in the *Readers Digest*. *The Nation*, son."

"Don't try to impress me, boy. You ain't even at college yet and already you're trying to sound like a college man. Anyhow, boredom is a disease I'd put up with for a million dollars. Gee, what wouldn't I do!" He lay back against the rock, running his hand over his crew-cut blond hair. He too tanned easily, but he never went as dark as Duke. He had none of Duke's litheness, but was squarely built, with a blunt, good-looking face that might have gone unremarked but for the occasional veil of curiosity that dropped over it, suggesting a depth to him that was not normally apparent. The world would never be his oyster, but he would be forever trying to open it. "First thing, I'd travel. See the world. London, Paris, yeah, even Berlin, if it's still there when this lousy war of theirs is over."

"Yeah, I'd travel, too. But not to any of those places. They're for *tourists*."

"Oh, *poddon me*, Marco Polo. Or are you that other character, that grand-daddy of yours, whatever his name was?"

Duke grinned. He had always been able to take Matt's ribbing, even if he had not been able to take it from anyone else. He had had several fights when the boys had begun to call him Duke; it was only after he had won the fights that he had begun to take pride in the name. "Yeah, well, he wouldn't want a descendant who spent his time looking at places like London and Paris. No, I'd go to some of those faraway places. Samarkand, Tashkent, Mecca."

"Yeah, they'd let you into Mecca. Just tell 'em you don't believe in God and they'd throw the whole joint wide open to you. That place is *holy*, don't you know that?"

"So? Any place that can't stand an unbeliever inside its gates, it can't have much confidence in itself."

25

"Okay, go to Mecca. I'll take London or Paris. From what I read, those French dames fall all over rich Americans."

"You read that in *Readers Digest*? Son, that's a corrupting magazine."

Then clouds began to come up from the south and by the time they were driving home the sky was grey, promising rain. A gun-blue haze smudged the sea and along the point the low pines had a look of iron to them, indestructible as the rocks below them. They skirted a cranberry bog, and a Negro boy with whom they went to school stood up in the middle of the bog and raised a hand, looking for a moment like a dark scarecrow. They drove through the grey-blue noon in one of the silences that close friends can enjoy, when words, for a time, are as unnecessary and irritating as sand in a bedsheet.

Then Matt switched on the car radio. An announcer, his voice punctuated by static, was giving the news: "The Germans continue to besiege the Russian city of Kiev, but the Russians, soldiers and citizens alike, are doggedly holding out——"

Matt turned down the radio. "You gotta admire them. They've got guts. Maybe the Nazis have bitten off more than they can chew."

"It's only a matter of time. The Russians are just peasants. Sure, they'll fight, but they can't win."

"You read *The Nation* and you're for Hitler?"

"Of course not! But I got a proper respect for brains. And no matter what we think of the Germans, they've got brains."

"I don't think Russia is full of dopes. That Stalin, he's no dope."

"Maybe not. But the Russians have never produced anything intellectual, nothing that required brains. Just a lot of dull books and, oh yeah, some good music. Tchaikovsky was no dope."

"They'll be glad to hear that in Kiev. You should drop them a note. Fight on, comrades. Tchaikovsky was no dope."

"Okay. But you wait and see. It's gonna take us Americans to beat the Germans."

"You don't think the British can do it? You should talk to my dad. He's a real Angloph—obe? Phile. He can't forget my great-great-grandfather came from England. Don't knock the British in front of my dad. You've done enough knocking for one day, knocking your mother and father the way you did this morning."

"Yeah, I guess so. I got my own war."

"And if you don't mind me saying so, you didn't show much

26

brains. A real Russian dope. You'd be at home in Kiev, boy, you and all them other atheists."

Duke said nothing, sitting low down in the old Essex as it took him home to the raw gritty atmosphere that would surround him till he went away to college. He felt suddenly cold, as if he had stayed in the water too long and its chill had just got through to his bones. His unbelief was sincere, he was not showing off; but it had hurt him to hurt his mother and father. He had begun the long journey to the heart of experience, a road that he would learn was strewn with the thorns of hurt. He felt an amusement older than his years, wondering if God had been hurt at being rejected. It was not a joke he could share with Matt, who was a believer.

"It's gonna be a lousy winter," Matt said.

He's not talking about the weather, Duke thought. *He's talking about us*. And it came as a shock to realize that he was going to hurt Matt by going away. For years Matt had depended upon him and now he was going to desert him. "How about writing me a letter occasionally?"

"Write you a letter? Geez, I've never written a letter in my life. Never had cause to," he said, and stared ahead down the long empty road as if wondering if he had missed something by never having written a letter. Then he looked at Duke. "If I write you, will you write me?"

"I'll try. I might be busy. You know what it's like at college."

"Yeah," said Matt, who didn't know. "Forget it. I'd probably write a lousy letter anyway."

"Well, don't despair, boy. Only another year and you'll be up there, too."

"It's gonna be the longest year I'll ever live," Matt said.

3

Two weeks later Duke went away to Massachusetts Institute of Technology. Julia had not forgiven him for his desertion of God, but she did not neglect her duties as a mother towards him. He faced eternal damnation, but he would face it in a clean shirt and with his clothes pressed: the Devil would never be able to sneer at her. She packed his bags for him and when he checked them he found she had not forgotten one thing, not even his old ball glove.

"I'll have to get a new glove." He would not need a new glove till next spring, but he felt he had to say something. She was

27

moving about his room, already tidying it up even before he had gone, impersonal as a maid in a hotel.

"You won't have much time for baseball. Not if you are going to study properly." Her frown seemed to have deepened over the past few weeks. She frowned at the photos of the sports stars on the wall as if they were pictures of various devils. "Do you want to take these with you?"

"I don't think so. It's kinda kid stuff." He took one of the photos down, looked at it for a moment, then quickly tore it in half and dropped it into the wastebasket. He looked sideways at his mother and again he had the feeling that he had hurt her. It was as if he were deliberately trying to destroy his boyhood in front of her, murder the child which was the only part of him that she now wanted to remember. But he could not approach her, she repelled sympathy, and so, unable to stop himself, he went on being cruel: "All study never got a guy anywhere, unless he was Einstein. And this family has never produced any Einsteins."

"I don't know the man, but I'm sure all his family, they're not geniuses."

He relented. "I'm sorry, Mom. I promise you I won't skip any classes. Don't worry about me. I won't flunk out."

She stopped and looked straight at him, the first time she had done that in two weeks. The frown lay like a deep dark scar across her brows, and he was surprised at how old she looked. "You believe in yourself, don't you?"

He nodded, all of a sudden knowing he was speaking the truth. "You get nowhere if you don't, Mom."

"You'll find out sooner or later that you need something else besides yourself to believe in." She spoke of her own truth: she didn't have to be Einstein to recognize the truth of what she had been taught all her life: "Self isn't enough, John."

She was gone from the room before he could think of an answer to her. He wanted to run after her, to tell her there *were* other things he believed in, but he knew it would be no use: you couldn't argue with someone who didn't speak your language. They used the same words, but in the language of ideas they were foreigners to each other.

His father drove him up to Cambridge, and Matt went with them. "I'm glad you got ambition," his father said, steering the car as carefully as if he were taking his boat into a gale wind. "There ain't no future in being a fisherman."

"You've done all right, Mr. Dalmead." Matt had a lot of

28

affection for Duke's old man: unlike a lot of old men, he seemed to remember what it was like to be a boy growing up.

"Pop, if we were all ambitious, who'd keep the country working? Don't knock yourself, Pop. Sure, I'm ambitious, but don't blame yourself for not having been the same."

Phil Dalmead shook his head. "Oh, I had ambitions, all right. I wanted to go to sea, be a ship's captain on the Atlantic run. But I never liked to study. I liked the good time too much. It was a good life out on the Cape when I was growing up, before the last war. Much better than before this war started. But it wasn't a good life for kids with ambition. You kept putting things off, always enjoying yourself, always gonna settle down to-morrow. It ain't like that to-day. You kids *work*."

"We got to, Pop. I mean, if you want to get ahead."

"Sometimes I wonder if it's worthwhile," said Matt, lolling back in the back seat like a man who had already got ahead, already made his fortune. "I mean, what if we get into this war to-morrow? What's the good of study then? I was reading in the *Readers Digest* about those Oxford and Cambridge guys in the Battle of Britain. Three or fours years of study and exams, then *wham*! Who wants a dead Bachelor of Arts or whatever?" He saw Phil Dalmead looking at him in the rear-vision mirror and he sat up quickly. "But don't get me wrong, Mr. Dalmead. I mean, we may not get into this war. Duke can't sit around waiting for it to happen."

Phil Dalmead smiled and looked at his son. "I don't think Duke will ever sit around waiting for things to happen."

Duke flushed under the compliment. He liked being compli-mented and had become used to it while at school, but having your father compliment you in front of your best friend was taking flattery too far. The old man still had too much Portuguese in him. "You gotta go after things to-day, that's all, Pop. I'm no different than a million other guys. Matt will be up here next year, going after it, too."

"Going after what?" Matt said, and there was no banter in his voice. It was as if with this departure of Duke for college, his own boyhood had also come to an end. He, too, would need an ambition.

Duke shrugged, feeling a little resentful of Matt's question: it was almost as if Matt were needling him. "Success? I dunno. Whatever it is guys need out of this world."

"What do you need?" his father asked, looking carefully ahead at the traffic as if each car in front of him was a rock trying

29

to sink the old De Soto. Traffic was getting out of control: soon there would be no pleasure in driving a car.

"I dunno for sure, Pop. All I want is not to keep standing still, nor to slip back. Just keep going up the ladder, that's all. If I'm gonna be an engineer, each year I want to be a better one than I was the year before." He wanted to be the best there was, but he didn't say that: all at once he had the feeling that his father and Matt were not as sold on success as he was.

"That's a good ambition," Phil Dalmead said. "Your mom and I will pray for you." He leant forward, straining to stare down the road ahead of him, knowing he had said the wrong thing. It was like salt in his mouth to know that his son would never be grateful for the prayers that would be said for him.

Later, when they were driving back to the Cape, Matt said, "Mr. Dalmead, do you reckon Duke will be happy at M.I.T.?"

"What makes you say that?"

"Geez, I dunno. But sometimes, talking to him, I got the idea he doesn't really know what he wants."

"Do you know what you want, Matt?"

"No, I guess not." Ahead of them a flight of mallards drew an arrowhead across the lime sky as they headed south towards the bayous along the Gulf country. Some day he would head south himself, and east and west, too. He would see the world, but like the mallards, he would always come back to the Cape. "But I don't have the itch Duke's got. I don't have the talent he's got, either. All my life I been an average guy, all my life I'm gonna be an average guy, I reckon. The itch will never worry me the way it's gonna worry Duke."

Phil Dalmead looked at the seventeen-year-old boy beside him with new respect. He had always liked Matt and thought he knew him, but he had never known him as well as he knew him in this moment. "We'll just have to wait and see, Matt. Just let's hope the itch don't take him too far away from us."

Matt nodded and hunched down in the seat, turning up his collar against the September breeze and the cold wind of loneliness.

He went back to school, impatient now for graduation. For the first week or two he was restless, unable to settle down to either study or play. He drove around in the Essex, being variously one of the rich kids from Boston, a Kennedy or a Saltonstall, or a racing driver, Wilbur Shaw or that Englishman John Cobb, but after a while even that began to pall. He tried going around with one or two fellows from his class, boys he had known all his life and with whom he and Duke had often gone sailing and to parties, but a day or two of their company only made him realise how much he missed Duke.

Then at the beginning of December Duke came home for a weekend. Matt picked him up at the bus station and drove him out to the Dalmead house. "Well, what's it like up there?"

"It's another world. They make you work for one thing. It's a lot different than school."

"Everything's a lot different than school. That's why I'm breaking my neck to get out of school."

"How's your mom? Had the baby yet?"

"Due any day now. She sits around the house fat as a barrel, and I find I'm playing nursemaid now. But if it comes to washing diapers, I'm leaving home."

"You're not the home-leaving type, son."

"And you are?"

"I don't know. There's a lot of freedom up there I never had before. I can do what I like, think what I like. It's a new world."

"You said that." There was a lot of traffic on the road, people coming in to town for their Saturday shopping, and he had to keep his attention on his driving. It gave him an excuse for not looking at Duke. "Got to know any guys up there?"

"One or two. You *know*. Takes a while to get to know a guy in a place like that. I don't rush my friendships. That way you get stuck with someone you don't really want." He was silent for a moment, and Matt had a sudden cave-in of emptiness, a feeling that Duke had grown tired of him, was now regretting the years he had wasted with him. Then Duke suddenly smiled and thumped him on the shoulder. "We're going to a party tonight. A guy I met up there, his folks have a place down here. It's his sister's birthday or something."

"How did I get invited? I don't know his sister. I don't even know him."

"Their name's Connolly. They own that big old place out near the freezing-works."

"Hey, we might get to meet one or two of those rich girls, the ones who aren't Puritans. Old Man Connolly's a banker or something, isn't he?"

"He's an investment counsellor."

"Well, I'll be glad to meet him. I got a couple bucks I want to invest."

The party was in full swing when Matt and Duke arrived there that evening. As soon as he stepped up on to the wide porch running right round the old timbered house, Matt wished he hadn't come. Every boy in sight was in casual clothes, slacks and a jacket, and beside them, in his new double-breasted blue suit, he felt stuffy and over-dressed, like a floorwalker at a store staff picnic.

"I told you," Duke said. "Where did you think you were going—a wedding?"

Matt looked at Duke's jacket, slacks and soft shirt. "How did you know they'd be dressed like this? I always thought the upper crust were fashion-plates."

"This isn't the upper crust, son. This is the doughy underside of the upper crust. And as for knowing how to dress, I just have an unerring instinct for the right taste. All Portuguese aristocracy have it."

"Balls," said Matt, "of style."

Two hours later, his collar wilted and his diffidence starched by one unaccustomed beer, Matt was sitting out in a dark corner of the veranda with a girl, telling her how the moonlight suited her and trying to get her to undo the front of her blouse.

"Your hands are cold," she said.

"You won't give me a chance to warm them."

"You American boys are always so forward."

"It's the pioneer in us. Cleo—is that really your name? Cleopatra?"

"I was born on the Nile. No, *really*. My father was stationed in Egypt then."

Cleo Mulligan was a blonde pretty girl with high cheekbones, a bosom that was obtrusive and an English accent that had Matt slightly puzzled at times, as if she were speaking at him into the teeth of a gale. She had told him that her father was the British Consul in Boston, that she was a friend of Peg Connolly, for whom the party was being given, and that she *absolutely adored* Americah.

"Listen to that running water! I just *absolutely adore* ice-works, don't you?"

"Eh? Oh, yeah. Adore 'em." Across the garden, in the neighbouring yard, Matt could hear the water dribbling and piddling its way through its honeycomb freezer. It had been built years ago for the fishing trade, but now it only made ice for the summer visitors and for those stores which couldn't afford to invest in large refrigerators. This summer home of the Connolly's had originally been the home of the owner of the freezing plant, a man now long since gone to the cold storage of eternity.

32

Cleo suddenly relaxed and lay back in the crook of Matt's arm. He began to work on the buttons of her blouse and she made no attempt to stop him. "My, that's nice!"

"Yeah, isn't it?" he said, working faster.

"No, I don't mean *that*, silly. I mean that running water, the sound of it. It's like a musical cistern."

English poets, he thought: *Byron, Browning, Cleo Mulligan.*

"Matt—Is that your name? Well, Matt. Are you a primitive? I mean, do you sometimes think there is something in the way savages live? I mean, running around with no clothes on, free as a dryer in the woods."

"*Who?*"

"A dryer. A nymph. Oh, I'm English, but I'm not one of the stuffy English. Do you ever think about sex, Matt?"

"Hardly ever," said Matt, undoing the last button of her blouse and feeling now for the catch on her brassiere. "Except on Saturday nights."

"I think it was being born in Egypt. They're very sex-minded in Egypt."

"I'd be at home on the Nile. Especially on Saturday nights." He loosened her brassiere and was amazed at what he felt beneath it. He was like his father to-night, a real Anglophile. Then suddenly she wriggled free of his arms and sat up, doing up her brassiere and blouse.

"Later. But listen—they're playing my favourite number. I *absolutely adore* it!"

He sat up, frustration filling his belly like a shovelful of grit. He turned a careless ear to the music coming from the gramophone inside the house: "Six Lessons from Madame La Zonga." "Okay. Care to trip the light fantastic?"

"What? Oh, you mean *dance*?"

"Yeah, I think that's the word. We speak a funny sort of English over here in Americ*ah*."

They went into the house and Matt took Cleo in his arms. He found she was the sort of girl who danced with her pelvis wearing the skin off his own; he had read *Beau Geste* and he wondered if Cleo had based her dancing on that of the Ouled Nail girls. Africa was all one to him: he could never distinguish between Egypt, Morocco and some place that had lately come into the news because of the war. Libya. He looked at Cleo again in the bright light of the room, saw the sultriness he had not seen before in her eyes, saw the full lips, glistening and expectant, as if between kisses, and was glad now that he had come to the party, even if he was only mingling with the doughy underside of the upper crust. He wondered if Cleo's mother was English, but thought it better not to ask. Maybe Cleo's father had been doing something else in Egypt besides representing the British government.

"Who's the terribly handsome boy over there, the dark one with the teeth?"

"Which one? Most American boys have teeth. It's a national characteristic."

"*That* one. The one who is looking this way."

Matt was only aware that most of the boys in the room seemed to be looking their way. Cleo's blouse featured a pattern of bright green butterflies, most of them on her bosom; the boys were watching her with the fascination of lepidopterists waiting for a new specimen to break out of its cocoon. Matt glanced over his shoulder and saw Duke smiling at them.

"Duke Dalmead. He's my buddy. Don't trust him."

"Your buddy? You mean your best friend? If he's your best friend, why do you say don't trust him?"

"He's ruined every girl on the Cape."

"Oooh!" Matt felt the shiver run right through Cleo and he waited for her to break into the Dance of the Seven Veils. He was beginning to curse Madame La Zonga: she had gone on for five too many lessons. He wanted to be back on the porch, taking up his love-making again to the accompaniment of the musical cistern. "He looks Latin. Is he?"

Then Madame La Zonga concluded her lessons, and Duke came across to them with the girl he had been dancing with, a little blonde condemned forever to anonymity. "Matt, Tim Connolly says they're running out of beer. I told him we know where we can get some."

"Why doesn't everyone drink that *absolutely lovely* rum punch? I've had three glasses of it."

"Duke, this is Cleo. From the Nile."

Duke flashed one of his most brilliant smiles; and Matt with his arm round Cleo, felt the shiver run through her again. "Glad to know you, Cleo. Egypt is one of my favourite countries. We're always talking about the Pyramids, aren't we, Matt?"

"He's a liar, Cleo. The closest he's ever got to Egypt is making dates." He waited for Cleo to laugh, to appreciate his wit, but she hadn't heard him: she was basking in the blaze of Duke's goddamned lousy smile as if it were the Egyptian sun.

"Will you excuse him, Cleo? We better get that beer for our host."

34

When they were outside and getting into the Essex, Matt said, "They're pretty big drinkers, this crowd, aren't they?"

"You're among men now, son. College men. The more you drink, the bigger you are."

"I haven't noticed you sinking too much."

"I don't have to prove myself that way. When every other guy is dead drunk at the end of the night, I'll just take my pick of the girls. I'll prove myself *that* way."

"Hands off the Nile."

"She's all yours, son. I like 'em subtle."

It was almost an hour before they returned with the beer. As Matt brought the car to a halt, they could hear shrieks of laughter coming from the rear of the house, and a whooping noise like that of Indians swooping down on the wagon train and Gary Cooper.

"They're playing cowboys and Indians?" Matt said. "Maybe they don't need this extra beer."

"Maybe they've made out with the rum punch."

They went into the house and found it empty. They went through and out on to the back porch. Tim Connolly, a tall thin boy with spectacles, dressed only in a topcoat, was running round and round the garden pursuing what Matt supposed was meant to be a dryer in the woods, a nymph very much errant, Cleo naked as Mark Antony ever would have wanted her. The rest of the party stood in a circle, the girls screaming with laughter and the men whooping like sex-thirsty Indians. Meg Connolly, dark, intense and half-drunk, stood with her arms wrapped round one of the porch posts, crying.

"Oh, Duke, stop them! The neighbours are complaining—they've sent for the police! If Daddy ever hears of this, he'll never let us have another party down here! Please stop them! Tim will listen to you."

"Tim might," Duke said. "But who's Cleo gonna listen to?"

At that moment Cleo caught sight of them and came running towards them, bosom bouncing like loose headlamps, hair flying and Tim Connolly panting on the back of her neck. "Duke!" she cried, but her aim was astray and she stumbled up the steps into Matt's arms.

"Easy, Cleo. You'll scratch yourself on my tie clip." Matt put his arms round her, since that was the only way of retaining his balance. He looked over her cold bare shoulder into the owlish countenance of Tim Connolly. "Sorry. I saw her first."

Meg Connolly was still weeping against the hard aloof breast of the porch post, clutching it as if it were a lover who was about

35

to leave her. "Please, *please*, everyone, be respectable! You're all from Boston, remember."

"Everyone except you and me," Matt said to Duke. "How are we supposed to behave?"

Above the laughter and whooping there suddenly came the scream of an approaching siren. Meg Connolly let out a loud wail and sank down, still clutching the post. Tim Connolly blinked behind his spectacles and looked as if he was suddenly afraid. "Geez, we better do something! The old man'll skin me alive——!" He made to come up the steps and fell flat on his face and lay there.

Matt let Cleo go. "Where are your clothes? Quick, go and put them on!"

Cleo blinked at him, as if seeing him for the first time; but Matt had turned back into the house as Duke called to him. Duke, a stranger in the house but sober, had taken command. He was bustling everyone upstairs, cautioning them to be quiet, and Matt was surprised to see that everyone was obeying him. Matt himself was sweeping bottles and cans under the chairs and sofas, doing his quick best to remove all evidence of the party. In less than two minutes Duke was downstairs again. He looked about the room.

"Good enough." He looked at Meg Connolly, who now sat in a chair, pale, big-eyed and frightened. She had been into the bathroom, been sick and was now doing her unsteady best to impersonate a Proper Bostonian. "Can you carry it off, Meg? We'll say a crowd gate-crashed in here, but they've now buzzed off. Okay?" Meg Connolly nodded dumbly. Duke then looked at Matt. "How's the whirling Dervish?"

"I told her to go and put her clothes on."

"You better check. I'll try and stall the cops," Duke said, and went towards the front door as the police car, its siren dying away to a moaning gurgle, drew up out in the road.

Matt went hurriedly out towards the back garden, wondering, if he should not keep going, over the back fence and on to home. He had never been in any trouble with the police and he could see the headlines in the local and Boston papers: SCHOOLBOY CAUGHT IN ORGY . . . CAPE COD CAROUSAL. . . . It would kill his mother, or at the very least bring on a miscarriage with her. He looked wildly around for Cleo, couldn't see her, turned for home and tripped headlong over her. She lay sprawled on her back, legs and arms spread wide, inviting rape or anything else that might happen to fill the mind of a passing male. Nothing

36

filled Matt's mind but panic. He remained on his knees beside her naked form, pleading with her: "Cleo, wake up! Put your clothes on—Where *are* your clothes? Cleo! There's a good dryad. Please, wake up and tell me where your clothes are!"

He looked back towards the house and saw shadows against the glass door that led out on to the back porch. The police would be out here in the garden in just a moment! He moaned to himself, shivering with cold and panic. Hurriedly he looked around for some bushes behind which he could hide; but the Connolly garden was bare of everything but a few tiny shrubs that wouldn't have hidden a midget. He bent down, picked up Cleo, staggering under her unexpected weight, slung her over his shoulder, and looked for a way over the fence into the yard of the freezing plant. A quick glance towards the house told him the door was about to be opened.

He found a tree stump in one corner of the garden that would serve as a rough ladder for getting over the fence. With Cleo lying like a sand-filled bolster round his neck, he clambered up on to the stump and swung one leg over the fence. Cleo's weight threw him off-balance and he came down heavily on top of the fence. He felt the fence bite into his crotch and he bit his tongue as he tried to strangle the cry that leapt to his lips. A wave of sickness exploded up through him and he almost fainted. He swung his other leg over and fell down off the fence, hearing his trousers rip as he did so. Holy Pete, what a night! Near-castration, and now a twenty-dollar suit ruined!

He leaned against the fence, hearing Duke, Meg Connolly and the police come out on to the back porch. "I told you, sarge," he heard Duke say, "Miss Connolly and I were just having a quiet evening when this crowd crashed in."

One of the policemen said, "The complaint said the noise has been going on for the last two hours."

"Was it that long?" Duke sounded incredulous. He's an actor, that boy, Matt thought admiringly, still sick with the pain of his bruised crotch, resting his face against Cleo's bare buttock as he still continued to hold her over his shoulder. "I thought we'd got rid of them sooner than that. When they left, they said they were heading over Chatham way."

"What happened to the naked girl?"

"What naked girl?" Duke said; and Cleo, as if acting on cue through a reflex action, stirred in Matt's grip and moaned.

"What's that?" Matt recognised the voice now: it was that of Sergeant Lucas, one of his father's best friends. Oh brother, this was it! Casanova must often have felt as he did at that moment, though he doubted that Casanova was ever caught with his women unconscious. He had achieved nothing but the squeeze of a bare breast, yet in a moment he looked like being branded a first cousin to Jack the Ripper. He looked wildly about him, glad of the dribbling water above him, certain that otherwise the foundry pounding of his heart would have given him away. Then he saw the door. He stepped towards it, swung it open and stumbled inside. Only as the heavy door swung to behind him did he realise that he and Cleo were in the freezing chamber. He was in total darkness, black as the inside of Jonah's whale, but he was certain that Cleo must have already begun to turn blue in his arms. He could feel even himself turning the same colour.

He stood Cleo up, hoping the cold might have begun to waken her, but she flopped against him. He slung her over his shoulder again and turned back to where he hoped the door was. He began to thump on it with his fist, yelling loudly at the same time. Ten years in Leavenworth or any Federal prison, even Alcatraz, was preferable to a night here in the freezing chamber.

He seemed to be banging on the door and yelling himself hoarse for an entire polar winter. When the door at last swung open he could barely lift his legs over the sill of the doorway and out into the, by comparison, tropical air of the Cape night.

"What the hell were you doing in there?" Duke demanded. He was laughing, but there was concern in his voice. "You could have frozen to death!"

Cleo seemed frozen to Matt's shoulder, and the tongue in his mouth felt like an ice cube. He shook his head, numb and dumb, and sank to the ground as Duke took Cleo from him. The police had evidently gone, because Tim Connolly and several other boys were now at the fence waiting to take Cleo as Duke lifted her up to them.

"She's frozen stiff! Quick, get her to bed!"

The other boys hurried away with Cleo, and Duke dropped on one knee beside Matt. "You okay, Matt?"

Matt's tongue had thawed out. "I'll be okay. I better get home, though——"

"You better get to the hospital. I'll come with you."

"The hospital? You crazy or something? I'm not dying or anything——"

"It's not you. It's your mother. The cops just told me. They had to rush your mother to the hospital. The baby's on its way!"

38

4

Anne Norma Crispin was born in the early hours of Sunday morning. There were no complications and she came into the world with no portent of what future lay ahead of her. She squawled when the doctor slapped her to bring her to life, then almost immediately she fell asleep. On one side of the world, in Europe and North Africa, other people, slapped by bullets and shrapnel, fell asleep into death; on the other side of the world, in the darkness of the ocean with the ironic name of Pacific, a fleet, loaded with the instruments of death, was headed towards Hawaii. Anne Norma Crispin, as innocent and untroubled as she would never be again, knew none of this. She slept on, and Bob and Nell Crispin, in a world of their own for that one night, as ignorant as their baby of what was going on beyond their horizon, thanked the Lord that she had been able to begin her life without handicap. She had no hare lip, no deformed limb, she was not a blue baby. She inherited only the disease of human events.

Duke and Matt were not allowed to see Matt's mother when they got to the hospital. They joined Bob Crispin in the waiting-room. "Do you want us to stay with you, Dad?" Matt was still cold, his crotch was still sore and he was very much aware of the tear in the seat of his trousers. Now that he knew there was going to be no crisis with his mother, all he wanted was to go home to bed.

"No. But I'll stay awhile. Your mom might want me." It was typical of Bob Crispin that his car should have broken down to-night and he had had to call on the police to rush his wife to the hospital. His life had been one of crises, most of them small; he lived in a state of perpetual emergency. He was smaller than his son, a compact man with straw-coloured hair that stood straight up on his scalp, adding to the effect of the whirlwind state in which he lived; and he had a red square face that showed more pugnacity than his character held. He tired both Matt and Matt's mother with his continual excitement, but it was his way of living: if crises didn't happen to him, he would have invented them. He puffed furiously on a cigarette, waiting expectantly for another emergency. "You never know. It's a long time since she had you. There could be late complications."

"Well, I better stay then——"

"No, no. Go on home. You look peaked." If there were an emergency, Bob Crispin would rather rush to the phone and tell his son to come a-running, than have him sitting here quietly on hand beside him. "I'll stand watch."

Outside the hospital Matt said, "I dunno how movies get along without Dad. Sometimes I feel like laughing right in his face." He got into the Essex. "Of course, I never would."

"Your mom never has, either, I bet."

"No," Matt said, starting up the motor. "She never has. You think that is what a good wife is—one who never laughs at her husband?"

"I'd walk out on any wife who laughed at me," Duke said, eighteen years old and already lord of all his women. All but his mother, that was. He had walked out on her, but there had been no victory in it.

When they drew up in front of the Crispin store, Duke said, "Can I borrow the car for the rest of the night?"

"What for?"

"I'm going back to the Connollys'. I got a date with Meg."

"How did you manage that? Didn't she bring a guy with her from Boston?"

"He passed out. I told you, I was gonna be the sober one and take my pick. I've picked her."

"Why her? She's pretty enough, I guess, but there were better ones than her at the party. Even Cleo, for instance."

"Cleo's father doesn't have the contacts Old Man Connolly's got."

"You're a cold-blooded bastard, aren't you?"

"I'm hot-blooded, too. I'm not gonna just hold Meg's hand and talk about investments. I'll bring the car back in the morning."

Next morning the two boys went to the hospital to see Nell Crispin, Duke taking a bunch of expensive winter flowers with him. Nell Crispin lay among the pillows, worn out, cheerful but a little frightened: after seventeen years could she learn again to cope with a new baby? "Are you pleased about the baby, Matt?"

"I guess so," Matt said, and Duke saw the shadow of disappointment cross Mrs. Crispin's face. Matt saw it, too, because he hurried on: "I mean, of course I am. She'll be an interest for you, won't she? I mean, next year I'll be going away to college. You lose one, you gain one."

"Don't talk like that, Matt. I don't want to think that I'll ever lose either of you. Duke, did you feel your mom was losing you when you went away to college?"

40

His mother had lost him years ago, but it wouldn't help at all to tell Mrs. Crispin that. He was aware of Matt watching him, but he wasn't embarrassed: he hid the lie well: "I don't think so, Mrs. Crispin. It's only a matter of adjustment. And then, my mother has all my brothers and sisters. No, I don't think she felt she'd lost me."

"Maybe I should have had other children, too." She had come up from Providence to marry Bob Crispin, a step she had never regretted making, and she had made her life on the Cape. She had grown accustomed to Bob's routine of crises, laughing quietly to herself at them, and she had made a world of her own in their small general store, enjoying the company of the customers each day and at night sitting back and looking with quiet pride on what she and Bob had managed to acquire. She had wanted other children to follow Matt, but for a long time her health had not been good and she and Bob had kept putting the matter off. Time had gone by and finally, when her health at last was good, she had begun to reason that they had left it too late, that it would not be fair to bring a baby into the world who would be separated by so many years from its brother. Then one morning this year she had gone to the doctor and had confirmed what she had hoped against, that she was pregnant. That had caused another crisis with Bob, but gradually he had adjusted himself to it, as he always did.

She reached now for Matt's hand, smiling. "You're almost old enough to be her father. Some day you may have to look after her like a father."

Matt blushed, and Duke grinned. "Geez, don't start talking like that! Maybe she won't want a brother acting like a father towards her. All the girls I know hate their brothers."

"I'll see that Anne doesn't hate you." Then she looked at Duke. "Thank you for the flowers, Duke. You're very thoughtful."

Duke winked at her, smiling broadly. "You're one of my favourite girls, Mrs. Crispin. Maybe I should've brought some for Anne, too?"

"She has all the time in the world yet for men to start bringing her flowers. Don't rush her." She was smiling, joking with them, and Duke tried to remember when his own mother had last joked with him. "I want her to get used to the idea that there *are* men, before she starts getting rushed by one man in particular."

"He's never rushed one girl in his life," Matt said. "He just rushes the field."

41

"At your age, it's not a bad idea. Good luck, Duke. But don't spend all your money on flowers."

"Only for my favourites," Duke said, and smiled again.

When they got outside the hospital Matt said, "Boy, you and your lousy charm. I better get my old man to keep an eye on you."

Duke grinned. "No, I meant it. Your mom is one of my favourite women." Then the grin faded, his face stiffened soberly. "You don't know how lucky you are, son."

Matt looked sideways, his own face sober. "How's it going at home?"

Duke shook his head and made a face. "It's worse. My mother has had time to brood while I've been away. She now thinks I was responsible for the Crucifixion."

Matt felt uneasy: he was never quite sure where blasphemy started. "Yeah, well, I know you didn't do that," he joked nervously. "You're not old enough."

"Oh, I'm old enough, all right. I'm very ancient this morning." They got into the Essex, which had their fishing gear and a basket of lunch in the back seat, and Matt started up the motor. "You been reading the newspapers this past week?"

"A bit. I see you got your name in them. Said that the Red Sox were interested in you. What would you do if they made an offer for you?" They headed out along the Cape. There was no traffic and Matt drove fast, enjoying the sensation of speed given by the rush of wind past the windscreen. Although he was not a wild boy, a speed hog, he enjoyed speed for its own sake, the excitement it afforded when the landscape peeled past so fast it was unrecognisable and he was alone in the small world of the car, committed to no other thought but that of keeping the car on the road.

"Slow down," Duke said.

"What's the matter?" Matt lifted his foot from the accelerator. "I thought you liked going fast?"

"Not this morning, son. I told you, I'm ancient this morning."

"The Red Sox are sure to make you an offer then. They're looking for an ancient first baseman."

"Yeah, well I might just join them. Would depend on their offer. DiMaggio got thirty-seven-and-a-half thousand dollars from the Yankees this year. They paid me that sort of money, I'd forget all about being an engineer to-morrow."

"You're no DiMaggio, boy."

"Who said I was? But I wouldn't become a ball player unless

42

I could be a top one. I wouldn't want to get myself lost in minor league stuff. I might wind up in Class D ball, down in Paducah, Kentucky, or somewheres like that. Paducah, Kentucky, is no place for a man with my ambition."

"I'll write to Paducah and find out whatever happened to the men down there with ambition."

"Do that, son. But that wasn't what I was getting at, I mean about the newspapers. I was talking about the Japanese. I don't think it's gonna be too long before we're at war with them."

"Is that the talk up at Cambridge?"

Duke nodded. "We're cut off from the world here on the Cape, Matt. Oh, we're not the only place in America that's like it. But we're isolated without being isolationists."

"I'm an isolationist. Leastways, I don't care about other people's lousy wars. When we were sophomores in high school, you think the Spanish War meant anything in my young life? All those demonstrations at colleges. They wouldn't have interested me if I'd been at college then."

"*This* war is gonna interest you, son. This one is gonna mean something in your young life, believe me. Look, Matt, you and I, we talked about the war over in Europe, but we never really knew much about it. Up there at M.I.T., guys my age know *all* about it. They've got magazines and newspapers up there I never knew even existed. They give you the background to *everything*. Not only about what *has* happened, but what's likely to happen."

"The *Readers Digest* gives me all the background I want."

"There are bits in the *Digest* you been skipping, then. Because we're gonna be in this war sooner or later, Matt. And I think we should be facing up to it."

Matt turned off the main highway and drove down towards the sea. A wind blew in from the sea, cold with the rumour of winter. The sky had the clear look of alabaster about it; you expected to see the world reflected in it. A few gulls were static against the wind, looking like white chips in the alabaster; and white horses rode the sea in mobs that galloped to destruction on the rocks along the coast. Monomoy Island lay like a grey-green cloud along the horizon. It was no more than five miles away, but on this cold unfriendly day it had a look of remoteness about it, as a true cloud has to a child's mind. Duke, gazing ahead of him across the sea, could remember when his child's troubled mind had sought refuge in the land of imagination that lay in the clouds.

They parked the car, got out their fishing tackle and headed

43

down towards the rocks. It was not a good day for rock fishing, but they had never really measured the success of a day on the rocks by the number of fish they caught. They both liked these occasional days of companionship on the lonely coast, the unobstructed slap of the wind against their faces and bodies and the rumble of the sea, like the echoing thunder of history, as it rolled in against their feet from the other side of the world. They found a flat ledge of rock, cast their lines, then stood leaning back against the wind as it bounced off the cliff-face behind them.

Duke took up the conversation again: "I been thinking. What's the point of me studying hard if I'm gonna be drafted pretty soon? It looks like I'm gonna have to go in anyway."

"You got the itch again, that's your trouble. They don't give you medals for that sorta patriotism."

"I'm being practical, not patriotic. What I want is to go in now, pick my service, instead of being shoved where they want to send me."

"What would you go into?"

Duke pointed. Far out at sea a plane, coming from God knew where, going to God knew where, a gnat in the vast eye of space, was heading south. "I think I'd like to be a flyer. I got it worked out. If there's a war for us, that's gonna be the service where promotion will come quickest. The Air Corps isn't overloaded with generals like the Army is."

"You gonna be a general, eh? An eighteen-year-old general. Boy, I bet they'd write you up in the *Readers Digest*. The *Saturday Evening Post*, too, maybe even in those magazines you'd never heard of."

"Okay." Duke shook his head to wipe the spray from his face as a wave, larger than the rest, smashed itself against the rock beneath them. "If that's your attitude, I don't know that I want to ask you what I was gonna ask you."

"What were you gonna ask me? Would I be your orderly or something? Nothing doing, boy. I've already promised General Pershing."

"He's retired, and he's eighty years old, for Christ's sake!"

"Yeah? Well, he should be pretty easy to get along with. Easier than an eighteen-year-old general. Sorry."

Duke shook his head again, this time in mild exasperation. "I don't know if you wouldn't be a handicap. I was gonna ask you, how about enlisting with me? But a wit like you, you oughtn't be piloting an airplane. You should be writing propaganda or something. Sarcasm is supposed to be some sort of weapon."

Up till now Matt hadn't thought Duke was serious. They had often had serious discussions in the past, discussed their future, but all the talk had been theoretical: nothing specific had been discussed beyond college. Matt tasted the salt on his lips, enjoying the flavour of it. "Geez, I dunno. I'm too young, to begin with. Then there's my mom and dad. They're pretty keen on me going to college."

"You'd be able to talk your dad out of it. You've told me yourself—the one big regret of his life was he never got out of the States in the last war. That was why he never joined the Legion, because he didn't have any battles to talk about with the other old guys."

"That don't say he's gonna let me rush off and enlist. There's no tradition of soldiering in my family."

"There's none in mine, as far as I know."

"If you'll pardon my *Mayflower* superiority, my folks have been over here a couple hundred years more than yours have. They've had more opportunity to do some soldiering. There's only one soldier ever been talked about in our family, a great-great-uncle or something. He was a Minuteman at Lexington. He had one day of it, then went across and joined the British. Figured they couldn't lose. In the Civil War, the war was over before my great-grandfather and uncles could make up their minds which side they favoured. Alongside us, the Quakers are like Jenghiz Khan and his gang."

"Well, your dad tried, even if he didn't get farther than Camp Dix or wherever it was." Duke began to reel in his line. There was no fish and now all at once he had lost interest in fishing. He felt trapped, here in this vast wilderness of sea and sky where the only fence was the white barbed spray that curled up from the rocks. He wanted to be back at Cambridge, where his own rebellious spirit was not a handicap, a barrier to communication, as it was here on the Cape. He looked at Matt as if he were a stranger, a guy he had once known and had forgotten. "You're never gonna escape from here, are you?"

Matt reeled in his own line, aware that the day had been spoiled. This morning he had called the Connolly house to find out how Cleo was, but they had already all gone back to Boston. He had been going to ask Duke about Meg, but now it didn't matter. Something bigger than Meg and the contacts her old man might supply, had come between him and Duke. "I've never thought of it that way. What've I got to escape from? The difference

45

between you and me, Duke, is I'm satisfied with what I got, you're not. But does that make me a dope or something?"

"Let's go back." He would never again get through to Matt, he was sure of that. He suffered from being eighteen, which was a century older than seventeen. He had told Matt the truth this morning: he *was* ancient. Ancient enough to know that the life he had planned, as much as he had ever planned beyond merely wanting to be successful and top of the heap, wasn't going to work out. Two months at M.I.T. and he had all the education he needed to know that life would never be the same again. Matt was trapped in the security of ignorance, but he could not feel sorry for him. Because sooner or later even ignorance was going to be blasted wide open like a vault with a flaw in it. Nothing is impregnable, he told himself, except the man who anticipates events and looks out for himself.

"Let's have lunch first," Matt said. "I'm hungry."

They ate in silence, sitting in the car with the curtains up against the now increased wind. The gulls had gone from the sky, and loneliness enveloped them like eternity. At last Matt said, "If you really wanted me to enlist with you, I think I would."

"Christ," said Duke, who had never used that word except in prayer till two months ago, "it's not me who wants you to enlist. It's your country."

"I thought you were being practical, not patriotic?"

"That's for me. Not for you. Don't enlist for my sake. Although I'll be glad to have you along with me. I mean that, Matt. Enlist for that great-great-uncle of yours, the one who went over to the British—but don't follow his example. Enlist for your old man, if you like. But don't enlist for me. Like I said, I'll be glad to have you along. But I don't want your life on my conscience, if you should get killed. I don't want anyone's life on my conscience."

"You're gonna have *someone's* life on your conscience. You go to war, you're expected to kill someone, not just fire your gun into the air. A man's trying to kill you, you don't try and avoid killing him. That's neither practical nor patriotic."

"That'll be different. So long as I never see their faces. I got no conscience about killing a faceless stranger. Especially a Japanese or German stranger. That's the beauty of being a flyer. Everything's so remote. You kill at a distance. What's the matter?"

Matt had thrown his sandwich out of the car. "Nothing. I just ain't hungry any more, that's all."

46

"Sorry. I shouldn't have talked like that. I'm not all that cold-blooded. But pretty soon it might be the way we'll have to think. No humanitarian ever won a war."

Matt started up and drove out on to the highway. The wind had increased, looting the trees of the last of their leaves. They were half-way home when Matt turned on the radio. He searched up and down the dial for music, but there was none, only a babel of voices strident with suppressed excitement. He switched it off, but immediately Duke leaned across and switched it on again.

"Who wants to listen to a lot of guys yacking?" Matt said.

"Some day you'll be sorry you said that," Duke said. "Listen!"

An announcer, his voice punctuated by static that sounded like faraway rifle fire, said: "I repeat the headline of this special bulletin—Pearl Harbour has been bombed by the Japanese!"

The wind increased, slammed at the car. *This is it*, Duke thought. *We are caught in another of the gales of history*. And was not sure whether he felt regret or exultation. Whatever happened, he knew he would survive.

CHAPTER THREE

MATT brought the B-24 round from the west and headed in towards the airstrip. He and Bert Swenson, the captain of *The Flying Foxhole*, had a system: Bert took the aircraft out and Matt, the co-pilot, brought it home. He was bringing it home now from Rabaul.

"Twenty missions up," said Bert, the big red turnip of his face split by a wide grin. "Man, I'm looking forward to that furlough! But I wish I was going home to Wisconsin. The Aussies can have Australia."

"Don't let Murrumbidgee hear you say that. He's very sensitive about his homeland. Especially since he's found out so many Yanks are so ignorant about it."

"I was surprised to find they spoke English. Although that goddamned accent of his makes it almost like another language."

Matt felt the landing gear go down as he adjusted the flaps, then he was taking the aircraft in to the final approach. He put her down on the first hundred feet of runway, right opposite the splintered old palm tree that had been his marker for the five months he had been flying out of Moresby.

47

"You've made a dent there, you put her down so many times in the same place," Bert said.

"I hope I can always put her down exactly where I want to," Matt said, grinning under the other's compliment to his flying skill. "Getting home is always the important thing about flying."

"Them's exactly my sentiments." Bert Swenson hated New Guinea, the tropical heat and the war. He had been homesick for Wisconsin ever since he had landed here, and looked on each mission only as a step nearer his return home. He did his job thoroughly and conscientiously, and *The Flying Foxhole*'s crew had complete confidence in him, but he was a most reluctant warrior. "The thrill of flying is strictly for the birds. I mean, literally. You heard from Duke Dalmead lately? I know he was your buddy, but he was one of those guys always drunk on flying."

Matt taxi-ed the B-24 towards its bay. He lifted his finger, Bert cut the master switch and they both sat back for a moment. There was some conversation over the intercom, but Matt took off his headphones, uninterested in it.

"He's still drunk on it, I guess. He's already got the D.F.C."

"If he doesn't get himself killed, he'll get every medal they issue. I don't mean he's any hero. He's just a crazy bastard, that's all."

Crazy is not the word for him, Matt thought. Ambitious was the word; but Bert Swenson was not a man who understood ambition. But he was not alone in that respect. There had been plenty of others like him, both at the training command camp and then at the combat-crew training centre in Arizona. Ambitious men in wartime were never understood by men for whom war was only a hated interruption to their lives.

Matt and Duke had not gone into the Army Air Corps immediately after Pearl Harbour. They had tried to enlist, Duke being practical and Matt now all at once patriotic. In Matt's family there had been some opposition from Nell Crispin, but Bob Crispin had been all for his son's enlisting: Matt had been intelligent enough to recognise that his father saw him as a late stand-in for himself, that Matt would see the action that he himself had been denied. What went on in the Dalmead house, Matt had never learned. Duke had just told him that it had all been settled, and had left it at that. But in the succeeding months Matt had noticed that Duke and his mother seemed to have grown even farther apart. Something more than a generation, and an ocean of different beliefs and heritage, now separated them. They were more than Portuguese Catholic mother and American atheist son. But Duke never discussed the matter now, and Matt, always diffident about prying into another's affairs, never brought it up.

The recruiting officers and sergeants, still dazed by the impact of the bombing of Pearl Harbour, still blind with anger at the Japanese treachery even though they had been expecting it for twelve months, were not interested in wet-behind-the-ears kids trying to choose their own service in which to fight. If you wanted to enlist then, you went into either the Army or Navy and took your chances on whether those services thought enough of you to put you in the air. Otherwise you waited till you were drafted, when, a recruiting sergeant told them, their chances of getting into the Army Air Corps might be better.

"Right now, kids," he told them, twenty years of booze and barracks experience sanding his voice, "you wanna get into the Air Corps, your old man's gotta know someone. Who does your old man know?"

"My old man knows his old man," said Matt.

"Ain't enough," said the sergeant. "Go home, kids, and wait till your number comes up. It's gonna be a long war. You still got time to make general."

"That's what he wants to do," Matt said, nodding at Duke, who smiled modestly.

"Well, good luck, kid. If you gonna be anything in this war, best be a general. Don't be a goddamned recruiting sergeant, that's all."

Then in the summer of 1942, by which time they were almost convinced the war would be over before they got into it, they had a marvellous stroke of luck. Meg Connolly's father went to work in Washington, in the Army Department. Duke, who had been seeing Meg only occasionally, now began to see her every free minute he could. Mr. Connolly came up from Washington to spend a weekend at the house on Cape Cod, and when he left on the Sunday night he had promised to see what he could do for them. Tim Connolly, 4-F because of his weak eyesight, would never need to call upon his father for any influence in a posting; so Mr. Connolly was glad to be able to help Duke and his friend, Young What's-His-Name. He saw the potential in Duke, and he also recognised that Meg, his daughter, was head over heels in love with this handsome Portuguese boy. Two weeks after Mr. Connolly returned to Washington, the boys got a letter from a colonel in the Army Air Corps asking them to see him in Boston.

"You see what I mean about contacts?" Duke said as they drove up to Boston in the Essex. "All this has happened because I went back that night after the party."

Matt was not experienced enough to differentiate between having a crush and being in love, but he had seen the effect that Duke had on Meg Connolly. "How does Meg feel about being used like this?"

Duke looked surprised. "For Christ's sake, who said I was using her? I like her, she likes me, we have fun. But that's as far as it goes. She doesn't expect any more."

"Okay, okay. Don't blow a fuse."

"Well, watch your language, son. I admit I picked Meg out because of her old man, but don't say I'm *using* her. That implies she's getting nothing out of it."

"And what is she getting? You?"

"It's enough, isn't it?" said Duke, then grinned, taking all the conceit out of his remark. "Meg isn't gonna get hurt, son. She'll forget me soon's I go away and in a year or two she'll be married to some nice solid Boston banker and a year or two after that she won't even be able to remember my name. Women never marry the first guy they go to bed with."

"You didn't have to say that last bit."

"No. I keep forgetting your Puritan background." Then Duke was instantly contrite. "I shouldn't have said *that*, either. I'm sorry, Matt."

"Forget it." Matt was hurt by Duke's remark, but he tried not to show it. There was a strong streak of the Puritan in him, he knew that, and he guessed there always would be. But Duke did not have to keep throwing it up at him, as if it were some goddamned lousy disease or something. He had come to notice one thing about Duke and the guys he went with from college: it was always the unbelievers who sneered at the believers, not the other way round. He had begun to wonder if the sneer was the one thing they did believe in.

"You hear that Cleo has gone back to England?" Duke said, glad to change the subject.

"I hope she's got her clothes on. From what I read in the *Digest*, England's no place to be running around with no clothes on."

"After that time you spent with her in the freezer, climate should be no worry for Cleo."

They were interviewed by the colonel, told that they lived up to Mr. Connolly's recommendation of them, and a month later they got their papers.

By the time they reached the combat-crew training centre in Arizona, Duke had achieved the role he had held all through high school: Glamour Boy Number One. At primary flying school he had established that he had a natural talent for flying airplanes; too natural, because he was carpeted twice for indulging in mild aerobatics to the shock of, and without the permission of his instructor. Matt, too, proved himself a good flyer, but he didn't have Duke's flair for it. It was the same when they reached the base in Arizona. Whatever the course, Duke came out on top, Matt half-way down the list. Bomb training, gunnery training, navigation training: Duke was just so much better than anyone else. It was even that way in the ground school courses, the dull routine stuff where the fancy flyers so often fell down. In engineering, ordnance, radio, Duke was always Number One, ahead even of the men specialising in those courses. The other men had begun to make sarcastic jokes about him, reckoning he was hell-bent to make general before he was twenty-one. The sarcasm was more good-humoured than rough, because for all his ambition, Duke still managed to retain his popularity.

They were in their sixth week of combat training when they were sent out on what was to be their last celestial navigation flight. Duke was flying as captain and Matt was co-pilot. They had their pattern—Fort Worth, Denver, then home—and it was a fine clear autumn night. It would be a breeze, a piece of cake, as they had heard the RAF pilots call it. Twelve months' training lay behind them and now they had the confidence of experienced flyers. Their only tension came from the knowledge that within the next few days they would be getting their postings, that at long last the war was really going to begin for them.

They had a good navigator and they hit Fort Worth right on the minute of their estimated time of arrival. Matt took the second leg of the flight, and again they were over the target dead on ETA. Duke took over again for the last leg from Denver to home.

"You heard the scuttlebutt?" Duke said. "We're going out to the Fifth in the Pacific."

"You were in the wrong latrine. I heard we were going to the Eighth in England."

"Well, anyway, we're going. There was a time when I'd begun to doubt it. I could see you and me, being just like your old man, spending the war sweeping out Fort Dix."

"Good old Mr. Connolly. You ever hear from Meg now?"

"Nup. I sent her a coupla postcards, but I never got an answer."

"Did you expect any? A girl who's nuts about you expects more than a postcard."

"Okay, so I was rough on her. Honest, I didn't believe she'd gone in that deep for me. Soon's I found out, I called it off. What did you expect me to do—marry her?"

"Say you'd got her pregnant—would you have married her then?"

"I took damn' fine care I didn't get her that way. But if I had—well, I dunno. Shotgun weddings never make out."

"You're a great one for maxims. But I've never heard you make one about yourself. What's your motto?" Young as he was, Matt had noticed the incongruity between himself and Duke. It was usually the contented, the unambitious like himself who spouted maxims and, quite often, endeavoured to live by them. But he had always distrusted maxims, knowing that each one had its own contradiction.

"I haven't worked one out yet. But stick around. You'll be the first to know it."

Colorado lay below them. The Rockies, highlighted by the snow-capped peaks, looked like a huge crumpled shield. East of the mountains a road was laid like a silver lance against the grey-blue of the prairie. Matt loved night-flying best of all; somehow there was less loneliness in the sky at night. He looked up at the blue-black sky, at the catherine-wheel of stars frozen round the hub of the moon. *They* were what relieved the loneliness, took the solitude out of this hurtling through space in an alien bird. In his mind he saluted the stars he knew, thankful for their presence: the Pole Star, Castor and Pollux, the constellation Perseus. In another month or two he would not have time to be saluting the stars, but would be painfully aware of the catherine-wheel of flak coming up at him from below.

"Just passed Silverton," the navigator reported. "I can see the railroad."

They were over Four Corners, passing out of Colorado into Arizona, Shiprock floating in the desert sea away on their port stern, when the trouble hit them. There was a shrieking sound from outside the aircraft, and for a moment Matt had the wild ridiculous idea that they had run into a flight of night-flying eagles. He sat up straight, ready to respond if Duke should call on him.

Duke was acting quickly and calmly. He leaned forward and pressed the button that would feather the air-screw on number four engine. He looked out, saw the prop losing its momentum and then stopping, then he gave his attention back to flying the aeroplane.

"The rev governor's gone on four." Duke had already adjusted the trim tabs to compensate for the loss of one engine and now he was trying to find the minimum throttle settings that would keep the aircraft at an even altitude. Matt had to admire the calm skilful way he had worked. The intercom was drumming with questions from the other members of the crew, and Duke told them what had happened. "Now shut up while I fly this thing! We're heading for base."

"Base? You mean home?" Matt's voice cracked with surprise. "Why, for Pete's sake? There must be a nearer airstrip."

"Skipper, I make it a hundred-and-eighty to Santa Fe on a bearing of one hundred and thirty." That was Cameron, the navigator, as usual with everything at his lip-tips.

"We're gonna make home." Duke had found the right throttle settings and could feel the aircraft responding to his jockeying of it. "No Santa Fe, no anywhere but home."

"I hope you're right," Matt said.

"Look," said Duke, in control of the aircraft now. "If we ever run into trouble like this over the Pacific or Europe, we're not gonna have alternative runways to make for. We'll make home or else."

"If I may venture a point, skipper." Cameron was five years out of Harvard, one year out of Wall Street, and as meticulously mannered as Emily Post's butler. "We are not now over either the Pacific or Europe."

"Your point is taken," said Duke, equally coldly polite. "But we are still heading for home."

"I'm for home." That was Sobieski, the bombardier, ten years out of the Chicago slums, two years out of driving a Greyhound bus. "There's a crap game going, and my luck is holding."

"Don't you ever go to bed, Sobieski?" Matt could feel the tension building up over the intercom, and he tried to ease it. He didn't agree with what Duke planned to do, but it wasn't going to help any by having argument and bitterness among the crew.

"Occasionally," said Sobieski. "But not to sleep."

There had been no comment on Duke's decision from any of

the rest of the crew. They were all enlisted men, one or two of them older by several years than Duke, and they kept their mouths shut. Matt had been surprised how rank-conscious and amenable to discipline were most of the enlisted men he had met. He had heard stories from his father of the wild behaviour of the enlisted men in World War I, and he had expected the same contempt for authority from the men of this war. He knew that the men beefed about officers, he had heard it and done some of it himself when he had been in training camp, but he had yet to see any outright rebellion against discipline or orders. Duke was the biggest rebel on this aircraft.

"Is she holding okay?" Matt asked.

Duke nodded. "We'll breeze it in. This is the sort of emergency training we need, son. You want to try your hand?"

"No, thanks. I'll cross my emergencies when I come to them."

"A sound philosophy," said Cameron over the intercom. "No offence, skipper."

Duke made a sour face, but gave no answer. Matt, keeping a wary eye on the altimeter, sat back. The mountains were behind them now and the wing of the plane moved like a black harvesting blade over the grey stubble of the desert. They flew on steadily, Duke riding the aircraft beautifully, and Matt began to relax.

They had been flying for perhaps fifteen minutes when the second and greater trouble hit them. The aircraft suddenly swung over and slipped downwards. Matt jerked up, feeling the belt cutting into him as the plane continued down in its violent dive. There were shouts over the intercom, but none of them made any sense; everyone was as confused and scared as he was. Everyone but Duke. *He* was working with the same quick calm skill as he had shown before, a little more urgently but still without panic. He kicked on the rudder, brought the wheel back gently and, after what seemed an age to Matt, had the plane once more on an even keel. But even Matt, just sitting there with no hand in controlling the plane, could feel how sluggish it was.

"We've broken the screw on one," Duke said. He looked at the altimeter, and Matt followed his gaze. They had dropped eight hundred feet in the dive. They were down to seventeen thousand and Matt knew they were going to have trouble staying at that altitude. "Where are we, Alan?"

"Just under two hundred from home, if we stay dead on course," the navigator answered.

"I had no intention of making any detours," Duke snapped; and now Matt could see the sweat shining on Duke's face. He

54

looked at the air-speed indicator and at once saw the reason for Duke's concern: their speed was down and was still falling.

"Have we got enough height to make it?"

Duke shrugged, all his attention concentrated on flying the plane. There was silence in the plane now, all questions ceased on the intercom. But the unspoken question pierced like a shriek against each ear: Will we make it? Matt looked again at the air-speed indicator, saw that it had steadied; but the plane was lumbering, held aloft, it seemed, only by willpower and the strength of Duke's arms. Their altitude now was twelve thousand: there was still plenty of time to bale out if the plane should suddenly decide it had had enough. Matt could feel the sweat running on him, and for the first time he was aware of a sickness in his stomach. Outside, he could hear the uneven beat of the two remaining engines, like that of a weak pulse. He wondered how his own pulse was rating, but now was no time for a physical check.

One of the motors ran rough, the plane seemed to stumble in the air for a moment and the air-speed dropped alarmingly. Someone said something over the intercom, but it was not intelligible: it could have been a prayer or a curse. The motor coughed and picked up again, but Matt knew there was no chance of picking up their lost air-speed. They must now be travelling at the minimum above stalling point.

Duke suddenly said, "Everyone prepare to bale out! Get base on the radio and tell 'em you're all jumping. Tell 'em I'm gonna try and bring the plane in." There was a babel of questions, but Duke snarled: "Shut up and do what you're told!" He looked at Matt. "You supervise the jump, son. And good luck. I'll see you back at base."

Matt hesitated, then unbuckled his belt, slid out of his seat and went back off the flight deck. He saw the men go out one by one, their parachutes opening like night-blooming flowers below the plane, then it was his own turn to go. He stood at the hatch-door, holding tightly to the grip above his head, feeling the wind snatching at him. He tried to remember all the steps of his parachute drill, but couldn't. He was not frightened; suddenly he knew he could not leave Duke alone here in the dying aircraft. He stepped back from the open hatch, cursed himself for a fool, cursed Duke for being a bigger fool, for having got them into this mess, and went back up on to the flight deck.

Duke looked up in surprise. "Forgot something?"

Matt slid into his seat, buckled his belt. "If we get out of this alive, don't quote any maxims at me." He was angry at Duke and, for some reason which eluded him right then, at himself. "I know a dozen. Beginning with, *Fools rush in where angels fear to tread*."

Duke was silent for a moment, and Matt could see the strain and sweat on the lean dark face. Then there was the brilliant smile, not so bright perhaps now and twisted wryly. "Okay, I made a mistake. But you're wrong about one thing, Matt. The sky isn't just for birds and angels. We belong up here, too."

"Is that what you're trying to prove, humping this cripple all the way back to base?"

But Duke didn't answer that, and after a moment Matt sat back in his seat, not angry any more, nor even afraid, filled now only with a resignation that was like a sickness he had never experienced before. He knew now why he had been angry at himself for coming back here to the flight deck, for not having jumped when he had had the chance. He was tied to Duke by some invisible cord and he would never be able to escape him. They were like the binary stars he had learned about in the elementary astronomy course, double stars that revolved around the same centre of gravity. He was the one they called the dark companion, the one always in eclipse.

They kept losing height all the way. Their air-speed remained constant, but only just; twice Matt tensed in his seat, waiting for the plane to dive earthwards. The desert flowed beneath them, pale and lonely as a moonscape in the light of what seemed an alien moon, one that was now a cold basilisk eye staring them into death. Matt turned his own eyes away from it, looked ahead and saw the lights of the base come into sight, glittering like friendly stars.

"I'll have to put her in flat," Duke said. "If I dip the nose too much, I'll never get it up again."

"Wheels down!"

Matt dropped the lever. He felt the plane stumble in the air as the wheels bumped down and locked. He released the flaps, felt them sliding down, taking hold of the air, and he saw Duke slowly drawing back on the wheel, lifting the nose as they came in towards the end of the runway. They were coming in at absolute minimum speed, yet the ground had never seemed to come up at them so fast. It rushed at them, seeming to come right up at them into the plane; they were going to smash right through it, through the Looking-Glass of the world into death. Matt drove his feet into the floor, felt the sickness turning into something

56

live in his gut, said a prayer to prepare him for oblivion.

Then the wheels had touched down, took hold of the earth and held it back, they were running towards the far end of the strip in as good a landing as any man had ever done on the base, they were safe.

A minute later Duke had shut off the engines, set the emergency brake and sat back. He dragged off his helmet and looked out at the two dead engines with a grin of triumph, as if they were living foes he had fought and beaten. Pride in what he had done shone on his face as bright as the sweat already there.

"Nice flying," Matt said.

Duke caught the note of restraint in the other's voice. "You still don't think I did the right thing?"

"I think we should have turned south to Santa Fe."

"Why wouldn't you have come home? You're not the type who scares easy. I've seen you bring a sail-boat home to Waquoit when it would have been easier to put in somewheres else."

"I was scared when that prop went on number one, don't think I wasn't."

"Well, to tell you the truth, so was I. But before that, were you scared?"

"No. But I don't think that's the point. We don't fly planes to prove we're not scared. That's for guys who get shot out of cannons at county fairs. The important thing is the guys who were with us. I just hope to God they all landed okay——" Vehicles were converging on the aircraft now from all sides: a crash truck, an ambulance, half a dozen jeeps. In a moment Matt knew Duke would be beyond him, would be swamped by the outsiders. He had to say what he had to say right now, this very moment, or he would never be able to say it. "You've got no sense of responsibility towards anyone but yourself, Duke. You never gave a thought to those other guys till that second trouble hit us, till it struck you that maybe you had done the wrong thing and we weren't gonna make it. Quite apart from what it cost in time and money to train them, how long it would take to replace them, there's the personal aspect. Those guys all have their own reasons for wanting to live. Maybe they've got no more reason than I've got, just that I want to stay alive. Maybe some of them have got someone who depends on them. Cameron, for instance —he's got a wife and a kid. You forget all that, just to prove you could bring this goddamned plane home. You've missed the point entirely, Duke. We're not here to prove how good you are."

57

He got up and left the flight deck as the first of the jeeps skidded to a stop below the wing. Duke's centre of gravity was himself, and he, Matt Crispin, nineteen years old and now dimly aware that every man had his own destiny, was no longer prepared to revolve round it.

Next morning Duke was called before the commanding officer. Matt sat in the Officers' Club, drinking beer, surrounded by excitement but curiously unmoved by it. He had been there a good half hour before Duke pushed through the door and looked around. Matt raised an arm and Duke came towards him. The dark face was even darker this morning, anger making him look even more foreign than the Portuguese blood ever had. Matt had never seen him like this before.

"It was as bad as that?"

"What do you mean?" Duke slumped down in a chair.

"My friend——"

"Who said we're friends? The way you shot your mouth off last night——"

Matt shrugged. "Okay, stranger then. Stranger, you have a face that shows your attitude towards the world. Right now it shows that you think the Army Air Corps can get stuffed. Am I right?"

"And you can do the same!"

"Biologically impossible, stranger." Matt pushed the beer in front of him across the table. "Drink that while I get two more." He got up, went away across the room and was back almost immediately with two more beers. "You had better talk to me, Duke because nobody else is gonna listen to you. They're all too full of their own news."

"What news?"

"It's just come through. We've been posted. To the Fifth, out in New Guinea."

Duke grimaced, as if the beer had turned to arsenic in his mouth. "Not me. I'm being transferred to fighters. I've gotta go back for more training."

Matt had been about to lift his glass to his mouth. He stopped, put the glass down and pushed it away from him. The room seethed about them like a cauldron, the men released from the tension of the last six weeks to boil over into an excitement that was a mixture of relief and a new fear. Cameron, who, with Sobieski and the other crewmen, had landed safely yesterday, waved to him across the room; but he ignored him. Matt felt he and Duke could have been in the desert beyond the limits of the

58

base, so intimate and shocking was the news Duke had just given him. "Why, for Pete's sake?"

Duke seemed to get some perverse pleasure out of the nature of his answer: "The C.O. thinks like you do. I haven't got enough sense of responsibility to be a bomber captain."

Matt felt the spear thrust in that one, but he was growing older by the minute: he was learning that the fabric of friendship had its threads of enmity, that you had to learn to ignore them or no relationship would ever survive. "What are you gonna do?"

Duke was staring down into the fifty-foot well of his beer glass: Matt knew he would be dead drunk before the day was out. "Matt, would you transfer to fighters, too?"

Matt ransacked his mind for some excuse that wouldn't sound like a betrayal. Duke had been hurt enough already; now it was his turn to rub salt into the wound. He played for time: "Duke, isn't there a chance the C.O. will reconsider?"

"Not a chance." Duke had already decided the finality of the C.O.'s decision, and Matt now recognised the attitude: Duke would perversely resent any last-minute leniency on the part of the C.O. *It won't be long*, Matt thought, *before his anger turns to pride, pride in being a martyr.* And began to feel a little less conscience-stricken about his own decision. "Maybe he's right. Maybe you're right too. It could be I've got no sense of responsibility." Suddenly he thumped his fist on the table, and almost at the same instant opened the fist to catch his glass as it toppled over. With one part of his mind Matt admired the action: *he's got the reflexes for a fighter pilot, all right.* "Christ, why couldn't they have told me back at primary training? Why did they have to wait all this time to scrub me?"

"Take it easy, Duke," Matt said, looking about him, wanting them not to be invaded till he had given Duke his answer. Three men rolled by them, drunk with thoughts of the future, hungover with regrets for what they had failed to do in the past. They slapped him and Duke on the back: they loved the world this morning, everyone but the goddamned Nazis and Japs. Matt waited till they were gone, giving them the mechanical smile of barrack-room camaraderie. "You deny your own potential, Duke. Maybe they had hopes that you'd get it into your thick handsome skull that you could be the best flyer in the Air Corps and still be responsible."

"You haven't answered my question," Duke said with a drunk's doggedness, although he had drunk less than half a glass of beer.

59

Matt sighed, felt unhappy, felt ashamed, as if he were confessing some weakness that was splitting their friendship apart. "I'm not the fighter type, Duke. They wouldn't have me."

The frown was cut deep into Duke's brow. His mother had disowned him, but she had marked him with her looks. "We enlisted together. I didn't think it would ever end this way——"

"Don't think I don't regret it." Matt crowded his voice with regret; suddenly young again, he tried too hard. "I'd give anything to come with you—no, honest——"

Duke was surprisingly accepting. "Don't push it, Matt. I understand. On the level——"

Matt relaxed, glad that for the moment there was going to be no bitterness. "Okay. But I do regret it. But it wouldn't work out, Duke. Not me in fighters. I've got only one aim in this war—to survive it. I wouldn't last one week in fighters."

Duke moved his head, as if trapped in a cobweb of accidents: the planner whose plans had suddenly been whirled away by an unforeseen gale. "I've let you down, Matt. You wouldn't have come into the Air Corps if it hadn't been for me——"

Matt looked at him soberly, feeling more certain of himself now, less a traitor. "That's right. But I'm here and I'm gonna make the best of it. That's what I think you had better do about the fighters—make the best of it." He stood up, careful now not to be sentimental: there would be enough danger of that when the final moment of farewell came. "You'll be okay, Duke. You always will be. You'll just have to change your ambition, that's all. Be the best fighter pilot in the Air Corps. Leave it to me to be the best bomber pilot."

"You really lay it on thick, don't you?" Duke looked up, smiling wryly, without bitterness: the dark blood of anger had gone from his face now and he looked less foreign.

"That's what friends are for," said Matt, smiling back at him, knowing now that the worst moment was past. "Sycophancy is for brown-noses."

"That's a good word, that sycophancy. You can say that for the Air Corps, it's educated you."

"I'd rather be back at M.I.T. I'd be a sophomore now. Maybe not educated, but struggling towards it. War isn't an education."

"Who's quoting maxims now?"

That had all been five months ago, and now Matt was here in New Guinea and he had begun to learn that war *was* an education, just as any experience was. He wondered what Duke had learned, flying out of England in fighters.

When he and Bert Swenson came out of the intelligence officer's hut, Murrumbidgee Finn was waiting for him. "I want a word with you, mate. Come on over for a grog."

Matt put on his sunglasses against the glare from the ground as they walked across towards the rest hut. He felt suddenly tired, and he knew it was not just from the mission they had just completed: it was the tiredness of twenty missions, of letting a body and mind relax after five months.

"I've got everything teed up for you in Sydney." Murrumbidgee was almost too big to be a flyer. He stood well over six feet and had a frame that crowded every hut or tent he entered. He had a nose that had been shaped like a door-knocker by a fist in a Rugby scrum, deceptively sad eyes and a huge moustache that was like a disguise, that made Matt believe he had never seen the real Murrumbidgee Finn. He was a squadron-leader, had flown in the Middle East and here in New Guinea, and was now the RAAF liaison officer with Matt's group. "We catch a Dakota out to-morrow morning, one that's going right through to Sydney. You could stay with me and the wife, but frankly, we wouldn't want you around. I haven't seen her for twelve months——" Matt grinned, still young enough to be embarrassed by the confidences of a married man. "I've booked you into the Officers' Club at Elizabeth Bay. Nice and handy to all the vice and temptation of Kings Cross. I've also asked my sister to tee up all the eligible young virgins under thirty—if there are any left. You should have a wizard leave, mate. It's up to you."

2

Matt had a wizard leave, the best but one that he was to have during the whole war.

"You could have bought the whole of the Palm Beach peninsular for twenty thousand pounds the week after the Japs shelled Sydney in 1942," Jane Finn said. "People deny it now, but there was a certain amount of panic in those days. I was still at school, but I can remember the girls coming to school and saying their parents were all packed and ready for the Blue Mountains if the Japs should come. I came home expecting us to be all packed, too, but Mum was busy having the bathroom re-painted."

"What about your father?"

"*He* was worried. He had twenty horses in training then and

61

he said he wasn't going to have any of them killed by any bloody Japs. Dad's not unmindful of the war, but I'm afraid he loves horses more than he does people. With the exception of Mum, of course. If the war hurt Mum in any way, I think he'd take on the whole Jap army with his bare hands."

"How does he feel about the war in Europe?"

"Couldn't care less, I'm afraid. And there are a lot of Australians like him. Unless they have relatives over there, in the Air Force or something like that, they're not really interested. I brought a boy home one night from the Uni, a German boy——"

"Uni?" These Australians spoke a language all their own. He was always having difficulty with Murrumbidgee's esoteric phrases. "University?"

"You're catching on. Anyway, I brought this boy home and he tried to tell Dad what it had been like in Germany before the war and Dad just wouldn't listen. When the boy had gone, Dad told me not to bring any more reff-os home——" She gave a quick smile. "Refugees. They call them reff-os out here. We cut the word down to a syllable or two, then add -o. Reff-os, Comm-os, bottle-os—they're men who collect empty bottles, garb-os—they're the garbage collectors, milk-os——"

"Am I a Yank-o?"

She shook her head, smiled and put her arm in his. From the first moment of meeting her he had realized that she was a remarkably affectionate girl. There was no apparent coquetry or sexual side to it; she seemed to shower affection without wanting any reward or ransom. She was a small neat girl, with none of her brother's heftiness; and she had grace, something Murrumbidgee lacked. Matt tried to remember when he had seen a girl move as gracefully as Jane Finn; each movement she made was a smooth continuation of a previous movement. She had dark auburn hair, pale smooth skin that she kept hidden from the summer sun as much as possible, hazel eyes in which the yellow of malice would never appear, and much better teeth than he had seen on most Australian girls. He was not sure if she was beautiful, because he had the feeling that she was a girl who was only halfway to her real self, who would be changing for a long time yet, whose looks that he saw now were only masks that would one day all be gone, to reveal the true face of Jane Finn, the one that was to be remembered.

They were standing on the front veranda of the Finn home at Randwick, looking out across the dark expanse of Randwick racecourse. Kingsley Finn was a horse trainer, a species of man

Matt had never met, a giant as tall as Murrumbidgee but twice as wide. He had a loud voice, a dogmatic air and, as far as Matt could see, only one redeeming feature: a consuming love for his gentle soft-voiced wife. Matt had been glad to escape him and the others in the room. Matt had arrived at the party, a welcome home for Murrumbidgee, by cab and Kingsley Finn had come out to the gate just as Matt had been paying off the cab-driver.

"How much did he charge you?"

"Thirty shillings," Matt said.

"Bloody robber!" Finn had leaned on the cab and for a moment Matt had thought he was going to push it over. "Where did you come from? The Cross? Five bob at the most." He bent down to look into the cab. "Give him back his change or I'll tear this bloody wreck to pieces." The cab driver mumbled something, gave Matt back his change, and drove off. Finn looked at Matt. "You blokes are easy marks. You chuck your money around much too free and easy. I'm Tony's dad. Come on in."

Tony, Matt guessed, was Murrumbidgee. He followed Tony's dad up the steps and into the house. "You know anything about horses? Never even ridden one? Stone the bloody crows, you don't know what you've missed! I thought all Yanks rode. I been seeing too many cowboy pictures. You've had one or two good jockeys. Not as good as our boys, but not bad. Tod Sloan, Earl Sande, they weren't bad." Matt could feel his hackles and his national pride rising, but he wasn't prepared to argue. For one thing, he didn't argue with his elders, especially strangers; and for another, he knew nothing at all about horse racing or jockeys. "Riding is the one thing I miss in life, since I put on so much flaming weight. I was a bloody good rider in my day. Now I can't find a horse strong enough to break into a gallop beneath me."

"He's the only trainer in Sydney who has a Clydesdale for a hack." Murrumbidgee, unrecognisable out of uniform and with his moustache trimmed to a neat brush, had come to the front door to meet them. "Have you had your ear bashed enough by him? Leave him be, Dad. He's got to get acclimatized to Aussies in their natural habitat. Come on, Matt. Meet the wife. Doreen, this is the Yank I was telling you about."

Doreen Finn was a tanned golden girl who exuded health, vitality and independence; she would never be lost in the shadow of her husband. "The wife. I love that introduction, he uses it

63

all the time. As if I'm part of his goods and chattels. Are Americans more appreciative of their wives?"

Matt grinned, blushing a little: all the Australians he had met so far seemed a little too direct, too overpowering, "I'm a bit young to pass an opinion, Mrs. Finn."

"The boy's only twenty," Murrumbidgee said. "He is probably still frightened by you women. Not all Yanks are wolves."

"Are you frightened of women?" Doreen asked.

Matt tried to hide his embarrassment, cursing his youth and his lack of experience. He had the feeling that Doreen was baiting him; or perhaps she was baiting her husband? For the first time he was aware of the undercurrents that could flow in a marriage. On the surface Murrumbidgee and Doreen Finn looked perfectly happy, but now he was not so sure. And felt further embarrassed, as if he had peeped through a keyhole and seen them in a secret argument. He looked at Doreen, and suddenly she seemed to realise that this boy was perhaps not as naïve as she had supposed. He was not sophisticated, but he would be a quick learner. She beat a shrewd retreat, turning him over to another woman, one who would keep his mind off Doreen herself.

"I think you had better meet my sister-in-law," she said, smiling quickly and taking his hand to lead him across the crowded room. "She's young, too, but she knows better than any girl I know how to put a man at his ease."

And Jane had put him at his ease immediately. Now, an hour later, they were alone here on the veranda and Matt was trying to remember if he had ever met a girl who had had the impact on him that Jane was having. It was not just that she was good to look at. *That* counted, of course: he would always be the sort of man for whom beauty was a necessary pleasure. His mother, defence counsel for all women, had always been telling him that beauty was only skin deep. He had brushed that aside with the old corny gag about not being a cannibal, mainly because he had known he would never be able to explain to her how much he needed beauty. He was neither poet nor aesthete, a word he had learned in his last year at high school; but in his fumbling way he worshipped beauty. And Jane had beauty, no matter how fleeting or unpredictable it might be.

She had something else, however, and it was this that Matt was trying to define. She had none of her father's dogmatism nor her brother's confidence; yet Matt was sure that, even at nineteen, she had come to terms with herself. She may have been wounded in the past, she would certainly be wounded in the future, but

64

she would never be crippled. Bemused by her femininity, it took Matt some time to realise that what he had found in Jane was courage; still a boy, accustomed to thinking only in terms of heroes, he had never thought to look for courage in a girl. Jane might never be a Joan of Arc, or a Harriet Beecher Stowe or (who were the Australian heroines? Come to think of it, he had never heard of any Australian heroes, except Ned Kelly, the bush-ranger); but she would battle for what she believed in, even if at this age it was only herself. She did believe in herself, that was evident; but somehow it was not the selfish faith that Duke had had in himself. She would never strive for the detachment that had been Duke's aim. At a distance of six months and ten thousand miles he had come to see Duke plainly now, although his affection for him still remained.

He told her about Duke. "I miss him. Murrumbidgee— Tony had been some sort of stand-in for him, but you know how it is, you gotta know a feller for years before you can really confide in him. It was that way with Duke."

"I know," she said, and he knew she would have dozens of friends who would confide in her—though he doubted if she would confide in all of them: she would spend affection lavishly, but not confidences. He was not to know it till a long time later, but the inner Jane Finn would only be exposed to the man she loved. "Did Duke confide in you?"

"Oh sure. I guess so," he added, now a little uncertain: had Duke always told him everything? "Why do you ask?"

"I don't know. Maybe because I think you're a person who'd give too much of himself away. You're very trusting, aren't you?"

He hesitated. "I don't know. I'm sympathetic, I guess. Is that the same thing?"

"It can lead to the same end," she said.

"What's that?"

"Disillusion."

"You know, you sound just like Duke. A cynic."

She shook her head, smiling: her smooth face was shadowed by dimples, making her look even younger. "No, I'll never be a cynic, Matt. I like people too much for that to happen. But I try to be wide-eyed about them." She was still smiling, still looking incredibly young now; somehow now he saw her as a very wise and worldly schoolgirl; and seeing her looking so young, his confidence in himself began to return.

"Looking at me with wide eyes, what do you see?"

She put her hand on his; he had to restrain himself from leaning forward and kissing her. "I see someone I'd like to know for longer—how long is your leave going to be?"

"Two weeks."

"You're lucky it's February and the Uni's on vacation. I can give you all the time you want."

"Had I asked you?" he said, grinning.

"No. But this is wartime. We might waste an awful lot of time if we observed the proprieties."

The next day, a Sunday, Jane borrowed her father's car and they used up half the family's monthly petrol ration driving down to Palm Beach, where the Finns had a cottage. They surfed, Matt marvelling at the warmth of the water and remembering the chilling swims he had had with Duke, then went back up to the cottage for a picnic lunch. They sat in old cane chairs on the veranda facing out to sea, the sultry afternoon, heavy with the threat of a storm, pressing down on them with an almost physical intimacy. Clouds stood like frigates along the horizon, ready to storm the land, and on the Barrenjoey headland the lighthouse, its lamp darkened by the war, stood like an empty and useless Roman watch-tower.

"I always think of it as a Roman tower," Jane said, "although I've never seen one. I hope to see one after the war. I'm going to Europe then."

"Do you think Europe will be worth seeing after the war?"

"Anything is worth seeing that has a connection with the past. Delphi has been in ruins for centuries, but that doesn't make it less interesting. At least not to me."

"You might be married by the time the war is over."

"I don't think so. Another year or two at the most, that's all it will last."

"I hope you're right," he said, without much hope. He was still trapped in the rutted mind of the fighting man, unable to envisage peace, the new peace, because he knew it would bear little resemblance to the life he had known. He had heard his father and mother talk of the difference between the days before the First World War and the days after. As they had remembered it, the years before that war had all been one long summer; winter had seemed to be the only season that had followed the end of the war. His father had told him about the Wobblies, the riots, the shiploads of poverty-stricken immigrants, the rise of the gangster kings; none of it, as far as he could see, had been even

66

remotely related to the America of Sousa marches, nickelodeons, Teddy Roosevelt, Taft and Wilson, and, the dream his father had never achieved, a Pierce-Arrow car. How much would remain of his own life, Eddy Duchin, Bing Crosby, the high school football games, the still-to-be-experienced life at college? Perhaps none of it, because what he was remembering were the things of boyhood, things he would have grown out of and maybe forgotten anyway.

"What are you thinking about?" Jane said after a while.

"My old car. I bought it for fifty bucks, had it for nearly two years and sold it for fifty bucks. I'm wondering if the guy I sold it to is getting the same amount of pleasure out of it as I got."

"Depends on the boy."

"Somehow I don't think he would. I had imagination. It was only an old beat-up Essex, but I could make believe it was a Duesenberg, a Stutz Bearcat, anything at all. I don't think this guy I sold it to, he could never do that. He'd never be satisfied with less than the real thing. If he dreamed about a Duesenberg, he'd want a Duesenberg."

"And you wouldn't?"

"If I could afford it, yes. But I'll never be able to afford one, so I'll never make myself unhappy pining for one. I'll always settle for the possible."

"You surprise me. I always thought all Americans were aiming for the moon."

"Most foreigners forget there are a hundred and sixty million Americans. *Some* of us must be different. Matter of fact, I think most Americans are like most people anywhere—all they want is a nice quiet comfortable life."

"What will you do when the war is over?"

He shrugged, careless of the future. The Americans and the Australians had begun to drive the Japanese back up the curve of the globe, the Germans were retreating in Italy; but the end of the war was still a long way off, the future was still a distant prospect. "I had ideas about being an engineer. Going through college, getting a job in a plant somewhere near Boston, still being able to get down to the Cape weekends. It might still work out. How about you?"

"I'm going to Europe, give myself two years there, pay my respects to history, then come home and marry and settle down."

"I know someone else who has life all worked out like you."

"Duke?" He nodded. "You talk a lot about him. Is he your standard for everyone? Don't you know anyone else?"

67

He felt he was being accused of weakness and he tried to assert his independence of the absent Duke: "Sure, I know a lot of people. But we were like brothers—we grew up together. Haven't you got a friend like that?"

She shook her head. "I tried to find a friend like that, but it didn't come out as I hoped. I should have known better. You don't *find* a friend. I mean you don't search for one. A friend finds *you*, just happens to you."

"Well, maybe that's how it was with Duke and me. We happened to each other." He grinned, changing the subject, feeling that if the conversation went on he might be trapped into some disloyalty to Duke. "What about boy meeting girl? Do they just happen to each other?"

"Of course," she said. "Love is the biggest accident of all."

The afternoon burned itself out. The air was thick with the smell of flowers: it wrapped them in a perfumed blanket. Occasionally a shout came up from the beach, breaking the heavy silence; but they were in a world of their own, insulated by their own lethargy. Slowly they came to know each other. Each was an explorer in the territory of the other: they discovered landmarks of humour, sympathy, dissatisfaction. They were alike only in their youth; their nationalities lay about them like a climate. Yet there was an accord between them, something that was not yet passion nor even the beginning of friendship; perhaps it was no more than an ease with each other, an awareness that too much explanation was not needed between them. Each was too young to recognise the seed of love. At that age love is only recognised when it bursts into instant full flower, alive with passion and reckless of the consequences. Matt did not have that impetuosity necessary for love at first sight. That was for someone like Duke, the calculating planner who would never be able to deny his temperament.

They were driving back to the city, going the long way up the Mona Vale road, when the thunderstorm broke. The rain fell with the force of a waterfall, hitting the ground in a spray of bright gems and almost instantly turning the road ahead of them into a torrent. Matt, who was driving, pulled the car into the side of the road. They were on high ground and far down to their left they could see the sea coming and going as a huge magnesium flare under the charge of the lightning. Thunder hammered the sky back, explosions and echoes merging into one continual bombardment. Jane moved closer to Matt and he put his arm about her.

68

"Storms frighten me," she said, her voice small against the barrage outside. The rain sounded as if it were trying to drive its way through the roof of the car, and the windows were blurred with water as it poured off the car. The world outside was no more than a blaze of light and an explosion of sound. "When I was young a nun told me they were the wrath of God. I've never got that idea out of my head."

"You're a Catholic? You Catholics are always looking for God somewhere. I'm an Episcopalian. I dunno whether other Episcopalians are like me, but I just enjoy storms as storms. We have some humdingers on the Cape."

"Ask your baby sister some time if she isn't frightened of storms."

"I'll do that next time I write her. At two-and-a-half she discusses everything with me. Probably be the only time in her life she ever will." Suddenly there was a terrific explosion and up ahead of them a tree was a momentary pillar of fire as lightning struck it. The car shook under the shock of the thunder clap, and Matt felt Jane leap in his arms. He tightened his hold on her, suddenly considerate of her. "Don't be afraid. What have you ever done to call down the wrath of God?"

She managed a weak smile, one that did not bring the dimples to her cheeks. "Nothing, I suppose. I——" Whatever she had been about to say was lost in another immense crack of thunder; the world seemed to split open right through to its core in a flash of blue light. She buried her face against his neck, her hair brushing his lips in the reverse of a kiss. She was trembling like a frightened animal in his arms. Manlike, he felt his own confidence growing; he felt more sure of himself when it was only a matter of combating the elements. He expanded with the charity of protection.

A car went crawling by, working its slow way along the road like a landing-craft. "How long do these storms last? You think we should be moving on?"

She mumbled something against his neck. He put a hand under her chin and gently raised her face. He did it with more gentleness, almost a compassion, than he had ever shown towards a girl before. She stared up at him, fear still clouding her eyes. "It hurts me to see you afraid. No, honestly——"

"I'll always be afraid of the elements," she said, her voice light as a frightened child's. "People, never. But storms, things like that——" She turned her head and looked out at the storm, now abating. "I can't help it. I *believe* in the wrath of God. It's

69

the Irish in me. I might just as well try to drain the blood out of me."

He kissed her lightly on the mouth. Thunder fell again and she jumped with shock, bruising her mouth against his. Her lips clung to his, in fear rather than in passion. Then abruptly she dropped back, as if recognising that a moment of declaration was suddenly facing her. She stared up at him and now there was another fear in her eyes. Caution entangled both of them like a web; neither would easily surrender the heart. She sat away from him as the rain began to ease.

"Will you see me Tuesday?" she asked.

"Tuesday? Why not tomorrow? You said I could have every day of your time——"

"Monday is my thinking day." With the passing of the storm, already galloping out to sea with its victory behind it, she was burying her fear, digging up confidence again. She could be frightened, but she was not a girl who would be cowed for long. She had reserves on which she could draw quickly. "Some people *wash* on Mondays. I *think*."

"What do you want to think about?" He could guess, but he wouldn't tell her so. All at once he wanted time himself to think.

"I'll tell you on Tuesday. Or perhaps I shan't. It depends on *what* I think."

He started up the car and drove towards the city, filled with a mixture of doubt and happiness. He would never mention it to Jane, but he wondered what Duke would think of a man who was cautious of a girl's desire to surrender.

3

Duke was near Liege, coming back from Cologne, when the flak, a carnival of flowers in the pale spring sky, hit the Mustang. He had been flying automatically, his mind on Cleo in London, and he was as angry at himself as at the gunners below when the shells began to bloom about him like orchids of death. That they exploded without sound around him, their blast silenced by the roar of the Mustang's engine, only increased his shock at seeing them. The aircraft shuddered as the air was blown apart about it, and for a moment he lost control of it. He acted with the instinct of the born flyer, making the plane once more responsive to him. But it was time to take evasive action.

The rest of the flight, canny as eagles, had already swung to

70

the south. Farther to the south he could see the bombers, flying in the prim precision that was always the epilogue to a successful raid. He tipped the rudder and went after the flight of fighters.

The ground batteries were flinging up their tracers, inviting him to sign his name on the dotted line of death. It was not the first time he had been fired on, had run the gauntlet of flak; he was familiar with the threat and presence of death, had hardened himself to an acceptance of it. This was his twenty-eighth mission and none of them had been a breeze, a piece of cake. In a moment this one would be only a memory like the rest.

Suddenly the whole plane lifted, as if punched up into the sky. He felt his stomach rise within him, like a suddenly expanding balloon, and for a split moment he thought he was going to be sick all over the cockpit. His mouth was a mixture of sickening tastes, a cocktail of shock, anger and, a new ingredient, fear. One part of his mind was stunned to find that, now the moment had come, he could not accept the fact of his own death.

The plane shuddered at the apogee of its lift, seeming to strain as if about to crack apart, then it fell over and slipped down into a dive. Desperately he fought to keep control, feeling the plane shudder again as it was hit a second time. When he brought the plane out of the dive he was down to less than five thousand feet, a sitting target for any batteries that could cone in on him. Below him he could see the flat fields of Belgium sprouting poppies of flame, all meant as a giant wreath for him. The sky was black with bursting shells, the air violent as a storm-wracked sea. He and Matt had often run before a Cape storm in their boat, enjoying every moment of it; but this was something else again, something only a suicide would enjoy. The rest of the flight was nowhere near him now, nor could they help him if they were. This was his own private war; only his own skill and luck could save him. He put the nose of the Mustang down; he had to get *under* the fire. Wind and shell ripped past him, each tearing at the plane; he only hoped it would not fall apart under the onslaught. The ground rushed up at him, became real and not just a distant map. It was time to pull out of the dive.

He felt the strain on himself as well as on the plane as he brought up the nose. He had come out of dives before, but he had left this one too late. He was going to have to come out of it too tightly; either he or the plane was going to crack apart. He could feel the skin on is face stretching like rubber, his mouth dragging open; his skull seemed to become empty, drained of blood and brain. In a moment he would black-out; already his vision had turned to a grey blur. He shrieked from deep down inside him, trying to keep the blood out of his bowels and his legs; he felt dead below his waist, the whole weight of his body pushed down there. He kept pulling up the nose of the plane, oblivious now of what might happen to the aircraft; then light burst into his eyes, he could see again, and the strain slackened from his body. The plane did not fall apart, and for the moment he was safe. He looked down, saw that he was right above a village on a main road. He had a quick confused impression of people running, of a truck plunging off the side of the road: ordinary people caught up unwillingly in the business of war, innocents trapped by geography. The people back home on the Cape could never appreciate how fortunate they were. Then the village was behind him and he was still headed in the right direction for home.

He checked his course: four degrees off. He drew deeply on the air, filling his lungs, trying to steady his nerves. The immediate panic was over; now he had to concentrate on getting home. The plane was sluggish, not responding to his manoeuvring of it; something must have snapped when he had come out of the dive. The wings were shredded and holed where the flak had gone through them; and he knew his tanks must have been pierced. He listened to the engine: it was rough, protesting like a bronchial old crone called upon to do too much. He was going to have to coax it every inch of the way, a hundred and fifty miles at least.

"How goes it, Duke?" the words in his earphones were a surprise: he had thought he had been abandoned. It was Bialoguski, the flight commander.

"I'll make it, I guess."

"Come up here with us." He looked up and saw the flight glittering like silver arrows against the sun. "You look like an egg-bound duck down there."

"No can do. If I lift the nose of this thing, the ass will fall out of it."

"What's your airspeed?"

"One-forty. I can't get any more out of her."

"Okay. I'll stay with you, but up here. Low flying gives me the jumps."

"Chicken," said Duke, but he was glad of Bialoguski's company.

He looked up and saw the flight commander peel off. The remainder of the flight went on, following the bombers towards home and celebration. They would be home by the time he was only half-way across the Channel. Home: a base outside a village in a county he had never heard of till six months ago. But it was a landmark of security, something you aimed for after each mission: like Matt's father he had become an Anglophile, but for a different reason. When you were in the air over enemy territory, England was home.

"Channel coming up." Bialoguski, many storeys above him in the sky, could already see the sea. "Still holding?"

"I don't know why I'm bothering to take her home. She'll never be any good again."

"If you don't take her home, you'll have to swim. And I'm not gonna ride herd on you while you do *that*."

Duke grinned, glad he had someone to talk to. He was maintaining his airspeed, but the plane seemed to be getting heavier in the air with every mile. Then he saw the coast coming up and a few minutes later he was passing over what looked to be familiar ground.

"Remember this?" Bialoguski said. "The rocket pads."

Sure, he remembered them now. They had come in here in the late afternoon, flying out of the sunset almost at sea level, blasting at the rocket sites before the Germans could get to their guns. When they had first been briefed on the mission, Duke had felt he had suddenly been catapulted into a war resembling the ones he had read about in *Amazing Stories* back when he was a kid. The buzz-bombs had been falling on London for some time: they were remarkable enough, but at least they were believable. He had seen them: that made them credible. But rockets that could travel between a hundred and fifty and two hundred miles—— "If this is war," Bialoguski had said, "I'm going home. I'm here only for the medals, and who wants to get a medal just for pressing a button?" The mission had been successful, and so far there had been no rocket raids on London. But since the mission he had done some reading on the subject and now he knew that rockets were feasible, were not something out of *Amazing Stories*. He wondered if the magazine was still being published, or if it had folded up because the world had caught up with it, made it obsolete.

The Channel glittered below him. If he had to ditch the plane now, he wondered if he could make it to the English shore. Gertrude Ederle had done it; would they give him a ticker-tape welcome up Broadway if he did it? He began to feel lighthearted, almost light-headed, as he got closer to home. He looked at his watch, surprised to find it was still only so early in the day. Cleo would be on her way to the office now, still maybe suffering from morning sickness. Or was it too soon for that . . . ?

He had met her in London two months ago. He had come up to London on a three-day pass with Bialoguski, determined to storm the town. They had checked in at a hotel near Gloucester Road where the receptionist, a plump blonde with the world in her eyes and a lisping innocence in her voice, rode up in the tiny lift with them, rubbing her belly against Duke in an absent-minded way and talking about the rhododendrons that were still growing in the garden of the house that was now just a pile of rubble two doors away.

"They're all like that," Bialoguski had said when they had closed the door of their room against her still unspoken invitation. "The English are garden-mad."

"She looked willing enough to be led up the garden path."

"All the younger ones." Bialoguski had had four three-day passes to London; he was an authority on English women. "English dames have just re-discovered sex, the first time for over a century. Since Victorian times they've thought it was just a music-hall joke. Some of the older ones still do it with their eyes shut, as if it's a form of national service, but the young dames are having the time of their lives. This chick I'm about to introduce you to is a fine example of emancipated English womanhood. She's been emancipated by a dozen fellers, from Poles to Aussies."

"I sound as if I'm joining the League of Nations."

"You can't afford to be fussy, bud. You have only three days."

But the League of Nations chick turned out to be in bed with the 'flu—"What nationality is he?" Duke had asked. "Never mind. You go out with your date, Bialoguski, and I'll find myself something."

He went out, shaking his head at the blonde receptionist when she looked inquiringly at him, and turned left along the street, walking aimlessly. A plaque on a wall caught his eye and he stopped: this, it said, was the house where W. S. Gilbert had lived and worked: a gondolier came along the street in his milk-cart, whistling off-key but happily. Suddenly Duke was not interested in a girl, at least not for the moment. Something took hold of him; time took him by the hand. Wasn't he a descendant of de Almeida, shouldn't he pay his respects to the past, even if the Portuguese had never been here to London? Christ, life wasn't made up of dames! The world was bigger than a double-

74

bed, sex wasn't the only excitement in life. He felt almost pious, fired with his suddenly acquired sense of history. He must write to Matt's father, tell him he had become an Anglophile.

He walked all day through the streets of history. A British general passed him and he saluted, and the general never knew that the American lieutenant was really saluting London and its heroes. Accept my homage, Shakespeare, Ben Jonson, Dr. Johnson, Hogarth, Dickens; take the salute, Donne, Garrick, Keats, Kean. He passed the bomb sites and the shelters, none of them new-looking and somehow as greyly ancient as the rest of the city, and came to St. Paul's, Wren's rock of ages. That evening, still piously cultural, still Anglophilic (he wondered if there were such a word: would Matt's father know?) he went to see a performance of *Twelfth Night*. He had never cared for Shakespeare, but tonight he was doggedly determined to be educated in every way. All the propaganda said that this was what he and a million others were fighting for: centuries of a way of life made up of Shakespeare, freedom of speech, Mom's apple pie, the Declaration of Independence, liberty, God, *The Saturday Evening Post*, Magna Carta—he wondered if the propagandists, safe in Washington, had a reminder list tacked on their office walls. What they wrote was mostly crap; he wondered if they believed it themselves. *He* was fighting the war for himself, because he didn't want to live under the Nazis or the Japs, and he was willing to bet that a million other guys were fighting for exactly the same reason, for themselves. But tonight he would pay his respects to Shakespeare: the old guy couldn't be blamed if the propagandists had borrowed his name. And he *had* written some good stuff, particularly that bit about: *To thine own self be true. . . .*

He watched the play with only one eye, bored by it now that he had come. The other eye was on the small shadow box at the side of the stage. There, as the second act began, a sign flashed *Air Raid Alert*.

"My stars shine darkly over me," said Sebastian, who couldn't see the sign; and the audience all looked through the ceiling of the theatre and waited. Then a while later the sign flashed *All Clear;* but Duke was distracted for the night and he got up and left the theatre. Even Shakespeare could not have counted on the competition of bombs.

He went out into the black streets, blinking in the brazen light of the harlots' torches, and found a pub. And there, the buxom candle to a group of RAF moths, was Cleo Mulligan. She

75

recognized him before he recognized her. She dived through the RAF types and flung her arms round his neck.

"More bloody Lend-Lease," he heard one of the RAF men say.

"Duke darling! It is Duke, isn't it, or is it Count? No, that's Count Basie. I'm terrible at names. How long have you been over here? Why didn't you get in touch with me?"

Duke was aware of everyone in the bar staring at them. He had heard that the English were great ones for minding their own business, which was why eccentrics could flourish so well in this country; but evidently Cleo was an eccentric they couldn't, or didn't want to, ignore. She hadn't changed, as far as he could remember, except to become a little more statuesque: even in the dowdy brown gown she wore there was something heroic about her, Boadicea disguised as the vicar's wife. "Let go my neck, Cleo. You're giving the United States Army Air Corps a bad name."

She released his neck, but grabbed his arm. "Who cares? You haven't become respectful, have you, Duke?" She waved a hand and he saw the ring sparkling on her finger. "I'm engaged, but that doesn't worry me. A boy named Christopher Thwing. He's with the Foreign Office. It's all a terrible mistake and I'm going to break it off the first weekend he gets off. We're not compassionate at all. Oh, it's good to see you, Count!"

"Duke."

"Of course! Wait till I say goodbye to these dear boys, then we'll go home!" She swept away like an albatross, a big expanse of white breast showing above the brown gown, and Duke waited for her. She was no intellectual, but tonight she offered more than Shakespeare. She was on no propagandist's reminder list in Washington, although she might be on a Foreign Office list in Whitehall. Tonight she was going to be on his own list.

She came back, grabbed his hand and dragged him out into the street. "Slow up, Cleo! What's the hurry?"

"I like to be home before the raids start," she said. "I'm not afraid of being killed, but if I'm going to be, I want to die in a place I know."

They plunged on through the streets, running the blockade of the prostitues, Cleo swearing at them in her high middle-class prep school voice, and came to a mews flat somewhere, Duke guessed, in Mayfair. Cleo opened the door, galloped up the narrow winding staircase ahead of him, then at the top spun round, wrapped her arms round his neck and gave him a kiss that almost suffocated him. "Oh Duke, it's so absolutely wonderful to see someone from Americah again!"

"London is full of Americans. You shouldn't have been lonely."

"Oh, I haven't been lonely! But I haven't been able to bring any of the boys here. This is probably the only respectable mews in the whole of London. Christopher picked it out for me."

"Am I honoured then, or don't you care about my reputation?"

She dug him in the ribs with her fist and devoured him with another kiss. "Take your tunic off! You look too regimental. How's that other divine boy, that buddy of yours, Mark?"

"Matt."

"Of course! I knew he was one of the Apostles. How is he?"

"Last I heard he was okay. He's out in the Pacific. I gather he wouldn't mind spending a night in a freezing plant out there. It's pretty hot and steamy."

He moved away from Cleo, bumped his head on one of the low ceiling beams and dropped dazed on a couch. When his vision cleared Cleo was taking her dress off.

"Still up to your old habits," he said, glad now that he had gone to see Shakespeare. If he hadn't, if he had gone to another show and not been bored, he would not have gone into that pub and found Cleo. He might have finished up back at the hotel with the garden-mad receptionist. Life, he believed, should conform to one's own planned pattern, but the occasional accident had its appeal. Cleo was an accident, but she looked like making the next two days more than just appealing.

She paused with the dress half-way over her head. She was wearing black lace underwear, which didn't fit at all with the vicarage dress she had been wearing: it was as if a Windmill chorus girl had been cast as one of the Brontë sisters. "What habits?" Her voice was muffled by the dress, and she wiggled her bottom as if to aid her diction. Then she tore off the dress and dropped it on the floor. She walked over it as if it were a mat and took a negligee from a closet in a corner. It was a black lace negligee, too tight and too revealing. Duke suddenly wanted to laugh, but restrained himself. Cleo was all ambition to be a siren, but there was something so healthy and direct about her that the impersonation would never be more than a caricature. Sex with her would never be a music-hall joke, but a romp, a non-blood sport, something to be enjoyed on the playing fields of Eton or wherever the opportunity offered.

77

"There, that's better." She dropped on to the couch beside him. "I still don't like wearing clothes."

"Do you still run around naked at parties, being a dryad in the woods? Matt told me that's how you liked to feel."

"Oh migod, no! Christopher would die if he knew I did anything like that. He's so conservative, even the Carlton Club thinks he's stuffy." She gestured at the dress on the floor. "He bought me that dress. He had a theory that the fiancées of Foreign Office men should look as much unlike spies as possible."

"How did you become engaged to him?"

Cleo shrugged, exposing half of one breast. "These things happen. One minute you're single and free, the next you're engaged."

Duke shook his head. "Not if you're careful. But I wonder if that's what happened to Matt? Yeah, he's going to be married. To some girl he met in Australia. I had a letter from him last week. I didn't think he was the kind of guy who'd rush into a thing like that. Just shows how little you know about people."

"Perhaps he loves her. Love can happen at first sight."

"I'm myopic. I like to have a really good look."

She giggled, got up and made drinks for them. They lolled on the couch and talked for another half-hour. Then all at once she was lying with her head in his lap and one arm, a lace-clad python, was pulling his face down to hers. "Two drinks and I always feel this way!"

"What way?"

"Sensuable!"

"Like a dryer in the woods?"

She giggled again. "Who told you that? Oh Duke, it's absolutely marvellous you're here! Are you going to see a lot of me while you're in England?"

"I'm seeing a lot of you right now." He undid the negligee, and she moved restlessly, *sensuably*. He had a lapful of Roedean passion, a hockey goalie with her guard down. Then the sirens went.

"Quick, it's a raid!"

She rolled off the couch and he stood up beside her. She turned and spun away from him towards the stairs; the negligee was ripped from her back and fell in a heap on his blundering foot. He lifted his foot out of its folds, thinking it had been a neat and original way of undressing a woman, and followed Cleo in her brassière and panties down the stairs. He was stiff with frustration, but he wanted to laugh. Cleo was a girl cast by her nature for comical situations.

At the foot of the stairs he found they were in a garage. A grey-and-green car stood there, filling the entire space but for a small section in one corner. In that corner there was a heavy antique table that served as a work bench for the owner of the car. Cleo had already dived under the table.

"Quick, darling, this is my shelter!"

He wanted to laugh and almost did. Then it struck him all at once that Cleo was frightened, really afraid. It came as a cold shock, as if he had suddenly learned she was legless or stuffed with straw. She was so big and healthy and foolish, he had not associated fear with her. But now she was cowering under the table, trembling in her black lace underwear, with fear and not with passion, looking up at him out of eyes as big as a lemur's.

"Quick, darling. They'll be here in a moment!"

It was a tight squeeze under the table, but he made it. He was sitting in what felt like a pool of oil and cobwebs curled on the back of his neck. He took the shivering Cleo in his arms and held her to him; she felt colder than the night she had come out of the freezing plant. He tried to take her mind off her fear.

"What sort of car is that?"

"A Rolls."

"Who's it belong to?"

"Christopher's father."

It was no use: she wasn't interested in conversation. Then she stiffened in his arms. She had heard the buzz-bomb before he had; he had the feeling she had heard it at the moment it had crossed the coast. She wrapped her arms tightly round his neck and he could feel her teeth biting into his cheek. The sound of the bomb suddenly cut out, and he felt himself stiffen now: when you could no longer hear it, they had told him, it was on its way down. *This is the way I'm going to die,* he suddenly thought, *with a half-naked dame in my arms and my ass in a pool of Castrol or whatever it is Rolls-Royce recommends.* It would make Matt laugh, if ever he got to learn of it.

The explosion went right through his head like a great wind. Cleo leapt in his arms and the floor heaved beneath them like a huge mattress. The single electric globe above the Rolls-Royce flickered like a cloud-swept star; then it went out and blackness and the world fell in on them. Duke heard the crack as the outside wall went, the crunch of metal as the flat above fell in on the Rolls; then the table sagged and next moment bricks were hitting the top of it and sliding off and Cleo and he were choking in a

79

black cloud of dust. The horn of the Rolls began to blow and it went on and on, like a pig in agony. The sound of the explosion died rapidly away, the bricks fell less tumultuously and the dust began to settle. They were still alive.

"The bastards," Duke said aloud and got a mouthful of dust and Cleo's hair. She was still in his arms, but she couldn't move; they were trapped beneath the table like twins in a womb. He tried to straighten out his legs, but couldn't move them more than an inch. Cleo stirred at last and said something, but he couldn't hear her for the monotonous shriek of the wrecked Roll's horn.

"What?" he yelled.

She twisted her head and managed to get her lips against his ear. "I thought we were dead!"

He nodded, and found he was rubbing his face up against her bare breast. Now the danger was past, he was grinning with relief. He bit gently on her breast and felt her jump. Then he felt, rather than heard, her giggle, and he knew she was now all right. She was over her fear of dying, ready to enjoy life again.

It was daylight before they were found and dug out. The car's horn had gone on for an interminable time and then the battery had at last run down. The silence immediately after was frightening.

"It's like being in a grave," Cleo said.

"An unfortunate simile at the moment."

"Your buttons are hurting me."

He had grabbed his jacket as they had come downstairs and had put it on. He was suffering the most excruciating cramp in his right leg, and he had a pain in his belly from the continued pressure of Cleo's knee. Her brassière had snapped off and his chin rested in the soft cushion between her breasts, but he was no more stirred by her bosom than he was by the pool of oil in which his behind still rested.

"I feel like a fluid fly-wheel," he said; but Cleo was not mechanical-minded.

"What?" she said; then they heard the sound of voices beyond the hill of bricks and rubble that buried them.

"Looks a write-off," a man's voice said. "Almost a direct hit. Hope nobody was home. Otherwise they've had it."

Cleo suddenly came alive. Her bosom pressed into Duke's face, almost stifling him, as she filled her lungs. "Somebody certainly is at home!" she yelled, and poked Duke in the eye

80

with her nipple. "And we haven't had it. Get on with the exhumus!"

"Why, that sounds like Miss Mulligan!" said a woman's voice. "The poor dear. Such a nice quiet girl."

It took half an hour to dig them out. Two men lifted Cleo out and, resting on the arm of one of them, she clambered down over the rubble. "Oh, the poor dear!" a woman said. "She must just have been going to have a bath."

Then Duke clambered out of the hole and, favouring his cramped leg, stumbled down the rubble after Cleo. "Who's that?" he heard a man mutter. "The plumber?"

Someone produced a blanket and wrapped it round Cleo. A car appeared, they were bundled into it and five minutes later a doctor was examining them at a first-aid post.

"You're both okay," he said. "Nothing shattered."

"Except Miss Mulligan's reputation," Duke said.

"Don't worry about that, Duke, darling." Cleo was her old self again. She let the blanket drop a little, and even the doctor looked at her unprofessionally. "I'll have to move anyway, since my flat's been demolished. May I use your phone, doctor? I'll call Mummy. She can come up from the country and get us."

"Why don't you call Christopher?" Duke didn't want her to call her fiancé, but he was curious as to why she didn't.

She shook her head, her hair falling down over her face. She was covered in dust and dirt still, she wore no make-up; somehow she looked less foolish, there was a suggestion of wild beauty about her. He looked at her again, wondering if he had been wrong about her: was there more to Cleo than he had suspected? "I think a day in the country would do the both of us the world of good, Duke. Please?"

He hesitated, then suddenly making up his mind, he nodded. "Okay. Forget Christopher. Call Mummy."

Mummy turned out to be a smaller, even more vague version of Cleo. She didn't question how Cleo came to be wrapped only in a blanket while entertaining an American officer; evidently life on the Nile those many years back had given her a broad-minded attitude towards the world. She drove them out into Berkshire, to a small village at the edge of which the Mulligans owned an old thatched-roofed house.

"This house was a Quaker meeting place at one time," Mrs. Mulligan said. "Are you a Quaker, Mr. Dalmead?" Many Americans are, are they not?"

"I wouldn't know, Mrs. Mulligan. I'm afraid I'm not very religious."

"Neither's Cleo. You young people are missing so much these days."

Duke looked at Cleo, but she was already hurrying inside to a bath and fresh clothes. He was certain, however, that if she had no time for religion she had not arrived at the denial in the same logical way as he had. She was too vague and illogical to have been converted to rationalism as he had. More likely she had discarded the more conventional religions for one of her own, hedonism. He tried to remember any girl he had ever met who had enjoyed living, the sheer pleasure of being alive, as much as Cleo; and couldn't. Well, as the English said, jolly good luck to her.

They spent the rest of the day together, and he came to know that there *was* more to Cleo than he had recognized. She had a fund of sympathy that many men, intent on finding their way about her body, had never bothered to explore. He wondered if the absent Christopher had known about it, but after a moment dismissed Christopher from his mind. Ex-fiancés, even if they were not yet quite ex-, should not get in the way of a man on a three-day pass.

"Do you get leave very often?" she asked.

"Not to London. But I could get up here occasionally. Maybe once a week."

"I work during the week in London. I'm a secretary in White-hall. No, not to Christopher. To a Navy commander, a dear sweet little man who would like to go to bed with me but is afraid to ask."

"Why don't you ask him?"

"Oh, I couldn't! He's married. I'm not an adulterer."

"No, you're certainly not that," he said, admiring the feminine shape of her: nothing masculine there, least of all an adulterer. "If I come up here, is your mother always at home?"

"She won't be next weekend. She goes up once a month to spend the weekend with Daddy when it's his duty weekend in town. Why?"

"I'll give you three guesses."

"Years ago I told Matt you American men are so forward. I'm glad. American girls must be glad, too."

"Not that I've noticed."

"Welcome to England, Duke. Kiss me. Properly this time. There are no bombs to interrupt us."

82

Next weekend they went to bed, in the house where the Quakers had held their meetings—"We're a two-member Society of Friends," Duke joked, trying to keep it light; and had been surprised to see the look of disapproval on Cleo's face.

"Don't say that! I'm not religious, but I don't believe in being blasphemious."

"I'm not being blasphemous." He almost made it rhyme with *abstemious*, as she had.

"Well, whatever it is. I never poke fun at anyone for their beliefs. Being an unbeliever is the easy way out."

"How do you know?"

"I'm an unbeliever myself. All my life I've looked for the easy way out of things. Come on, darling. Love me!"

"Is that an easy way out?"

"Not always. But love is something you don't have to get intellectual about. I'm not an intellectualist."

"No, you're a sensuablist. And I'm glad."

He had seen her each weekend since then. She was ideal company for an airman on leave, someone to take his mind off the business of war with her unintentional funny chatter, her uninhibited love-making, her lack of pretence towards being an intellectual. She was a weekend girl, someone he met on Saturdays and left on Sundays before he could grow tired of her. She made no demands on him, asked no promises. She was a girl for the present, one he would kiss and say goodbye to with a minimum of regrets when the time came for farewell. Theirs was a wartime romance, not meant to last. . . .

Then last night she had phoned him to say she was pregnant.

He thought about her now as he battled to bring the crippled Mustang home across the Channel. He could see the white cliffs of Dover, coming out of the morning haze like the battlements of home. The engine was really sick now, coughing spasmodically, threatening to give up at any moment and die on him. He *had* to get home, for Cleo's sake.

"Not far to go," said Bialoguski, safe at five thousand feet on a sound engine.

He was not afraid once he had crossed the English coast. He might still crash, but at least it would be in friendly territory; he knew now that he had been as much afraid of being taken prisoner as he had been of crashing. He would go out of his mind if he were confined in a prison camp for the rest of the war. Flying was the greatest freedom a man could know, and once having tasted it, any sort of enforced confinement would be like a

83

tight band round the brain. The worst danger was past, the one to which he would have had no answer, and all he had to do was keep the plane flying for another twenty minutes. He was confident he had the skill to do that.

He was down to two hundred feet, still in the air but not really of it: the ground was reaching up to claim him. He roared over a village, saw the clock face clearly on the square Norman tower of the church: it was stopped at noon on some day in the past, yesterday, a year ago, four or five centuries ago. People in the fields beyond the village raised the flat white mushrooms of their faces towards him, astonishment rooting them there in the dark brown earth. Then they were gone, scythed by the wing of the plane.

If he had to go down, he would see that he crashed in some open empty field. If he had to die, and all at once he began to think about it, he would not want other people to die with him. Death was not something to be shared. His mother had called him selfish: well, he would prove her right in that at least. He would not share his death with innocent strangers.

"Field in sight," said Bialoguski.

Duke was sweating now, holding the plane up by willpower, aware of the strain all through his body. This was worse than the Arizona training flight had been; there was no wide open desert here in which to crash-land. The plane was as sluggish as a mortally wounded beast, a mustang pierced by Indian arrows. He saw the field ahead, the crash truck and the ambulance standing by the runway: everyone was prepared for the worst. He had no altitude now; if the engine gave up he could not glide in. He gunned the engine, asking for another ounce of power, enough to lift him over the trees at the perimeter of the field. The engine groaned, shuddered, then abruptly cut out.

He felt the landing gear brush the tops of the trees, but the nose of the plane held up. The ground rushed up at him, a grave ready to open as soon as he hit it. He could feel the plane dropping, no longer held in the air, the propeller stiff and unmoving as a paralyzed arm. He braced himself for the shock that would come as the plane broke apart under him.

The wheels touched with a squeal of rubber, the plane bounced, stayed upright, then he was rolling gently towards the end of the runway, safe at home.

"Nice going," said Bialoguski, still aloft.

"I've had practice," said Duke, but the irony of his smile was hidden in his face-mask.

84

On 8th September of that year, when Cleo was almost five months pregnant, she lost the baby in the first of the V2 raids that fell on London.

She had been adamant that she would not marry Duke because of the baby. "No, we've never said once that we love each other. I know I'm foolish at times, darling, but I'm not a complete nitwit. I went to bed with you with my eyes open——"

He was ashamed of himself for his weak argument, but he couldn't bring himself to fight her. "But we owe the baby a name——"

They were sitting in Hyde Park, the spring twilight fading out now over the dark cliffs of Kensington Palace. Lovers struggled in the grass, reckless of consequence: arrest, pregnancy, a broken heart, meant nothing: you took love while you could, on a twelve-hour pass. An old man came down the path, medals clinking on his chest like metal teeth; his war, his loving, were over, but he wanted to belong; he smiled and winked at them understandingly. Traffic spun a humming cocoon round the outside of the park, not disturbing the shell of quiet here beneath the trees. Up north now the RAF bombers were taking off for Berlin, Hamburg, Düsseldorf. Duke wondered how the lovers there were faring.

"The baby will have a name. Mine. Mulligan isn't the best name in the world, but it's nothing to be ashamed of. He may be illegitimate, but he won't be incognitum."

"O. Incognito."

"Well, he won't be that. No, it's sweet of you to suggest marrying me, Duke, but I shouldn't want to marry a man who didn't love me. Just as I wouldn't marry Christopher because I didn't love him." She raised her hand, devoid now of the engagement ring.

"Well, I'll see you get a certain amount of money every week. If you put him in a home, there'll be charges——"

"A home? Oh Duke, how could you be so callous! How would you like to spend all your life in a home? You've told me how you felt bringing your plane home yesterday—that you were more afraid of being taken prisoner than of crashing. Would you want your son to be a prisoner in a home?"

"I don't want my son to be anything!" he said angrily, suddenly bitter at the way events had trapped him.

"Are you suggesting I should have an abortion?" He was

surprised at the look of horror on her face. Then he realized that, though she had no religion, she still had religious principles. She had reacted exactly as his mother, the devout Catholic, would have.

He shook his head, all at once tired, all at once young enough to wonder if a crash yesterday might not have been the best solution, for him if not for her. Then he shook himself free of the thought. That would have been a really selfish death. The sour taste of it would have remained in the mouth of his corpse till the worms had reduced him to nothing but a memory. He did not believe in the hereafter, but he knew now that conscience must be the last thing in man to die.

"Okay." He sighed and took her hand, linking his lean fingers in her plump ones. "No abortion. Have the baby, give him your name, or mine if you like, and I'll see you get enough money to keep both of you."

"No, darling. Not both of us. I'll always have enough money to keep myself—my grandfather left me five hundred pounds a year. But I'd like you to help keep John—that's what I'm going to call him, after you. I'd like to call him Duke, but Duke Mulligan might cause some confusion in this country. He'd always be getting invitations to Buckingham Palace and West-minster Abbey or somewhere. But I'd like you to help keep him. That would convince me that even though you didn't love me, you did like being with me."

He smiled, suddenly coming close to loving her, and kissed her on the cheek. "Do you need to be convinced of that?"

"A girl looks for gestures," she said, for a moment no longer foolish. "It's all that some of us ever get from men."

It was the only show of malice he had ever seen in her, but she was entitled to it. "I'll see you next weekend."

She shook her head. "No, Duke, it's over. I'll let you know when the baby is born, what it is, a boy or girl. But it's better we call it off now. I know you have a conscience, and it might get bigger as you saw me getting bigger——" She made a curving motion above her stomach with her hand. "A conscience-stricken bridegroom is no bargain."

He looked at her, smiling gently. "You're not really as dumb as you make out, are you?"

"Oh, I'm dumb all right, darling. I'm just not insensible, that's all."

No, he thought, *you're not insensible nor insensitive*. She used the wrong words, made up her own; but in the vocabulary of

86

the heart she was educated. She probably had her own word for philosophy, but she was more a philosopher than he was.

He wrote to her each week through the summer, but got no answer. He persisted with his letters, writing them as a sort of penance. He had given up his religion, but he still thought in the old terms: a penance of a decade of the Rosary, a penance of one letter a week. The God the priests had talked about had never answered him; he could expect no more from Cleo. Then in September Cleo's mother rang him at the camp.

"She has lost the baby, Duke." On the wire Mrs. Mulligan sounded as vague as ever; it was impossible to tell if there was any condemnation of him. "She's out of danger now, thank God."

"Where is she?" She named a hospital in London. "I'll come up right away."

"I think she might like that, Duke." For a moment the vague voice sounded even vaguer; then he realized she was crying. "She almost died, you know."

He had no trouble getting a twenty-four-hour pass. A RAF staff car was going up to London and the C.O. wangled him a lift. He rode up with a grey-haired air commodore, a man with last war ribbons on his chest and the D.S.O. from this war. "Going up to see your girl, eh?"

"Yes, sir. She's in hospital."

"Hurt in a raid? These damned rockets. It's an abominable way of fighting a war." Duke looked at him, wondering if the air commodore was one of those old professionals who thought that war was okay, so long as it was fought on decent sportsmanlike lines. But the older man just looked tired, tired of war on any lines. "Although I don't suppose one can blame them. We plaster Berlin, they plaster London. It's so bloody impersonal, that's the damnable thing about these rockets."

Duke looked out at the English countryside, the trees still heavy with summer, the fields looking like small parks. Men were building haystacks in some of the fields, and a cart moved slowly up a hill, possessed of all the time in the world to reach wherever it was going. It was like a calendar scene of peace: you looked for the saccharine thought for the day inscribed across the cloud-dappled sky. Then in the trees along the crest of a ridge he saw the ack-ack guns, the harvest of shells stacked beside them under the camouflaged covers. He looked back at the air commodore.

"Excuse me, sir, but I've never felt very personal about the war."

87

"You should now, my boy. Now your girl's been hurt."

Duke made no reply, and the air commodore, after a glance at him, opened the brief-case on his knee and began to pore over some papers. They rode in silence the rest of the way to London.

When the car pulled up to drop Duke, the air commodore looked up from his papers. "Cheerio, my boy. I hope your girl isn't too badly hurt."

"Thank you, sir." Duke got out of the car, stood on the pavement and saluted.

The air commodore leaned forward. "When you are as old as I am, you'll come to realize that all wars are personal. Even those you are not engaged in. That is, if you have any feeling for humanity at all. And I think you have. Otherwise you would not look as concerned as you do for your girl."

Duke stood on the pavement and watched the car drive off. He felt no resentment at what the air commodore had said, only surprise that his feelings should have been read as they had been. He *was* concerned for Cleo, but it had not crossed his mind to be concerned for all the others who had died in yesterday's raid. He wondered if Cleo would give a thought to the dead of yesterday, and at once knew the answer. Cleo, dumb as she was, did have a feeling for humanity.

He found the hospital without any trouble, a grey dreary institution that, in the appropriately minded patient, would have encouraged death rather than cure. They ushered him into the ward, telling him he could have only ten minutes with her. He felt resentful of the time limit put on him, but when he saw Cleo he understood why.

She seemed the same colour as the wartime sheets that covered her; and he could not guess at how much weight she had lost. She smiled when she saw him and her eyes lit up with surprise, but the only movement she could make was to lift a thin weak hand.

"Darling, what a lovely surprise! How did you know?"

"Your mother phoned. And I'm glad she did. You wouldn't have let me know, would you?"

"I don't think so, darling. Remember what I said about your conscience?"

"Conscience didn't bring me here today. I'm not callous, Cleo, no matter what you think." He looked about the ward, saw the other patients, some of them lying within earshot of death, and felt a tide of sympathy well up within him. The air commodore, the stranger who had met him only once and would never meet him again, had been right: these other strangers here did concern him. "Are these all raid victims?"

"Every one." Cleo looked about the ward and her eyes glistened. "Four died last night. And some will be dead by tonight. Oh Duke, it's terrible!"

She began to weep, and clumsily he picked up her hand. It felt as weak and bony as a crippled bird. He remembered how plump it had once been, how much pleasure it had given in their love-making. "Did it upset you much, losing the baby?"

She lay looking at him for a moment, blinking back the tears. "Darling, I was really looking forward to having it. I *wanted* to be a mother. I never thought I'd be that way, but as it started to grow inside me—Do I sound soppy and maternal?"

"Cleo," he heard himself say, "will you marry me?"

Her hand gripped his for a moment; he felt the strength of shock. "Duke, you don't know what you're saying—you're just being kind——"

Later he would know that he *was* being kind, that it somehow seemed more cruel to walk out on her now than when she had told him about the baby. She had almost died because of him: the rocket had been only an outside instrument, a fantastic curette wielded by Fate or whatever it was that sparked the accidents in a man's life. Conscience that morning wore the mask of love, and he allowed himself as well as her to be deceived by it. Matt had written him that he was now married to the Australian girl, and he wondered if Matt's decision had been as sudden and unexpected to himself as this decision was. And even as he wondered knew that it would not have been: Matt would never have staked the future happiness of himself and another on the gamble of an impulse.

"You talked me out of it once before and I shouldn't have let you do it. You're not holding anything at my head this time, Cleo—no baby, no gun, no promises. We get on well together, we could be happy——"

"But you don't love me." She searched his face hopefully: she was prepared to accept only a hint of love.

"I do love you," he said, straining for truth.

She stared at him for a long moment, then he saw the tears start in her eyes. "Oh Duke darling! You'd better get the doctor! I'm going to be delirious in a moment!"

"Just don't feel sensuable," he said, smiling at her, feeling the

tears start in his own eyes, really loving her at that moment.
"Not in front of the other patients."

CHAPTER FOUR

DUKE and Matt both survived the war and began to prepare to
survive the peace. Duke was back in the United States waiting
for a posting to the Pacific when the atom bomb was dropped on
Hiroshima. He and Matt would argue for long afterwards the
justification for dropping the bomb. Matt, still flying missions in
the Pacific, had reserved his opinion after the news of the first
bomb. Like millions of other men, on both sides, he had grown
tired of the war and any end to it, no matter how horrible it
might be for the other side, was welcome. His first considered
reaction was one of relief that he had not been the pilot chosen
to drop the bomb. His doubts, then his condemnation of the act,
grew after the dropping of the second bomb on Nagasaki, and
when the real horror of the bombs at last began to be understood
by those who hadn't witnessed them. Duke, for his part, welcomed the bombs and the end of the war without any reservations
at all: the Japanese were the enemy, they had bombed Pearl
Harbour without provocation, they deserved to be beaten in any
way that offered itself. He had finished one war in Europe and
he had no desire at all to enter a second in the Pacific. The atom
bomb was the answer, and he would never blame the new
President, Harry Truman, for ordering it to be dropped.

A year later, when they were both back at M.I.T., they were
still arguing about it. "We'd have won the war anyway," Matt
said. "A few more months and it would have been over."

Matt was a mature man, calm, easy-going, looking a little older
than his years: his professors were often surprised to find he
had not yet had his twenty-third birthday. His hair had darkened
a little, but perhaps that was because he could no longer afford to
spend as much time as he once had on the Cape Cod beaches. The
occasional veil of curiosity that had once masked his face had now
been replaced by a mildly quizzical air that still had more question than mockery in it. He did not doubt the world, but he
wanted to be fully informed before he made decisions.

"Look, I know you think I'm callous about this," Duke said
and remembered when he had had to defend himself against the
same charge with Cleo. His and Cleo's marriage had been more
successful than he had expected; not perfect, but he had never

been as romantically minded as Matt in thinking there could be a perfect union. Cleo loved him without reservation but at the same time without possessiveness; and because she allowed him to call his heart his own, he gave her the love she craved. He was honest enough to realize the selfishness of his outlook, and to know that it was a shaky foundation on which to build a lasting marriage; but he was of the opinion that all beginning marriages were undermined by secret doubts, and he sincerely believed that he and Cleo would in time have a happier and more compatible marriage than that of his own parents. He was even more handsome now than he had been as a boy, and girls from Radcliffe and Wellesley, seeing him on the streets, would turn and look after him, half-inviting him to speak to them. He was egotistically pleased at his faithfulness to Cleo: he was content to go home to her, to her bumbling attempts at cooking, her vague understanding of what he was doing at college, and the wild hungry love she offered him in bed.

"I'm not callous," he repeated. "I'm just being practical. People who start wars, who acted the way the Japs did against their prisoners, they can't expect mercy." He held up a hand as Matt went to say something. "Don't start quoting Christian ethics to me. I'm not a Christian. I'm rational, and reason tells me we had to end the war in the quickest way possible. There are too many soft hearts in this country, too many brains made of strawberry chiffon pie—take the spine out of this country and you'd find the vertebrae is made up of those conversational candies, all saying the same thing: *Please love me.* I'll bet the Russians would have had no qualms about dropping the bomb."

"They don't have to consider the problem. They haven't got the bomb. We Americans are going to be the world's leaders from now on, whether we like it or not. I just wish we hadn't had to start with such a bloody great bang." He had picked up the so-called Great Australian Adjective from Jane and Murrumbidgee: it seemed to be a password in the Finn family.

"You're looking too far ahead. The bomb was meant to end a war, that was all, not start a new era of American dominance."

"That may have been the original idea, chum, but that's not the way it's going to work out."

"Okay, I'm not going to argue that with you. It's still in the future, still theory, not fact. I just repeat what I said—reason tells me the bomb was the quickest possible way of ending the war. It had to be done."

"Not by killing tens of thousands of women and kids. Not by

maiming tens of thousands more for life. Don't give me that—not even a rationalist can be as cold-blooded as that!"

"Look, son, you spent the war bombing uninhabited islands. If you didn't hit a Jap, then all you blasted was a palm tree. I flew escort on five bombing missions to Berlin, besides all the other missions I had. I didn't notice any pin-pointing of military targets on those trips. They let the bombs go and God help anyone who got in the way."

"God? How did He get into the act? Or have you had second thoughts about Him now?"

"A figure of speech, son. Our whole life is coloured by myth symbols. I kiss girls under the mistletoe, but that doesn't mean I believe all the balderdash about it."

"Balderdash? Why not plain bull? Cleo will have you talking Olde English next."

"It was a pun, son. All you Christians are the same—you don't know anything about the myths you live by. You're afraid you may find out you're more heathen than you care to admit."

"Let's go to classes, chum. You'll be quoting maxims again in a minute."

"Maxims? Wouldn't it be great to be going to dinner there tonight? Why couldn't we have taken our courses at the Sorbonne instead of here at M.I.T.?"

"If you're in a Gallic mood, we'll go to Howard Johnson's tonight. You can have French fries."

Duke made a grimace of mock agony, then laughed, punched Matt on the shoulder and moved ahead of him towards the classroom. Matt, following, smiled at the dark head in front of him with affection. They still argued, they always would, but their friendship would survive the cracks of their divided opinion.

They had gone back to M.I.T. under the G.I. Bill in the fall of 1946. By then both Jane and Cleo had arrived in the States: Jane with John, aged one year, and Cleo with Caroline, aged one month. It had been impossible to find accommodation for families with children in Boston; landladies, vinegar-faced viragos with barren wombs, slammed doors in the faces of Matt and Duke when they went looking for rooms. Then Matt's father had learned of a furnished house that was for rent outside Falmouth on the Cape: it meant Matt and Duke being separated from their families for five days of the week, but it was better than nothing. Duke and Matt shared a room in a lodging house in Cambridge, driving down to the Cape each Friday afternoon in a 1938 Chevrolet they had bought from a fellow student who had married a girl with her own car. It was not an ideal way of life, far less than they had fought for, but there seemed no alternative. It was no consolation to know that thousands of other young people were living in the same, or worse, conditions. The war was over and they were enjoying the fruits of peace.

"Ninety bucks a month," Matt said, lying beside Jane in the huge old iron bed that, the realty agents had assured them, was a real genuine old antique. Each bed post was topped by a brass knob that rattled in a broken rhythm every time they made love, a discordant accompaniment that had more than once reduced Matt to laughter and temporary impotence. He had been threatening to remove the knobs for months, but Jane had insisted that they remain. The house was furnished throughout in the same real genuine old antique fashion, and years later Jane would find herself paying ransom prices for chairs that had come as part of the house for sixty dollars a month in that fall of 1946. The rattling knobs did not worry her: she was uninhibited by the knowledge that Duke and Cleo slept in an identical bed on the other side of the house. She and Cleo giggled to themselves during the week and referred to it as the *Weekend Symphony;* it had pleased both Matt and Duke to find how well the girls got on together. They had even discovered a mutual interest in cricket, an esoteric pastime beyond the comprehension of Matt and Duke.

"Ninety bucks. Do you think we'll get by on it?"

"No," said Jane, practical but not bitter. She had come to the States with a good many of the illusions of a girl who had been brought up on the Hollywood version of America. Matt had done nothing to strengthen those illusions; indeed, he had tried to deny them. Jane was not a foolish girl and she had been prepared for some disappointment; but nineteen years of living with a doting and comfortably well-off father and mother had not prepared her for what she looked upon as poverty. She did not complain to Matt, because she understood that he felt even worse than she did about the way they had to live; and she did not write to complain to her mother and father because she understood quite clearly that they would never understand. Her father, blinded by xenophobia and his bigoted Irish Catholicism, had been against the marriage right from the start. He had wanted to know why she couldn't marry some good Australian Catholic boy instead of some American Protestant whose own parents had probably voted against Al Smith just because he was a Catholic. He had only been stopped from trying to prevent the

93

marriage by the determined intervention of Jane's mother and brother. Murrumbidgee, who had known by this time that his own marriage was headed for the rocks, had seen how much in love Jane was, and had made up his mind that she should have her chance at happiness. Matt, head over heels in love and just as determined as Jane to be married, had agreed to be married in a Catholic church, a concession that had not been appreciated by Jane's father, who had only remarked it showed just how bloody fickle the Protestants were about their religion.

"We've got no hope of getting by on it," Jane said.

"Well, do you think I should go to college? Dammit, what's the good of being an engineer if my wife and kids have died of malnutrition before I graduate?"

John, the baby, whimpered in his cot, as if already afraid of the starving future that faced him. "Of course you should go to college," Jane said. "What else can you do? You can become a salesman, but what future is there in that? I mean for you. You couldn't sell a square meal to a starving millionaire."

Matt rolled away in indignation; the bed provided a clanging accompaniment. "You've got a great deal of confidence in your husband, haven't you? Look, I'm not exactly a—what's that favourite word of your brother's?"

"No-hoper?"

"That's the one. I'm not exactly a no-hoper. I may not be the brightest of wits, but I'm not dim. I could sell things if I had to——"

"But you wouldn't want to, would you? No, be honest, darling. You could never be a *successful* salesman. And there is no point in being a salesman if you aren't going to be successful."

"You're taking the dignity out of an American institution. I know salesmen in your country don't amount to much, they're second-class citizens, like your aborigines, but over here, well, they're right up there with Davy Crockett, Buffalo Bill Cody, Admiral Byrd. They're *heroes*. You want to watch yourself, you're likely to find yourself classified as subversive."

"Where did you get that word from—Murrumbidgee?" Jane had given up calling her brother Tony.

"It's a good old American word, just coming back into fashion. But you still haven't answered my question. Do you think I should continue at college?"

"I did answer it. I said yes. There's nothing else you can do."

"I could go back to flying."

"You know that wouldn't be easy. The airlines are flooded

with boys who can fly. No, I'll get a job—Keep still! Duke and Cleo will be thinking you're extra passionate tonight."

"I'm passionate all right!" The brass balls rattled. "I didn't bring you all the way across here to have you go out and keep me! Your old man would declare war on the United States if he heard about it."

"He won't know a thing about it, unless you open your big American trap. I've talked it over with your mother and dad and with Cleo. Your mum and dad want some help in the store and were going to put a girl on anyway. So now we'll just be keeping it in the family—Keep still! As for Cleo, she doesn't have to go out to work—she has her allowance from her grandfather's estate, it comes to something like forty dollars a week. She'll look after John——"

"She's got her time cut out looking after Caroline. If she's a typical English mother, I wonder how English kids ever learn to survive. Or maybe it's because they do survive that they find building Empires a breeze."

"Cleo is all right. You men are all the same—the only women you ever understand are your mothers. Or so you think."

"What's it like being in bed with Oedipus?"

"Noisy," she said, giggling, and the brass knobs began to rattle again.

On the other side of the house the second bed was silent. Duke and Cleo lay there, each with his own thoughts, each nursing the wound of a recently discovered truth. Duke, for his part, had discovered that the prospect of four years of college was as frightening as the prospect had been of years spent in a German prison camp. Peace, not war, had defeated him; the question of survival still faced him. "I'll never survive it," he said aloud, to himself more than to Cleo.

"What?" One brass knob rattled as she turned her head towards him. The other three knobs were on the floor somewhere under the bed, had been for more than a week. Cleo was not a slovenly girl, but ordinary housekeeping seemed to her a specialized science in which so far she was making no headway. She had no system, and the house would have been a mess had it not been for Jane.

"College. Four years of study. Living on ninety bucks a month."

"We have my money." She was not arguing with him, only stating a fact. The other argument was still lying in ambush in her mind, waiting for the right moment.

"It still adds up to just a bit more than sixty bucks a week. I'll be twenty-seven, nearly twenty-eight by the time I graduate, still living on sixty bucks a week. I had plans once. I was going to be earning ten thousand a year by the time I was twenty-five, fifteen by the time I was thirty. So what'll I be? A graduate pauper."

Cleo said nothing, lying there with a resignation that surprised even herself. Her own discovery was not a sudden one: it had been no shock to her to learn that Duke was still a stranger to her. The knowledge had been creeping in on her like a slow tide, something she had been able to see but not able to escape: she was marooned now on the rock of her own love for him. "Duke, why did you marry me?"

The brass knob rattled again as he turned his head quickly. "For Christ's sake, what's that got to do with me going to college?"

She had not meant to spring the question like this: the ambush had gone off at the wrong moment. "Nothing. It's irrevelant, I know." The bed rattled again. "What's the matter?"

"Irrelevant. I wish to Christ you'd speak English. Or stick to one-syllable words." He was shocked at her question: he talked while he tried to retreat.

She sat up, leaning on one elbow. The knob rattled, then fell with a clang to the floor and rolled around for a moment. "And I wish you wouldn't keep swearing at me! I didn't ask you to marry me, Duke—I was getting all my words wrong when you first went to bed with me, you didn't complain then, in fact you used to laugh about them——" She flopped back on her pillow: the bed was silent now. "You don't laugh at anything any more."

"What is there to laugh at, for Christ's sake?" It was not swearing if you didn't believe in the man. He was not going to give up his disbelief because it might offend someone else's faith. The Catholics hadn't given up their Mass, and that offended him. "I'm a middle-aged sophomore. How obsolete can you get?"

"Don't be ridiculous. You're not the type for Hamlet or whoever you think you are. Your trouble is, you want everything in such a hurry. I can't say all Americans are the same—Matt isn't, for instance——"

"Don't start comparing me with my friends. That's an old wives' game."

"Righto, we'll leave Matt out of this. Let's talk about you and me. You still haven't answered my question—why did you

96

marry me?" Now she had sprung the ambush she had to go through with it. Suddenly she was afraid, not really wanting an answer. She was beginning to discover, as others had, that love was born of illusion and yet could sire disenchantment; and she was afraid of the desert that might lie ahead, not wanting to be cast out by the truth of his reply.

He told himself now that he had known from the moment he had proposed to her that some day the question would have to come. But not so soon: she had penetrated his impersonation ahead of schedule. He had no answer right now. He could tell her the truth, but that would hurt her immeasurably, and—he told himself again—he was *not* callous: he didn't want to hurt her if there was some other way out. He had deluded himself into thinking that the façade of happiness was enough for Cleo, that she could make do with that and no more; it was a shock to him to learn that the jerry-built structure that was their marriage had not deceived her. He pondered when her disillusionment had set in, but he would gain nothing by questioning her on it. He had hoped that by the time she came to ask *her* question, in six or seven years' time maybe, there would have been a way out, an answer that wouldn't have hurt her. He was still a sophomore in the art of love, still learning how to accept failure as well as success. He had failed Cleo in every way possible.

He countered with a question: "Do you think reasons are necessary for a thing like falling in love?"

"They are with you. You're always posing as a rational man."

Posing angered him; but there was no point in starting an argument over that. It was impossible to explain to anyone as irrational as Cleo the merits of rationalism. "I married you because at the moment you were the girl I wanted to spend the rest of my life with."

"At the moment? That's not a very rational reason."

There was no anger or bitterness in her voice. She lay quietly in the bed, arms by her side, staring at the ceiling. Duke lay on his side looking at her lit by the bright moonlight coming through the big window. The moonlight lay aslant her, blue and soft, taking the colour from her; suddenly he was reminded of the stone queens he had seen lying on tombs in English cathedrals, their passions and griefs withheld with that damned English reserve. He *wanted* her to be angry, to be bitter. That way there might be some release for his own pent-up frustration.

"But then I wasn't very rational, either." Her voice was quiet, meditative. "I think I knew you didn't love me, but the last thing I wanted was to be rational about it. I tortured myself being rational when I turned you down the first time."

Caroline, the baby, let out a single cry, chased by the devil she had inherited in her sleep. Cleo slid out of bed, crossed to the cot, murmured to the baby, then came back towards the bed. She put her foot on the brass knob, it rolled from under her and she went down with a loud thump on her behind. Duke jumped out of bed and knelt beside her as she lay on the floor.

"You all right?"

She was giggling, aware of what her clumsiness could do to her: even the tragedies of her life wore the mask of comedy. Then she was angry at herself for giving away to giggling, and she turned her anger on him. "Why don't you fix those damned knobs? You're supposed to be an engineer."

"I'm not going to M.I.T. to learn how to fix brass knobs," he said pompously, and felt foolish; then he, too, was angry at himself and in turn turned his anger on her: "Get back into bed before you catch cold!"

"I never catch cold, you know that."

"It's a wonder. The English accent is one long goddamned sniffle."

"Of course Americans are so marvellously *healthy*."

They got back into bed and lay there, the width of the Atlantic between them. After a minute or two Duke, still conscience-stricken, made a peace approach: "I should have guessed you'd never catch cold that first night I met you. Remember?"

She was politely formal: *she's being goddamned British now*, he thought, *being the daughter of a goddamned minor diplomat*. "I went out there the other day with Jane to show it to her, the iceworks, I mean. They've pulled them down. Everything is disappearing. You Americans have no time for traditions."

"Who said there was any tradition in a freezing plant?" He was angry again; peace fell under the bed with the brass knobs. "Christ, sometimes I *do* wonder why I married you!"

"There you go again, swearing." Their argument was following the pattern of so many domestic fights, zig-zagging a dozen ways in order to avoid the point they both feared. "Jane's a Catholic—do you think she likes to hear *that* all the time?"

"I don't swear, if that's what you like to call it, at Jane."

"No, only at me." She pulled the bedclothes up to her chin, rested her arms at her sides again. "Duke, what are we going to *do*? In another year *I'll* be swearing at *you*. Can't we do something to avoid that? It won't be much future for Caroline if the first words she learns are what she's heard her mother and father hurling at each other."

The mention of Caroline silenced him for a moment. They should have waited before having her; that way there would have been no chains on either of them. But as soon as Cleo was well again after the miscarriage she had suffered in the V-2 raid, she had wanted another child. In those months he had desired her, had been prepared to give her anything she asked: her ambition for happiness, her devotion to what she thought could be got from marriage, had almost convinced him that they would make a success of it. Now he knew they would never make a success of it, and Caroline would be the innocent victim.

He said slowly, carefully, "I might be easier to get on with if I left college, took a job."

"Doing what?"

"I'd like to go back to flying."

"All the flying jobs are filled. You told me that."

"I don't mean fly for someone else." He propped himself up on an elbow, restless again; enthusiasm could rush through him like a brush fire. The ceiling of the room suddenly became the skies of America; he could reach up and touch them, conquer them if only he had the chance. "Fly my own plane! Buy a C-47 and run a non-sked company. Fly freight anywhere, any time. The field is wide open if I could only raise the cash!"

"Sixty dollars a week. How much does a whatever-it-is cost?"

"If you shop around, look at war surplus stuff, you can get one for ten thousand bucks. Then you would need another ten thousand to get started. What are you doing?"

She was murmuring to herself. "I'm terrible at mental arithmetic. I'm dividing sixty into twenty thousand. Seeing how many weeks we'd have to starve before you got your plane."

"Forget that." He lay back, the blaze of his enthusiasm dying down. "Once I started flying, we wouldn't get ninety bucks a month from the government. We might be living on your forty a week."

"Where would you get your twenty thousand dollars then?"

"My father. Not all of it. But if he guaranteed me with the bank, and if Matt could get his pop to do the same——"

"Have you discussed this with Matt?"

"Not seriously. You know how cautious he is. He'd rather starve on ninety bucks a month——"

"Than starve on nothing a month? I shouldn't call that being cautious. That's being rational."

He turned his head on the pillow to look at her. She was still lying flat on her back, still staring at the ceiling, still looking like a cold stone queen. "Sometimes I wonder if your dumbness isn't just an act. I'm beginning to wonder if I really know you——"

"You don't, Duke. I hope you never do. I don't think your ego could stand the shock."

She turned away from him, so that he could not see the tears running down her cheeks. He had not answered her question as to why he had married her, and she guessed now that he never would. She had discovered that in the depth of love there is the ever-present root of despair; she yet had to learn that out of that root could sometimes grow a better love. She did not understand the currents of the heart, only where they led one: to pain, regret and a slowly growing wisdom about men that might one day wither to cynicism. Then she and Duke, if they were still together, would be perfect partners: cynics making a parody of love.

"You're wrong——" But then Duke lay back, saying no more. He had seen the tears on Cleo's cheeks, something he had never seen on the cheeks of the stone queens of England. *They* undoubtedly had wept, but in the privacy of the royal bed-chamber: public tears were for lesser people. But he felt that Cleo was entitled to the privacy of *her* tears: tonight he felt the lesser of the two of them, the traitor in the royal bed.

He lay on his back staring at the dark ceiling, at the black American skies. No American Presidents were ever commemorated that way, he mused. They were always standing up, just about to make a speech, playing the politician even in death; or they were peering out of the side of a mountain, as on Mount Rushmore, American sphinxes spoiled by their undisguisable shrewdness. Come to think of it, the only President he could remember who had ever looked relaxed in his statues was Lincoln. And he was not a man who had had the best of marriages. He would model himself on Lincoln. Be patient, tolerant, wise.

But at once he was wise enough to know that the ambition was impossible. Cleo was wrong: his ego *could* stand the truth of himself. It was the only way he would survive. The rational man never denied the truth of anything that was self-evident. And it was evident to himself that so far he had been anything but a success, as a husband or as a man.

From outside, from somewhere up in the real American skies, there came the sound of a plane, a gentle hum that was like

100

music to his ears. He closed his eyes and was the pilot of the plane. Cirus cloud stretched away, shining in the moonlight like a wind-rippled beach. The port and starboard wing lights winked at him, his own stars. And above him the sky extended upwards forever, the only real freedom. . . .

He slept, his dreams as simple and unshadowed as that of a boy. He would fly to the stars and beyond. . . .

2

It took Duke twelve months to argue Matt into leaving college and joining him in partnership in a one-plane airline. Once they had decided to leave college, they gave up the idea of studying hard and did only enough to keep up their grades. They each got a part-time job, Duke as a checker in a supermarket and Matt as a grease monkey in a service station. They spent some of the extra money they earned in taking refresher flights, then they took their tests for their commercial licences and passed easily. It took them another three months to convince their fathers and a Boston bank that their scheme had a chance of success. Then, over the opposition of both mothers, both fathers put up the collateral required by the bank.

"Your mother isn't speaking to me," Phil Dalmead said, smiling wryly, secretly pleased at the spirit of adventure his son had shown. He had not been too disappointed that neither of his two eldest sons had wanted to come into the fishing business with him; it was a tough life and he had long ago lost his own zeal for it. But he had sometimes wondered what he would have to talk of with Pete and Duke, when one was perhaps a monsignor or even a bishop and the other a highly successful engineer. He had respect for both professions, but neither of them would lend themselves to the sort of reminiscence in which he took delight, the taking of risks, the battling with the elements. The saving of souls and the building of bridges were not his idea of topics of high adventure. He was still a romantic at sixty, still secretly wishing he had been born in the sixteenth century, when being a Portuguese had meant something.

"That makes it tough for you," Duke said.

"Oh, she will get over it. I point out to her, I am a good arguer, we offer prayers every day for Pete's career as a priest. Why can't we offer you dollars for *your* career?"

Duke grinned. "I wonder how the Europeans would feel if the Marshall Plan offered them prayers instead of dollars?"

"Even the Vatican doesn't deny the efficacy of the dollar," Pete said. "But don't quote me to the Archbishop."

"I'm sorry you had to do my arguing for me, Pop. But Mom and I just can't talk to each other any more. I come here to visit with you——" The three men were sitting on the front porch of the Dalmead house, relaxing in the warm fall sun. From the side of the house came the hum of the lawn-mower as the youngest Dalmead boy, Tom, earned his pocket money at the chore he had taken over when Duke had gone away to college the first time. He was fifteen now and in another few years he, too, would be moving out into the world. Then Julia Dalmead, who hated strangers about her house, would have to be employing a stranger to cut her lawns.

"I feel bad about it," Phil Dalmead said. "But what can we do? Your mother is a very stubborn woman. She'll never forgive you till you come back into the Church."

Duke looked at his brother. "Why don't you try and tell her that charity isn't a sin, that a little forgiveness might get her a plenary indulgence?"

Pete shook his head, smiling. He was taller and thinner than Duke, a good-looking man who might have been mistaken for an æsthete but for the wry grin he always wore, an inheritance from his father. He had just gone to his first parish in Boston as curate, and secretly he was glad that his mother was not among his parishioners. The Boston Irish had their bigotries, but they were universalists compared to his mother. Secure in his own faith, he did not understand Duke's denial of God and the Church, but he was neither embarrassed nor hurt by it. He had learned years ago that he had to accept his younger brother on Duke's own terms or not accept him at all. His mother had no charity, but he had inherited his father's share of it. "I'm in someone else's parish, Duke. A matter of protocol."

Duke grinned in reply. He liked his brother and had never resented the fact that Pete, because of his zeal for religion, had always been their mother's favourite. In a way he admired Pete. The latter had survived the constant pressure of the daily Masses, the daily Rosaries, the daily admonitions against sin, still to retain his faith. They had had the opposite effect on him. What would his mother say if he told her that she was partly to blame for his leaving the Church?

"I'll say some prayers for your success," Pete said, then held up his hand as Duke went to say something gently sarcastic in reply. "Don't be offended by a heretic's intervention in your affairs. I'll really be praying for the safety of Pop's collateral."

Phil Dalmead sat between his two sons, enjoying the good humour between them, not always quite understanding the dialogue that went on between them. Education made strangers of your sons, some of the fishermen on his boats had warned him. But it was a risk he had been glad to take and he had no regrets. If Duke had had no education, he could not have become an airline pilot, not even a pilot for a one-plane airline.

"When do you start operating?" Pete asked.

"Beginning of next month," Duke said, and felt a sudden expansion of confidence: success lay just beyond the clouds, the clouds that had been the other country of his childhood. "We'll be operating out of Newark. There's more work down there than up here around Boston. But in a couple of years we'll have our Boston branch."

"I think I better say some prayers for Pan-American," said Pete. "They don't know it, but they're going to be pushed out of business."

Then Julia called from inside the house that lunch was ready. She did not come out on to the porch; all the Sunday mornings Duke had been coming here she had stayed inside the house. He had brought Cleo home to supper the night she had landed from England and that had been such a silent, uncomfortable meal that he and Cleo had never come again to the house to eat. Cleo came occasionally with the baby, and surprisingly was welcomed by Julia; it was as if she had already recognized that her daughter-in-law was disappointed in her son, and so they were sisters under the hair-shirt. Duke came once a week to see his father, sitting out on the porch when the weather was good, going into the front parlour when it was bad, always seeing only the back of his mother as she retreated deeper into the house.

"I better be getting back," Duke said, standing up, trying to alleviate his father's pain and embarrassment. "Matt was to come by——"

"There he is now," said Phil Dalmead, rising a little too quickly, glad of the face-saving advent of the Crispins. He hurried down the steps and across the lawn to the car as it pulled up at the kerb. "Matt, you're looking fine! Bob, Nell. Hallo, Anne!" It was as if he hadn't seen them all for months. He looked at the Crispin family with secret envy: why couldn't his own family be as happy as them?

"We're all going over for Sunday dinner with Jane and Cleo.

Pity you can't come, Phil," said Bob Crispin, and flinched as his wife kicked his ankle.

"We must do it some time," Phil said. "Well, don't let us keep you."

Duke said goodbye to his father and brother, got into the front seat of the car and put his arm round Anne, who sat between him and Matt. "How's my girl?"

"All right, Uncle Duke." Anne was a pretty child, startlingly blonde, quiet and intense. She played alone a lot, secure in a world of her own that she had allowed only Duke to enter. She, too, escaped beyond the clouds, already a dreamer.

"Did you see your mother this morning?" Nell Crispin asked this question every time she met Duke. It hurt her physically to see a mother and son separated as Duke and his mother were. She looked at the back of Matt's head, thankful for her own good fortune.

"No," Duke said. "It's hopeless, Mrs. Crispin. I've just given up."

"She'll come around," said Nell Crispin with a woman's optimism. Possessed of the gift of forgiveness, she could not imagine another woman's being without it. It was only a matter of time, that was all.

"How's Cleo?" Bob Crispin asked.

"She's well," said Duke, avoiding Matt's eye. He and Cleo had reached a truce in their relationship. They no longer fought, still enjoyed the act of love; but they were no longer lovers, only partners in a play. Matt and Jane, living with them, had become aware of the collapse of the marriage; they had been embarrassed by it, then had come to accept the hollow replica that had replaced it.

"We're going to miss you all when you move to New Jersey." Nell Crispin had developed a fondness for both the boys' wives. When Matt had written her from the Pacific that he was marrying an Australian girl, she had worried herself to the point of sickness for a month or two. She had known nothing about Australians, except that a good many of them were aborigines and spent most of their time chasing kangaroos. She had been relieved to learn that her new daughter-in-law was all white, spoke English and was actually attending a university. On Jane's arrival, it had taken her only two days to fall in love with her daughter-in-law; Bob Crispin had done likewise, extending his love of England now to be a vociferous admirer of the British Commonwealth in general. When he came to visit Cleo and Jane in the one house, it took all they knew to restrain him from singing "God Save the King."

"I'll miss you, Uncle Duke," Anne said, smiling shyly up at him.

He squeezed her shoulder. "I'll send you a postcard once a month. Give you a report on what new things I find up there in Cloudland."

"You two," said Nell, smiling benevolently at both of them. "You're spoiling her, Duke. She'll never turn out a practical girl at this rate."

"The world can always suffer a dreamer or two," said Duke. "Don't ever let them make you practical, Anne."

Matt looked sideways at him above Anne's head, wondering how long the Dalmead marriage would have lasted if Cleo had been a practical girl.

3

"It's too much of a risk," Matt said. "What if the Russians decide to get nasty and start shooting? Our insurance doesn't cover being shot down."

"Who said they'd start shooting? They're bluffing, son, and we're calling their bluff. Look, flying in and out of Berlin we can make three, four times what we're making now. This blockade is likely to go on for months, maybe even years. They're stubborn, the Russians, and one thing about Truman, he's stubborn, too. Right now we're doing no better than breaking even, paying off the aircraft and getting a lousy hundred bucks a week each to live on——"

"I'm still better off than I was a year ago. I'm in no rush to be a millionaire. We didn't expect to make a fortune out of this business right away."

They had been operating out of Newark six months, flying freight anywhere on the North American continent. It was a cut-throat trade, much worse than Duke had pictured it; to make it pay, they had to spend much more time away from home than Matt had reckoned on. They had a mechanic, Vic Borsolino, who also doubled as freight checker and anything else they called upon him to do. He was a small happy-go-lucky Italian from Astoria, on Long Island, with a nose like a blade and black hair that was always as shining and immaculate as a helmet. He had spent one year in the Army Air Corps, had appeared to have done everything and to have paid the penalty for them, and was crazy about women. He was a one-man multitude of small sins, but he knew as much about planes as any man—or so he claimed. Involved with three girls at once, he had welcomed Duke's suggestion that they should try for a contract on the Berlin airlift.

"I never did get to see those fräuleins close up. I was always looking down on them from ten thousand feet. No dame looks good at that height."

"If you never got any closer to them than that," Matt said, "you might get into less trouble."

"Who wants to stay out of trouble?" asked Borsolino.

"How do you think Jane and Cleo will feel?" Matt said to Duke. Sometimes he and Duke had been away from home three weeks at a time, flying oil drilling gear to Houston, picking up leather goods there for San Francisco, taking on scientific instruments there for Mexico City, leaving that city with nothing aboard but heading for Los Angeles to pick up vegetables for Reno. Cleo and Jane had begun to complain about being left alone so much in the neighbouring apartments they had rented in Passaic. "If we go to Berlin, we could be there for months. Years, like you said. Who wants to be a rich man if his wife and kids are on the other side of the world? I'm not like Vic here, running away from my responsibilities."

"Who's got responsibilities?" Borsolino demanded indignantly. "None of these dames of mine is pregnant. I'm just a magnificent lover is all——"

"Okay, you Italian stallion," Duke said, and looked back at Matt. "Why can't we take Cleo and Jane and the kids to England We could fly them over with us——"

"We're not licensed to carry passengers, even non-paying ones." Matt shook his head. "So help me, Duke, don't you ever stop to *think*? You're always talking about your plans, but you're always in such a hurry to get what you want you overlook all the contingencies that can come up——"

"You and your goddamned contingencies! We'd never get off the ground if we started preparing for those. Flying is full of contingencies—you just have to take your chances with them."

"I'll take my chances in the air. But not with the CAB. What happens if they scrub our licence? No, we'll leave the women and kids here, at least till we see how things work out over there——"

"So we'll take the Berlin job?"

106

Matt looked out at the rain sweeping down from the Rockies, great sheets of water that enveloped the world, threatening to smother it. They had come into Denver yesterday with a cargo of hospital equipment, and had waited till this morning in the hope that they might pick up a return load of freight for some city on their way back East. But there had been nothing when morning had come; nothing but this storm which had now kept them grounded for six hours. Any place, even Berlin, was preferable to Denver on a storm-swept day, especially with an empty aircraft, that was still unpaid for, standing out on the tarmac.

"I think you have a point about the dough we'll make. There's just one thing. The money we make, I take charge of it. It goes into the bank as a sinking fund, okay? You'll never be a millionaire, despite your ambition, because even now you spend like a millionaire. So I'm the treasurer, okay?"

Duke grinned, not resentful, just glad of the opportunity to go to Berlin and make the extra money. "You're the treasurer. But put a little aside for an occasional contingency, eh? Like a night out on the town."

The women greeted the news with considerably less than enthusiasm. "What sort of married life is this supposed to be?" Jane demanded. "In the last six months, that damned plane has seen more of you than I have. I've been feeling very bloody-minded about you lately, if you must know."

They were driving back from Manhattan, where they had just been to see *Mister Roberts*, their first night at the theatre in twelve months. Cleo was looking after the children, John and the new baby, Bunty, who was now three months old; this was Jane's first night out since her pregnancy and she had felt as thrilled as a young girl going to her first ball. She had come to the United States with the idea that, after the theatrical desert that had been Sydney, she would sate herself on Broadway plays. Living on Cape Cod she had managed to see a summer stock revival of *Dear Ruth*, and she and Matt had once driven up to Boston to see the try-out of a play that, she read later, had folded before it got to Broadway. She had begun to wonder if she had not done better back in Sydney; at least there one could go regularly to see *Maid of the Mountains* or *White Horse Inn*. She had enjoyed *Mister Roberts* tonight, had fallen for Henry Fonda, whom she had not liked in movies, had wept when he had been killed, had indeed got as much out of the evening as she had hoped. Now Matt had spoiled it all for her. So spoiled it that she was not even grateful to him for having saved his news till they were driving home.

"Whose idea was it?" she said.

They were crossing the George Washington bridge, a cold autumn moon turning the cables above them to silver trellises against the night sky. "Do you think I *want* to be away from you?"

"So it was Duke's idea? I might have guessed it. He'd go to the North Pole to get away from Cleo. I don't know why she has put up with him as long as she has. Tell me, does he play around with other girls when you and he are away on trips?"

"Why don't you ask me if I play around? Or is that what you're subtly doing?"

"Don't dodge the question. Does he? Ah, never mind," she said disgustedly. "You wouldn't tell me anyway. You're so bloody loyal to him——"

"Now you're really annoyed. I can always tell when you start swearing."

"You're enough to make a nun swear. Don't you ever think to question Duke occasionally, look at him without your blinkers on?"

They were off the bridge now, running the gauntlet of the tavern signs: Pull up Here! Stop Here for Beer! *I could get drunk on occasions like this*, Matt thought. He hated arguing with Jane, and over the past few months they seemed to have had quite a few arguments over Duke. "He doesn't lead me around with a ring in my nose, as you seem to think." The tartness in his voice matched hers. "But maybe I'm a bit more tolerant than you are. Women have never been noted for their tolerance."

"Where did you read that? *The Charter Pilot's Bulletin?*" He gave a dry ha-ha to that. Australian sarcasm, he had noticed, was like the Australian character: blunt and direct, full of rocks. Sometimes, especially tonight, it was a little hard to live with. "What has he ever done to deserve your tolerance?"

"Nothing," he conceded. "But that's not the point. I don't condemn him quite as much as you and Cleo do because I realize that, in my own way, I may have just as many faults as he's got."

"Oh, no you don't! You don't get out of it that way. You only want me to defend you, to say you haven't any faults. I'm not falling for that."

He sighed. "Now I know why governments are against women diplomats. No argument would ever get anywhere."

"You think you men have done any better? If women had been handling the world situation, there might be no need for the Berlin airlift."

"There is a need for it, you think?"

"Of course there is. We can't leave all those people there, even if they are Germans, to starve or freeze to—— Ah, no you don't!"

He grinned at her, thinking how lovely she could look when she was angry. "Someone's got to fly in the food and fuel to them, honey. Why not us? It'll satisfy your humanitarian instincts and make us some money at the same time. It'll be three months at the outside——"

"You want to go, don't you?" He recognized the resignation in her voice. They had come to know each other completely over the past four years since their marriage. They had made a delayed start because of the separation enforced on them while they had waited on the end of the war; their letters to each other in those months had been no more than tentative charts of the mental topography of themselves. But once they had been re-united, had been able to settle down to married life together, each had slowly eliminated the stranger in the other. There were still discoveries to be made, the unsuspected surprises that are the fissure-veins in human nature, but for all practical purposes they now knew each other as well as they ever would. A look, a note in the voice, said as much now as words ever had.

"In a way, yes. I'm tired of flying about the States. I might just as well be driving a bus. There's no kick to it any more."

"You fly for kicks? That sounds like a responsible, family-loving husband."

"You know what I mean," he said, patient now about her sarcasm. "I'm not one for aerobatics or taking off in a hurricane just to see if I can beat it. But a man has to get *something* out of his job. There's more to a job of work than just *doing* it."

He had come to love flying: not for the thrill of it, but because of the skill it required and which he had found he had. He took a craftsman's pride in doing a thing well, and it was not conceit that told him he did the job of flying well. He would never be the artist that Duke was nor did he have any desire to be; but he had begun to find some of the poetry in flying that so often took hold of Duke. How long that poetry would remain he did not know. Already he had heard some of the old-timers regretting that the days of *real* flying were past, that sheer speed was taking all the enjoyment out of it. When the new jets finally made the skies, maybe all the excitement and feeling would be gone from flying. But jets were a long way off, especially for the Dalmead-Crispin airline.

"I think you should have stuck to engineering. By now you would be building something, bridges, roads, a dam, doing something *and* getting a kick out of it."

Jane had been pleased when Matt had told her that it was his ambition to be an engineer. She was not a girl whose own ambition was to set up house, build a home both in bricks and atmosphere, and never move from it. She had the urge to travel, a curiosity of strange places and strange people. In those months in Australia when she had been waiting to join Matt after the war she had dreamed of them, with their family, moving about the world, helping to build the new peacetime world, doing something more than just finding a niche and making it comfortable for their old age. She would never confess to him her disappointment when he had gone back to flying.

"Look," he said, "a dozen times already I've admitted I made a mistake, I should have stayed at college, got my degree. You've won that point. Women are never satisfied with a victory, they got to keep turning it into an annual admission of defeat by the other party."

"You should be writing for the *Ladies Home Journal*. You know more about women than any man I've ever met. Where do you get all your information? Maybe you do play around when you're away on these trips——" Then she stopped and moved closer to him. "I didn't mean that, darling. I know you wouldn't."

"Will you trust me in Berlin? Trust me not to fraternize? What a word for it!"

"It's more polite than some I know."

"Watch that bawdy Australian tongue of yours." He took his eyes off the road for a moment to lean across and kiss her on the cheek. "Honey, I promise this will be the last time we'll be separated. Duke did suggest bringing you and Cleo and the kids to England, but I don't think it would be feasible. Too much expense. But what we make out of this deal, I'll see that it goes into getting our airline——" he grinned at the grandiloquent title "—on a firm footing. When we come back I'll take over the administration, and we'll hire another pilot to work with Duke."

"You mean you'll give up flying?"

He was not blind: he knew how much their separations wounded her. "That's what you want, isn't it?"

It was what she wanted most of all, but she knew she must not make her victory too complete: she had learned the value of compromise: "It's not the flying, darling," she lied, remembering the nights spent wondering and worrying where he was, what storms he was fighting, "it's just that I don't like you being away from me and the children so much. If you could get a flying job where I saw you every night, woke up every morning with you beside me, I wouldn't mind at all."

"Those sort of flying jobs don't exist. Maybe I *should* have been a bus driver."

A month later he and Duke got their contract and flew to Frankfurt.

4

"It's just like driving a bus," said Duke, "only the pay is better."

"Do Greyhound buses have flight mechanics?" Borsolino said. "When we get back Stateside, I think I'll get me a job with them."

"You'll never go back," said Matt. "You've got too many responsibilities here. Half this load of powdered milk is for fräuleins made pregnant by you."

"I wish you wouldn't keep jinxing me like that. I've never made a dame pregnant in my life."

"You mean you're impotent?" Duke asked.

"I mean I'm careful," said Borsolino indignantly. "That's why the dames appreciate me. They also appreciate my Latin blood. These Kraut dames go for it. One of them was telling me the other night she couldn't have gone to bed with Hitler, not even for the Fatherland, but she'd have done her patriotic duty for Mussolini any time he put up his hand."

They were coming down through a light fall of snow into Templehof. This was their second flight today, their fifth this week, their fiftieth all told. It was as Duke had said, like driving a bus: dull, boring, monotonous. Planes took off in waves from various bases in the American Zone and came into Berlin one behind the other like a convoy of buses. You put your plane down and kept rolling right to the end of the runway because you knew there was another plane coming down right behind you. The Army Air Forces were in charge of the operation, and Duke and Matt had early had it brought home to them that they were expected, while in the air, to respond to military discipline. In the crowded entry and exit corridors they had come to appreciate the need of such discipline.

Matt, who was acting as navigator as well as co-pilot, gave

Duke the course as they came in over the centre of Berlin. "That snow is getting worse," he said. "I'll ask them the ceiling over Templehof."

Control at Templehof came back a moment later. "Seven hundred and closing in. You're forty seconds behind schedule."

"Relax, son," Duke cut in. "I've never missed it yet."

Each plane was allowed a landing margin of only ninety seconds either side of touchdown time. If you were too early or too late you overshot the airdrome and went back to your base. It was an error that reflected on your flying skill and every pilot tried to avoid it.

"We're Number Five in the pattern," Matt reported.

Duke switched over to direct communication with Control. "This is Able four-three-three. How is the visibility?"

"Three hundred yards, but decreasing. Come in on G.C.A."

"Okay. I'm all yours."

There was a moment's silence, then Control said, "Okay, I've got you. You're on glide-path . . . you're sixty feet below . . . bring her up . . . up . . . that's it! On glide-path . . . come left two degrees to two-four-zero. . . ."

Matt sat with the same tension building up inside him that he always got when they landed on Ground Control Approach. Reason told him it was the safest way of landing when visibility was poor, but he hated the idea of some remote stranger piloting the plane in which he was flying. He looked out at the snow clouds through which they were descending, then looked back at Duke. The latter sat relaxed in his seat, his eyes never leaving the instrument board, trusting completely the man at Control talking him down through the white blindness that enveloped them.

Then they had burst through the cloud and there was the runway right below them, the snow on it black with the welts of the tyre-marks from planes already down. Duke lifted the nose and the C-47 settled on the runway as gracefully as Matt had seen some of the fighters land on the sun-bright strips of Arizona. At the far end of the runway, dimly through the falling snow, Matt could see the plane in front of them turning off to taxi back towards the apron where the trucks, manned by the German labour crews, waited for it. Their own plane rolled right to the end of the runway, Duke swung it off to the right and a minute later he had cut the engines and the Germans were already backing their truck up to the door.

"Take-off in fifteen minutes if the weather breaks," Duke said, taking off his headphones. "Here's the coffee."

A young German boy, in patched coveralls and a ragged old American flight jacket, came scrambling up past the crates of powdered milk to the flight deck, bringing coffee and buns. "Okay?" he said, his guttural voice tinged with an American accent. "I tried to get some rum, Captain Dalmead, to put in the coffee, but they thought I wanted it for myself."

"Forget it, Karl. I'll bring some with me when we come in next time." Duke watched the boy as he poured coffee for Matt and Borsolino. He was big-framed, but he was not a big youth; there was not enough flesh on him, and even at seventeen he walked with a slight stoop. There was no colour to his complexion and when he smiled you could see the damage that had been done to his teeth by poor diet. *I should feel sorry for him,* Duke thought, *but I can't.* "Were you in the war, Karl?"

The boy looked up as he stood in front of Matt. "Everybody in Germany was in the war, captain. It was difficult to avoid it."

"How old were you when it finished?" Matt asked.

"Thirteen, sir. But I was big for my age. I told the army I was sixteen and they took me. They were glad of anyone in those last days of the war."

"How have you felt since?" Borsolino said. "I mean about fighting for Hitler?"

"I wasn't fighting for Hitler, sir," the boy said, straight-faced, unsure if the men were baiting him but determined not to show his apprehension. "I was fighting for Germany."

"How do you feel about the Russians?" Duke asked.

The boy hesitated, then he said, "We Germans lost the war, captain. We're not entitled to feel anything."

Duke flushed. Borsolino leaned forward, his dark Italian eyes flashing. The boy stepped back a little, as if afraid that he had said too much. But it was Matt who got in first: "You're for neither the Russians nor us Americans, is that it, Karl?"

Again the boy hesitated a moment, then the stoop seemed to disappear from his back. "That is correct, sir. I am for Germany. May I have your cups, please?"

He took the cups, bowed stiffly and left the plane. Borsolino banged his fist on the shelf in front of him. "Goddamn, don't they beat all? Still arrogant, still no regrets—Geez, and here's us risking our lives twice a day to keep the bastards alive!"

"What do you expect from them?" Matt said, suddenly disgusted with himself and the others for their baiting of the German boy. "Would you like them any more if they licked your boots? At least that kid's honest."

113

"I'll never forgive them," Duke said slowly. "If it hadn't been for them, we wouldn't be here."

"We didn't have to come in on this deal," Matt said. "You twisted my arm, remember?"

"It was for the money, son, only the money. But I'm not talking about just this. If these bastards hadn't gone to war back in '39, you and I would be out of college now, sitting pretty as engineers——"

"I was gonna be an actor," said Borsolino. "I was gonna take Joseph Calleia's place, be the Wop villain in every movie made. Look at what Hollywood missed, all because of these lousy Krauts."

Matt looked back down through the plane, at the Germans working methodically and industriously as they cleared the freight from the plane on to the truck outside. They were mostly middle-aged men, old enough to have shouted *Sieg Heil* at the Nuremberg rallies in the Thirties, old enough to have had stomachs strong enough to take the horrors at Dachau and Auschwitz and Belsen. Whether they had been at those places, he neither knew nor cared very much; he did not feel that the judgment was his. Perhaps they had just been soldiers who had done what they were told, fought for their Fatherland as he and Duke and Borsolino had fought for America. Two of the men wore old Afrika Korps caps: from what he had heard from men who had fought in North Africa, there had been great respect for the Korps. You couldn't condemn a whole nation: sixty-six million people couldn't all be bad.

"I can't believe it's all that simple," he said. "War is like love. If there aren't two sides to it, it doesn't happen."

"War is hell and so is love, if that's what you mean," said Borsolino. "Or anyway, some of the time. But are you trying to tell us we're as much to blame as Hitler was? You wanna watch out, feller. You can't criticize Americans. Not this year, anyway."

"I'm not critizing anyone. I'm just saying that history isn't all that simple, you can't pin-point any major event down to one specific cause."

"Are you being tolerant again?" Duke asked good-humouredly, and looked across at Borsolino. "He's always being goddamned tolerant. That's what he donates to the Community Chest back home every year. Tolerance."

Their argument was broken off when the foreman of the labour crew shouted from the doorway of the aircraft, "All finished, sir!" Borsolino went back to lock the door, and Matt looked at Duke. *He'll never appreciate the irony of that last remark*, Matt thought. It was only his own tolerance that had kept their friendship cemented together. Jane abused him for it, and now Duke himself was making fun of it. It was the ultimate test of his tolerance that he could smile at the irony of it all.

Duke adjusted his headphones. "Able four-three-three to Control. What's the drill?"

"Visibility is lifting and is clear for you to land at Frankfurt. We're sending you out. Okay to taxi out."

Duke nodded at Matt and switched on the engines. They coughed, spluttered like some of the tubercular men who worked on the labour crews, then picked up. Duke ran them for a minute or two to warm them again, meanwhile looking out at the falling snow. "What do you reckon—is that snow thinning out?"

"It's thinning," Matt said. "But I hope they're right about it clearing at Frankfurt."

Duke spoke to Control. "Able four-three-three ready. How's the exit corridor?"

"There are four MIGs reported cruising at around four thousand."

"That's our level. What do we do—ignore them?"

"What else?" said Control. "Unless you were thinking of trying to persuade them to come over to our side? Taxi out."

"You comics in Control," said Duke. "I wonder why they bother to bring Bob Hope out here."

"Cut out the chatter," a third voice chimed in, crisply and authoritatively. "That means you, Able four-three-three. This isn't some municipal airstrip in the Dakotas. Button your lip and get going."

Duke grinned and raised his eyebrows at Matt. The rebuke meant nothing to him. In the air he responded to the discipline of the traffic controllers because he knew he would be stupid not to; on the ground military discipline was something that, borrowing a habit from Matt, he tolerated.

Five minutes later they were taking off into the fine snow still blowing down from the north. They climbed steadily into the grey murk, turned at their given point and headed for the exit corridor.

"What's the matter with those crazy Russian bastards?" Borsolino said. "Cruising around on a day like this? Ain't they got something better to do?"

"They could be holding ack-ack practice like they did last

week," Matt said. "Be just dandy flying through this soup with ack-ack bullets tickling your ass."

"You fellers are natural-born worriers." Duke was peering out into the grey swirl of cloud through which they were flying, a look of anticipation more than concern tightening his face. All his life he had delighted in the spice of danger, aware of the treacherous temptation of it but unable to resist it. He did not look upon himself as daring, although he would never have denied the compliment if anyone had mentioned it; he knew that danger held a fascination for him and that it was a weakness, like drug-taking. Deep down within himself he was now beginning to realize that his inability to resist any sufficiently strong temptation would always be the weak link in his chain of ambition. But he still felt he could succeed despite this weakness, and it was this conceit and the further inability to recognize it as such that was the worst weakness in him. He was remarkably obtuse when it came to recognizing the danger that lay in pride.

They had been flying for ten minutes when suddenly they burst out of the cloud. There was still cloud below them, obscuring the ground, and away on either side of them and above them the grey murk still contained them like the walls and ceiling of a tremendous prison. They were in a vast hall of air, utterly remote from the world. Germany lay below them somewhere, a focal point of the world's worries, but from here it didn't exist. All dimension was lost here in this secret grey world; and with dimension went perspective, both physical and mental. Matt, half-dozing, fancy swirling in his tired brain like the distant walls of cloud, saw themselves as between planets, relieved of responsibility, worry, memory, prognostication. Germany and the world meant nothing to the three of them here in the plane; the guilt of nations and the judgment of mankind were only tremors in the passing of time: continents and commonwealths were no more than specks of dust in the eternally recurring explosions of the universe. As a boy Duke had tried to interest him in the immense imaginative landscape of cloudland, but he had always laughed and turned away; he had been too interested in the world then, too curious of reality to want to escape from it. But maybe Duke had been right; maybe there was some sort of escape here. He dozed even deeper, his brain and the plane now one, flying into oblivion.

"Bandits three o'clock!"

Matt snapped awake at the old wartime warning. In the Pacific he and the other pilots had never used the cry of

"Bandits"; but Duke and other Americans in the European theatre had often used the RAF warning. They were over Europe now, no longer remote from it even though it still couldn't be seen, and the enemy was bearing down on them. The Russian planes came straight at the C-47, flying close together, two of them, so close that to Matt, still blinking awake, they looked like a twin-hulled aircraft.

"They're gonna ram us!" Borsolino had left his seat and come to crouch in the doorway of the flight deck.

"Get back to your seat and strap yourself in!" Duke snapped. He was holding the plane steady on course, watching the Russians as they came at him from the side and slightly above. He had no fear that they would ram him, but he wondered how close they would come. If he moved the plane the wrong way, he could throw them off course; they might be green kids who would panic, would turn inwards instead of out; the three planes would meet, burst like an exploding star. He watched them, holding the C-47 steady, tensing but keeping control of both himself and the plane. At the last moment the noses of the Russian planes lifted, they went over like flashes of black lightning, the C-47 rocked suddenly in their backwash, then everything was smooth again. Borsolino tumbled back out of the doorway, and Matt twisted in his seat.

"You okay?"

Borsolino picked himself up and buckled himself into his seat. "I'm okay. Where are they now?"

"Coming back, Duke said. "Hold tight."

"If we can make those clouds up ahead, we'll be okay," Matt said. "They won't chase us into that sort of soup."

"We're not going to make the clouds. They've got too much speed for us." His voice had suddenly become higher; there was almost a note of laughter in it. "Sit tight. I'm going to give the bastards a shock."

There was no time to ask Duke what he was going to do. The MIGs were already on their way back, boring down from above the port wing in a flat dive. Matt watched them come, his head turned away from Duke, tension stretching his body like bones that had suddenly grown too big for the flesh. He was afraid because he was helpless; this was much worse than any fear he had felt while coming in on GCA. Behind him he could hear Borsolino asking what was happening. Borsolino's high, excited voice pinged against his eardrums, but made no impression on his brain. All he could hear was the imagined sound of the Russians as they screamed towards him, wing-tip to wing-tip, like two arrows fired from the one bow.

They seemed less than two hundred yards away, coming in at five hundred miles an hour, when he felt the plane lift, swinging up and to port, *towards* the Russians. For a moment he didn't believe it, *couldn't* believe it; he was suffering from vertigo, it was he who had gone off balance. Then he saw the two fighters suddenly shy, pulling up swiftly, trying desperately to avoid their target that had crazily shifted to meet them, as if correcting their aim. He let out a yell, a cry of fear and farewell, and swung his head, not wanting to be facing death as it hit him. For a split second he stared into the masked face of Duke, saw the wild look in the dark eyes; then Duke's head had turned quickly to watch the two planes as they swept overhead, so close that for an instant the three planes seemed one. The C-47 rocked and vibrated in the storm of the MIGs' passing; but she had weathered rougher storms than this. The Russians went away, still locked together, bits of wing flying from them like dark feathers, then they were peeling away from each other, plummeting down to disappear without explosion or trace into the sea of cloud below, plunging on into the snow-clad land far below that their government claimed was theirs by right of conquest.

Duke brought the plane back on course. "Sorry if it shook you up. But it worked, eh? It worked!"

Matt felt relief rushing through him like a spasm of sickness. He sat back in his seat, feeling sweat breaking all over him. "Don't include me in your next suicide attempt." He was surprised at how quiet and level his voice was. He was suffering from a mixture of shock, fear, relief, and anger; but none of those emotions came through in his voice. "I'd rather wait till my number is called."

Duke looked at him, but spoke first to Templehof. "Able four-three-three to Control at Templehof. Buzzed by two Russians, took retaliatory action, got them to tangle with each other, both planes crashed. Proceeding to Frankfurt as scheduled."

"You mean they both——?" Borsolino, strapped in his seat, had seen nothing of the second buzzing by the Russians.

"We'll talk about it later," Duke said and looked at Matt.

"I don't want to talk about it at all," Matt said, still shaken. "I've made my point. I'm not interested in suicide."

"What did you expect me to do?" Suddenly Duke was now

the one who was angry. The decision to flirt with disaster, to test his nerve and skill against that of the Russians, had been a sudden one; one moment he had been content to stay on course and ignore the Russians, the next he had known he had to respond to their challenge. And he had responded the only way he knew: by turning towards them, not away from them. "Sit here and let them maybe knock us out of the air? They did that to that British plane a couple of weeks ago. He followed orders and look where he finished up."

"We're not the first plane that's been buzzed."

"And we may not be the last! But after today those Russians will think twice before buzzing too close. Christ, why are you always so goddamned negative?" He turned back to flying the plane, his voice sour and grating. They were in the cloud again now, remote once more; it was as if they were arguing only an hypothesis, that the Russian planes had been no more than swift points of argument in the mind of each. Even Borsolino, intent on establishing contact with Frankfurt, which they were now approaching, seemed as distant as any man on the obscured earth below.

How can I tell him I'm not negative? Matt thought. How did you explain that a respect for other men's lives was not a negative attitude, especially when the other men included yourself? To explain would sound like an explanation of cowardice; and he knew from experience as boy and man that in the eyes of some men cowardice and a negative attitude were one and the same thing. Twice now in Matt's company Duke had proved he had no thought for the lives of others, that his own gesture of achievement, of defiance, of whatever it was, meant more to him than the right of other men to go on living.

"We're still here," Duke said, speaking over the intercom, his voice lying like acid in the cup of Matt's headphones. "Isn't that the important thing? Isn't anything worth the risk if it comes off?"

Matt shrugged, having no answer to a philosophy based on the nod of Fate, or whatever it was Duke believed in, if he believed in anything but himself. He had never known Duke to gamble as ordinary people gambled, on a racehorse, a basket-ball game, the numbers game. Once, delivering a cargo of lettuce to Reno, they had had to stop overnight in the town that advertised itself as the Biggest Little City in the World. They had gone down to Harold's Club and wandered through the gambling rooms. Matt had won ten dollars at a faro table, drawn there by the spiderweb of suppressed excitement that pervades a gathering of gamblers like a cold fever; he had taken up his winnings and passed on, glad to have escaped before he had been drawn in too far, but glad, too, that he had chanced his luck and won. Duke had moved through the crowd, cynical-eyed, contemptuous, impervious to the lure of the tables as a feudal king to the lures of democracy; sarcastic to the change girls, silently cruel to the gamblers who looked up hoping to find a glint of luck in the eye of a passer-by. He had spat as he had come out of the club.

"Christ, what a way to fill in your time," he had said. "Open up their heads and you'd find they had piggy-banks for brains."

"That's the first time I've heard you sneer at money," Matt had said.

"I'm not against money. But I believe in *earning* it." Strangely he hadn't sounded priggish when he had said it. "These are bums, getting their money and their kicks the cheap way."

Matt had had no answer to Duke's comment that time in Reno, and he had no answer now. Then and now Duke seemed illogical; it was part of the contradiction in him, the planner who could not resist the impulse. Matt was no gambler himself, he knew that his ten dollars win at the faro table had been a big night for him; but he had some sort of understanding of what brought people to the gaming tables and held them there all night: the devil was in the dice and the cards and everyone had to flirt with him. But Duke had to flirt with the devil's partner, death, and that Matt could not understand. Duke was always talking of survival, yet time and again he turned in the other direction, towards suicide.

Then they were interrupted: "This is Control at Frankfurt to Able four-three-three. You are not to leave the aircraft till Security has talked to you."

"Satisfied?" Matt looked at Duke, couldn't resist the cheap jibe, and felt disgusted with himself.

"You won't believe it," Duke said evenly, "but I didn't do it for any glory. I didn't think that far ahead."

There was a group of Air Force officers waiting for them when they landed at Frankfurt. It had stopped snowing now and a chill wind had sprung up, cutting the cheeks and watering the eyes, making everyone look bad-tempered, especially the officers who had been sent out to bring in a civilian pilot who had disobeyed orders. Cars were waiting on the tarmac, and Duke, Matt and Borsolino were escorted to them as soon as they stepped from the plane.

"What about checking in to Control?" Duke asked.

"That will be done for you," said one of the officers. "This is more important."

They drove through the battered city, the scabbed ruins looking a little more decent under their gauze of snow, to the unmarked I. G. Farben building that was U.S. Army Head-quarters. There hadn't been total war on this city, Matt thought cynically. Something had been spared, to be used for the comfort and convenience of the conquerors. He got out of the car, looked up at the building, now brightly-lit in the quickly descending evening gloom, then followed the others inside. Clerks and typists stopped to look curiously at them as the party crossed the main hall to the elevators.

They were taken up in an elevator, down a long corridor past more curious clerks, and into a large room where a dozen more officers stood waiting for them. A brigadier-general sat behind a desk, flanked by two colonels and a covey of lieutenant-colonels. The rest were majors and a solitary lieutenant, who looked ill-at-ease and very conscious of his lack of rank.

"Sit down, gentlemen," said one of the colonels.

Then a young major stepped forward, a short thin fellow with a Southern accent and glasses with the thickest horn-rims Matt had ever seen. He was the most unmilitary-looking man in the room, an owl that hadn't learned to fly, and Matt wondered how he had managed to survive amongst the tall eagles that surrounded him.

"Cap'n Dalmead, Ah'm gonna ask yo' the questions, but yo' will direct yo' answers to the General heah. All we want are the facts at this stage. No opinion, yo' understand, suh?" Duke nodded, and the major adjusted his glasses. The weight of them seemed too much for the thin bridge of his nose and for the next half hour he would be adjusting them before he asked each question. "Yo' claim yo' plane was buzzed by two Russian MIGs and that yo' caused them to collide and crash?"

"Correct," said Duke, answering the major, then remembering to look at the general behind the desk, who said nothing but nodded almost imperceptibly.

"Do yo' verify the incident, Mr. Crispin?" the major asked, and Matt sat up, blinking a little. He had expected Duke to take over the interview, indeed had wanted him to, and for a moment now he was confused. "Well, Mr. Crispin, do yo' verify the incident or not?"

"Oh, it happened all right," Matt said, remembering to look

at the general. "We were about fifteen minutes out of Berlin, I think, when it happened."

"Mr. Borsolino?"

"I didn't see a thing." Borsolino seemed awed by the rank that surrounded him like a tall picket fence. It was a shock to Matt to learn that the cocky little Italian could be silenced by a display of brass. "Mechanics never do."

The major looked at Borsolino as if he wasn't sure what a mechanic was, then he looked back at Duke and adjusted his glasses again. "Cap'n Dalmead, did yo' take any sort of evasive action?"

"No."

"Why not?"

"I had instructions to ignore them."

"Did you go on ignoring them?"

Duke hesitated only a moment. "No, I didn't. I——"

But the major had turned away from Duke. "Mr. Crispin, yo' were flying co-pilot, is that correct? Did yo' see everything that went on?"

"Yes, sir," said Matt, speaking to the general.

"Describe it, Mr. Crispin."

Matt looked at Duke, but the latter was staring straight ahead. *You bastard,* he thought, *even the Air Force is on your side.*

"Go ahead, Mr. Crispin. Describe the incident."

Matt did, adding no opinion nor embellishment, but even as he talked he saw the officers in the room beginning to lean forward, interest and something approaching excitement now taking the stoniness out of their faces. A memory came back: this was what he had seen on the faces of the gamblers in Reno. Only the general remained impassive, still sitting unmoving at his desk. He was a man in his fifties, small, compact, hair stiff and grey as wire, his fighting days over, yet faced now with fighting a war that was still undeclared. The syllabus at West Point, back in the days before World War I, had never allowed for a discussion on tactics for a cold war.

"Did yo' plane actually touch the Russians?"

"We went close, but we didn't touch them." There was a tart edge to his voice, and he saw the general raise an eyebrow. His anger at Duke was growing, shortening his patience with the meticulous questioning of the owl-like major. "We wouldn't be here if we had."

"Just the facts, Mr. Crispin," said the major, the treacle in his accent suddenly turning to vinegar. "No opinions."

One of the colonels looked at the general, who nodded. Then the colonel looked at Matt. "It would seem that Captain Dalmead judged the moment perfectly to throw the Russians off? In other words, would you say he had executed a beautiful bit of flying?"

"Yes," said Matt, and saw the officers about the room nod, one or two of them breaking into smiles of approval. *Their necks hadn't been risked,* he thought. *All they are concerned about is the end result.*

The questioning went on, of Duke, of Matt, occasionally of Borsolino, but the atmosphere in the room now was much more relaxed. Even the general spoke once or twice; the colonels became almost garrulous; the major, tired of adjusting his glasses, took them off and at once looked twice as efficient and twice as human.

At last the general summed up: "When we brought you in here, Captain Dalmead, I was prepared to have to dress you down, maybe even have your contract cancelled. For reasons best known to Washington——" He looked around the room and all the officers nodded: they were fighting men, even if some of them were only temporary fighting men, and they had no time for pussyfooting statesmen. "For reasons best known to them there, we have to avoid a shooting match with the Russians. But you can't be blamed if, because you are a better pilot, you cause two of their planes to collide. Correct, gentlemen?" The officers nodded emphatically. "Mr. Crispin's graphic account leaves no doubt in my mind that you were not to blame. In fact, I'm glad he was there to witness the incident and be able to describe it to us. Otherwise I think modesty might have tempted you to underplay what you have done. Frankly, I think we could do with a more aggressive attitude towards these Russian attempts at buzzing our planes. What you have done today might teach them a lesson. Now I am going to turn you over to the newspaper correspondents, who somehow have already got wind of what has occurred." He looked around the room again and all the officers smiled. *If he pushes his tongue any farther into his cheek,* Matt thought, *he's going to bore a hole there.* "While working for us, Captain Dalmead, I must remind you you are under military discipline. So don't offer opinions to the newspapermen, nor repeat anything of what has been said in this room. Just give them the facts of what occurred this afternoon and let them speak for themselves. If you need any support I'm sure Mr. Crispin will be glad to fill in. Good evening, gentlemen."

123

Three-quarters of an hour later Duke, Matt and Borsolino had emerged from their session with the newspapermen. Duke was on top of the world, Borsolino was already drunk on the intention of getting drunk, and Matt was plain angry.

"I think this calls for a party," Duke said. "I'll call up Trudi, get her to get a couple of her friends——"

"I got my own," said Borsolino. "Nice little bit of chinaware out of Dresden last year. Fragile, but oh so friendly. Name the place and I'll bring her along."

"Forget me," said Matt. "I got letters to write."

"Forget the letters for tonight," Duke said. "Jane won't mind waiting a day. Don't be so goddamned puritanical. I'm not asking you to lay the girl, whoever Trudi brings along. It's just a nice friendly party——"

He had found Trudi, who had wanted to be found, a few days after they had landed in Frankfurt. She was a tall good-looking girl from Munich who had come to Frankfurt to work in U.S. Army Headquarters there. She was looking for a rich American husband, but until she found him she was prepared to go out with and to bed with any American, rich or otherwise, who responded to her inviting eye. She was frank about her amorality, calling it her American education, and Matt could not stand her at all. So far he had managed to contain his disgust at Duke. He was not disgusted with him for his unfaithfulness to Cleo, because he knew now that the Dalmead marriage was almost at an end; but he was provoked by Duke's two-faced attitude towards the Germans, his bitter animosity towards them in general and his urge to climb into bed with the first good-looking German girl he had met. Perhaps Duke saw it as some sort of revenge, but Matt didn't think so. Duke's attitude towards women was always the same, whether they were allies or ex-enemies. Sometimes he wondered how Duke would have treated a Russian girl.

"I'm not interested," Matt snapped, and turned and walked off into the snow that had begun to fall again. He had contributed enough to Duke's triumph today; he did not have to spend the night toasting him. Trudi, with the body that was dedicated to America, could do that.

5

Matt re-read the letter to Jane, put it in an envelope and sat back wearily in his chair. There were two or three other letters he had meant to write tonight, to his parents, to his sister Anne, to

Murrumbidgee, now a RAAF liaison officer in London. But he knew that the letters would have been tired ones; and he knew how unsatisfying, almost insulting, a tired letter could be. He would write to them tomorrow: by then he might not be so bitter about tomorrow's hero. For Duke would surely be a hero by then.

He got up, made himself some coffee and took the steaming cup back to the old leather arm-chair, the only comfortable piece of furniture in the room. He, Duke and Borsolino were quartered in an old apartment building, one of the few houses that had escaped destruction in the old part of the city. Matt and the other two men occupied one big room between them; the rest of the building was taken up by other flyers on the airlift and by several Air Force officers and their families. Often during the day Matt saw the wives and the children coming out of the building, heading for the PX or towards the park; the wives pink-cheeked and healthy and beautiful, he thought, and the kids bursting out of their skins and their snow-suits to be at the tobogganing that lay ahead of them in the park. He would think of Jane and his own kids, John and Bunty, and at once become homesick and, occasionally, angry at himself for having allowed Duke to talk him into coming here. He would hear an American wife welcoming her husband as he came home in the evening, and his ear would ache for a similar greeting from Jane.

He looked at the battered telephone standing on the huge and ancient chest of drawers in the corner. It would be three o'clock in the afternoon now in Passaic, not a good time for calling your wife to tell her you missed her; the kids would be waking from their afternoon nap, she would be changing diapers on Bunty, she would be in no mood for comforting a lonely husband whom she had not wanted to go to Germany anyway. Besides, he could imagine the irritation at Headquarters when he asked for a connection to his wife.

"What is the emergency, sir? You understand of course, personal calls are only allowed in the case of emergency."

"I'm homesick and lonely."

"Sorry, sir. Homesickness and loneliness do not count as emergencies. The line is required for more important matters."

"Such as?"

"Reporting to Washington the brave deed of Captain John Delmead in causing the collision of two Russian planes this afternoon."

Yeah, that would be important, all right. In the city of Goethe

125

the suffering of the human heart no longer counted. You had only to look around to see what had been spared in the bombing raids: the I. G. Farben building, for instance. *Do not destroy what can be useful*, he could hear the bombing planners saying back in the war years. *Goethe's house, the Römer, the Church of St. Bartholomew : bomb those, they are of no use.* Bomb tradition, bomb history, bomb the human heart. Save only what can be used for housing the conquerors, for propaganda, for stopping the Russians. *Oh, I'm bitter tonight*, he thought. *Bitter, un-American, subversive towards my friend and buddy, the All-American hero, Captain Duke Dalmead.*

The door opened and the All-American hero came in, dusting snow from his coat as he took it off and dropped it on his bed. "That coffee smells good. Any more in the pot?"

"Help yourself. It's open house for heroes."

"You drunk?"

"Just on treason."

Duke looked at him, but said nothing more. He went to the gas-ring, took the pot from it and poured himself a cup of coffee, came back and sat on the edge of his bed. He sipped his coffee, looking at the pin-ups tacked on the wall above Borsolino's bed: Jane Russell, Lana Turner smiled invitingly, good American propaganda. His mouth had the reddened, slightly bruised look of a man who had been kissed long and hard for an hour or more and then had had difficulty in removing the traces of lipstick. There was still a lipstick imprint, the faint outline of lips, on the back of the hand that held the coffee cup, but evidently he hadn't seen that yet. Matt wondered what had happened to Trudi. But he was not going to ask, he told himself. Tonight he was not interested in Duke or his German whore.

At last Duke spoke. "I came home early." He took another sip of his coffee. "Trudi sent her love."

Matt raised his cup. "She's a girl who can afford it. A real philanthropist, that girl, in the disposal of love."

Duke said nothing for a moment, then he stood up, walked to the window and looked out at the falling snow. "Christ!" he said, still staring out at the city, lying like a crippled beggar under its ragged blanket of snow. "What have I got to do, beg your forgiveness?"

Matt looked up surprised. "Who's asking for an apology?"

"Okay, so you didn't ask." Duke turned back from the window, put his cup down on the chest of drawers. The top of the chest was ringed with stains of the coffee cups of a hundred men who had slept in this room since the end of the war, men who had made love here to fraternizing fräuleins, had pined for their wives, had fought with their best friends. *This room has a pattern of behaviour*, Matt thought, watching Duke closely. *And I'll bet we're conforming to the pattern.* For the first time Matt was aware of the atmosphere of the room: it was stained and impregnated with loneliness. It was difficult to think of Duke as being lonely, but now all at once he seemed part of the pattern of the room.

He began to walk about, hands jammed deep into his pockets, his voice hoarse with (anger or despair? Matt couldn't tell which). "But you are expecting an apology, aren't you? Don't think I don't appreciate the irony of it, son. I mean about you acting as my public relations officer this evening there at Head-quarters. Oh, I appreciated it, all right. I've been telling Trudi about it, drinking your goddamned health——"

"You've been drinking too much."

"You're so right! Drinking so much I couldn't lay Trudi. Rendered impotent by my best friend."

"It's me who owes you an apology then. I've never been one to stand in the way of love, true or false."

Duke held up a protesting hand, continued to walk around the room. His gait was not unsteady, but he seemed to have become drunker now that he had begun to talk: his tongue flapped on in a spate of words: "No, no. It was a good thing. Impotency is the answer to immorality. And I knew how immoral you think I am, how my unfaithfulness to Cleo, darling simple-minded Cleo, offends you. But not tonight, Brother Matt, not tonight. Tonight I was moral. If you will forgive the pun, there was no sementing of international relations tonight. I got out of bed, leaving Trudi there frustrated and angry, and came back here, son, to apologize. I apologize——" He thumped his fist on his chest. "*Mea culpa*, as my priestly brother would say, *mea culpa*. It's all my fault you're here——"

"Sit down before you fall over."

Duke had begun to stagger now; he lurched towards the bed and sat down heavily.

Matt got up and put his own cup on the chest of drawers. "It's not your fault I'm here. Or if it is, I've forgotten all about that. But while we're having a straight man-to-man talk——" Duke looked up and nodded; there was a look of sickening expectancy on his face, like that of a man asking to be punched. "I'm going back to the States if you pull any more tricks like

127

you pulled this afternoon. I've got no more time for the Russians than you have, but I'm not going to war with them. Not yet anyway, not till the government declares war first. I told you once before, that time at combat training in Arizona, I've got things to live for. I'll take a calculated risk, I'm not scared of those, but what you did this afternoon wasn't a calculated risk. It was a suicide attempt that didn't come off, that killed two other guys instead——"

Duke shook his head, wildly, emphatically. "No, no, Matt! Suicide never entered my head. It was just that I couldn't sit there and let them buzz me—I had to do something—I'd have fired a gun if we'd had one——"

"I'm glad we didn't then. I wouldn't have been your public relations officer if that had happened. I'd have kept my mouth shut and you could have talked your way out of that one on your own."

Duke put his head down into his hands and sat without speaking. From the apartment next door, through the thick walls, there came the faint sound of a radio tuned to the Forces network: the dead and gone Glen Miller was making a sentimental journey. But there was no sentimental journeying in this apartment: Duke looked more despairing than Matt had ever seen him before, like a man who regretted everything he had ever done.

The phone rang cracking the stillness of the room. Duke did not raise his head, and Matt took the receiver off the hook. Then he turned to Duke. "It's Trudi."

Duke shook his head without looking up. Matt stared at him for a moment, then he turned back to the phone. "He's not well. He's gone to bed. *Gute Nacht*." He hung up the phone and turned back to Duke. "She said she'd be at home all night if you wanted to go back."

Duke lay back on his bed, one hand over his eyes. "She can find someone else. I'm finished."

"Just for tonight?"

"For good."

"I'm glad," said Matt, adding with a touch of malice that he could not help: "For Cleo's sake."

"Don't go puritanical on me, Matt. Not tonight." He still lay with his hand covering his eyes, the imprint of Trudi's lips showing on the back of the hand like an invitation that had been refused. "I didn't come home here for a lecture."

"Why did you come home?"

128

Duke took his hand away from his eyes and lay staring at the ceiling. The furrow cut deep into his brow: he was the twin of his mother, burdened by sin. "I don't know for sure. I think I wanted some sort of reassurance."

"You've never asked for *that* before."

Duke looked at Matt without turning his head. His dark face was sallow in the weak glow of the electric light; the black eyes were dull with hopelessness. "I've never needed it before."

"Why now then? You're a hero. It came over the radio——" Matt gestured at their own radio on the table between his and Duke's bed. "You'll be a national figure in the States tomorrow. If you went back home tomorrow, they'd give you a ticker tape welcome up Broadway. Isn't that what you've always wanted? America is always looking for heroes and you'll fill the bill for this week."

Duke sat up suddenly, the bed rattling beneath him. "For Christ's sake, can't you bury your sarcasm for a while?" His voice was harsh, but it was a brittle harshness. *He's vulnerable,* Matt thought with surprise, *he's suddenly discovered he's vulnerable and he's frightened.* "I could talk to you once——"

"Duke, take it easy," Matt said gently, and sat down at the table. "What's eating you?"

Duke got up from his bed and went to the window again. The snow had thickened now and it was impossible to see the gutted shells of the buildings opposite. The street lamps stood like ghosts on the street corners, the snow forming an aureole round each of them as it fell through their glow. Nobody was out tonight: this was a night for home and home truths.

"I need you, Matt," he said slowly, the words coming thickly, like the words of a language he didn't know at all well. "I'm sorry about this afternoon. I couldn't help it and it might happen again if I was buzzed again. I don't know. But I'm truly sorry. I'd never forgive myself if ever I caused you any harm. I mean that. That's when I *would* think of suicide, if I caused your death."

Matt held his letter to Jane in his hands; it was as if he were holding hands with her five thousand miles away. *He* needed *her*; but then he had never claimed to be self-reliant. The shock of what Duke had just said was not that he needed someone, but that he had admitted it. It was the sort of surrender he had never expected from Duke: it proved once again that there was always one more secret left in every man.

"I'll see that you avoid that fate—that we both avoid it." He did not mean to sound sarcastic, but as soon as he said them he realized that the words sounded that way. Duke looked at him, and he hurried on, trying to make his voice gentle: "I'll help you all I can, Duke. But how? I'll lend an ear to you any time, but that's not much——"

"It's enough. Don't go home, Matt—You were thinking of it this afternoon, weren't you?"

Matt hesitated, then nodded. "I was. But I've calmed down a bit since then."

"I need help, Matt, I can't exactly explain it——"

"Why do you have to explain it?" Matt said, trying not to argue, trying to make it easier for Duke. "Everyone needs help. I've believed that for years. You don't have to explain it to me. I'm here to help the Germans—Okay, I'm here for the money, too," he said defensively as Duke looked at him. And was angry at himself: why should a man be on the defensive when he made some claim to altruism? Had that become a dirty word in today's lexicon of materialism? Everyone suspected the charitable man. "But all I ask is that you have a little respect for my point of view. I'll help you, be a sounding-board, a listening-post, whatever you want. I'm not going to be a door-mat, that's all."

"Have I ever wiped my feet on you?" It was not a challenge: it was a sincere question.

"No. But several times you've come close to it. If it ever happens, Duke, that'll be the end of us."

"It'll never happen." Duke smiled for the first time since entering the room. The strain went out of his face; something like relief, a new spark of hope, gleamed in the dark eyes. "If ever it comes close again, just knock me down, son."

"I'll do that," said Matt. "Now do me a favour, will you?"

"What's that?"

"Wash Trudi's lipstick off the back of your hand. That is, unless you're going back there tonight?"

"I told you, I'm finished there." He went to the basin in one corner, poured water from the old-fashioned china jug and began to scrub his hand. "There's no flight for us tomorrow. Let's go down to the Club. I'll buy you a drink, we'll talk about old times. Boy, what wouldn't I give for some good clam chowder on a night like this! Remember that time we went out to Truro——?"

Matt was tired, but he recognized that there would be no sleep for him if they stayed here in the apartment. Duke would talk far into the night, his despair gone now, making his sentimental journey to a boyhood when he had been independent, before he had discovered the need of help. Borsolino would not be home at all tonight, to bring a welcome interruption to the slightly maudlin reminiscences; he was spending the night somewhere with his bit of Dresden china, building up his own memories for the future. There was nothing for it but to go out with Duke, help him recapture some of the past that he, Matt himself, didn't need. It would be easier to stay awake sitting up in the noise and glare of the Blue Angel Club. Just the place for boyhood reminiscences, among the drunks and tarts.

They went out into the snow-filled night, walking silently through the silent streets, Duke now happy and young again. Matt trudged beside him, half-happy, half-angry, caught once more in the pull of gravity that was Duke's own centre. But he no longer felt that he was the dark companion. He knew now that if ever he had to break away from Duke, he would be capable of doing it.

CHAPTER FIVE

DUKE *was* a national figure for a week. No complaint was received from the Russians, nor even an admission that any of their planes had crashed. They had learned both the negative and positive values of propaganda: when there is nothing to be gained by opening one's mouth, it is better to keep it shut. The American press took the positive line: Duke's photo appeared on the cover of *Life*; *Time* and *Newsweek* wrote features on him; the daily newspapers devoted columns to him and his brave wife who kept the home central heating going while he fought the battles of the Cold War. Hollywood sent its agents to Frankfurt to buy the rights to Duke's story; but within a few hours of their arrival the agents were on their way back to their offices in Paris and London. Word had come through from Washington that no official co-operation was to be given to the companies should they want to make a movie of Captain Dalmead's story.

Duke cursed. "I could have got fifty, a hundred thousand dollars! We'd have paid off all our debts, been in the clear. Is our government scared of the Russians?"

"Ours not to reason why, ours but to do and fly," said Matt.

"You're a great help! You'd have got your cut of this dough— doesn't that mean something to you? When I think that I voted for Truman, too——"

"I think I might have liked seeing you in a movie," Matt mused. "I wonder who would have played you? Humphrey Bogart? No, too old. Van Johnson? Too many freckles for a Portuguese. Mickey Rooney?"

"Okay, break it off. But just bear it in mind—you and I might never again get as close as that to a hundred thousand bucks."

"I don't believe they'd have given you that much," Matt said. Secretly he was pleased that Washington had, indirectly, vetoed the making of any movie based on the incident with the Russians; the less perpetuation of Duke's action, the better he felt. He understood now that what Duke had done had been an impulse that he could not control; but that did not mean that he, Matt, had to condone it. If this hero worship went on too long Duke would begin to believe that what he had done was right, that other men's lives were his to gamble with. "You might have got fifty, but I doubt it. More likely twenty-five or even ten."

"So what's wrong with even ten thousand bucks?"

Matt looked directly at him. "If you want to know the truth, I think you'd have given them the rights for nothing. You're starting to think about glory now, chum. Something you told me wasn't even in your mind when you took on those Russians. You *want* to be a hero, don't you?"

"Christ, you can be insulting when you want!"

"It's one of my lesser talents. It's an old Puritan strain. Another name for it is telling the truth. I thought an old rationalist like you would have appreciated it."

Then a week later Harry Truman, the outsider, the man everyone had written off, was sworn in again as President. The newspapers took up the chant that once more it had been proven that *anyone* could be President of the United States; last week's hero was forgotten and this week's, the underdog President, took his place.

"Console yourself," Matt said to Duke. "If you are going to be upstaged by anyone, who better than the President of the United States?"

Duke, now an ex-Democrat, replied with a Republican oath.

In succeeding weeks the President, too, was given his come-uppance, for no President must remain a hero too long: that might lead to a second term. News turned into history and was forgotten. One of the new six-jet B-47's flew across the United States at more than 600 miles an hour, breaking the record, the sound barrier and half a dozen windows in Ohio. Communist leaders in Italy, France, England, Germany and the United

States urged the workers to welcome the Russian army when it began its invasion: the message did not appear to have got through to the Russian army and the workers of the world waited in vain and capitalist comfort, garlands at the ready. The Chinese Communists swarmed like a disciplined locust plague over the land already eaten bare by the Nationalists: people began to ask the Chinese laundryman how to pronounce Mao Tse-tung. In Brooklyn a man was discovered who had spent ten years in a closet because he hadn't liked the way the world was going: people wrote to the newspapers asking if there was space to let in his closet. And the Russians, at long last, lifted their blockade of Berlin, and two weeks later Rita Hayworth married Aly Khan. Things looked brighter all around.

"Now all we've got to do," said Duke, who had quickly recovered from his eclipse, being rational about it, "is to go back and pick up where we left off. Only we're richer."

"Have you had a good look at the crate lately?" Matt asked. "It's taken a beating over these past few months."

"What are you suggesting—we buy a new one?"

"We haven't got the dough for that. No, I'm suggesting that by the time we've got it fixed up good enough to pass the CAB, we're not going to be as rich as you think."

"For one thing," Borsolino chimed in, "nearly all the wiring is gone. It's got that way sometimes I carry the current myself from the front of the plane to the back. I'm known as DC Borsolino."

"Well, we've got to get the plane back to the States first. Once we're back there, we'll see what's got to be done——"

"I think we'll see what's got to be done before we leave Germany," Matt said.

"I thought we were all in a hurry to get home?"

"I'm easy," said Borsolino. "I'm still being kept warm nights by Hedy. Frankly, Duke, I'd rather be in her bed than in the Atlantic. The way the plane is now, I don't think we'd make it home across the water."

"Oh, nuts! We can take it in easy stages, I'm not going to try and do it non-stop. There'll be nothing to it——"

"We're going to fix the plane up before we leave," Matt said. "It'll be cheaper to have it done here. And I'm treasurer, remember?" He kept his voice light as he added, "Vic is right about not wanting to finish up in bed in the Atlantic. What's the point of suicide if we don't get paid for it?"

Duke flushed, but had turned away before Borsolino had seen

the spark of resentment in his eyes. "Our contract doesn't end till we're back in the States."

"Sure," Matt agreed amiably. "But do you think the Air Force is going to let us fly home without some sort of inspection? The pressure is off them, now the air lift is over. They'll even be reading the commas in the regulations now. There's no one more bureaucratic than the services in peacetime."

"That's treason," said Borsolino. "But I agree with you one hundred per cent."

"Maybe I should have sold myself to Hollywood," said Duke, an ember of rebellion blazing up for a moment. "They would have paid at least enough to fix up the plane."

"Yeah," Borsolino said. "I had a talk with one of those agents that day he was here. He said they would of got Victor Mature to play me. The Latin type."

"It would've been an improvement on the original," said Matt. "Who was going to play me, he say?"

"Minnie Mouse," said Duke sourly, and Matt smiled and bowed in acknowledgment. He could afford to be tolerant: the insult was nothing to the one he had handed Duke when he had accused him of being a glory-chaser.

So they had the aircraft repaired in Frankfurt. They saved money, but not as much as they had expected; parts were not as readily available as they had hoped. They flew back home, had the plane passed by the CAB, and prepared once more to enter into competition with United, TWA and the five hundred and one other airlines all battling for business in the American air space. They were up-to-date on their payments, they had eleven thousand dollars in reserve in the bank and they were now making a hundred and fifty dollars a week each.

"Excepting that he's got Rita Hayworth," said Duke, "I wouldn't swap places with Aly Khan. I'm twenty-six years old and life is just about to begin."

"With Cleo or without her?" Matt said.

Duke's face clouded over for a moment; the frown appeared between his eyes. "That's something I've got to talk over with her."

A few nights later he and Cleo went to a drive-in movie. The summer had been hot and dry, and people, not yet rendered immobile and unsociable by television, were flocking to the new outdoor movies. The fact that quite frequently you were seeing last year's films meant nothing; you were out in the open air, catching a cooling zephyr, even if sometimes it was only the breeze of an argument from a neighbouring car. If it was still too hot to go to bed when you got home, you could turn on the television set and sit back and endure an ancient British movie, one in which the speech and pictures were as indistinct as each other and in which the commercials were a welcome break. The summer of 1949 caused eyestrain, day and night, across the American continent.

"I don't like this sort of picture," said Cleo after she had been looking at the movie for some time.

"Well, for Chri——" Cleo nudged Duke with her elbow, and he looked over his shoulder into the back seat of the car. Caroline, aged four, lay there half-asleep. He lowered his voice as he turned back. "For Pete's sake, *you* suggested this movie. *You* said you'd like to see *The Snake Pit*."

"Well, I didn't know it was going to be about an asylum. I thought it was going to be an Indian picture, you know, rajahs and all that."

Duke shook his head in exasperation. He had long got past being amused by Cleo's dumbness. He was not amused by it because he was still unsure if it was not just a good act; she still had the disconcerting habit of occasionally being as intelligent and penetrating as he liked to think he himself was. Unlike Matt and Jane, he and Cleo had grown farther apart, had come to know each other less and less. He still made love to her and she allowed him to, but they were strangers in the same bed. They had become no more than partners in a physical act they both enjoyed. In the ordinary routine living that made up the rest of their married life they had lost contact with each other. Sex was the only code they shared and each was becoming tired of that.

Duke turned down the sound from the box hung on the car door. "Cleo, I think it's about time we had a talk. Would you like to go back to England?"

Cleo was silent for a moment; Olivia de Haviland moaned gently in the background. "Do you mind if I say no? Things aren't very good in England at present. I don't think I could put up with all that austerity, I mean not after living here for four years."

"Look, I'm not trying to *send* you back there. I just thought you'd prefer it. Your mother's there——" Cleo's father had died in the winter of 1947-8.

"I'm not the sort of girl who runs home to mother when her marriage breaks up." She spoke softly, not wanting to waken the now-sleeping Caroline; but there was a bitter challenging note to her voice. "And that is what you are getting at, isn't it? Our marriage is about to break up?"

"We can't go on like this, Cleo." He stared through the wind-screen of the car at the huge movie screen: Olivia de Haviland crawled across the sky, insane among the stars. Life could be worse, he guessed. At least Cleo had all her faculties about her, she would have no trouble in getting another man. "I admit I'm the one to blame. I've let you down, I've been a son-of-a-bitch—"

"Abusing yourself isn't going to make it any easier for me," she said quietly, the bitterness now swallowed. "Don't bother to do that."

He tried again. He was genuinely regretful that he had hurt Cleo; there was no self-pity for himself. There was no attempt at self justification, no attempt at easing his conscience: he was intent only on saving her from himself. "It's better we break it up now. You're still young, you can still find another man, have a chance for happiness——"

"I had my chance. It was a terribly slim one, I think I knew it when I took it, but I did take it. You see, I don't really blame you, Duke. If anyone is to blame, it's me. Oh, I'm not sorry for myself. As you say, I'm young, I can still find another man. But what about Caroline? Can she find another father?"

He glanced over his shoulder at Caroline. She was a pretty child and he loved her, but like many egoists he was secretly afraid of responsibility. "I know broken homes are tough on kids. But won't it be tougher on her later when she wakes up that you and I are only living together for her sake? Kids don't like to be reminded they owe a debt to their parents. And she'll feel she owes you something because you'll have been the one who's suffered."

Cleo began to weep softly and without moving. "Why do you have to be so kind and beastly at the same time? Why can't you be a straight out son-of-a-bitch?"

Some teenagers in the car on their right snickered, but they were not laughing at the Dalmeads: frightened and cruel at the same time, they were laughing at the inmates of the asylum on the giant screen fifty yards away. Duke looked at the screen, saw a close-up of a woman sitting in a corner, smiling secretly to herself, mad but happy, confined but self-contained. He remembered some lines from an English poet that had stuck in his mind when he was in high school: *There is a pleasure sure in being mad, which none but madmen know.* Maybe the poet—had it been Dryden? He couldn't remember—had known something.

"I think it would be best if I moved out now," he said.

She stopped weeping, dried her eyes and sat without speaking for several minutes. Then she said, "How much a week will you give me?"

He looked at her sharply, surprised. She had never worried about money before; she was neither extravagant nor mercenary; money had been only another of the vague things in her life, to be used if she had any, not to be missed if she had none. "How much do you want?"

"Half of what you make each week and half of your share in the company if ever you sell out."

"For Christ's sake——"

"Don't swear in front of Caroline!"

"She's asleep."

"It doesn't matter. Words can often make an impression on the unconscious."

"Subconscious," he said automatically. "But I'm not here to argue child psychiatry with you. One thing I always admired about you, you never seemed to be interested in that crap."

"I've changed while you've been away."

"I can see that. Look, I don't want to be lousy mean, but if I give you half of what I earn each week, that leaves me only seventy-five bucks to get along on."

"You'll be rich. Remember when you got only ninety dollars a month?"

He was beginning to get angry now: she was making him feel a real son-of-a-bitch. "But you're already getting eighty a week from your grandfather's and your father's estates! I thought of giving you fifty—you'll still have more than me each week——"

"There are two of us. You don't want Caroline to grow up an underprivileged child, do you?"

He switched on the car motor and in his anger drove away without disconnecting the sound-box. There was a screeching sound, a rasp of metal against metal; too late he slammed on the brakes, brought the car to a halt. Swearing to himself, being sworn at by other members of the audience in their cars, he got out, picked up the box and its broken cable, got back into the car and drove out to the entrance.

"Okay," said the attendant. "I got your name, address and your car number. We'll send you a bill, mac. But if you gonna keep coming here, just remember, willya, we're running *talking* pictures, okay? That was Olivia de Haviland you were watching tonight, not Pearl White."

"Ha ha," said Duke sourly, but Cleo was laughing heartily as they drove away towards home.

She said nothing but continued to giggle softly to herself. After half a mile Duke, too, began to smile, then to laugh out aloud. Their laughter woke up Caroline. She sat up, heavy-eyed and puzzled, then stood up, leaning on the back of the front seat between them. "What's funny, Mummy?"

Cleo looked at Duke before answering. "I don't know, darling. Perhaps it's just life."

"What's life?"

Duke looked sideways at Cleo. "Answer that one. Or haven't your magazines got around to that yet?"

"Don't let's argue in front of her," Cleo said gently.

"What's argue, Mummy?"

You could drown in a child's questions: you never had enough knowledge to keep you afloat. "It's one of the things you'll do when you grow up," Duke said.

"Like kissing? I don't think I'll like that." She sat back on the seat, a wide-eyed serious child who had a bit of each parent in her yet looked like neither of them. There was a quality of repose about her that was in neither Cleo nor Duke, a solemn waiting for the future to unfold for her.

They drove home to the apartment in Passaic. They called it home because convention demands a label for everything, and neither of them wanted to advertise their unhappiness to the neighbours. Cleo put Caroline, now asleep, to bed, then came into the main bedroom. Duke was already in his pyjamas.

"I'll sleep in the living-room," he said.

She sat down before the dressing-table, began to brush her hair. She felt ridiculous, but if they were not going to sleep together, she was not going to undress in front of him: she would wait till he had gone out of the room. "I'll start looking for another apartment for me and Caroline tomorrow."

He stopped at the door. "Why? You can stay here."

"One thing you men never learn is that it is us women who have to live with the neighbours. You men can ignore them, but we can't. No. I'll find a place, something a bit smaller than this one. I'll have to learn to count my pennies now." She stopped brushing and looked up at him. "I still want seventy-five dollars a week from you, Duke."

138

He turned and went angrily out into the living-room. She stared at herself in the dressing-table mirror, looking at the stranger there whom she was now coming to know. Suffering, she was learning, could strip the shell from oneself. She was becoming conscious of her limitations: the stranger in the mirror had less capacity for forgiveness than she herself had supposed.

She began to weep silently, the tears rolling down her cheeks like the first moisture of a long-concealed wound that had at last begun to suppurate.

2

Duke found a one-room apartment close to Newark airport, a shabby cave that cost him thirty-two dollars a month and a good deal of his dignity. Cleo moved to Fresh Meadows, a new development on Long Island, bought new outfits for herself and Caroline, and settled down to a life for which she had to find a new meaning, something that could not be bought. Matt and Jane stood helplessly on the sidelines, still friends to both, unable to help either of them. The web of human relationship, continually broken, found, as it always does, a new pattern. Life, the element Caroline's parents had not been able to explain to her, went on.

The British government, harassed by the rising cost of international living, devalued the pound. Cleo's remittance from England was cut from eighty dollars a week to fifty-six dollars; her American friends asked what more could she expect from a Socialist government; for a month or so she became a true-blue Tory, then once more her political opinions faded out into limbo. President Truman announced that the Russians had exploded their first atom bomb, a matter of only small concern to Cleo, still getting over the effects of the British bomb.

People began to worry about the decline of the West, a lament that was put into articulate terms for them by weekly columnists and by academic Cassandras in the literary quarterlies. Russians were no longer to be laughed at as a bunch of bortsh-supping hicks trying to better the Model-T Ford. They had developed their atom bomb three years ahead of schedule; God, if He recognized the Russians, knew what they would produce next. A lot of people, who should have known better but were perhaps blinded by patriotism and shock, said that of course the bomb had been developed for the Russians by captured German scientists. Sober, less jingoistic voices asked if that was the case why hadn't the German scientists who had come to the West developed a bigger and better bomb for us? Washington said nothing. In later years Americans would come to know that President Truman, who passed opinions on everyone from businessmen to music critics, could be as close-mouthed as Calvin Coolidge on really important matters. People worried for a month, then went back to reading their brown-paper-covered copies of the Kinsey Report. A cold wind blew from the east, raising gooseflesh in the suburbs of the West, but the human condition is nothing if not adaptable. It had survived the ice age; it would survive the atomic age. In the meantime democracy would once more apply itself to the everyday things of life: sex, battling the rising cost of living and dying, betting on the World Series, making a profit.

There was little profit in the Dalmead-Crispin airline. Matt came home one night in June, 1950, from a flight to Atlanta. He slumped down in his chair and Jane brought him a beer. The children were already in bed and there was no need for him to act the kind, loving, confidence-breeding father. He acted as he felt himself to be, an airline owner on the brink of bankruptcy. That he had only one plane to lose provided no comfort.

"Half a load to Atlanta and nothing coming back." He sipped his beer, its taste lost in that of the resigned despair that filled his mouth. "The second time this week, the sixth time in the past month. We're only joy-riding."

"How does Duke feel about it?" Jane settled herself in what she called her pregnancy chair. Their third child was due in September and she had begun to wonder how she had allowed herself to miscalculate to such a degree that she was passing through the worst of her pregnancy in a New Jersey summer. She and Matt had wanted a third child, but lately she began to wonder if they could afford it. For the past three months Matt had come home with nothing but bad news about the one-plane airline.

"Like he usually does. Things have got to get better, he says. I wish that guy would wake up that optimism can sometimes be a crime."

"Is he still on your back about having a negative approach?"

"I keep my mouth shut now. I quote only figures and facts, not opinions. How are the kids?"

"John has heat rash and Bunty is breaking in another tooth."

"How's the baby?"

"He hasn't been heard from today. I think he's suffering from heat prostration. Same as his old lady."

Jane took a mouthful from her fourth glass of milk for the day. She had begun to loathe it, had begun to wonder sardonically, if it wouldn't be improved by being strontium flavoured. Like most women in the late months of their pregnancy, especially those who had been pregnant before, she had begun to question the joys of motherhood. She had acquired a temporary cynicism: she was convinced that mankind was defeated before its birth, she wanted to paint the walls of the world's nurseries with the distemper of disillusion. Worn out by the heat, her own weight and that of the baby, she was prepared to agree with Matt that optimism was an extravagance that many people, including themselves, could not afford.

"What are you going to do?" she asked. "I mean about the business?"

"I'd like to sell out while we're still in front."

"What else would you do?"

He finished his beer before he answered, then poured what remained in the can into his glass. Jane sat and watched him patiently, knowing this was how he always acted when he was going to tell her something of which she might disapprove. Tonight she felt so cynical and dispirited she would accept anything he told her, even defection to the Russians. Anything that would get them out of this airless hole that cost them more money than it now seemed they could afford.

"How would you feel if I went back into the Air Force?"

That was something she had *not* expected. "I thought you said you hated service discipline during the war?"

"That was during the war. I did hate it, but I didn't rebel against it. Never as much as Duke, anyway. But over in Berlin and Frankfurt, we were under Air Force discipline, up to a point, anyway. I found I could get along with it."

"You want more than a job you can just get along with, don't you? And I thought you didn't have much time for peacetime soldiers."

"I don't have to be a drum-beater, wanting to rush into action all the time. I'm not a flag-waver nor a fighter. All I want is a nice steady job, one that will give me the chance to go on doing what I like to do—fly."

"You sound a dedicated patriot."

"How many patriots do you think there are in a peacetime

141

army? No, all I'm interested in is the money, the security. I'd go back in as a captain——"

"How do you know you would?"

He took a mouthful of beer, swallowed, then said, "I've already made inquiries. They'd be glad to have me. They didn't inquire about my patriotic qualifications."

"How much would you get?"

Matt grinned. "Who was it said that only Americans are dollar-minded?"

"I have two American children to support and a third on the way. It's them I'm thinking of. How much?"

"With my basic pay, my flight pay, my dependants and subsistence allowance, we'd have about five hundred and sixty bucks a month."

Jane looked at the ceiling, figuring in her head. "That's a hundred and forty a week."

"Then there's the security. The pension and things."

"There's no security for a pilot. Don't try and sell me that sort of bull's wool." She finished her milk, building for the future: children owed their mothers more than they would know till they were mothers themselves. "All right, if that's what you want. But how are you going to talk Duke into it?"

"I'm not going to talk him into it. Not into the Air Force, anyway. I don't think he'd even consider it. No, all I've got to talk him into is selling the business."

"Will that be hard?"

"I don't know. I mentioned it on the way back from Atlanta tonight."

"What did he say?"

"Nothing. We were over Roanoke, Virginia, when I brought the matter up. He didn't open his mouth till he said. 'Flaps down' at Newark."

"Then it *is* going to be tough. It may take you months to talk him into it." She got up and moved heavily across the room to the television set. "Want to look at Dagmar?"

The blonde with the huge bosom and the minute brain took shape on the screen. Matt looked at her. "You think someone as dumb as that has problems?"

"Everyone has problems," said Jane, returning to her chair. "She probably worries about her figure." She sat down, spreading her legs out, relaxing as best she could. "That's about the only thing I *don't* have to worry about right now. Nobody expects a pregnant woman to look anything else but slommicky."

"That's a new word. What's it mean?"

"You're looking at an illustration right now," said Jane, spreading herself in her chair like a bundle of cushions.

"The Air Force won't stand for a slommicky wife."

"The Air Force knows what it can do, then. But don't start practising your salutes just yet. You still have to talk Duke into selling the plane."

The United States government saved Matt the trouble. A week after his talk with Jane, the Korean War broke out. A week later both Matt *and* Duke got their call-up notices. The accidents of history had once more determined the pattern of Duke's life.

"Fate is always working against me," he said bitterly, staring at his call-up papers. He sat behind the desk in the small office that they rented at the airport. Borsolino was outside working on the plane, and Matt stood at the window watching him. "Or have you got the goddamned government working for you? It's that bastard Truman. He seems to spend his time screwing up my life."

"Not Truman," said Matt, grinning, careless of hiding his pleasure. He was not pleased to be going back to war, but he felt confident that the war, or peace action as it was being called, would be over before he and Duke were ready for combat. Neither of them had had any experience of jets and there was at least six months' training ahead of them. He was pleased because he had been saved the necessity of a showdown argument with Duke over the disposal of their air freight business. "It was Jane. She's been praying every day this past week."

"For a war? Rosary beads should be declared subversive propaganda. No wonder the country has never wanted a Catholic President."

"She'll fix that, too, some day. She wants John to be President."

"He'll never make it. You should have had him christened an Episcopalian."

"I'm happy. I never argue about religion."

"Well, if she was going to pray, why didn't she pray for the success of our business?"

"She doesn't believe in miracles, Duke. Be sensible, chum. The way business has been going, in another six months that plane would be so loaded with debt we couldn't get it off the ground. A one-plane airline can't make it today, let's face it. Not here in the States, anyway. Maybe somewhere in the East, yes, out of Bangkok or somewhere like that——"

143

"With this war on, we could get a lot of charter work. We could have these call-up papers deferred——"

"Duke, it's only putting off the evil day, can't you see that? Look, I'm not being a pessimist, adopting a negative attitude. I'm the treasurer, every day I stare at facts and figures, more and more of them written in red ink. I'd *like* to be a successful airline owner—I'm not against success, believe me. But I don't want to be a flying bum, and that's how we'll finish up if we try to keep battling on in this business."

Then Borsolino, wiping his hands on a rag, came into the office. He took a letter from his pocket and threw it on the desk. "My country needs me."

Duke looked up. "You too?"

"What are the dames like in Korea?"

Duke shrugged and looked at Matt. "Well, that settles it, I guess. I'm not illiterate. I can read the writing on the wall."

"You won't regret it," Matt said. "You might even make general this time."

3

Duke and Matt went off to Arizona to learn to fly jets. Matt, after some consideration, asked to be trained for fighters and was accepted. Jane was not happy when she heard of it, but she didn't question him and he was glad of that. He could not fully explain even to himself why he had asked for fighters; he had some half-formed guilt complex that he owed Duke some debt. He could perhaps make it up to Duke by staying with him. After all, Duke had said that time in Frankfurt that he did need him.

Jane left Passaic and moved to Fresh Meadows on Long Island, to an apartment just around the corner from Cleo. Matt was refused a pass to come home when Jane went into hospital to have her baby. Nell Crispin came down from the Cape to look after John and Bunty, and the children were spoiled extravagantly. Cleo went every day to the hospital to see Jane and would sit beside her, soft-faced and moist-eyed with vicarious motherhood, wishing that she might have other children to keep Caroline company.

Duke had gone to see Cleo and Caroline the night before he had left for Arizona; the meeting had been friendly but nothing more. When he had gone that night Cleo had cried herself to sleep. She was resigned now to the fact that they were separated for good, in both meanings of the term; but she did not have to sacrifice the bitter-sweet luxury of regret. No love, once it has burned, is ever dead; not even when it turns to hate, as it never would with Cleo. She would continue to give herself to Duke even when he was no longer there to take her. She had learned that the deepest part of loving is the giving; the taking is only the ecstacy, the fulfilment that comes and goes like a flower with the seasons. The love that is perennial is the love that contains suffering.

Duke wrote her an occasional letter from the training base, being more the dutiful father than the ex-loving husband. Matt wrote Jane almost every day, being at once father, husband and lover. Before and again after Jane's confinement the two women spent most of their time together, began to buy a library of newspapers and magazines to build up a picture of the country where the men would be going to fight. Cleo revealed a surprising knowledge of geography: she even knew where Korea *was*, a fact that had escaped ninety per cent of the American population till June, 1950. She and Jane began to learn strange place names: Seoul, Inchon, Pusan. The 38th Parallel became as well known as the Mason and Dixon Line: better known to Cleo and Jane, who had never been interested in that other boundary. War had made the maps of Europe and the Pacific come alive for most Americans; now they were continuing their education by the same means in Asia. They were beginning to major, painfully and still a little resentfully, in a compulsory subject, world leadership.

In January Matt and Duke each managed a five-day pass and were fortunate enough to get a lift to New York in an Air Transport Command plane that would be returning to Phoenix on the day their passes expired. Duke checked in at a hotel in Manhattan and Matt went home to Jane and the children.

The apartment was a ground floor one that faced out on to some parkland, now covered by snow. It had taken Matt and Duke some time to sell their plane, but they had at last managed it; after paying off their debts, they had come out with just over three thousand dollars each. Jane had spent some of their money to add to the furnishings she had bought for the Passaic apartment; this Fresh Meadows apartment, newer and bigger and with the extra furnishings she had bought, was a great improvement on Passaic. It took Matt only twenty minutes to realize that, barring his own absence, Jane was very happy here.

The older children, John and Bunty, were now old enough to miss their father: they greeted him with hugs and questions, the welcoming salutes of every child. Matt sat with one of them on each knee while he looked at the baby, now four months old and still only aware of its mother.

"I remember Anne was born on Pearl Harbour Day. You think wartime babies feel any different than peacetime babies?"

"Anne looks normal enough," Jane said. "When I saw her at Christmas, I couldn't get over what a beautiful child she is. And so happy."

"I like Anne," said John, five and a bit, still young enough to be publicly candid in his opinion of girls.

"I like me," said Bunty, two and a bit, young enough to be completely and egotistically candid. She pointed at the baby. "I not like him."

"She's had her nose pushed out of joint since he came along," Jane said. "But then women of all ages are having that done to them all the time."

"Who said that—Dr. Spock or Mrs. Roosevelt?"

"Actually, it was Eve."

Then Jane herded the children off to bed. Matt got up and began to wander about the living-room, picking up a book, handling an ornament, running home through his fingers. He noticed that the number of books in their small library had more than doubled since he had seen it last; and recognized that they were Jane's comfort in the lonely nights. He felt guilty, and when she came back into the room he took her in his arms and kissed her with the passion of a man who knew he would always be in debt to her.

"That's what I've missed," she said. "Some good old domestic rape. There should be more of it."

"Do you blame me because there's not?"

She looked soberly up at him. "Darling, you weren't responsible for this war in Korea. Sometimes I get bloody-minded about it all, but I try to be rational——"

"Don't be rational, for God's sake. I get enough of that from Duke."

"Are you sharing a room or whatever it is you share with him?" He nodded. "How is he?"

"Number One Boy. He took to jets as if he'd been flying them all his life."

"How do you like them?"

He sat down on the couch. She lay down beside him and put her head in his lap. He looked down at the face that had been as sharp in his mind as a vivid photograph all these months. "One thing I like about fighters, there's less responsibility than flying a bomber. That used to worry me out in the Pacific, that I had eight or nine other guys depending on me. Of course fighter pilots depend on each other, too, but if you lose confidence in the other guy you can always peel off and go your own way. You couldn't do that as part of a bomber crew."

"What are jets like to fly?"

He shrugged. "It's not flying at all. It's just moving through the air at a helluva bat in a sealed container. The C.O. at the base, he's an old-timer, he used to fly Ryans, Bellancas, Vegas before the last war, says that was real flying. He hardly goes up now, says there's no fun to it any more. And there's a *real* old-timer, the exec officer, he was in the first World War, flew with the British in Sopwith Camels. He reckons that's the only real flying."

"Then jets must be easy to fly?"

"Not too easy. You can't relax, if that's what you mean. Stability isn't one of their best features. You have to watch your trim——"

"Righto, that's as far as we go. I've gone as far as I'm going to go as the politely interested service wife. I couldn't care less about your jet's stability or whatever it is. So long as they stay up in the air when they're supposed to and come down nice and easy when you want them to, that's all I care about. If I'm going to be an Air Force wife, don't expect me to be technical minded. I'll salute generals, and their wives, too, if I have to, and perhaps spit on Army and Navy types, if that is required, but that's the limit. I am not, repeat not, going to listen to you talk shop."

He bent his head and kissed the dimples in her cheeks. "Okay, no shop talk. Just one thing, though, don't ever worry about me, will you?"

She stared up at him. "Are you out of your crew-cut head?"

"You mean you don't worry?"

"Of course I worry! What woman wouldn't except one who wanted to get rid of her husband? Look, I'm not going to be one of those stiff upper lip wives now we're in the services. I worried when you flew the old C-47 and I told you so. I'm going to worry now, when you're flying these jets, either here or in Korea or wherever you'll be. If it's what you want to do, I don't mind— or rather I do mind, but I'm agreeable to it. I don't want to be selfish or demanding. But don't expect me to act like those wives in films about the British Navy. The stiff upper lip has never been fashionable in the Finn family. We are the greatest bloody moaners and whiners ever to come out of Ireland, and there's been a few of them. We used to spend Sunday nights keening round the old piano."

He smiled despite his concern that she should worry so much over him. "Stiff upper lips are no good for kissing."

"Where did you learn that?"

"During the war. I dated a girl whose family were old Annapolis types. No passion at all. We made love standing up, as if we were performing to some sort of national anthem, and all I got was a rash on the mouth. She had lips like wooden louvres."

She laughed, not believing a word of what he said. Then she pulled his face down to hers and kissed him with a fierceness that frightened him. Women were always capable of more passion than men; that was something he had learned in the first months of marriage to her. He knew that his love for her was equal to her own for him, but always he felt that his expression of it was less than hers. A woman could love with tears of happiness, something Matt knew he could never achieve himself; he was not incapable of weeping, but they were the easier tears of sadness and regret. He could taste the salt now as it ran down her cheeks to their joined mouths. He tasted the tears, assured by his own heart that he was entitled to share them.

That five-day leave was a short tremendous season of love: the children included completely in it during the day, the nights reserved for themselves. They marked each other with the cicatrices of passion, trying to squeeze a year's agony of love into four nights. They had no inhibitions about sex; for them it was the natural expression of what they felt for each other. They would fall asleep exhausted, bruised and smarting, destroyed and yet victorious, having triumphed over the small death that is the act of love. In the mornings they would wake to the cries and laughter of the children, the fruit of what they felt for each other.

"I'd like a dozen kids," said Jane, looking beautiful even in the morning, her dark red hair spread like a giant crushed flower on the pillow beneath her head. She was twenty-five now and all the promise of her beauty had matured. With the coming of the children her body had rounded, had become fuller but had remained firm; she exercised regularly, almost devotedly each day. She had been meticulous about her post-natal exercises and her belly was as smooth and firm as when Matt had first seen it; Matt, himself a physical fitness addict, had been pleased at how well she took care of herself. She was no faddist, did not diet nor smother herself in creams guaranteed to make sirens out of sows;

148

she was candidly pleased with her beauty and was determined to hold on to it for as long as she could without being a slave to it. Matt, twenty-seven, still not within sight of the descending slopes to middle and old age, still seeing only the beauty of the moment, not yet able to trace the lines in the fallen flesh of the years to come, was certain she would be beautiful till she died. And he deliberately never thought of her as in death. That was a thought he could not face.

"A dozen kids," she repeated. "How would I go as a matriarch? Shall we give it a go?"

"It wouldn't be an economic proposition on a captain's pay."

"Hurry up and be a general then."

"By the time I'm a general, you'll be in no fit condition to bear kids. I probably won't be in any fit condition to get you pregnant. Not unless I wear an oxygen mask."

"Louis the Fourteenth was doing it when he was in his eighties."

"That's the French for you. Preoccupied with it."

"What are you going to do in your eighties?"

"Not you," he said, then slid his hand under her and pulled her to him. "But I'm not eighty this morning."

"Watch it," said Jane, and pulled the covers up round her as John and Bunty came into the room.

"Hey, Mummy, you got no clothes on!" shrieked John, for the benefit of the neighbours. "Neither has Daddy!"

"Where's his camera?" asked Matt with mock sourness. "He's got the makings of a good private eye. Why don't you teach your kids to knock on bedroom doors?"

"Why, Daddy?" Bunty said. Hers was not only the bluntness of a child: she had inherited the direct approach of her mother. She looked wide-eyed at the world, a child whose seeming innocence would later on delude men into thinking they could take advantage of her. Curiosity would never trap her, as it does so many, but would only educate her.

"It's polite," Matt told her.

"What's polite?"

He shrugged resignedly. "You win. Come in any time you feel like it." He looked out the window through the venetian blinds that John had opened; snow was falling, confetti for another happy day. This was the last day of his leave and he wondered when the next would be. "How about some sledding today? Is Stevie awake?"

John nodded, bouncing on the end of the bed. He had his

149

father's compact build, but more energy than Matt could remember ever having owned; the apartment crackled with the electric liveliness of him, sometimes wearing thin Jane's patience with him. "He wants his bottle."

"Did he tell you?" Jane said.

"No-o-o."

"Righto, then let him speak up for himself. I'm not going to have you telling me I'm a neglectful mother. Now go on, buzz off and get dressed before I get the wooden spoon to you."

"Do you still use that on them?" Matt said as the children skidded out of the room in a blast of laughter and shrieks.

"Why not? Spare the rod and spoil the child. Shakespeare, I think."

"Oh? I thought it was de Sade."

"No." She got out of bed and looked at a bruise. "De Sade is the man I've been sleeping with." She closed the bedroom door as he also got out of bed. She came and stood close to him, putting her arms round his neck. "Will you be faithful to me in Korea?"

"Is that a serious question?" She nodded, and he put his arms round her waist, locking his hands together in the hollow of her back. "You shouldn't have asked it this morning. Not after last night."

She smiled lovingly at him and nuzzled her lips against his chin. "That's what I love about you, darling. You're the romantic type. No, I mean it. In the morning you can feel how a woman can feel about a wonderful night of love."

"Then why did you ask such a question?"

"Because I *am* a woman. Torturing ourselves is part of our loving. Jealousy is just another way of cutting our wrists."

He stared at her, frightened of the stranger in his arms. "Do you ever think of suicide?"

"No."

"Would you?"

She hesitated, then looked up at him honestly and directly. "It depends. If I lost both you and the children, yes. There wouldn't be anything else left to live for. I'm not a girl who could make a go of two or three lives. I've got only one life, the one I started the day I met you. It's the only one I want to live. So far I've had more happiness than any woman deserves. I shouldn't complain if it was taken away from me. I'd be sad, heartbroken, but I shouldn't complain that anything was owed to me. Oh, I've been separated from you more than I've wanted, things could have been better that way—but, well, do I sound morbid or something because I feel that God has already been too good to me?"

"I wish you wouldn't bring God into our bedroom. You make me feel like a Heaven-sent gift, some sort of two-legged manna."

"Oh, and what a manna!" She laughed suddenly, feeling the mood had to be broken; if it went on too long, it would spoil their last day together. She broke away from him. "Come on before I get carried away again! You have your shower first, while I get the baby his bottle." She put on a housecoat, ran a comb through her hair, then went to the door of the bedroom. She stopped there and looked back at him. There was no coquetry, no passion on the broad-cheeked, satin-skinned face, the full-lipped mouth bruised from the night's love-making, the deep-lidded eyes still a little heavy from the sleep of exhaustion. There was only humility, the charity of a woman who offered the gift of herself. "I love you, darling."

Matt went into the bathroom, stunned that he should be the object of such a love, fearful for the future when a suicide might be laid at the door of his own death. He had survived one war: it was even more imperative that he should survive this one.

4

The men went to Korea in March, 1951. Cleo, who had seen Duke only once on his five-day leave in January when he came to see Caroline, got only an occasional letter from him from then until the end of the war. For other news of Duke she had to rely on the picture postcards Caroline received, and what mention of Duke was in the letters Jane received from Matt. Sometimes she would look at Caroline, asleep in bed at night, and would weep silently, feeling she had failed the child in not having succeeded in making its father love her.

Divorce had not been mentioned between Duke and herself, and she was grateful for that: it gave her some hope that some day he might come back to her. She was birthmarked with hope; nothing was ever entirely lost. All her life she had believed that tomorrow would be better; but unlike so many optimists she had not ignored today. She had always got as much as she could from the moment: for her, *living*, the mere fact of being alive, had been important. Even now, when life was only half a life without Duke, she got the most from living.

She came round to the Crispin apartment, bringing Caroline

with her, one afternoon in late October. She still had a summer tan, and in the yellow wool dress she wore and with her blonde hair shining, she looked rudely and beautifully healthy. Any normally healthy man would have been attracted to her, and that was how it was with Murrumbidgee Finn.

He had arrived in the United States only a week before. He was now a wing-commander and had just taken up his post as one of the RAAF liaison officers at the Australian Embassy in Washington. He had come up to New York this morning and had come out to Fresh Meadows at once. He had not seen Jane for six years, and he had been delighted, and a little envious, to see how successful her marriage had been. His own marriage had now been finished for five years; he had agreed to Doreen's divorcing him for desertion. He was no longer in love with her, but he had decided that he was not interested in another marriage; the decision was due in part to his Catholic beliefs, in part to his lack of faith in being able to make a success of another marriage. Like Cleo he had planned to spend his life with only one partner; it would take more readjustment than he was prepared to undergo to settle down with someone else. The truth was that he was looking for another Doreen, the ideal that the good-deal-less-than-perfect Doreen had proved not to be. In moments of candid honesty with himself he recognized the futility of his search.

"It's a pity I have to go back to Washington first thing tomorrow morning," he said after Cleo had been telling him what he should see while in New York. "Perhaps you could have shown me around."

"You've still got tonight," said Jane, suddenly deciding to act as matchmaker. She had no thought of her brother and Cleo as a future married couple, but like most happily married women she found it distressing to see two people whom she liked without partners. She did not know how Murrumbidgee had been entertaining himself over the past five years, but she did know that Cleo had not been out with another man since she and Duke had separated. With the naïveté of a lot of sisters regarding their brothers, she thought Cleo would be safe with Murrumbidgee. "You've told me all the family news. Take him out and show him the town, Cleo. I'll look after Caroline."

Caroline was quite happy to stay the night at the Crispin apartment; she welcomed any escape from the lonely life of an only child. "Go with the man, Mummy."

Murrumbidgee laughed, a blast of sound that scared the

Crispin baby into crying. "By God, what a country! What an effect it has on women! Even the infants are trained to trap a bloke."

"Don't you want to go out with Cleo?" said Jane, wondering if she had made a mistake.

"Of course I do! But give a bloke a chance to make his own dates, will you? I was going to ask you, Cleo, but I was beaten to the jump."

"So was I," said Cleo, who had come to appreciate American ways; gentility was an English habit that had never fitted her very well. "I mean, I was going to ask you myself."

Murrumbidgee looked at all the women, young and old, then looked at John. "How can a man win?"

"Win what, Uncle Tony?"

"Get your father to tell you, John. He no doubt feels he's a loser, too. Well, where are you going to take me, Cleo?"

Cleo, no conformist, took him to few of the usual tourist haunts. This avoidance of New York's pride was not planned; she just didn't know how to get to most of the places. She was the worst guide any stranger to New York could have had; the ghost of Henry Hudson would have found his way about with more certainty. She did manage to show Murrumbidgee Rockefeller Center, but that was only accidental; she thought she was taking him to Grant's Tomb. Twice they made the subway trip to Long Island City: the first time they were supposed to be heading for The Cloisters, the second time for Wall Street. Murrumbidgee saw the Chronic Disease Hospital on Welfare Island, the Municipal Asphalt plant, the Fulton Street fish markets and (neither Cleo nor Murrumbidgee would ever know how they got there), the New York Central's freight yards across the river in Weehawken, New Jersey. When Murrumbidgee at last managed to put his aching feet up, he found he was watching a roller derby in some cavernous building that, for all he knew, could have been in the middle of Lake Superior.

"Where are we, love?" A horde of roller skaters thundered by, making the building tremble, and he had to repeat the question, shouting at the top of his voice. Other members of the audience, most of them less than half his age, looked at him curiously, then went back to watching the derby.

Cleo waited till the skaters were on the opposite side of the arena. "Some armory, darling, I've forgotten which. I thought you might like to see this. It's terribly thrilling. It's New York via London."

"*Via* London?" All afternoon and evening he had had trouble with her use of language.

"Via?" The skaters came by again, the Golden Horde on wheels: they went round and round in circles, looking for something to lay waste to. Cleo screamed at Murrumbidgee, "Versus?"

He nodded, and absently bit into the hamburger that looked as if it was going to be dinner. He wondered what the Ambassador would say if he could see one of his officers, a wing-commander in uniform, munching hamburgers at a roller derby and screaming at the top of his voice at a dumb blonde. Well, being a diplomat meant making contact with the natives. Except that Cleo was only a naturalized native.

"Do you come here often?" he yelled. The question sounded ridiculous, a parody of the question he had often asked girls at dance halls in his youth, and suddenly he roared with laughter. A lone girl skater, hopelessly out-distanced by her rivals, threw him a dirty glance, thinking he was laughing at her, as she rolled past.

Cleo laughed with him, not knowing why he was laughing but enjoying his company and glad that he, too, seemed to be enjoying himself. It was a long time since she had laughed in the company of a man. "No, this is the first time. We came by the armory twice today. I saw the sign outside then."

"You mean you managed to find your way back here?"

Cleo nodded, unoffended. "Incredulous, isn't it?"

Murrumbidgee was slowly becoming accustomed to the noise inside the echoing cavern of the armory: the rolling thunder of the skaters on the boards, the shrieks and yells of the audience, the sham excitement of the commentator as he blared his voice over the amplifiers. He looked good-humouredly at Cleo, put a huge hand on her arm and squeezed it and said, "Cleo, you're incredible yourself, bloody incredible. But I'd rather believe in you than in a dozen other crows I've met over the past five years."

"Is that a compliment?" Cleo shrieked as New York and London skated by.

"Too bloody right it is!"

Cleo turned, smiled at him, then impulsively leaned across and kissed him. Then she turned back and looked at a woman skater who had rolled to a stop in front of them. The skater, wearing the Union Jack as a jacket, was leaning on the rail, sneering and making rude noises at the other skaters as they whizzed by. Cleo reached over and tugged on the Union Jack.

154

"I'm English, darling. Why aren't you skating? Are you giving up?"

"Shaddup and mind ya bizness," said the skater, a Cockney from the Bronx.

"I was only going to wish you lots of luck," said Cleo.

"Shove ya luck," said the lady skater.

At that Cleo stood up, reached across, took the Union Jack in both hands and ripped it from the shoulders of the skater. "You aren't fit to be wearing that flag!" Cleo yelled as the skaters whirled by again.

The lady skater stared at Cleo for a moment, as if wondering how this Boadicea had got by the immigration authorities. Then she proved her heritage, if not her nationality, with a flood of Anglo-Saxon language.

"Break it down, love," said Murrumbidgee. "There may be one or two ladies in the audience."

The lady skater looked at his uniform. "What bus line do you drive for, buster? Shaddup and mind ya bizness!" She looked back at Cleo. "Gimme back that flag!"

Cleo dropped the flag in Murrumbidgee's lap. Then she leaned forward and gave the skater a push. The skater let out a yell, then skidded down the steeply inclined track to land on her rump in the middle of the arena. She clambered to her feet, hampered by her skates, and made to come back up the track; but the other skaters, strung out now in a long weaving line, came round once more. By the time they had gone, so had Cleo and Murrumbidgee.

Outside the armory Murrumbidgee said, "Is that how you usually entertain your boy friends—by starting a riot?"

Cleo clutched the Union Jack to her bosom. "You shouldn't have pulled me out of there, darling. She had no right to be wearing this flag. I'll bet those others haven't, either. My grandfather, he was an admiral, he'd have had them shot."

"Well, I'm glad *he* wasn't here tonight," said Murrumbidgee. "Love, I admire your British patriotism, but I'm an official Aussie representative in this country. I can't afford to get caught up in demonstrations against the debasement of the Union Jack."

Cleo giggled and stuffed the flag in her coat pocket. "I'm sorry—must I go on calling you Murrumbidgee? That's too long for a girl to wrap her tongue around. I mean, it's not an intimate name, is it?"

Murrumbidgee grinned. "Are we going to be intimate?"

"Who's being forward now?" She put her arm in his as they

walked across town towards Fifth Avenue. At least she *hoped* they were headed towards Fifth. "I used to think that about American men once," she said pensively, regretting one American man who was no longer forward towards her. "Jane told me all about you. How did you feel when your wife left you?"

He stopped and looked at her, standing in the middle of the sidewalk while people streamed past them. "I thought the English were supposed to be ultra-reserved about private affairs?"

"Have I offended you?" Cleo did not look apologetic.

"No-o," he said slowly, beginning to walk on. "But you surprised me. Why did you ask that question?"

"I don't know, actually," she confessed. "Perhaps I just want to know if the way I feel is wrong."

"How *do* you feel?"

"As if it's all not quite true, like a dream. My husband has been gone quite a while now, but I still can't believe he's gone permanently." She looked up at the street-sign above them. "Oh, this is Fifth Avenue!"

"Congratulations. We made it."

"Where did you think we might finish up?"

"I really don't know. But I wouldn't have been surprised if it had been Piccadilly or the Champs Elysées."

She stared at him, then suddenly she burst into a loud peal of laughter; passers-by turned and looked back at the happy, laughing woman without a care in the world. "You're pulling my leg!"

"I could think of worse ways of spending the rest of the night," said Murrumbidgee.

She was still smiling when she said, "You're really trying hard, aren't you?"

He shook his head and pressed the hand that was now in his. "Not really, Cleo. I like my bit of fun, but I'm not a bastard. I don't go around putting the hard word on lonely wives."

"You're terribly frank, aren't you?"

"You mean my language or my attitude? I gave up beating about the bush a long time ago, love." They saw a subway entrance farther along the block and began to walk towards it. "I think perhaps it's why they sent me over here on this liaison job, why they sent me to London a couple of years ago. Little countries like us can't afford to be polite, we have to speak up for ourselves or we get pushed into a corner. You English tried it on us for years, now the Yanks are doing the same."

"You're big enough to speak up for yourself."

"Australia or me? Personally I can hold my own. Not too many people pick on me——" He grinned. "Excepting women skaters. That's one advantage to being a big bastard—people think twice about picking a blue with you. But as for Australia, we're not a big country, despite what a lot of people back home like to think. No one would take any notice of us if we didn't do a bit of yelling now and again."

"Daddy used to say the Australians were always complaining about something or other."

"If we hadn't, you English would have sat on us forever. The Yanks tried the same act last year when this business in Korea got going. Some stupid bastard in the Defence Department made the announcement that America was going to stockpile blankets. So all the other countries rushed in to buy our wool before the Yanks copped the lot. The prices went sky-high, so high they were bloody ridiculous. A good merino was practically a walking gold mine. So the Yanks told us they wanted us to cancel our auction system at our wool sales, let them buy it at their prices. We said no, our system had been operating for years, and if they didn't like it, they could lump it. So they got nasty and cancelled our quota of sulphur, said they didn't have enough to supply us. But they soon backed down when we said we'd do a bit of yelling about *that*. They thought we'd knuckle under, but they came a gutser."

"A gutser?"

"Came a thud. Made a mistake. The Yanks have got quite a few things to learn when it comes to handling small countries like us. You English were never entirely successful at it, but you did have one advantage—you never cared a damn what the rest of the world thought of what you did. If it was right for you, then it was right for everyone else."

They went down into the subway and Cleo said, "I hope we don't finish up in Long Island City again."

"If we do, I'm staying there the night," said Murrumbidgee.

A train came in, they ascertained from another passenger that it was indeed going where they wanted to go, and they got aboard. One or two people looked curiously at Murrumbidgee's uniform, then went back to reading their newspapers or dozing. Murrumbidgee was learning that New York was a town that minded its own business, was not really interested in the rest of the world or even in the rest of America.

"Where was I? Oh yes. The Yanks do care a damn about what the rest of the world thinks." He looked about the car again: only the New Yorkers had achieved the indifference to opinion of the English. But every American was always telling him that New York was not America. "They're so bloody busy trying to keep up their image of being a nice friendly country, it's a wonder they ever get around to doing anything constructive. They try this business of getting you to knuckle under, then hastily back off as soon as you snap at them and tell them you'll broadcast what a lot of bastards they are."

Cleo shook her head. "I don't understand you. I don't know whether you are for them or against them."

An elderly Negro, dozing in a window seat, opened one eye and looked at Murrumbidgee. The latter was sure his voice hadn't carried as far as the old man, but he didn't want to start any riot. He lowered his voice still further: he sounded as if someone was treading on his throat. "I'm for them. But they're still bemused at finding themselves Number One Nation. They've been boasting about it for years and now when everyone else—everyone but the Russians, of course—admits it, they don't know what to make of it. They don't know whether to use the Big Stick or play Big Uncle. It might take them twenty years to make up their mind. What amuses me is that for years they slung off at the English for bumbling through. So far that seems a pretty good description of their own foreign policy."

"You're so different from Daddy," Cleo said. "He was a diplomat all his life, a very minor one, but that was all he ever learned to do. He had the polite approach."

"It's not a bad one if you're a diplomat from a big or strong country. But we'd just be patted on the head and told to go away if we were polite." The elderly Negro raised a head like an old goat's; he rolled a satyrical eye at Murrumbidgee and Cleo. Murrumbidgee lowered his voice still further. "Anyhow, I'm no diplomat. I'm just over here to see that Washington gets the word now and again that the Yanks aren't fighting the Korean War all on their Pat Malone. That's why I wear this uniform everywhere I go. In this country you've *got* to advertise."

"How do you get on with Matt?"

"I haven't seen him for years, but I used to get on well with him. I think I get on well with all Yanks. There are two images to every man—his national one and his individual one. The newspapers are usually responsible for the national image and generally they don't do a good job. The individual is usually a much nicer bloke than the newspapers make him out to be. No American is as loud-mouthed as the *Daily News* here makes him out to be, and no Englishman is as conceited and jingoistic as he sounds in the *Daily Express*."

"How do you get on with the English in London?"

He grinned. "How am I doing tonight?"

"The bonds of Empire are very strong tonight."

"You'll do me, love."

They got up as the train drew in at the end of the line. The old Negro stood beside them as they waited for the doors to open. Murrumbidgee looked at him, then took the plunge: "I hope I didn't offend you with some of my opinions?"

The old Negro cupped a hand to one ear. "Excuse me, sah, Ah'm very deaf."

Murrumbidgee felt an almost uncontrollable desire to laugh, but he knew the old man would never understand it if he did. He searched wildly for something to say, then shouted at the top of his voice, "God bless America!"

"That's a funny thing to say, sah," said the old Negro. "Coming from a furriner."

He raised his hat to Cleo and plodded off ahead of them up the stairs to the street above. Murrumbidgee took Cleo's arm. "That'll teach me to keep my mouth shut in a foreign country."

"Daddy always said that was the most effective way of being a diplomat."

They came out into the crisp autumn night. They walked towards the parking lot where Cleo had left her car, a 1946 Pontiac that Duke had left with her when he had first gone to Arizona. She was not a good driver, and the car was scarred and bent where she had scraped it against posts, fences and other cars. So far she had managed to avoid any serious accident. Murrumbidgee opened the door of the car for her.

"Shall I drive?"

"Do you think you had better come out to the apartment with me? It's a long way back to Manhattan if you miss the last train."

"Somewhere under this uncouth exterior, love, there's a gentleman. He's never let a lady go home unescorted yet." Then he looked at her soberly. "Or would you rather I didn't come home with you?"

"No," she said, just as soberly. "I'd like you to come home."

When they pulled up outside her apartment she said, "But how are you going to get back to Manhattan?"

"Don't worry about it. Once in the Middle East I pranged a

159

kite behind the Italian lines. I walked home, forty-two miles of it. I can do it again if I have to."

She sat for a moment looking out at the stars, the stars that stretched right round the globe to Korea. Then she said slowly, "Would you like to stay the night?"

5

Next morning Cleo went round to the Crispin apartment to pick up Caroline. "Murrumbidgee must have got away early," Jane said. "I rang his hotel, but couldn't raise him at all."

"He wouldn't be back at the hotel yet," Cleo said without embarrassment.

Jane looked at her, then turned to the children. "Righto, outside all of you! Quick!" She swept the children out of the apartment, closed the door and went into the small kitchen. Cleo followed her and sat on a stool by the serving bench. "Coffee? Or do you want something stronger?"

"Darling, I'm not going to have a breakdown or anything like that. Coffee will do."

Jane put on the percolator. "True Confessions has never been my line. Do you want to talk about it?"

"Of course," said Cleo. "That is, if you want to listen?"

"Of course," said Jane. "Well, you wouldn't have let him stay unless you'd wanted him to. Or were you drunk?"

"Cold sober."

"I'm glad to hear that. I'd hate to hear my brother was a cad. Although come to think of it, I don't suppose there's any reason why a brother should be any different from other men."

"Darling, I didn't think of him as your brother last night."

"Have you fallen for him?"

"No." Cleo lit a cigarette and puffed on it for a moment or two. She looked thoughtful, a mood she did not often achieve in public. "You must think I'm terribly loose or unmoral, do you?"

"I mind my own business when it comes to morals."

"When I was younger I was always taking my clothes off," Cleo said reminiscently, almost a little sadly: life had been very uncomplicated then, if sometimes a trifle cold. "I used to think I was a dryer—a dryad. You know, in the woods. A nymph."

"A nympho?"

"Good God, no!" Cleo was horrified. Then she thought for a moment, once again looking candidly at herself. "Although I suppose some people thought I was one of those, too. No, Jane,

I used to just love being in love. I suppose it was terribly unmoral but I never thought of it that way. I was being happy and I was making someone else happy. Maybe just for the night, but it was something. But you must believe me, darling—after I met Duke, it was never like that again. Till last night."

"Was that what you were doing last night—making Tony happy?" Jane used the name by which she had known her brother for most of her life: Murrumbidgee was a stranger, a man from whom she had grown apart in the years of her absence from Australia.

Cleo looked out at the leaves falling like yellow shavings from the trees beyond the kitchen window. "In a way, I suppose. I felt sorry for him. He's lonely, and so was I. But—does this sound silly?—I'm more in love than ever with Duke this morning. If that's possible. It was a sort of lesson to me."

Jane poured the coffee. "There's Danish pastry, sponge cake or cookies. What do you want?"

"Danish pastry."

Jane spread butter thickly on the pastry, knowing Cleo's taste for it. "There's no doubt about you. You may die of a broken heart, but you'll never let yourself starve to death."

"I always eat twice as much when I'm unhappy."

"Are you unhappy this morning?" Cleo nodded and bit into the pastry. Jane sat beside her, nibbling on a cookie, happy and not in the least hungry. "I can't suggest anything. I'm no Dorothy Dix. There's just one thing——" Cleo looked at her, her mouth full of pastry. "I wouldn't try last night's party too often. I mean, using another man as a substitute for Duke. Unless——"

"Unless what?" asked Cleo, dribbling crumbs.

"Well, I mean—well, do you have to have sex? I mean, do you sometimes feel you can't do without it?"

"You mean am I really a nympho?" Cleo's candidness was almost an innocence. "No, I'm not, Jane. I shan't go round the bend *that* way."

"I'm glad to hear it," said Jane, relieved. "I think it must be dreadful when a girl's like that. I mean, I feel sorry for her—it must get them into situations that they curse themselves for later on. I must admit I get pretty sick for Matt sometimes." She, too, looked out the window, at the children frozen with curiosity as they stared at a squirrel planted on the broad trunk of a tree like a fur door-knocker. Suddenly she, too, was unhappy. "I know it's sinful to say it, but sometimes I wonder what Matt and I have got out of our married life. Oh, there's the kids. But what else? Always separated from each other. Last time he was home I told him I was thankful for what we had had. Now—worrying if he'll be shot down, if I'll ever see him again——" She sipped her coffee, feeling it going down past the lump in her throat. The heart can turn into a goitre, she thought, can choke you with your own feeling. "Do you think we married the wrong men, Cleo?"

Cleo shook her head slowly. "Not you, darling. Nor even me. If I had to do it all over again, I'd do exactly the same thing."

Jane smiled. "So would I. I don't know what the hell I'm complaining about."

"Neither do I," said Cleo without malice, smiling and wiping pastry crumbs from her lips. "I'm stupid, I suppose. Instead of envying you, you give me hope. I see what happiness is available when two people hit it off together like you and Matt do."

Jane continued to stare out the window, embarrassed by her own happiness. The squirrel had now retreated to the higher reaches of the tree and the children, their curiosity and their patience both gone, were once more at play. They chased each other through the fallen leaves, creating their own whirlwind, so that they seemed to be running through a swiftly flowing golden stream. Their voices came in the open window, light and musical as tinkling glass. Was innocence real happiness? Jane wondered; or must you have suffered first to know it? If the latter was the case, then Cleo had more than her share of happiness coming to her.

"What about Tony—are you going to see him again?"

Cleo shrugged. "Do you want me to?"

Jane hesitated. "It's your business, Cleo. Yes, I think you should see him. He won't be coming to New York so often that he'll become a habit with you. But you need some sort of diversion. Your life is aimless enough as it is."

"Not mine," said Cleo, with another of her moments of insight into herself and Duke. "I know what I want, even if I can't have it. Duke is the aimless one."

"You may be right," said Jane, surprise that she had not thought of that fact herself. "But he'd hate to hear you say it."

Cleo put on her coat, went to the door of the apartment and called to Caroline. Then she turned back to Jane. "Have you heard from Matt this week?"

"A letter this morning. Duke's all right."

Cleo patted her hand, once more the happy careless girl who

fooled the world. "You have more than an ordinary woman's share of intuition, darling."

"That was what you wanted to know, wasn't it? How Duke was?" Cleo nodded. "He's enjoying the war, Cleo. Or so Matt says. That's a terrible thing to say, but it seems to be true."

"What about Matt—is he enjoying it?" Then Cleo shook her head at her own question. "Of course he wouldn't. Matt isn't that sort of man."

"He's not. He's a very unhappy mixture, I think. He's a pacifist at heart, but he's also a realist. A good deal more of a realist than Duke."

"You don't have to tell me, darling." Caroline came to the door and took her mother's hand. John and Bunty crowded past them into the apartment. Inside the apartment the baby began to cry. The two women stood among the living reminders of their menfolk. Cleo looked down at Caroline, then back at Jane. "Some day I'm going to have to explain her father to Caroline. I think it's going to be terribly difficult."

Jane smiled. "Cleo, I'm on your side all the way. I even say prayers for you every Sunday at Mass."

"Do you think prayers do any good?"

"I don't know. But it's a comfort to say them."

"Like taking aspirin?" Then Cleo smiled apologetically. "No, I should not have said that."

"No," said Jane. "You're not a cynic, Cleo. Not even when you try."

"It's a pity. It might be some sort of help."

"Do you really think so?"

Cleo ushered Caroline ahead of her out the door. "I lived with a cynic for five years. It didn't help him. No, darling, I don't think there has ever been a really successful cynic. Give Matt my love when you write to him."

"And to Duke, too?"

"No, darling. He wouldn't appreciate it."

6

Julia Dalmead died on the same day as Joseph Stalin. The coincidence escaped her, and perhaps it was just as well; she would have spent the rest of eternity wondering if there had been any connection. Twice a day for the last five years she had been praying for the death of Communism; with the egotism of some pious people, she had begun to look upon herself as a life member of the circle of Our Lady of Fatima. Senator McCarthy, she had been certain, was destined for sainthood; the State Department, she had been equally certain, was only an annexe of the Kremlin. When Duke had gone off to fight the Communists in Korea she had said prayers for him, but this had been a secret between her and God. Duke could personally and with his bare hands have killed Stalin, but he would never have been fully forgiven till he had returned to the Church.

Duke and Matt, now back in the States and training other pilots in Arizona, flew back East for the funeral. Cleo and Jane, leaving the children with an elderly Irishwoman, a neighbour, who was delighted to act as baby-sitter for two days, drove up from New York. The funeral, as funerals so often do, promised to be an uncomfortable reunion for several of the mourners.

"How do you feel about seeing him again?" Jane asked as she and Cleo drove up the Merritt Parkway.

"Thrilled," said Cleo, honest as ever.

Jane looked at her, then said, "Be careful, Cleo. I'd hate to see you get hurt even more than you have been."

They reached the Cape in the late afternoon. Duke and Matt were not due in till early the following morning, arriving on a transport plane that was coming to the Air Force base farther out along the Cape. Jane dropped Cleo at the Dalmead house, then drove on to the Crispins'. As she drove away, she wondered what further unhappiness Cleo was exposing herself to by staying in the Dalmead house.

Phil Dalmead took Cleo's bag and led her up into the house. The house had been re-painted only a week before Julia's death; it was as if she had been preparing her own memorial. Phil held the door open for Cleo to enter ahead of him. "I've given you Duke's room, Cleo. Or was that a mistake?"

In the hall Cleo turned and kissed her father-in-law, something she had hesitated about doing on the sidewalk. All her life she had kissed people without discrimination; often it meant no more than a handshake to her, a way of showing people she was glad to meet them. But she had never kissed Phil or Julia Dalmead. When she had first met Julia she had left it to the older woman to set the tone of relationship between them; and Julia had greeted her with no more than a smile and a handshake. Phil had followed his wife's example, and that was how it had been up till now. But now was different: Julia was dead, and Cleo could set her own example. And she felt an affection for this old man, not all of it born out of sympathy, that required more than just a smile and a handshake. She kissed him as she had once kissed her own father. And Phil, for his part, recognized the warmth of feeling in the kiss, and had difficulty in holding back the tears. He was an emotional man whose feelings had been too long damned by his wife's frigidity.

"It was no mistake, Pop." Cleo had taken easily to calling him Pop; but she had never been able to call Julia Mom: it had always been the more formal Mother. "It was where I was hoping you would let me sleep."

"Not many of his things are left in there," Phil said as they climbed the stairs to the second floor. "It's been Tom's room for some time now, that is, when he comes home from college. Duke and Pete used to share it before Pete went away to the seminary." He opened the door to the bedroom. "I guess it's got a bit of each of the boys in it."

"A priest, a pilot and a college boy. Not many other women can say they've shared a room with such a mixed lot of men." Then she put her hand to her mouth. "I'm sorry, Pop. Terribly sorry. I shouldn't joke at a time like this, not jokes like that——"

Phil put her bag on the bed and turned round to face her. "Maybe not in public, Cleo. But between you and me, a little joke ain't wrong. I never got to know you well, Cleo, and believe me I wanted to. It broke my heart, you and Duke broke up——"

"Oh Pop!" Tears sprang to Cleo's eyes.

"You could have brought a lot of laughter into this house. It needed it, believe me. I loved Julia and she was a good wife to me. And a good mother, too, except——" He looked up at the faded photo of Duke on the wall, taken years ago. "Well, they were both to blame there. We had some laughter here, maybe not as much as I'd liked but enough, till that day when Duke and his mother fell out. I never told Duke, but he spoiled things for all of us that day, not just for his mother."

Cleo went to him and laid her head on his shoulder. She was weeping unrestrainedly now. He put his arm round her and kissed her hair. Downstairs were his own two daughters: what sadness lay ahead of them? He would never have the words to express it, but he knew only too well the dangers that lay in the web of human relations. Sometimes, feeling ashamed of himself for the thought, he wondered if Pete's going into the priesthood had been a retreat from such dangers.

Supper that evening was a sad meal. Cleo had gone into the kitchen to help Isabelle and Maria prepare the meal; five minutes there had shown her she knew less about cooking than they did.

Julia had prepared them well for the drudgery of married life; they would have to learn their own pleasures of it. The two girls had been very quiet, both affected by their mother's sudden death, and after a while Cleo had left them alone and had gone in to set the table for the meal.

Pete and Tom had both come home; when Duke arrived tomorrow morning it would be the first time in five years that all the family had been together. Cleo sat in Julia's place at the table; she felt like an outsider, but none of the family treated her that way. Tom, twenty now and looking startlingly like a younger version of Duke, sat beside Cleo, with Pete on the other side of her.

"How is college?" Cleo asked.

Tom shrugged. "I'm beginning to wonder why I bothered to go there. I graduate, what happens? I go into the army, maybe get sent to Korea. Who needs a college education for that?"

Cleo noticed the pessimism in the boy and didn't blame him for it. Duke, early in their marriage, had told her of his own unsettled state of mind while at M.I.T. She remembered boys she had met in London during the war who had told her they had had the same feelings while at Oxford and Cambridge. For a generation now youth had been growing up in a time of crisis; they studied for a future that might never be available to them. She sought to comfort Tom, feeling totally inadequate, aware of whose chair she was occupying. "Perhaps things will be better now that Stalin is dead. We'll have a new start with him gone." The words suddenly seemed to ring in her ears; it was almost as if the body in the coffin in the front room had stirred. She looked about the table at the faces all raised towards her. She wanted to say something more, to wipe the echo of the words from the room, but she could think of nothing.

Then Pete said, "We can only pray it will be so."

"I suppose," Cleo said, stumbling on, wishing now that she had stayed at a hotel in Falmouth; she had never been in a mourning household before, not even when her father had died. "I'm afraid I'm not terribly good at prayers, though."

"Who is?" said Phil, smiling kindly at his daughter-in-law. "No one is ever expert at it, not even the bishops. Eh, Pete?"

"Mom was good at prayers," said Maria, aged thirteen, afraid of the death in the front room. "She knew them all, even the prayers at Mass."

"Knowing the prayers and having them answered are two different things," Tom said, and Cleo detected a note of cynicism in his voice. She looked at him, once more saw the remarkable resemblance to Duke, and wondered if Tom was going the way his elder brother had gone. If he was, Julia had been spared the further pain.

"We'll never know if Mom had her prayers answered," Pete said. "Just let's hope she did."

Cleo went to bed that night in the room that had been Duke's when he had first met her. She tried to remember what he had looked like that first night at the Connollys' party, but could remember nothing of it. The party and her own adventures had been described vividly to her by both Duke and Matt, but she had no memories herself of it. She wondered how much she herself had changed since that night. She doubted very much if Duke had changed: the twenty-year-old Tom downstairs was a reminder of how little Duke had changed in looks.

She undressed and got into bed. Downstairs she could hear the Dalmeads saying the Rosary in the dining-room; the voices came up through the floor to her like the murmur of a dark sea. She picked up a book from the small bedside table and at once put it down again. It was a small Bible, something she did not want to read tonight. Once again she was looking for pain, not comfort.

Downstairs the Dalmeads had finished their prayers. The house was still, tuned now to the silence in the front room. Cleo began to weep, not for the dead but for herself, the living.

When she came down for breakfast in the morning Duke was already there. He rose from the table where the others were and came round to greet her. He kissed her lightly on the cheek and held her chair for her while she sat down. "You're looking well, Cleo. How's Caroline?"

"She's fine, thank you. Did you have a good trip?"

"A bit bumpy."

"You look well, too."

"It's the easy life I lead."

They exchanged empty bon-bons of conversation, putting up a front that would save the others at the table from embarrassment. It was what Cleo had heard referred to as being civilized, as if civilization had something to do with the heart.

"Congratulations." Cleo nodded at the major's gold maple leaves on Duke's shoulders.

"Matt got his, too. I guess we were both a bit slow. It's taken us nearly three years to get them."

"When will you be a colonel?" Isabelle asked. She was sixteen, old enough to be rank-conscious: it would be really terrific if her brother made colonel before she left high school.

"That may take quite a while. The jump to colonel is a big one. The Air Force isn't overloaded with guys with silver eagles. I may make lieutenant-colonel in the next five years."

Isabelle made a face. "At that rate I'll be an old woman by the time you make general."

"Quite probably." Duke laughed; he seemed careless of what lay in the front room. "Never mind, Belle. If it's glamour you're looking for, you can tell the girls at school I'm going to be a test pilot. Maybe they'll settle for that."

"I wasn't going to tell them——" Isabelle was embarrassed that Duke had so easily seen through her pride in him. But then pride rapidly overcame embarrassment. Nobody, but nobody, had ever had a brother who was a test pilot. "You really mean it? You're going to be a test pilot?"

"We report the first of next month. Out to Edwards Air Force Base in California."

"We?" said Cleo.

"Matt and I."

"Does Jane know?"

"She would by now," said Duke. "Unless he's holding back."

Then it was time to go to the church. The coffin had already been taken there; Julia had left home for the last time. Cleo and Duke rode with Matt and Jane, who had called for them in the Crispins' car. It was a fine clear day, the trees green with spring, putting on weight for summer. The sun shone with almost irreverent cheerfulness. Duke looked out at the sky, a blue page of oblivion, the old idea of heaven towards which his mother had aspired. Well, now she knew the truth of eternity, the truth that there was no eternity, only oblivion.

"Did you tell Jane?" he said, looking at Matt, suddenly not wanting to think about where he would be in the next ten minutes.

Matt, who was driving, nodded. "Didn't you notice we're not speaking?"

"Why *should* I speak to him?" said Jane, quietly angry. "Here we are on our way to a funeral and he tells me he's taken a job that practically ensures his own. Did you talk him into it?"

"We discussed it," Duke admitted. "But I didn't talk him into it, Jane. Honest."

"Whose idea was it in the first place? Let me put it that way."

Duke looked at Matt, but the latter was staring straight ahead at the Dalmead car in front of them. "This is going to surprise you. It was his idea."

"My buddy," said Matt.

"Well, what the hell do you expect? Jane's all set to kick me in the ass——" He sank back in the seat, rolling his eyes to his mother's heaven. "I get blamed for everything. Anyone wants a patsy, they just name me."

"And the name usually fits," said Jane. "Okay, I'm wrong this time. But why didn't you talk him *out* of it? You know he's got three kids. *And* a wife."

Duke shook his head in mock despair. "A man can't win. I'm always saying that." Then he smiled, and Cleo, sitting beside him, felt as if her heart had turned over within her. "I'm sorry, Jane. No, I mean it. Maybe I should've talked him out of it. But your old man, he's a dedicated flyer now. It's always been me in the past who's had the bug for it. But he's got it, too, now."

Jane looked at Matt. "Is that right?"

Matt hesitated, then said, "I thought you would have got the idea from my letters."

"I didn't read the bits about flying. But I can recite from memory the bits where you said you were dying to get back to me and the kids. *Dying* is right. Do test pilots get suicide pay?"

"Here's the church," said Matt, pulling the car into the parking lot beside the white clapboard church. The lot was thronged with cars and more were still arriving. Julia herself had never had many friends, but Phil Dalmead had made friends all his life and still had most of them.

The two couples got out of the car and went into the church. Duke nodded at Bob and Nell Crispin, and sank down on his knees between his father and Cleo. This was the first time he had been into a church for a service in—he paused while he tried to remember—almost twelve years. He had survived: no lightning bolt had struck him down. It was what his mother had expected; he wondered if she had prayed to have him saved from it. He could not offer her thanks, since he did not believe in the wrath of God. He did not believe in God, period. It always caused comment when, on his service papers, he put himself down as an atheist in the column marked *Religion*. The U.S. Air Force would have pleased his mother: it officially recognized the existence of God.

He knelt staring straight at the coffin standing before the altar. There was no thought of prayer in his mind; he knelt because he was less conspicuous that way. And after a while he began to feel a sense of loss. But it was not for his mother herself: it was for the relationship that might have existed between them. There had been a time when he had loved his mother, but that was way back now in the mists of childhood. He did not know how to act now; the dead gave you no encouragement. He stared at the coffin, wearing a mask for the benefit of the others in the church.

He turned his gaze towards the altar. Pete was saying the Mass, moving with measured progression through the ritual. His face, too, was a mask: a priest was allowed no emotion on the altar. *I wonder if he loved her?* Duke thought; but knew he would never embarrass his brother by asking him. Then he was aware of his father beside him, weeping silently into the rough cup of his hands. He hesitated, then he put his hand on the old man's elbow and pressed it. And almost as if by osmosis, as if by touching his father some contact had been made with his mother, he felt a spark of the dead love come alive. He looked once more at the coffin where his mother lay and suddenly grieved for her, for the life that had never been fully enjoyed, for the death that had come too soon.

Then the Mass was over, and half an hour later Julia Dalmead had been buried, committed to history, part of the earth out of which the future would grow. Then the Crispins and the Dalmeads all went back to the Crispin house for lunch.

Bob and Nell Crispin had moved from the dwelling behind their original store. Bob now owned a supermarket, the largest in town; and a year ago he and Nell had bought a house with two acres of land a mile out of town and overlooking the bay. Nell had bought new furniture, her first in thirty years; and Bob had given her a car for herself, a Morris Minor that she drove as if it had all the lethal potential of a tank. Sometimes Nell, mindful of their early struggles, thought they were spending money a little too freely, but Bob was enjoying his small success so much she did not like to spoil it by hinting that it might ever come to an end. She read all sections of the newspapers and magazines they had delivered, and she knew that some Cassandras were wondering what would happen to the American economy when the Korean War ended.

Even more than his own success, Bob enjoyed the success of his son. "I think we can be proud of the boys, Phil, what do you say? Look at 'em, both of them majors. I never made better than private first class. And look at those decorations! Look at 'em—each with three D.F.C.'s. And the Air Medal—how many clusters have you got, Matt? Fifteen, sixteen?"

Matt grinned. He had felt proud when he had won his first D.F.C. in the Pacific, but after that he had come to look on his decorations as GI issue. He still remembered the caustic remarks of Murrumbidgee and other Australians at how freely "the salad" was doled out by the American forces. "Just pick a number out of the air, Dad. No one will ever question you."

"No, I think you boys have done real well. I wish I'd had your opportunities."

"What he means is," said Nell, making sure there were enough places at the table for everyone, "he might have made corporal first class. They shouldn't have stopped the first World War when they did. He was just getting into his stride."

Bob could take his wife's ribbing. He had produced a son who was a hero of two wars, and not many men could claim that. He had slowed down over the past couple of years; life was no longer a continual crisis. His hair had now turned grey and had begun to thin; he wore it cut short in crew style and his pink scalp glowed through it. He had surrounded himself with some of the small luxuries he had coveted all his life, and he was now developing a smug complacency that sometimes annoyed Nell, but which she found easier to bear than the false alarms of their earlier life.

"I wonder if this war in Korea will finish in a stalemate now that Stalin is dead?" Bob, like so many men whose army career had been frustrated, was an arm-chair general. He had been emphatically against Truman's dismissal of MacArthur. If he had been in MacArthur's place, he would have done exactly what the general had advocated.

"Depends on who succeeds him," said Pete, sipping a beer, glad now that the requiem Mass for his mother was over. There would be others to say, if he survived the other members of the family, and it was a task he did not relish. He would gladly have surrendered the altar this morning to the parish priest, but that would have looked both a dereliction of duty and an insult to his mother. He knew it would have pleased his mother to have him say the Mass over her, but that had not made it any easier. He had not yet achieved the impersonal attitude towards death that priests and doctors, if they are to be successful, must have.

"I hope you guys in the Church have been praying for a peaceful type to take over," Duke said.

"You read the papers this morning?" Tom said. "It's like picking the winner of the Kentucky Derby. The front runner looks like some guy named Malenkov."

"Where do these guys come from?" Matt said. "One day they're nobodies, next day they're world leaders."

"Who'd ever heard of Truman?" Bob Crispin said, and looked as if he were about to spit.

"What we ought to do," said Matt, "is send them Joe McCarthy."

Phil Dalmead smiled as the other men laughed. "Julia would have liked that. Only she wouldn't have meant it as a joke."

Duke was pleased to see that his father was not going to be prostrated by grief: he would miss Julia, but he would not stop living because she had gone. "Well, whatever happens the war is over for Matt and me." He looked at Tom. "It's your turn next, if it lasts long enough."

"Thanks," said Tom.

"That's right, they're finished with the war," said Jane, her voice as tart as the sauerkraut she brought in from the kitchen and set down on the table. "So they're going to take a nice steady job of test piloting."

"Is that so?" Bob looked at Matt with pleased surprise. "Say, that's something I've always wanted to do——"

"Come off it, Dad." Jane was as candid with her father-in-law as she was with her husband. "Even when you fly from Boston to New York, you sit with your seat belt on all the way."

Bob blushed and grinned; he loved his daughter-in-law and could never be offended by her. "Well, what I mean is, I've always dreamed about it——"

"These young 'uns, they forget us old folk like to dream," said Phil, coming to Bob's rescue.

Nell saw that everyone was seated, then she sat down and looked at Matt. "I think you ought to be ashamed of yourself, taking a risky job like that. Whatever got into you?"

"Test piloting is not as dangerous as you think," Matt said. "Sure, you take your chances, but so does any flyer. Matter of fact, a test pilot is usually more cautious than an ordinary pilot."

"That's right," said Duke: all the men seemed to be coming to each other's rescue this morning. "He's interested in making sure a plane can fly."

"How did you get accepted then?" Jane asked. "Whoever said you were cautious? Matt's told me himself you're one of the Fanciest Dans he's ever seen in an aeroplane."

Matt looked at Duke, but the latter was not offended. "Now

172

the truth's coming out," he said, grinning widely. "And I used to think you were my pal."

"I was talking about you ten years ago," Matt said, looking at Jane, silently trying to ask her to keep this discussion, or argument, whatever it was going to be, till they were alone together. "Trust a woman to dig us some forgotten remark to bolster her argument."

"You still haven't told us why you applied for the job," said Nell, coming to Jane's aid.

Matt looked at his father and Phil Dalmead. "Maybe you'll understand better than the womenfolk. Flying ordinary jets has just become routine stuff nowadays. Space is the next target."

"You mean you want to fly to the *moon*?" Jane said.

"Your voice has just cracked," said Matt. "You're getting old."

"My voice isn't the only thing that's cracked in this room. I could name a couple of sets of brains that are the same way. What sort of bloody—sorry, Mum——" with a glance at Nell. She looked around the table at Isabelle, Maria and Anne: the young girls were hiding smiles behind their hands. "Don't take my language as an example, girls. But when you grow up and have husbands of your own, you'll find out how difficult it sometimes is to keep from swearing." She turned back to Matt. "What sort of crazy idea is that, to want to go to the moon? Heavens above—notice the restraint in my language there, girls —the kids and I see very little of you now. How long does a trip to the moon take?"

"I haven't said anything about going to the moon," Matt said patiently. "I'll be too old to make the trip by the time they get around to putting a man on the moon. But when they do, it won't take as long as you think. The journey will take only about three or four days."

"There and back?" Pete asked.

"Now you've asked him an embarrassing question," Jane said. "Coming back isn't on the schedule. Oh, don't I envy those wives of the future! Kissing their husband as they step into their planes——"

"Not planes," said Duke, amused by Jane's temper. "More likely rockets."

"Whatever they are, they'll really be coffins." Then she stopped, looked around the table at all of them, then down at her plate. "I'm talking too much. Sorry."

Cleo had been silent up till now, content to sit beside Duke and be warmed by the presence of him. There had been no strain between them: it was like meeting an old boy friend from whom she had drifted apart. Now she said, "Why do men want to go to the moon? Or Mars or Venus or any of those other planets? What gives us the right to send all our diseases, all our crazy mixed-up notions, all the things that are wrong with us, why should we visit them on other planets? Aren't the people there or creatures or whatever they are, entitled to their privation?"

"Privacy," said Duke gently, smiling at her. "But spoken like a true Englishwoman. Privacy is everything."

"Well, perhaps not privacy. But aren't they entitled to their own world?"

"Cleo," said Matt, not unkindly. "If Columbus had thought like you, there wouldn't have been an America."

Cleo laughed, unembarrassed. "Oh, now you're putting me on the spot! Trying to make me say, would that have mattered?"

"Okay," said Matt, laughing with her. "Let me put it another way. If Drake and Frobisher and Clive had thought like you, there wouldn't have been a British Empire."

"So that's all you aim to be?" Jane said. "That will look good when I take the kids to enrol them in school and they ask me what their father does. Oh, he's an Empire builder, currently planning to take over the moon."

"Here we go again with the Australian sarcasm," said Matt, giving up and looking at Duke. "Shall I carve you off a slice? It's thick enough."

"Leave me out of it," Duke said, and winked at Cleo. "Cleo and I are on the sidelines."

The discussion dissolved into mumbles as they all began to eat. Cleo hardly touched any of her food: she was happy, therefore she was not hungry. Jane, looking up, saw Cleo only toying with her food and recognized the sign. She shook her head, but Cleo only smiled at her: if Duke asked her to go to the moon with him, she would do so. Matt had been right. If you didn't explore, you would never discover anything. And she desperately wanted to re-discover the happiness she had once known.

Beside her Duke had turned to answer a question from Anne. "Was it a beautiful funeral, Uncle Duke?"

Duke looked across at his father, then back at Anne. The sad occasion of the morning had been pushed to the back of the mind for the time being: tonight would be the time for meditation on it, the tears that still remained to be shed.

"No funeral is beautiful, Anne. Not when you look beneath the flowers."

"Anne," said Nell Crispin, "get on with your lunch."

"I'm sorry," Anne said, and brushed the long blonde hair away from her forehead. She was eleven-and-a-half now, and already a brilliant student at school; Bob and Nell Crispin were continually amazed at the seeming genius they had produced. "I oughtn't to have asked that question. But I never see you, Uncle, to talk to."

"That's the complaint of the women of my life," said Duke, but his back was to Cleo and she could not see whether he was joking or stating a smug fact.

7

Matt, Jane, Duke and Cleo drove up to Boston in the late afternoon. Jane had taken Cleo aside after lunch and said, "How is this going to affect you? I mean, where you spend the night. I don't want you falling into bed with Duke and have you blaming me for it tomorrow."

"Darling, don't worry. If anything happens, it won't be your fault, I promise you."

"I could leave you here and drive back for you in the morning after they take off——"

"No, I'm coming with you. I don't want to stay in the Dalmead house. They don't want an outsider there, not tonight."

"You could stay here with the Crispins. They'd be glad to have you."

"Jane, stop *worrying* about me."

Jane nodded and bit her lip. "You're right, I suppose. I've got enough problems of my own. I was looking forward to tonight as another honeymoon night, but it looks as if I'll be spending all night trying to argue Matt out of this test pilot job."

"Do you think you'll be able to?"

Jane smiled ruefully. "I'm like you. I have my weaknesses, and they're mostly physical. I'll hate myself for giving in, but I know I'm going to."

Duke showed no discernible reaction when he learned that Cleo was coming up to Boston with them. He sat in the back of the car with her and talked about Caroline as if he were the child's devoted uncle instead of her father and the husband of the woman sitting beside him.

"What's she like at school?"

"Like her mother, I'm afraid," said Cleo. "Dumb."

He grinned and patted her hand: it was a friendly gesture rather than an affectionate one: she could take no encouragement from it. "I told you many times, Cleo—you're not dumb. You just have perfectly illogical reasons for logical occasions."

"Who doesn't?" said Jane from the front seat, looking at Matt, who was driving.

"Okay," said Matt. 'You've made your point a dozen times about the test pilot job. Now let's discuss the weather."

So the two married couples rode up to Boston in an atmosphere as brittle and uncertain as that which might surround two unmarried couples going away together for their first illicit weekend. Three of them were uncertain, even a little nervous: Cleo had begun to wonder now if she should not have stayed on the Cape. Only Duke seemed unconcerned by the night that lay ahead of them.

They checked in at the Ritz. "We can afford this on a test pilot's pay," Matt said in answer to Jane's raised eyebrows. "You'll find it has some compensations."

"Well, if we're going to spend the night arguing, I'd just as soon do it in comfort." Jane then looked at Cleo, but Duke had already stepped to the desk.

"A double for Major and Mrs. Crispin. And two singles."

The desk clerk was a Proper Bostonian when it came to discretion: not a flicker of expression passed across his face when he saw that Major and Mrs. Dalmead wanted separate rooms.

Duke's and Cleo's rooms were on the same floor. When the elderly bellboy opened the door to her room, Duke said, "I'll be back," and went on down to his own room. He returned in five minutes as Cleo was unpacking her bag.

"*Two* black dresses?" He looked at the black wool suit she was wearing, then at the black silk dress she was hanging in a closet.

"I just like black. You'd forgotten?"

"I can remember you always liked black underwear."

"You *would* remember that."

He walked to the window and looked out at the Common, turning into a dark lake now as the dusk came gypsying in over the city. He had enjoyed Boston when he had been at M.I.T. out at Cambridge and lately a nostalgia for the city had begun to affect him. Its bigotries and social distinctions irritated him, but it had a charm that no other American city could evoke in him. New

York and Chicago were the foreigner's example of American cities, but for him the heart of America was in the less brash cities like Boston. It was symptomatic of his nostalgia for Boston that some of the brashness had gone out of his own personality in the past couple of years. He sometimes grinned at the thought of his retarded development, but the process of his growing up had been completed in Korea.

He turned back to Cleo. "I'm afraid you are going to be saddled with me for the evening. Jane and Matt won't want us around. This is a big night for them—no, not in the bed. I think they're going to have a Godalmighty fight. You may have Jane knocking on your door in the middle of the night asking to be let in. And it's just as likely I'll have Matt doing the same thing. I think you and I might have to play the role of trusted friends, lend a shoulder for them to bawl on."

"You think it's *that* serious?"

"I know just how keen Matt is on this new job. It really was his idea that we should apply for it."

"You mean you aren't as keen as he is?"

"Oh sure, I'm keen all right, every bit as much as he is. But it was he who first got wind that they wanted men out there in California. He'd got all the dope on it before he came and asked me if I'd be interested, too."

"But *why*? I mean why should he want to take on such a job? Has he——" she hesitated, then went on "—has he got tired of being married?"

"You mean has he got like me?" He sat down on the bed, then quickly looked up at her. "You mind? I mean, do you want me to get out?"

"Of course not. Make yourself at home——" She had another of her clear moments of insight: she smiled to herself at the irony of it: home was a hotel bedroom that she wasn't even going to share with him. "Shall I send down for something to drink?"

"Make mine beer."

"Nothing stronger?"

"I've given up hard liquor. I found out I was relying on it too much in Korea. It wasn't good, either for my system or my flying."

"You must have more strength of character than I gave you credit for." Then she looked directly at him. "Sorry."

He was not offended. "Three or four years ago you'd have probably been right."

She called room service, then sat down in a chair and eased off her shoes. She was beginning to feel more comfortable with him, but she was aware of a growing sense of disappointment. She had not yet made up her mind if she would surrender to him if he tried to make love to her, but already it looked as if he was more concerned with what might happen between Jane and Matt than between themselves. She felt like the girl with whom the suspected rapist had turned out to be a gentleman. She might not even get the opportunity to test her own strength of character.

Duke took off his own shoes and sat back against the headboard of the bed. He had undone his jacket and loosened his collar and tie. They looked like a completely married couple accustomed to taking each other for granted.

"No, getting back to your question, he hasn't got tired of being married. In fact, when he applied for the job, that was one of the things he was thinking of. Out at Muroc, at Edwards, there's good accommodation for Jane and the kids. It's in the desert, but it's healthy. They'll see him every day and he could be there for three or four years. Test pilots don't get moved around like other Air Force flyers. Most of their flying is done over California, so they're home every night. It's the nine to five job Jane was always after him to take."

"That's not the only reason he took it."

"No," he said slowly. "It's more than that. But I don't know if he's going to be able to explain it to Jane. You were always more understanding about flying than she was. I mean you could understand the hold it gets on a man. It's—well, remember those records we used to play when we shared that house on the Cape right after the war? Jane and I liked Beethoven and Bach, you and Matt liked Irving Berlin and—who was that other guy?"

"Ray Noble. 'The Very Thought of You' was my favourite."

"Yeah, you played it all day every day. Well, anyway. One couldn't explain to the other what it was that moved them about the music, what got *inside* them. Flying is like music—you *feel* it, it gets inside you, and trying to explain the feeling of it is like trying to explain the feeling of a piece by Beethoven to someone who can't take anything but jazz."

"You used to like jazz."

He looked at her. "How did you know that?"

"I slept in your old room last night. There were some old records with your name on the sleeves in a cupboard." She smiled candidly. "I'm afraid I poked around."

He made no comment on her admission, as if he wanted to

avoid the inference that she had been so interested in him. He had begun his own retreat: he had recognized by now that she was half-way to surrender. "Yeah, I remember those records now. Some Artie Shaws? A couple of Benny Goodman, right? Well, I can still listen to that sort of stuff. But it doesn't get inside me. Not like the other music."

"Nor like flying?"

"No, nor like flying. That's the *real* music, as far as I'm concerned. And for Matt, too. But I don't know how he's going to explain that to Jane. She's tone deaf in that direction."

Then the drinks came and a little later Duke said, "Well, we better eat. You think we should call them?"

"Will they appreciate it?"

"If they're in bed, no. If they're still fighting, maybe they would."

"*You* call them."

He reached for the phone, asked for the Crispins' room, then said, "Matt? We're going to eat. You want to eat with us? Okay. See you at breakfast. Seven. Say good-bye to Jane for me." He hung up and looked at Cleo. "Looks like Jane has surrendered."

"I'm glad."

He stood up, tightened his tie and began to button up his jacket. "I think you are. Is that your idea of love? Total surrender?"

She looked up at him over the rim of her glass. She had had two gin-and-tonics, her British courage, and she was feeling a little reckless now. "Are we going to argue?"

"No," he said, smiling. "Let's say that was a rhetorical question. It's the only sort of question you can ever really ask about love, because there's never any true answers."

She stood up, putting her glass down on the table beside the bed. She wondered when he had ever stopped to ponder the nature of love, but she would not provoke him by asking him. "Come back for me in half an hour."

"Half an hour? You never used to take that long to get ready."

"I'm out of practice," she said, certain now that she could handle anything the night might bring. "It's been a long time since you took me out to dinner. Where shall we eat—here in the hotel?"

"We'll go out. Matt and Jane might decide to come down to eat, after all. I think it would be better if we left them to themselves."

"You can be so thoughtful at times. It's a pity you're not always like that, Duke." She opened the door. "Half an hour."

Half an hour later right on the minute he knocked on her door. She was ready and waiting for him. He looked at her for a moment, then he said, "You look lovely. And I'm not just being thoughtful. You really do."

"You like my dress?" It was black and low-cut, exposing more bosom than ever would have been seen at a wake; if she had stayed at the Dalmeads' tonight, it would have had to stay in her bag. She was honest, too honest as she so often was: "I went out and bought it specially when I knew I was coming up here to see you. Bergdorf Goodman's, and I shan't tell you how much it cost me. The girl asked me if it was for a special occasion and I said, yes, I was going to a funeral to meet my ex-husband. I think she thought I was making a sick joke." They waited for the elevator to come up. "I'm sorry, Duke. I mean I shouldn't have bought a dress like this, coming to your mother's funeral."

"I'm glad you did," he said, and ushered her into the elevator as the doors opened before them. "I don't know how Mom would feel, but I'm sure Pop would be glad to see the two of us going out to dinner like this."

"Yes, I think he would," said Cleo, and knew then that the hundred and forty dollars on the dress had been well spent.

They went to Pierino's and Duke ordered champagne to drink with their lobster Newburg. "To go with the dress," he said, raising his glass to her. "It's a special occasion."

All evening she had been working hard not to call him Darling. It was her favourite term of address, for strangers as well as for friends and lovers, but tonight she knew that if she used it, it would have an accent to it that he could not miss. She was prepared for surrender, but she wanted to be challenged by more than just a glass of champagne.

"I wish Caroline were here with us." She looked about her, aware that other diners were glancing at them. She tried to imagine herself on the other side of the room, looking at the dark handsome Air Force major with his row of ribbons and his blonde wife in her new black silk dress celebrating (what? Her birthday, his promotion, a wedding anniversary? What stranger would guess the truth?)

"So do I," he said honestly.

"Duke, I wish you could come East more often to see her. She asks about you, and I've run out of answers. She's seven now, old enough to want to have a father, even if only a part-time one."

"I'll make it as often as I can. I can manage it at least three or four times a year, I think." He was softened by the whole day: his mother's funeral, this reunion with Cleo, even the champagne. At that moment he wanted to be a full-time father to Caroline, to take up again his responsibilities towards her. He felt exactly as he had felt when he had proposed to Caroline's mother in the London hospital years before. Conscience once again wore the mask of love.

The food was excellent, the dinner a success. There was no strain at all between them now; they talked freely, exchanged jokes, enjoyed each other. Then suddenly someone was standing by their table, a thin dark woman in gem-encrusted glasses and a red dress and a tall heavily-built man who looked as if he had had too much to drink.

"It *is* Duke Dalmead, isn't it? *And* Cleo Mulligan?"

Duke stood up, trying to place the couple but unable to recognize either of them. It was Cleo who said, "Meg Connolly! What a lovely surprise!"

"Meg *Noonan*. This is my husband Bill."

Bill Noonan shook hands with Duke and bowed an unsteady head towards Cleo. "I've heard a lot about you, Dalmead. *Major* Dalmead." There was no mistaking the antagonism in his voice. "Been hearing about you for years."

Duke smiled affably. "I didn't think Meg would remember me."

"Oh, she remembers you, all right."

"*You* didn't remember *me*," Meg Noonan said.

"It was the glasses, I think. You weren't wearing them, how long ago was it? Twelve years?"

"Ten years," said Noonan. "We've been married nine years. Nine years tonight. I been hearing about you all that time, major. You married?"

"You just said good evening to my wife," said Duke, no longer smiling, hating this big red-faced man as much as the latter must have hated him all these past nine years.

Meg Noonan blinked rapidly behind her glasses, suddenly reminding Duke of her brother, who had always been blinking drunkenly behind *his* glasses. "You mean you two married?"

"Almost *eight* years," said Cleo, standing up and taking Duke's arm. "We're an old married couple, too."

"Who does *he* talk about?" said Noonan, but Meg Noonan had suddenly stopped blinking, had grabbed her husband's arm and was pushing him ahead of her out of the restaurant.

Duke looked at his watch. "Time we were getting back, I think. I've got to be up early tomorrow." He paid the cheque, and escorted Cleo out of the restaurant. When they were standing on the sidewalk, the cool night air lying like curved glass against their cheeks, he said, "I'm sorry they spoiled our evening."

"You never told me about her."

"You knew I knew her."

"Not *that* well. She really must have been terribly in love with you. Did you ditch her to marry me, Duke?"

"Will you believe me if I say it was never like that between us, at least not on my part? Sure, we had an affair, if that's what you call it. So did you, as I remember. But this was no more serious than any of yours was."

"It was to her."

He was surprised at his own patience: the day and evening *had* softened him. "Don't blame me for the way she feels, Cleo. We had stopped writing to each other a couple of years before I met you in London. I expected her to have married, settled down and forgotten all about me by now. Maybe if she had got some other guy but that son-of-a-bitch, she would have."

"That's the risk you take when you marry on the rebound," Cleo said, and was glad now that she had not tried to find a substitute for Duke. There, but for the grace of God. . . . "I wonder how Jane and Matt have made out tonight?"

"She'll probably tell you on the way back to New York," he said, relaxing now that she had changed the conversation. He hailed a cab and they got into it. "You girls still have your heart-to-heart talks, don't you?"

"Of course. We need them occasionally."

"Ever discuss me?" He was smiling as he said it.

"Occasionally," she said, smiling back at him. "You'd be disappointed if we didn't, wouldn't you?"

They bantered with each other all the way back to the hotel, the banter of two people who now all at once realized that soon a serious word would once more have to be spoken. At the door of her room he took her key from her and opened the door.

"Do you want to come in for a nightcap?" Cleo asked the question lightly, but this was no longer banter: she had decided to surrender.

Duke stood close to her, one hand propped against the door jamb. A man and a woman went by them and he waited till they had gone. "If I come in, Cleo, is one of us going to be hurt?"

"You mean am I going to be the one?" Cleo slowly shook her

head. "The hurt is still there, darling. Whatever you do won't make it worse."

"I don't want to be any more of a son-of-a-bitch than I have been. I *want* to stay the night with you, but I don't want you to think that means—well, I don't think I could ever be a married man again."

She felt the pain, that had been quiet all day under the sedation of hope, come back. "There's just one thing, darling—and please be honest with me—have you fallen for another girl?"

"No, Cleo. That's the truth. In that way, there's never been anyone but you. Meg Connolly's torch, notwithstanding."

"In what way? You never really loved me, Duke."

"I don't honestly know. But if I didn't, I came as close to loving as I'll ever get with anyone."

She took his hand down from the door jamb. "Come in, darling."

He hesitated, and for a moment she thought he was going to refuse. Then he grinned, leant forward and kissed her hair as he followed her in and closed the door. "As mehitabel said, wotthehell."

"That's one of the nicest things you've ever said to me," Cleo said, and prepared for total surrender, her definition of love.

In the morning Duke rose early and was gone before she awoke. When she did wake she lay in the wracked bed savouring the sweet pain that he had left her: the pus of bitterness might not come for hours or even days. He had been both tender and brutal with her, the physical gestures of true love: that had caused the sweet pain. What might eventually make the pain suppurate was the memory that not once throughout the long wild night had his voice mentioned the word *love*. And that had been worse than if he had used the word as a lie.

Driving back to New York she said to Jane, "How did you and Matt make out last night?"

"I gave in," said Jane. "I knew that I would. How about you?"

"I gave in, too. I knew that I should."

Jane smiled wryly. "No woman should ever attempt to advise another. We never learn from our mistakes." Then she said, "I'm going out to California."

"To live?" Jane nodded. "I'll miss you, darling."

Jane swore. "I wish to God there was something I could do to make that no-hoper Duke see what he's missing! The stupid, bloody selfish fool——"

183

"He's going to come East more often to see Caroline," Cleo said. "That will be something."

"It'll never be enough, Cleo. You may kid yourself, but it will never be enough. Not for a woman as one-eyed about love as you are."

CHAPTER SIX

THEY passed 10,000 feet and Duke plugged his mask into the bomber's oxygen supply. Another half an hour, another 25,000 feet, before it would be time for him to get off. He sat back on the uncomfortable bench seat, stretching his legs, looking disinterestedly at the sergeant and the corporal, his two linetenders, sitting opposite him. This was the sixth drop he had made in the US-XP and each time Grabowski and Fuller had come up with him. They knew their job and he could depend on them. This was his last flight and he wondered if they were as bored with the test flights as he had now become.

Midge Filene, the bomber pilot, looked back over his shoulder His voice, flat and croaky as a Jewish mynah bird's, came over the intercom. "You got a good day for it, colonel. Looks like the cover will be less than predicted. About two-tenths, I'd guess."

Filene, a bald wiry little man who looked like a plucked eagle, had been twelve years in the Air Force and was a major. He called both Duke and Matt by their first names down on the base, but here in the air they were always "colonel" to him; he was proud of his own rank and he respected other men's, especially that of those above him. He expected some day to be called "colonel" himself.

Duke had been pleased when his and Matt's promotions had come through on the same day five months ago. He knew that the silver maple leaf of a lieutenant-colonel meant more to him than it did to Matt; but he would have been genuinely upset had he been promoted ahead of Matt. The latter was not unambitious, but he looked upon promotion primarily as a source of more money; he had not become mercenary, but he and Jane were now putting money away for the children's later education. Duke himself, while not careless of the extra pay, *was* ambitious, as he had always been. It was not improbable that he would make brigadier-general within the next ten years, before he was forty-five. He might some day even make general, although he had missed his chance of being one at eighteen.

"Twenty thousand," Midge Filene said over the intercom. "Just crossed the Utah State line."

"How do you know, skipper?" said Begley, the co-pilot.

"It's that dotted line running down the desert there, see?" said Filene.

Grabowski and Fuller grinned politely at Duke, showing they appreciated the humour of their superior officers. Filene was loaded with corny old jokes: Duke sometimes wondered if he had studied Joe Miller's Joke Book instead of the Officer's Manual. Every time Duke went out of Filene's bomber in a drop, he was presented with a corsage of corn; he was pretty sure that Filene stayed up half the night looking up suitable jokes. Duke grinned back at the two men opposite him, wondering what they really thought of him, Filene and the other officers on board. As a test pilot he had little to do with the enlisted men. Each time he went up they presented him with a plane; when he came back he returned it to them. The rest of the time they were strangers.

He and Matt had now been four years at Edwards Air Force Base at Muroc Dry Lake in California. Their tours of duty had been extended twice, but they knew now they were in their last innings. Next week they were both going to the National Aeronautics and Space Administration's Laboratory at Langley Air Force Base in Virginia for two months to assist in experiments on spaceflight simulators. After that it looked like desk duty in Washington for an indefinite period.

It had taken Duke less time to settle down out here in California than it had Matt; the latter had been worried for months about Jane's attitude towards the job. Both men had had their escapes during the test flights; it would have been remarkable had they not over four years of such flying. But Jane had never asked questions of Duke as to what went on, and he and Matt had an implicit agreement that the day's work would never be discussed in front of her. They had adopted the façade that every day was routine flying; and to all outward appearances Jane was now reconciled to the job. She and Matt had taken a house in Lancaster where the children could go to school, and Matt drove out every morning; one or two weekends a month, if Matt wasn't needed for duty, they drove up to Lake Mead in Nevada, where Matt kept a power boat. Duke guessed that it was a drab life for Jane, but she did not appear to complain. She, Matt and the children seemed to have a happy and contented life, and he was glad for them.

He had tried to tell himself that he was happy and contented with his own life, but there were times when doubts pricked at him like exposed nerve ends. Never when actually flying: *then* he was happy and content. sometimes excited to the point of ecstasy. He had become bored with test piloting because of the isolation here at Edwards; as a virtually bachelor officer he lived on the base. The desert was fine for flying, but it offered no social life nor diversion: not unless you were an amateur naturalist which he was not. He was sick of the sight of bare mountains, Joshua trees and cactus trees. Washington, even at a desk, would be welcome. At least for a while.

The doubts had begun some months ago. He could not be sure when he had first felt the irritation of them: on the long drive back from Malibu, after a weekend with Debbie Fairfax, or coming back from the three or four visits a year he made East to Cleo and Caroline. There would be no emptiness of feeling, but more a feeling of non-fulfilment; it was as if he had climbed a mountain to find there was no view. He would have enjoyed his time with Debbie, and even more so with Cleo and Caroline; but the taste of enjoyment would be gone before he was half-way home.

Part of the rut was Debbie Fairfax. He had met her at a party in Brentwood, where he had gone with one of the other officers from the base. She was a film editor, working for one of the better independent producers, a dark-haired plumply good-looking girl who had come out from Pennsylvania to be a film star and had never made it past the extra ranks. She was a sensible girl who had some creative ability, and after two years of being no more than a passing flash on the screens of the world she had looked around for another job. She had slept with an aging film editor, whose fading virility had not allowed him to make love all the time; on his tired days he had taught her to cut films, had explained to her other rhythms than the ones they had practised in bed. She had then met the independent producer, who had fortuitously had a vacancy in his bed and on his staff. She had proved her worth in both places, and though the producer had stopped sleeping with her after three months, when he had gone back to his wife, he had kept her on as an assistant editor. Now she was his senior editor and his wife's best friend.

"Thirty thousand, colonel. We're over Wendover. Time you got ready. Mind the step as you go out."

Filene must be getting bored, too: that was one of his earliest jokes and one of his worst. Duke stood up and Grabowski and Fuller rose from their bench, looking men glad at last to be getting to work. They took hold of the long oxygen-line and followed him to the bomb bay. Fuller bent down and pulled back the door of the bay. The wind blasted in at them, cold and sharp as a huge blade of ice. Below the opening, like a white needle-nosed shark that had been caught in the ocean of the sky, hung the US-XP. The wind shrieked past it, making it sound almost as if it were alive. In another twenty minutes it *would* be alive and far more dangerous than any shark.

The US-XP was not the latest of the experimental aircraft being tested for the Air Force. There were five or six later proto-types, all of which had been flown; but the US-XP had not been junked as being superseded. Soon it would be obsolete, but as of now it still had something to teach the designers. Duke had an affection for it because it was still a *plane*: some of the later prototypes did not deserve the title of airplane and offered very little that resembled real flying. In the US-XP the pilot still had a sense of being in full control of his aircraft, even if the margins for error were razor-thin.

Duke slid down through the opening into the cockpit below, feeling the wind tearing at him, trying to blow him out into the open sky. The oxygen line whipped against his helmet; in-stinctively he turned away so that the line would not hit his face plate. Then he was in the cockpit, out of the worst of the wind. He nodded up at Grabowski, and behind the pig snout of his mask the sergeant winked encouragingly. Duke took a deep breath, then quickly disconnected the oxygen line from the bomber's supply and plugged it into that of the US-XP. Fuller and Grabowski pulled the hatch cover into place and locked it. The roar of the wind was suddenly gone and in its place was the deeper thunder of the bomber's engines. Duke sat in the dusk beneath the bomber, cocooned in his own world, his own master again. This might be the last flight for a long time and he would make it a good one.

He plugged in on radio communication. "All set, Midge. All set, Ground Control. Beginning checking."

Acknowledgment came from Filene and from Ground Control five hundred miles away at Edwards. Duke went through his checking exercise: he did it thoroughly, as if this were his first time in the plane: he and Matt had told Jane the truth when they had said that a test pilot had to be a cautious man. As he worked the sounds outside faded from his consciousness; he was aware only of the sawing sound of his own breathing in the oxygen mask. From the corner of his eye he could see the oxygen indicator breathing with him: a black circle with two white slits for lips that always reminded him of a blackface Al Jolson silently mouthing "Mammy".

"Five minutes, colonel." No jokes now; when they were getting down to business, Filene always became serious.

Duke watched the stop-watch on the panel in front of him. A minute passed: it was time to prime the jet engine. If there should be a fire warning now, he had already rehearsed in his mind the drill he would have to go through. The warning would get through to Filene, whose decision it would be to drop the US-XP. Duke would blow the canopy and leap for the sides of the bomb bay as the experimental plane would fall away beneath him. It was all very risky, but they had decided it was safer than staying in the falling plane and trying to use the ejection seat once it was away from the bomber. By the time there was enough air room to let fly the ejection seat, the US-XP might have blown itself out of the sky. Several prototypes had gone that way, but so far the US-XP had behaved itself.

The jet engine was rumbling now, its sound puny against that of the bomber's engines. Duke leaned forward, peering at the dials on the instrument panel; he switched on the small light that was necessary because of the dark shadow of the bomber. He could feel the cold getting at him, and he would be glad to be gone.

"Chase plane with you, colonel. I can see him at four o'clock."

Matt's voice came in over the radio. "On time all the time, chum. Let's get this thing under way."

Duke could not see Matt's aircraft, but it was comforting to know he was around: there was no better chase pilot in the business than Matt. "I'm going upstairs a while, son. You want to come?"

"Nix on the chatter. Countdown about to begin." That was Ground Control, the guys who never seemed to appreciate that a little levity helped a man up here. They were always ready with the jokes when he was on the ground, when he needed them least, but once they had put him in the air they were all business.

"Teacher's talking, son."

"See you after school, chum."

Countdown was Filene's responsibility. "Okay, colonel, you're all alone now. Ten—nine—eight—" Duke reached for the data switch, pressed it; glanced again at all the dials "—three—two —one—*zero*!"

The US-XP dropped like a stone spear hurled at the heart of the earth. The sky exploded as an immense burst of white light about it, so bright that Duke was sure that the white plane must be lost in it. He blinked, accustoming his eyes to the glare, saw by the altimeter that he had already dropped a thousand feet. He reached for the switches on the rocket tubes. He felt the kick as they blasted on, but he was used to this by now; the extra G's were something he had learned to live with. But at this fierce acceleration the plane became alive, wanting to yaw if you didn't watch it. The plane was still headed down, but he had it under control now. Then it was time to pull her up, to begin the climb towards the dark purple sky above. He would be already almost half-way back across Nevada and he always aimed to hit his apogee just north of Lake Mead.

"Looks good from here, chum." That was Matt, a mile away on the starboard side. "Take her away!"

Duke drew back on the wheel. The long needle nose of the plane began to quiver; a tremble passed down the length of the plane like a shiver of dread. He felt himself being forced down into his seat, the blood draining down into his stomach; his jaw hung open like that of an idiot screaming in animal terror. He had stopped breathing: the Al Jolson cartoon face stared at him close-mouthed. His eyeballs felt as if they wanted to shoot back into his skull; he was aware of the greyness creeping over him that told him his brain was not getting enough blood. Then the pressure began to ease, his sight suddenly cleared and ahead of him the needle point of the US-XP was steady and pointing upwards. He glanced at the dials in front of him: air speed, Mach needle, altimeter: all working perfectly. Al Jolson began to sing "Mammy" again.

He felt the buffeting as the Mach needle climbed; then she was through the barrier and had smoothed out. Sixty thousand, 65,000, 70,000 and still climbing. There was still slight vibration in the aircraft, but it was no more than a projection of what he himself felt: a tremble of excitement, the quivering that a man feels when he approaches consummation with his one true love. Above him the sky was a colour that earth-bound people would never know, a blue-purple that was the coloured edge of eternal darkness. The sun was behind him and he could see the stars like inviting diamonds in the dark curtain ahead of him, a curtain that he knew would keep retreating the farther he flew into it. The US-XP was climbing faster now, streaking through the thin unresisting air, but there was no sensation of speed, no dimension

189

at all. Time and space had become one, yet did not exist at all. There was a serenity here that transcended all understanding. He could never explain it to Cleo, but *this* was happiness, and suffering was not necessary.

Experience told him that the plane was climbing at a speed that could, ridiculously, bring him close to stall point. He and the plane, now one, were balanced on a fourteen-mile-long invisible pole whose fulcrum was the earth. So long as he kept the balance he was safe. He was not afraid. It was almost as if somewhere between earth and sky, he had passed through a barrier where fear was shucked like an unwelcome weapon at a customs post. He was detached from himself and all the emotions that cloaked him when he was aground. You did not take fear with you into eternity.

Eighty thousand feet: almost the end of the climb. He turned his head and looked out into the brightness that stretched away like an extension of the sun itself. This was not day, it was something far brighter: perhaps *this* was eternity, and not the darkness of legend. In the cockpit the shadows were blacker than one ever knew shadows on earth; he put his gloved hand into a shadow and it disappeared completely. There was no reflection, no greyness: everything was black or white, existent or non-existent. He hated the admission, but if there was a God, this was the light of God.

He was on the edge of reality: the feeling was both uncanny and pleasant. Perception was heightened till it gave the paradoxical feeling of being wide awake in a dream; every experience of every second he had lived had been drawn into this fine core of intelligence. There was no understanding: he *knew*, but he did not understand. He was aware not only with his mind, but with every cell of his body; here in this silent world the mind and the body thought together, came to no conclusion. There were no reflexes, nothing was born out of conditioning, all reference was gone. There had never been any time but now: past and future were encumbrances that had been dropped at the border where fear had been checked. Nobody but he lived or ever had lived.

"Don't hang around up there too long, chum. I know the feeling, but think of me down here in this crate." That was Matt, one of the earth-bound in the chase plane, a man who knew the sublime joy of flying at this height but who, today, had to be practical and think of getting them both back to Lake Muroc and the ground.

Matt's voice was the one link with the world, with memory and the past. It was needed: otherwise Duke knew he would have flown on forever. "Okay, son. I'll bring her down."

He eased off, rolled to starboard and saw the world come back into view, into being: he created the world whole with a wave of the plane's stubby wing. California lay below him, flat as a brown beach holding back the dark tide of the Pacific. Somewhere down there were cities, mountains, lakes: they were only blemishes on the long vast beach stretching down the curve of the world. Down there were people, ordinary people, film stars, generals: fame was a message that couldn't be read at this height. Down there was Hollywood, Escape Capital of the World; but it could never manufacture the escapism that one knew up here. Down there was Debbie Fairfax, a girl whose bed could never give him the euphoria that existed for him here in the lonely ocean of the sky.

He turned the aircraft earthwards, reluctantly like a man turning back from a suicide that he had welcomed, that would have offered no pain at all. He turned his head sharply for one last look at the dark oblivion above him, it might be months, even years, before he was flying this high again; then he was moving down through the gradually diminishing brightness towards Muroc and the convulsions of human nature that were what people called living. He could see the frost melting on the canopy as he got lower: California ran off the map into the Pacific. All at once he did not want to return to earth: *up there* was where he wanted to go! There had been no clouds in the sky, but now a long way south he could see mountains of them building up on the Mexican horizon. He lifted the nose of the plane: he would keep going south, seek the cloudland of long ago, then pull the nose right back and head for the stars.

A mile away in the chase plane Matt saw the nose of the US-XP lift. "No tricks, chum. I'm running out of gas. I've got to put this thing of mine down pretty soon."

"Go on home, son. You're not needed."

Matt at once noticed the slurred speech. "Duke! Check your oxygen indicator!"

"No time for that." Duke sounded annoyed, impatient, like a man being held against his will. "Other things to do. Go home, son, go home."

The US-XP had begun to weave, almost waltz through the sky. Matt felt the sweat break on him as he saw the danger that Duke was heading for. The US-XP was not meant for fancy flying:

191

it could stall at any moment, go into a spin and Duke would be in the ground before he knew where he was. Matt glanced at his altimeter: 28,000. He had to get Duke down to an altitude where he could get oxygen from the atmosphere.

Ground Control came in, sounding like a petulant parent. "What's going on up there? Ground Control to Sitting Bull. Answer!"

"He's in trouble," Matt interrupted, still watching Duke's aircraft anxiously. "Stay off the air and leave him to me. This is urgent. Stay off the air!"

"Go home." Duke's voice was now almost incoherent; he sounded like a tired drunk, a man suddenly weary for a resting place. "Going home. Home."

Matt took the chase plane in as close as he dared to the weaving US-XP. He rode above it, his own aircraft throwing a deep shadow over the experimental plane; he just hoped that Duke would get no ideas about giving the US-XP full throttle because the chase plane would stand no chance of pacing with it. They were well off course now and for a split second he sensed another danger: for all he knew they might be right in the middle of the commercial lanes and at any moment a DC-6 or similar aircraft, one that could not take quick evasive action, might loom up right in their path. But he could not watch out for such a possibility: other than his own, there was only one plane in the sky for him right now.

"Duke, this is Matt! I'm right above you!"

There was no response from the man in the cockpit immediately below. Duke was all alone in the sky, lost in the cloud-land that would soon be the blackness of unconsciousness.

Matt looked at his fuel gauge: five minutes' flying at the most. "Duke, I'm running out of gas! I'll never make it home!"

"Home." The word was almost indistinguishable; in less than half a minute Duke would be gone beyond call. Matt could see the helmeted head rolling a little like that of a drunken knight; he wanted to reach out and beat with his fist on the glistening canopy below him. He could feel the sweat pooling in his palms inside his gloves; his breathing was just a series of quick gasps. He looked at the oxygen indicator, saw the white lips on the black mask opening and shutting like a darky minstrel gasping for help——

"Duke! Duke! Is Jolson singing?" He was screaming into his mouthpiece now; it was like a tight hand over his mouth trying to keep his cry from getting to Duke. "Is Jolson singing? Duke!"

Below him he saw the helmeted head lift for a moment; light gleamed on it, a spark of understanding in an orange eyeball. "Not singing." The words were slurred almost beyond recognition: they rubbed against the ear, understood only because they were the words he *wanted* to hear. "Shut."

"We've got to get him singing! Duke! Follow me down! You hear me, follow me down! We got to get Jolson singing!" It was like shrieking through a thick wall of wool; the hand over his mouth seemed even tighter. He was bathed in sweat and his throat was tightening up; pretty soon he might not have a voice to continue shouting. "Follow me down!"

He gunned the chase plane and moved ahead of the US-XP, knowing that he was now at the limit of the chase plane's speed. He could feel the buffeting beginning to run back along his plane; she was beginning to be hard to handle. He looked back and down, saw Duke looking up at him, said a prayer, then swung the chase plane over to starboard and down. If Duke didn't follow him down, this was farewell.

"Going down, Duke! Gotta get Jolson singing!"

For a moment the US-XP continued to weave, then slowly the starboard wing tipped. Matt watched anxiously in his mirror. If Duke went too far over, went into a roll, he would never pull it out before his brain was sufficiently cleared for him to be able to control the plane. "Keep right on my tail, Duke! Watch Jolson!"

Matt continued the slow downward curve, turning them so that they were heading back towards Edwards and the safe dry bed of Lake Muroc. He could not hurry the descent for fear that Duke would build up too much speed and go plunging past the chase plane before he had fully recovered consciousness. Away to the west of them Matt saw a big plane climbing out of the smog above Los Angeles, rising like a pterodactyl out of brown swamp mists. He could only hope they were not in its lane. He watched his altimeter as the needle slowly crept down: 18,000, 15,000. He had cut his power to the minimum, trying to conserve his fuel. If he got home at all it would be on a dry tank.

"How's Jolson?" He talked to Duke all the time, no longer screaming because he was unable to: his voice was just a hoarse croak. He watched in his mirror, now and again turning his head to check more directly, as the US-XP continued to follow him down. The experimental plane was weaving slightly, but it *was* following him. He continued to talk, trying desperately to think of things to say, filibustering to save a man from death. He even began to sing "Mammy": his voice cracked against his own ears. He saw the commercial plane from Los Angeles coming up at them on his port wing, and now he was certain they were in its lane. But he was no longer worried about it: if it was going to hit them, it was going to hit them and there was nothing he could do about it. He could take evasive action himself, but Duke would not be able to; Duke was still half-unconscious, still flying by instinct in the grey fog that had enveloped him. And if Matt did peel away to avoid the commercial plane, he would never be able to pick up Duke again, not in time to save him and assuming he missed colliding with the commercial plane.

Out of the corner of his eye he watched the big plane—it looked like a DC-6—coming up towards them. He wondered if the commercial pilot could see them, but there was nothing he could do to warn him: their radios were on different frequencies. There was not time to call Ground Control and have them call Los Angeles Control Centre; the planes would meet in the sky before the message was half-way through its circuit. For a moment Matt had a clear picture in his mind of the unsuspecting passengers relaxing in the warm comfort of the airliner; the *Fasten Seat Belts* light had probably just gone off and the passengers were getting out their cigarettes, opening their books, settling down for the long dull haul to Chicago, New York, wherever. Their last moments, like meteors, were rushing through the sky towards them. In a few seconds now life and the cigarettes would be snuffed out together; bodies and books would be shredded, all stories ending in the same tragedy. But there was nothing he could do about it. With unutterable regret, he committed his own life, Duke's and that of the people in the DC-6 to the whim of God. He prayed but with little hope.

He looked in the mirror again: Duke was still following him. "Duke, can you hear me?" A mumble answered him. "Duke!" It seemed to him that he no longer had a voice: his throat had closed and the words screamed only in his mind. "Check Jolson! Check your oxygen!"

He waited, and for a moment he thought that Duke had at last passed out completely. Then there was a murmur in his ears, the dazed muttering of a man coming awake. The DC-6 was still climbing towards them, easily recognizable, heading up the incline of sky as if on a prearranged date to meet them at a given point. Matt knew now that the commercial pilot could not see them: they were above him and against the sun. The three planes swung almost lazily through the air, drawing nearer and nearer to each other: in a moment they would meet, become an exploding black star in the shining daylight sky.

"Duke, check your oxygen!" They were down to 13,000 feet: Duke should not need the oxygen mask now.

"Okay, Matt." Duke's voice was still slurred, but it was coherent. "The tube pulled loose. Where have we been?"

"Never mind that. Snap out of it! Eight o'clock—bandit! Take action!"

He flipped the chase plane over and away from the path of the still climbing DC-6. He looked back and saw Duke do the same with the US-XP. Both planes plunged down and away from the commercial airliner; it passed above them, no more than two hundred yards away. Matt imagined he saw a flash of faces against the windows, but he couldn't be sure; maybe the passengers were still unaware of how close they had come to death. But the commercial pilot must have seen them, and Matt could guess at the language that must be going on on the flight deck of the DC-6. The pilot would already be on the air to Los Angeles: there would be a report to the CAB tomorrow that two Air Force planes had buzzed a commercial airliner in its own lane. Matt, still a little weak with relief at their narrow escape, shrugged at the thought. He grinned at the anticipation of what the newspapers would make of it if the story got out: Lieutenant-colonel Duke Dalmead, hero of the Berlin airlift episode who had sent two Russian planes crashing to their end when they had tried to buzz him, now accused of buzzing an American airliner. Maybe Duke would make the cover of *Life* again: he would be a national villain for a week.

"How you feeling now, chum?"

"Still a bit woozy, but I'll make it. I thought for a minute there we were going to book a couple of seats in that DC-6."

"I don't think that Joe liked us. We'll probably have the National Guard waiting for us when we land."

"Well anyway, thanks, son. Do we go home now?"

"If we can make it." Matt glanced at his fuel gauge. "I've always wondered what it would be like flying a glider. Looks like I might get a chance to try it. Chaser to Control. We're coming in. I am about to prove it is possible to fly a jet without gas. But in case I'm wrong, better have the emergency equipment standing by."

Ground Control acknowledged, coming in with what sounded like a mixture of relief, impatience and apprehension: it had not relished being told to shut up and get off the air while the previous emergency had been going on. But it cleared its throat and got down to business: "All aircraft in the local flying area—keep clear of Muroc Dry Lake. There is an emergency. Keep clear of Muroc Dry Lake."

Duke was once more wide awake, fully conscious of what was going on and aware of the risk Matt had taken in staying aloft so long in order to guide him down to a safe altitude. His oxygen tube hung loose, a dead snake, and he tried to remember what might have caused the disconnection. Had it been when he had turned his head for a last look at the darkness of space before he had headed his aircraft down? He had almost died because of the fascination the outer reaches of the sky held for him. And now Matt's life, too, was in danger. Conscience weighed on him with the force of several G's.

Ground Control came on the air again. "Wind is south-southeast. You had better come in on the northern runway."

"You sending someone up to carry me in?" Matt sounded irritable. Duke knew now that Matt was worried. "I'm coming in on the first runway that offers itself."

"What is your approximate position?"

"About eight miles south of the lake bed, I'd guess. I have just gone over to gliders. How are you, chum?"

"I'm okay," Duke said, anxiously watching the chase plane as it slid down through the air. It struck him that he was now flying chase for Matt, but Matt wouldn't want it brought to his notice, not right now. He looked back and saw Lancaster, a rash of buildings on Route 99, the railroad tracks glinting like a trickle of tears. He wondered if Jane had witnessed the near-collision in the air: if she had she would have guessed who were in the two smaller planes. "I'll come in with you."

"Better stay out of the way, Duke. If I fold this thing, I may be all over the runway like a jumble sale. They'd never forgive us if we fouled up that crate you're flying. The last costing on it was four million bucks. You got that sort of money?"

The desert slid by below them: they followed the road in from Lancaster. Duke could see the cactus and sagebrush quite clearly now; the Joshua trees raised inviting arms. The lake bed came up ahead of them. "You're going to make it, Matt. Put your gear down."

"Gear going down. Locked."

"Okay. Good luck, Matt."

Duke could feel the US-XP losing speed. He swung up and

went out in a wide turn. He was at the far end of the turn when he saw the chase plane touch down on the end of the runway, bounce a little, then begin to roll, shepherded by the fire truck and ambulance trailing their long trains of dust as they sped down beside the runway. He saw the chase plane roll to a stop, then Matt said, "Thanks, chum. Now it's your turn."

Duke brought the US-XP round and headed in towards the lake. He felt a strange disquiet: not a feeling of fear, nor even of relief that he had escaped death. Death itself did not frighten him; but what lay beyond death now, suddenly and unaccountably, had become something real. Not tangible, but nonetheless real. For years he had denied the myth of The Beyond; but today for a moment he had been outside the gate to The Unknown. Whether they were one and the same, he did not know. But for the first time he began to wonder at the meaning of his own life. It was as if a page had been turned in the wind and for a moment he had glimpsed the word *Truth*.

2

Duke jumped down from the US-XP as Matt got out of the jeep and came towards him. "Any bruises or anything, son——?"

"The Russians have just put a satellite into orbit," Matt said. "A Sputnik."

Duke put on his sun-glasses against the glare from the desert. "A *what*?"

"Sputnik. We better get used to the word."

"We better get used to a lot of Russian words." Gerry Stevens, the test project co-ordinator, motioned Matt and Duke into the jeep and got in behind the wheel. "Looks like they've already made that obsolete." He nodded across at the US-XP, now surrounded by mechanics. "What Mach number did you hit, Duke?"

"One point nine. Same as last time. That was all you asked for."

"This Sputnik—what a word!—is supposed to do around 17,000 miles an hour. What's that? A hundred miles up, it could be Mach 30, 40. I don't know. My slide rule doesn't stretch up that far." He grinned wryly, his tanned potato-nosed face opening to show his tobacco-stained teeth, but it was evident that his joking held no humour for him. He and other men had been working for ten years on planes like the US-XP and now all at once a doubt had been raised as to whether their efforts had been worthwhile.

"This Sputnik, is it big enough to carry a man?" Duke asked.

Stevens turned the jeep and headed back towards the administration block. "Hell, no. It only weighs a hundred-eighty-odd pounds. But if they've done it once, they'll do it again. With bigger and better Sputniks. With men inside them."

Neither Duke nor Matt accused Stevens of being pessimistic: they knew that he was probably right. Duke could already guess at the possibilities that lay beyond the Russians' achievement: they could in time control space, take over another battlefield in the Cold War. Duke leaned back and looked at Matt. "Well, if ever we develop a Sputnik, you want to fly chase for me?"

"Not if you do fool things like this morning."

"What happened up there, anyway?" Stevens said. "All the brass is gonna be waiting down at the admin. block for you. Los Angeles has been on the wire to us, threatening to sue us for everything but rape."

"How did they miss out on that?" Matt said. "Or isn't rape in California a credible crime?"

"Don't be too goddamned witty when you make your report." Stevens seemed unusually glum, as if he personally had suddenly become a failure with the Russians' success with their orbiting satellite. "Just give 'em the plain unvarnished facts. By tomorrow every goddamned Congressman in Washington is gonna be hollering why aren't we up there with the Russians, hurling our own Sputniks or whatever we're gonna call 'em around the goddamned earth. The less bad publicity we get right now, the better. What happened to you this morning, Duke, could have happened to anyone, even a Russian. But it might be just a bit hard to convince some people, especially those Congressmen who think we should have foolproof planes flying to the moon by now. Tomorrow morning everyone in America is gonna be a space expert, you wait and see. Geez, I knew I should've stayed down on that farm with my Pappy. Tomorrow *he'll* be a goddamned space expert, too."

Duke wanted to thank Matt for saving his life at the risk of his own, but the presence of Stevens held him back. He waited till they had both seen the impromptu committee waiting for them in the administration block, where they learned that everything would be straightened out with the CAB. There had been several crashes and near-misses over the past few years between

Air Force planes and commercial airliners; the civilian pilots were very sour on military pilots who acted like sky hogs. But the quickly convened committee of Air Force brass seemed to realize that, with today's news of the launching of Sputnik, the Air Force and its development programme would be looked at with a very critical eye tomorrow. It would not help if the newspapers got hold of a story that implied that Air Force test pilots could not even keep their planes on course. Duke and Matt were assured nothing more would be heard of the matter. Duke, though himself now a career man, had noticed that occasionally the American military mind, scratched through its thick coating of pride and smug certainty in its own necessity during the cold war, was sensitive to public opinion.

As he and Matt walked across to the officers' bar Duke said, "Thanks for what you did today. For your sake, I hope I never have to do the same for you."

"Well, that's our last flight. Stevens told me when he picked me up in the jeep. There are no more flights scheduled before we leave here. You and I have to have a couple of talks to the new boys and that about wraps it up for us."

"Then I think we ought to celebrate. You got the weekend off? How about you and Jane coming into L.A., having dinner with me and Debbie tomorrow night? Can you get a sitter for the kids and stay overnight? Debbie's got an invitation to a party out at her producer's house in Brentwood. We might go on there. You could talk to Cecil B. De Mille about those home movies of yours."

Matt's home movies, continually out of focus and taken by a camera that seemed to move around more than the people it was photographing, were a joke. Matt ignored the remark. "The break might do Jane some good. She tells me she's sick of talking to the Joshua trees."

"Okay, let's try and make like something more entertaining than a couple of Joshua trees. Drive your own car into L.A. and I'll pick you up wherever you're staying. Beer?"

A minute later Matt raised his glass and said, "Here's to the end of four years of it. You're looking at a man who's going to be a test pilot for chairs from now on."

"Here's to Sputnik," said Duke, grinning.

"Careful, chum. That may already be a subversive word."

When Matt got home to Lancaster and told Jane where they were going, she said, "Is he bringing Debbie with him?"

"Sure. Why not?"

"Because every time he does, I keep looking at that girl and resenting her, thinking Cleo should be in her place. Oh, I don't mean I resent the girl *herself*. She's nice enough, though sometimes I think she hits the bottle a little too much. But he could do a lot worse. That floozy he met when we first got out here, what was her name, Flo——"

"Okay, lay off. All I asked, do you want to go to L.A. for the weekend? I'm not interested in Duke's love life, past, present or future. Sometimes I think you should have been a Mother Superior."

"If I had been, I'd have been excommunicated, some of the things you've seduced me into." She leaned forward and kissed him. "Actually, I think a weekend in Los Angeles would do me the world of good. Rose Sharmon will look after the kids for me. You can go to a baseball match tomorrow while I luxuriate in I. Magnin's——"

"Ball *game*. When are you going to learn to speak American? And they don't have ball games in October——"

"Is it *October*? I didn't know. What year is it? Out here in the desert——" She sat on the arm of his chair and kissed him again. "I'm kidding, darling. But I'm glad we are leaving here, I don't think I could stand another year of this——"

John, quick as a desert road runner, freckled as a buzzard's egg, burst in the door. "Oh gosh, more love stuff! It's embarrassing." He was twelve now, looking more than ever like his father but twice as energetic; wide-eyed with curiosity, he chased through his small world in search of knowledge. He recovered quickly from his embarrassment, exploding with the little more knowledge he had gained this morning. "Hey Dad, have you heard about the Sputnik?"

"Sputnik? Is this one of those jokes you've been bringing home from school lately?" Jane said. "You're growing up too fast, sonny boy. Keep your crudities till you're older——"

John looked at Matt, man to man: what could you do with a woman like that? Were *all* grown women like that? Matt winked at his son, then gently explained to his wife what a Sputnik was. "Don't you listen to the radio? All the way back in the car I've been listening to nothing else."

"She never listens to the radio, Dad, you knew that——"

"Who's *she*? The cat's mother? Watch yourself, my boy, or you'll get a clip under the ear. This may be the dawn of the Space Age, but don't let's forget respect for our earthbound mothers." Jane turned back to the cake she had been mixing when Matt

200

had come in. "This Sputnik may just turn out to be a nine-days' wonder."

"No, Mom, this is the real thing." John moved about the room, excited and voluble. *He's not troubled by this bruise to our national pride,* Matt thought. John was a man of the future, careless for the moment of the cold war, thrilled only by the new frontier opened up for his generation. "They put it up in the sky with a rocket, and rockets aren't new. We put a rocket up into the stratosphere in 1949, in New Mexico. And Dr. Goddard fired a liquid-fuel rocket 'way back in 1926. The Germans had rockets during the war. And the Russians know a lot about them. A man named Ziolovky—gee, I've just remembered, he was born a hundred years ago this year——"

"Where did you get all this dope?" Matt was accustomed to the odd bits of esoteric information his son dropped like candy wrappers around the house, but this morning the boy was excelling himself. Matt tried to remember his own interests at twelve, and felt as if he had been lacking in intellect, a moron of the 1930's. The Ethiopian war had just ended, the civil war in Spain just begun; Hitler was on the march and King Edward of England had abdicated. And what had been his interests? Fishing with Duke off the point at Waquoit, going to see every Randolph Scott movie that came to town, glued every Wednesday night to the radio to hear Fred Allen, so that you could use his gags, slightly changed, a week or two later and be the school comic. The dirigible *Hindenburg* had flown the Atlantic that year, but Matt would not have been able to quote a single statistic about it, nor any statistic on air travel. But he would have been able to give you the lifetime batting average of Lou Gehrig or the number of strike-outs by Walter Johnson. Kids today were too sophisticated. But then maybe they needed to be, if they were to survive the future.

"Oh, I been reading it up for months. You see, Dad, science fiction isn't so crazy, after all——"

"Okay, don't let's get into *that* argument again. I know when I'm licked. Scram for a while, will you? I'll come out later and talk to you about Sputnik."

"Some of the other kids want to talk to you, too, Dad. Can I ask them in? Billy Sharmon thought we oughta have a space symposium——"

"Okay." John whirled and was gone, disappearing as a flicker of brown in the glare outside. Matt looked at Jane. "A *symposium*? Twelve-year-olds?"

"I was talking to the teacher the other day about Billy Sharmon. He's got an I.Q. of seven hundred and fifty or something. Anyhow, *he* teaches *her*, so she says."

"What am I going to say to them? They're sure to know more about it than I do. Gerry Stevens said something this morning. He said everyone in America would be a space expert by tomorrow morning. I've got one in my own house, and a genius besides living next door. Where's that encyclopedia that smart-alec college boy talked you into buying?"

"What are you going to look up?"

"Ziol-whatever-his-name-was-ki. Who wants to look ignorant in front of a bunch of twelve-year-olds? I'm supposed to be a hero of the wild blue yonder. Only the wild blue has suddenly got a bit too yonder for poor old Dad. I may have to go back to school."

"It's your problem," said Jane, turning on the cake mixer. "How was it today?"

"Okay. We got a bit off course, but that was all." He had become practised in sounding casual, but not too casual; he knew that Jane had also become practised in recognizing the deceit behind too much understatement. "But you'll be glad to know I've had my last flight as a test pilot. I am now going to retire to a desk and ponder about Sputniks."

"Sputniks are not going to make much difference to a woman who has to cook for a husband and three kids, keep the desert out of her house, never gets to talk with anyone but Joshua trees——"

He kissed the back of her neck. "If I didn't know you so well, I'd think you were happy here."

"I'll be happier in Los Angeles, even if only for a weekend. Are you going to do the right thing by me and book us into the Beverly-Wilshire or is it some motel down in Santa Monica?"

He did the right thing by her, and Jane appreciated the temporary luxury. She had grown tired of life in the desert, indeed had been tired of it now for three years, but she had managed to keep most of her complaints to herself. She had come to realize how much Matt loved his job; and she was not so insensitive as not to appreciate his dedication to it. She knew there were many men for whom their jobs were only a means of earning a living, and they brought their dissatisfaction with their jobs into their home life. Matt never neglected her and the children, and his satisfaction with his job was reflected in his contentment around the house. It had been a surprise to Jane how much the children loved living in the desert. They had been fortunate enough to rent a house with a small pool, and Matt had bought air-conditioning units for the house: except for the continual intrusion of dust and sand, actual living conditions were not bad. But the monotony of the landscape, the almost ceaseless glare of the sunshine, had begun to wear on her nerves. A weekend of luxury was a welcome relief.

The four of them went to dinner at Romanoff's. Jane wore a dress Matt had bought for her that morning at I. Magnin's; there being no ball games in October, he had come with her while she had luxuriated; then, partly to his own surprise and very much to hers, he had laid out a hundred dollars for the dress that had taken her eye. By the time they got to Romanoff's, she was in such a good mood she could not have been more friendly to Debbie Fairfax. But Debbie, who appeared to have been drinking before she and Duke came to pick up the Crispins, did not respond too well to Jane's approach. She was not rude, but she just did not seem to have her mind on the evening ahead.

After dinner they drove out to Brentwood, to the party at the home of Sol Hoban, the film producer. After they had been introduced to their host and hostess, Matt and Jane were left alone for a moment.

"Is this a gag?" Matt asked. "This being so nice to Debbie?"

"No. I just feel sorry for her. I've just realized that tonight will be her last night with Duke."

"And you feel *sorry* for her? I thought you'd have been cheering."

"Which just goes to show how little you know about women. Or anyway about *this* woman." She tapped her bosom. "I feel sorry for any woman who gets herself tied up with a man she can't marry and settle down with."

"Debbie doesn't look the type to me who'd want to settle down."

"I don't know how you ever got accepted as a test pilot. You're as blind as a bat." She looked across the crowded room at Duke and Debbie, standing in a corner, carrying on what looked like a desultory conversation with each other. "She's head over heels in love with him."

"When did you make this discovery?"

"Tonight. You wait and see. She's going to get drunker tonight than you've ever seen her."

"I won't look at her, then. I hate the sight of drunken women."

"I'm glad to hear it, even if in this community that would make you sound narrow-minded. A little narrow-mindedness occasionally is a good thing."

"That's the Irish bigot in you talking."

"Talking of talking, what does one talk about with movie people?"

"Movies."

But the movie people were not talking about movies that night. They were talking about the Russians and their Sputnik.

"I hesitate to venture an opinion for fear of being called un-American," said a stout bald director who wore a red-white-and-blue striped tie and a lugubrious expression. He downed his third Scotch in twenty minutes and looked across the room at his wife who had insisted on wearing her new red dress tonight of all nights. "Back in 1951 I expressed admiration for the work of Eisenstein and that brought me to the notice of that great American, Senator McCarthy. What do you think of the Russian effort, Mrs.——?"

"Crispin," said Jane, wishing that the tall thin man beside her would not lean so close to her.

"I understand your husband is a test pilot in the Air Force," said the director.

"He is," said Jane. "But we don't talk shop. Do you talk films all the time with your wife?"

"What else has he to talk about?" The tall thin man was a writer who had just decided to leave films for television. His agent had guaranteed him seventy-five thousand dollars for the coming year, and he felt he could now look on himself as a successful failure: in that year anyone was a failure who left films for television. For years he had been working at being a cynic and tonight he thought he had achieved full status. "Old Harry came out here to the Coast thirty—thirty-five, Harry?—years ago. Harry Langdon was a star then, and Brentwood, right where we are now, was Indian country. Hollywood is Harry's world, isn't it, Harry? He didn't know Roosevelt was dead till he saw a newsreel of the funeral at the première of one of his own pictures. You should go to their house some time for dinner—even the food comes from the studio commissary."

"I think television deserves you, Sy," said the director. "Your kinda humour is just the kinda crap they're buying."

Jane left them and wandered on through the rooms. It was a large house, furnished with much more taste than she had expected. She had a prejudice against film people, one based on hearsay and gossip rather than on actual experience; in their time in California she and Matt had met a few people from the industry, but this was the first time she had been to the home of someone in the top bracket. It was a large party and no one seemed to take any notice of her as she moved from room to room. She came to a heavy panelled door that was slightly ajar, and tentatively she pushed it open. A man was sitting at a desk in the room, silhouetted against a small reading lamp on a shelf behind him.

"Oh, I'm sorry. I've just been stickybeaking around——"

"Stickybeaking? What sort of word is that? No, don't go, Mrs. Crispin. Please come in."

Jane went into the room, which appeared to be a small study, and half-closed the door behind her. The man switched on another lamp, and Jane recognized her host. Sol Hoban was a small neat man with small neat features and grizzled curly hair. He had a soft lilting voice and beautifully manicured hands that he used as expressively as his voice. There were laughter wrinkles at the corners of his eyes, but the eyes themselves had a dark sadness to them.

"Why were you stickybeaking? I presume you mean you were poking your nose into things?"

"I liked your house. For most of my married life I've been living in furnished houses and apartments—well, you wouldn't know much about those."

"You'd be surprised, Mrs. Crispin, how much I *do* know about them. I couldn't always afford this——" A hand waved expressively in the air, a fluttering white bird above the dome of light on the desk. He motioned for her to sit and she sank down into a deep leather arm-chair. She ran her hands over the grain of the leather and wished she could afford to buy something like this for Matt. "My wife and I lived in a furnished apartment in North Hollywood for twelve years. And when I first arrived in this country from Russia twenty-eight years ago—twenty-eight years this very day—I lived in one room above a furrier's loft in downtown Manhattan."

"You're not an American?"

He smiled, the wrinkles covering the top half of his cheeks like a domino of net. "Oh, I'm an American, sure enough. How long have you been here, Mrs. Crispin? What are you, English?"

"Australian. I've been here eleven years." Two years ago she had taken the children back to Australia for the first time, and she had been shocked and a little upset to find how much she had grown away from her parents, her old friends and even Australia

205

itself. Everything seemed to have changed, and she had not been sure it had been for the better. Sydney seemed to have become very Americanized, something she had regretted; she was not anti-American, but she did not want to see a world made over into America's image. Especially her home town.

"And don't you consider yourself an American now? No, I can see you don't. Oh, I don't blame you. Did you come here to marry Colonel Crispin?"

"I married him in Australia during the war."

"That explains it. You married a man, not a country. I married America, Mrs. Crispin. I paid court to it as a teenage kid in Smolensk, where I come from, and I came here twenty-eight years ago and married it. Today is our anniversary."

"That doesn't sound very complimentary to Mrs. Hoban."

He looked at her, the wrinkles fading from around his eyes. "Do you usually rush to the defence of other wives?"

"All the time."

"You're very candid, aren't you? We aren't used to candidness in this town. Oh, we get plenty of insulting frankness, but that isn't candidness. No, you're wrong, Mrs. Crispin. I don't mean to sound uncomplimentary to my wife, I love my wife——" A hand went up, almost like a traffic signal. "Why do you look so quizzical?"

"I'm afraid you've forgotten whom we came with. Debbie Fairfax."

He sighed, folding his hands together. "No. I hadn't forgotten whom you came with. I had just forgotten how women talk to each other."

"Debbie has never talked to me. But she talked to the man she's now in love with, Colonel Dalmead. And he talked to my husband. And my husband talked to me."

Again the wrinkles covered his upper cheeks as he smiled. He raised his hands and a white cap of fingers rested for a moment on his head. "Every little progression of the subject was probably no more than an innocent remark. I don't believe Debbie has any malice towards me, in fact I'm sure of it. And now the subject is back here in my house, in my lap. Notwithstanding what you have heard, Mrs. Crispin, I do love my wife. Another wife, such as yourself, will probably find that difficult to believe. But it is the truth. A man can get into bed, but not take his love there."

"Would your wife forgive you if she knew?"

"I don't know. But I would never want her to find out. And

she never will. Not unless the cycle of innocent remarks lands it in *her* lap."

"I am surprised that you keep Debbie working for you."

"Debbie is one of the best editors in the business. That is one of the reasons I keep her. Another is that I am not a ruthless, callous man, Mrs. Crispin. Debbie never loved me, but she was kind to me when she thought I needed consolation. You see, my wife and I had separated at that time. We thought our marriage was finished. Three months apart from each other convinced us how wrong we were. That was seven years ago and we have never spent a day apart since."

Jane looked around the dimly-lit room, then back at Hoban. "Then why are you sitting in here on your own? You look sad, Mr. Hoban. Too sad for a man who is throwing a party—is it to celebrate your anniversary with America?"

He nodded seriously, although her question had been half-joke. "Every year I give this party for this reason. Very few people know why, and I don't like to broadcast it. Sentiment is in the blood of most Americans and they do a terrible lot of blood-letting. But in that respect I am not a good American. I hate public exposure of one's sentiments. And tonight I could not afford to expose my sentiments."

She looked puzzled. "What do you mean?"

"Mrs. Crispin, I've told you I married America. But I can't forget where I was born. Russia is my mother, if you like to put it that way. My flesh and blood parents are still there, and happy, too. My father fought in the Revolution in 1917. I was ten years old then and I can remember we had pictures of Lenin all about the house."

"Has your father forgiven you? I mean for getting into bed with America."

"It took him years. When I ran away from home, he told everyone I had been caught in a blizzard and eaten by wolves. The wolves of Wall Street, I presume he meant. But then by the time I had become successful, made one or two pictures that were artistic as well as financial successes, he was prepared to forgive me and resurrect me. A lot of people forget that Russians, even the Communists, admire success as much as we Americans do."

"*We* Americans? You were half-Russian a moment ago."

"I guess I always will be." The eyes went almost black with sadness; the hands were still on the desk in front of him. He was impregnated with Russia's history: he could hail Columbia with sincerity, but his raised arm would be arthritic with memories of

Russia. "I can't help the pride I feel in what the Russians have done with Sputnik. But I could never tell anyone that."

"Why are you telling me?"

"I don't really know, Mrs. Crispin. Unless it was that you were so candid about not being an American. There are a lot of people out there tonight—" he waved a hand towards the door "—who are no more American than you are. But they are sounding off like speech-writers for Eisenhower, trying to prove they are more American than anyone else. There is an air of doubt in America tonight, Mrs. Crispin, a questioning as to whether we are really as good as we think we are. We have this inner feeling of inferiority despite our outward air of superiority. When someone beats us to the punch on anything, we doubt ourselves, instead of going quietly ahead with our own schemes. Have you read the newspapers today, listened to the radio, looked at television? Oh, no one has said we have failed—that would be treason and they'd be shot at once, if not by the Government, at least by some crank. But the doubt is there. And the answer seems to be: when in doubt, shout. For the next few weeks there is going to be a terrible lot of shouting in America. Everyone shouting how proud he is to be an American, how by tomorrow or the day after we'll not only have caught up with the Russians, but we'll be ahead of them. If they're not shouting, they're making sour grapes remarks about what the Russians have done. Including our esteemed President. It is no wonder the rest of the world only half-heartedly accepts us as their leader."

"My husband, fortunately, is not a shouter. Nor is he given to sour grapes remarks."

"Perhaps he doesn't need to be a shouter. An Air Force colonel doesn't have to prove he's a patriot. All he has to do is put on his uniform."

"You notice he isn't wearing his uniform tonight?"

"I did notice it. And I admire him for it. My own temptation, and I'm sure that of more than half my guests, would be to put on any uniform we owned, even that of the Boy Scouts. Americans take their patriotism very seriously. Or at least the expression of it."

Jane smiled. "You know, Mr. Hoban, tonight you're not an American. You're like me, a foreigner. I think it is just as well you chose me to say these things to."

He shook his head, returning her smile. "Tonight, Mrs. Crispin, I think I am more garrulous than I have been in years. But then so are many of my guests, I think. I don't venture very many opinions. Look at my record in the picture business. The business has its ups and downs, its good and bad pictures, its scandals, but I've never made a comment. The men who have lasted longest in this town have been the ones who have kept their mouths shut. It is a good policy, not only in Hollywood."

"Doesn't your conscience worry you, I mean about keeping your mouth shut on things you feel strongly about?"

"Of course. But what man answers every call his conscience makes? He would be on the run all day. There are a lot of consciences on the run out there now——" Another wave of his hand towards the door. He seemed contemptuous of most of his guests and Jane wondered why he had invited them. But she would not ask him; she felt she had already been treated to too much of the man. Tomorrow he would probably regret that he had talked as freely as he had to her. "But they're really doing no more than shouting. A shout is no more than the voice of the mob, Mrs. Crispin. It never won a revolution, corrected an injustice. Behind all the shouters in history you'll find a few quiet men who got the job done that needed to be done. When all the shouting about Sputnik is over and America at last has a satellite up there with it, you will find it will have been the quiet men who got it up there. Not the shouters, not the politicians in Washington or the editorial writers or the professional patriots. It will be the quiet men. Maybe like your husband."

"And what about you?"

He smiled again and stood up. "I might answer my conscience then. Patriotism is born out of conscience, and I might have to prove to myself, if to no one else, that I am now an American and no longer a Russian. Maybe I'll make a picture about the quiet men. My own sort of memorial to them. Unfortunately no one would pay to come and see it, and then my bankers would ask me if I was out of my head for making such a picture. The quiet men of history don't make good movie material."

He took her arm and led her out of the library. "I'm glad you like my house. If you hadn't, you would not have come—stickybeaking?—and I should not have met you." His wife came up to them. "Darling, Mrs. Crispin and I have been closeted in the library for the last half hour. Were we missed?"

"If you were, no one mentioned it." Beatrice Hoban was a small, full-figured woman whose dark hair was liberally streaked with grey. She was handsome rather than pretty, but there was an animation to her face that made one look at her before looking at more beautiful women. "I hope Sol didn't bore you, Mrs.

Crispin. He is so faithful, a lot of women find him boring."

"On the contrary, I found him very interesting," Jane said, then smiled reassuringly. "But not in that way. Actually, I don't find faithful husbands boring. I have one of my own."

"I've noticed him. He's had one of the young girls from Warners hanging around his neck for the last half hour, but she is getting nowhere at all. But only an older woman, a wife, would recognize that."

"I'm glad to hear it. I mean, that she's not getting anywhere. But I think I'll go and remove her, anyway. You never know, he might weaken."

She moved on across the room and Beatrice Hoban looked after her. "That's a lovely woman. Fortunately she doesn't have star quality. I'm tired of beautiful women with star quality."

"Mrs. Crispin has her own quality."

"What did you talk about with her?"

"Conscience."

"Do you have one?"

"Not about you," he said, and squeezed her plump arm.

On the other side of the room Jane had joined the group where Matt sat with the young blonde actress almost in his lap. Matt looked up at Jane, winked and shrugged to indicate that he could not make room for her on the couch where he sat nor could he stand up without disturbing the people who sat around him. He was obviously the centre of the group; he was chairing another symposium on space. Jane stared hard at the blonde, but the actress was accustomed to stares and knew how to ignore those she did not welcome. She was giving her undivided attention to Matt, smiling at him with a cinemascopic flash of teeth, exposing her bosom to him like two melons hanging from a tree.

Jane felt someone standing beside her and looked up to see Duke. "Put your knife back in your garter. She's not worth going to gaol over."

"I was going to knife *him*. He's encouraging her!"

"Don't be crazy. He's enjoying it, but what middle-aged man doesn't——"

"He's not middle-aged. He's only thirty-three."

"And she's twenty. It flatters a man to know he can still have the young ones make a pass at him. Let him have his fun. It won't lead to anything you need worry about."

Jane looked about the room, then back at Duke. "Where's Debbie?"

"She's gone home."

"You let her go home on her own?"

"I offered to take her, but she wouldn't listen to me. I think it's better this way. It would have been a pretty messy night."

"For you or for her?"

"I told you, put your knife away. Can I get you a drink?"

Jane watched him as he crossed the room to the bar. He was better looking than ninety-per-cent of the men in the room; he was handsome enough to have been an actor. His dark hair, which he wore rather long like an actor's, was streaked with grey along the temples: it did not make him look older than his years but only added a certain distinction to his looks. He was lean and lithe: there was a suggestion of animal in his movements. Jane could see women turning to look at him, and for a moment she wondered how she herself would have reacted to him if she had not already been so deeply in love with Matt when she had first met him. It was not difficult to understand how women fell for him. What she did not understand was how they could continue to be in love with him once they had discovered the shallowness and selfishness of him.

He took two drinks from the bar, turned round and nodded towards a door leading out on to a terrace. Jane hesitated, looked at Matt and his blonde vine clinging to his arm, shook her head in warning to him, then turned and followed Duke out on to the terrace. It was a mild autumn night and a few stars glimmered through a gauze of cloud. To the south the lights of the city threw a glow on the cloud ceiling, like a reflection of fever. From somewhere below the house there was the sound of passing cars on Sunset Boulevard, a swishing tide that came and went quickly.

Duke handed her a drink. "You shouldn't pick on me so often, Jane. You do it out of habit. You nag me instead of your husband."

"I'm sorry, Duke," she said, but there was no real apology in her voice. "Perhaps I'm just on every woman's side, that's all. You must admit you don't have a very good record for chivalry."

"I was being chivalrous tonight. That was what started our argument."

"How was that?"

He walked to the edge of the terrace, stood leaning against the wrought iron railing. From inside the house talk escaped to scrape against the ear: he had noticed before that all party chatter seemed to have a metallic tone to it, as if uttered by tinfoil tongues. "I asked her not to get drunk. She was going to get drunk so that she could say good-bye in the way she thought I wanted her to say good-bye. In bed."

"And you didn't want that?"

"Don't sound so incredulous," he said without rancour. He was not in a good humour, but she noticed that so far he did not appear to have resented her remarks. And, she admitted to herself, he could have had cause to. "I don't find bed the answer to everything. I may not take it as seriously as a woman does, but I know it doesn't solve very many problems. It wouldn't have solved Debbie's problem."

"Which is?"

"Being in love with me."

"Oh my God!" Jane bumped her hip against the railing as she straightened up with surprise; her exclamation was one of both indignation and pain. She massaged her hip while she stared at him. "Duke, you have the most colossal ego I've ever come across. How can you stand there and say a thing like that?"

"Isn't it true?"

"About her being in love with you? Well, even if it is——"

"Even if it is. You know goddamned well it is." He sounded angry with her now; rage began to burn in him. "Jane, you've never liked me, but I'll tell you the truth, I've always liked you. I liked your respect for the truth, even when you were being a bit too goddamned truthful towards me. But why can't you respect the truth when I tell it? Why accuse me of being egotistical when you know that what I say is the truth? Is it because most women hate to hear a man claim that a woman, *any* woman, is in love with him. Does the war of the sexes go that far with you? No admission of surrender by any woman on any terms?"

"Cleo's never denied your claim."

"I knew we'd get around to her sooner or later. She's got more advocates working for her than the Department of Justice. You, Pop, my brother, my sisters——" He turned away for a moment, then abruptly looked back. "Cleo has never made any secret about how she feels and she'd let me boast about it as much as I wanted. *If* I wanted, which I don't. And I'm not boasting about how Debbie feels, either. I'm stating a fact, a fact that I feel more sorrow about than I do pride. You seem to think I get some sort of kick out of tossing women over.

"Why do you get yourself into situations, then, where you have to toss them over?"

"Would you rather I came here to town every weekend, spent it with some whore? Would you think more of me if I did that?

You know goddamned well you wouldn't. Married women hate the professionals—they hate the amateurs, too, but not quite so much. If I bought my time in bed, you'd have less respect for me than you've got now. And that's small enough."

"Does that worry you, Duke? That I don't have much respect for you?"

"Why shouldn't it, for Christ's sake? You're my best friend's wife. You're not mean or malicious—and I'm thankful for that— otherwise you'd have split me and Matt years ago. But what sort of fun do you think it is for me to come to your house and know all the time you think I'm a heel, a prize shit—I'm sorry. I shouldn't have said that." She had never seen him so emotional before. He gulped his drink, then visibly tried to calm himself. "Cleo was always on my back for swearing in front of you. I mean, saying Christ and things like that."

"That's the first time you've used a four-letter word in front of me."

"Well, I'm sorry. I mean it."

"Apology accepted." She turned to stare out at the garden that dropped away below them. All at once she felt unsure of herself with Duke. For years her antagonism to him had given her confidence with him; there was something positive in being so critical of him. She was not yet ready to forgive him for what he had done to Cleo and Caroline: she had a single-minded attitude towards one's family duty, an almost Victorian prejudice against those who shirked their responsibilities. Yet now she had begun to see a glimmer of the truth of Duke, the insecurity that he would be the last to admit but which was as much part of him as his external charm and good looks and restless ambition. Ambition towards what? she wondered. She had met ambitious men before, but each had had a single aim: to be rich, to be famous, to be top in their profession. She knew that Duke had told Matt it was his ambition to be one of the great pilots, but she had never believed him: womanlike, she could not bring herself to believe that a grown man could still cherish what, to her, were the dreams of a boy. Men, she knew, were constantly trying to prove themselves in physical action; the novels of Hemingway, which bored her, had proved that. But something goaded Duke: what, she did not know, nor could she be sure that he himself knew. For all her long opposition to him, she now suddenly felt a wave of sympathy for him.

"Jane——" There was a pleading note in his voice, one she had never heard before. Had he pleaded with other women, with

Cleo? She did not think so; and she wondered why he should plead with her. "I once told Matt I needed him. It was true then, and it's true now. I won't say I need you—it would sound like empty flattery and you wouldn't believe it anyway. But you are Matt's rudder——" She smiled at the description and he smiled, too. "That's not very flattering, is it?"

"No. But I know what you mean. I don't know if it's true, though."

"Oh, it's true, all right. I've seen him when you haven't been around. In Germany that time, and Korea. Even when we've had to go away from Edwards to Washington or somewhere for a couple of nights. He's lost without you."

Jane glanced inside the house: the vine-like blonde was now almost smothering Matt. "He doesn't look lost right now," she said, but there was no ill-humour in her voice. She had never suspected Matt of any unfaithfulness, but a wife always liked to hear what Duke had just told her.

Duke's gaze followed hers. "That blonde wouldn't be trying so hard if she stood any real chance with him. She has a thing or two to learn. One of them is the difference between indifference and playing hard to get. She thinks Matt is playing hard to get."

"Would you play hard to get if she sat in *your* lap?"

"Tonight? Yes. In fact, I'd be indifferent. But maybe not some other night."

"What's the matter with you, Duke?"

He looked at his empty glass, debating whether to have it refilled, then decided against it. He had tried to tell Debbie tonight that there was no solution in the bottom of a glass; he should try and follow his own advice. Down on Sunset there was a squeal of tyres as a car took one of the curves too fast: the sound came up at them like the scream of some jungle animal. Above the lights to the west he could see the fog beginning to roll in like a fleet of grey-yellow sails. Everyone was being invaded tonight by fog or some sort: the fog of love, the fog of doubt that clouded himself. The experience of yesterday morning was still with him: infinity had begun to take on a dimension, hazy though it was. "I don't know, Jane. It's not that I don't care about anything any more—it's more like there's nothing to care about. And it worries me."

"What about Cleo and Caroline?" She knew she must sound as if she were harping, plucking the one string of criticism; but now she felt more an urge to help him than to criticize him. For the first time she began to be aware of the seeds of disaster

214

buried in him; perhaps it was an inheritance from some ancestor, sprouting now like corn seeds suddenly germinating when exposed in the tomb of a long dead Egyptian king. She believed in destiny because she believed in God; she found no contradiction in the two. Cause and End were the same, God; so what passed between was also God. But it would be difficult to explain this to a man who did not believe in God. Especially when your explanation implied that it was God who had planted the seeds of disaster in him.

"I care about Cleo and Caroline. Or at least I have a conscience about them. Is that the same thing?"

"I wouldn't know. I've just been talking to someone else. He seems to think conscience is another name for patriotism. Or was it vice versa?"

"Conscience has a dozen names. Sometimes it even masquerades as love." She noticed the harsh note in his voice, and wondered if it was the sound of self-criticism. "Not with Caroline. With Cleo, I don't know for sure. I wish I did."

"Can't you recognize love when you feel it?" It was as recognizable to her as the moon, the stars, the shape of the human heart: all the symbols that accompanied it. "If you feel it towards Caroline, why not towards Cleo?"

He smiled with good-humoured patience. "You're a woman, you shouldn't ask me that. Do you feel the same towards Matt as you do towards the kids? You love them all, but I bet it's not the same sort of love."

She acknowledged his point. "Righto. But it seems to me that a man—or a woman—should know whether they're in love with another person. You're past the age of infatuation."

"Not past it. Between it. There are two ages of infatuation. When you're too young to know true love and when you're too old to hope for it."

She looked at him. "Where have you been spending your time lately? With one of these California intellectual cults? When did you become a bloody philosopher?"

"Don't swear at me," he grinned.

"Bloody isn't swearing. Not in my book."

"Okay, I'm not a bloody philosopher. I'm just trying to prove I'm not the dope you think I am. I've made a mess of my love life, but in the process I've learned a thing or two about love."

"You sound like a dope to me. A man who can't tell whether he's in love with his wife or not." Then she looked at him, suddenly curious, even a little apprehensive for him. "Or is it that you aren't capable of love, Duke?"

He shrugged. "I wonder that myself sometimes. It happens, doesn't it?"

"More than we guess, I suppose. If that's the way it is, Duke, I'm sorry for you. But I wouldn't have a clue how to help you."

"Just a little understanding now and again, that's all I ask." Then he turned as Matt came out on to the terrace towards them.

"What happened to the blonde?" Jane said. "Did you have to cut her off or did someone pour Kill-Weed on her?"

"You get a nice meaty note in your voice when you're jealous," Matt said. "Like a carnivorous canary."

"A family row is brewing," said Duke. "Exit the Duke."

Matt watched him go. "What have you two been batting the breeze about?"

"Him. Me. You."

"Are we a triangle? I never knew."

"All of a sudden I'm beginning to understand why some women fall in love with him."

He put a finger against her cheek and turned her face towards him. "Not you, too?"

"Don't be silly. No, I can see now why Cleo and Debbie and what was that German girl's name——?"

"The one who bawled her eyes out when we left Frankfurt? Trudi. Boy, was I wrong about her. I thought she was just a tramp—well, maybe she was. But when it came to saying good-bye to Number One Boy in there, she was really in love with him. Why don't women go for me like that?"

"That blonde was going for you like that, the bitch. Anyhow, I'm not quite so much against Duke as I was. He's asked me to try and understand him a bit better and I'm going to. Does that please you?"

He looked at her, smiling gently. "Does a man kiss his own wife in Hollywood?"

"You could do much worse." She offered her lips to his, then said, "What was the topic that had everyone hanging on your every word and the blonde hanging on everything else?"

"I love you when you're jealous. Sputniks was the topic. That talk yesterday afternoon with the kids has made me an expert."

"How much of an expert?"

"Just an arm-chair one. Maybe I'll know a bit more after a week or two at Langley."

"Darling, where do we go from here? I mean, is there any more flying for you?"

"Honey, I'm only thirty-three. There's sure to be more flying. I *want* there to be."

"In a Sputnik?"

She noticed the slight hesitation before he answered. "It may be years before they get a manned satellite up there. We haven't even got an unmanned one up there yet."

Then Sol Hoban came out on to the terrace, his sad dark eyes lighting for a moment as he saw Jane. "Stickybeaking at the view, Mrs. Crispin? I come out here every night before I go to bed. Have you a sense of history, Colonel Crispin?"

The question surprised Matt. He considered for a moment, wondering if this were some sort of Hollywood joke. The group he had been talking to inside the house had been a mixed lot. Most of them, with the exception of the blonde starlet, had been intelligent and concerned with the implications of the Russians' success with their satellite. Some of them had contributed reasoned comment, but others had been irritatingly flippant, as if their whole life was geared to the wisecrack. Hoban did not sound that type of man, but you couldn't be sure of any face or personality in this town of make-believe.

"I think I have. If you mean am I conscious of the men who passed this way before me, yes."

"Exactly what I mean. I come out here every night and listen to the ghosts of Portola and Serra moving up the coast. I often wonder what they think of a little Russian Jew from Smolensk who feels grateful to them for what they discovered." He looked up at the sky, now covered with fog. "Tonight I wonder what they think of the Russians who have put the first footprint in space? Do you think, colonel, that when you are dead you still have a sense of history?"

Matt smiled. "You have me, Mr. Hoban. But if you should go first, I wish you'd let me know. You can always get me care of the Air Force."

"We must find a medium then. Mrs. Crispin? Do you think you could get in touch with the hereafter?"

"I doubt it," said Jane, with a glance at Matt. "I have trouble in keeping in touch with the present."

3

Duke and Matt went East to Langley Air Force Base in Virginia the week after the launching of Sputnik. They found that the scientists and engineers there were not surprised by what the Russians had achieved; they had much more respect for Russian potential and achievement than did American Congressmen and editorial writers. They were not unduly depressed by their own lack of success so far; they felt reasonably certain that the United States would have its own satellite in space before very long. Duke and Matt were both impressed by the scientists' and engineers' practical outlook towards the Russians, and their quiet determination to be not upset by the general mild hysteria among uninformed public voices.

In November, by which time Matt knew he was to go on to Washington for desk duty for an indefinite period, Jane and the children also came East. Matt met them at the airport. "I've got us this house in Chipp Falls, out past Falls Church. A big one, without sand in the carpets and not a Joshua tree in sight."

"It's nice to see some greenery again," Jane said. "And all those lovely autumn colours! See that, kids? That's a silver maple. There's a buttonwood sycamore. Oh, I learned all my American trees when I first came here. To impress your father, but he couldn't have cared less. Joshua trees are just about all he deserves."

The children, grown accustomed to the desert, looked out with wide eyes as Matt drove them through the green Virginia countryside. When they at last pulled into the drive of the house, the children leapt from the car and vanished round the back of the house to see what diversions this new home would offer. Jane sat in the car and looked at the low fieldstone building set across the wide lot and surrounded by a blaze of trees.

"It's lovely, darling. But what's the rent—two hundred, three hundred a month?"

"Nothing."

"You mean someone has *lent* it to us?"

"I mean we own it."

She looked at him, tired after the long plane trip and in no mood for silly jokes. "Are you pulling my leg?"

"No, I'm fair dinkum, as your illiterate brother would say. We own it."

"How much did it cost?"

"Thirty-two thousand."

"Now I'm sure you're pulling my leg. Oh Matt, I'm too tired for acting the goat——" She looked at him irritably, then stopped. "You mean it? But thirty-two thousand dollars! You're out of your head. We can't afford that sort of money. And what if we're moved again? We'll be up to our eyes in debt at the bank or wherever you borrowed it——"

"Relax," he said gently, thinking how careful she had always been with their money, how worried she had been when their airline had been losing money those so few years ago. His mother, with her New England respect for money and its proper use, had thought a great deal of Jane for her non-extravagant outlook. "Dad financed us on the deal. I went up to see him and Mom just after I came East, one weekend, and Mom asked me what sort of house we'd had out in California. Or rather, she didn't ask me what sort of house *we* had. She asked what sort of house did *Jane* have."

"I love your mother. She understands how other women feel."

"Well, the next morning Dad put the suggestion to me. He said I should buy a house for you and the kids, and he would finance us. We pay him back over the next twenty years at no interest. His argument was that with me in the Air Force and Anne likely to marry someone who might not want to live on the Cape—evidently she doesn't want to live there herself—there would be no one to leave the business to. I mean to run it. He's already had a couple of offers for it, so it will be sold and Anne and I will split the money. He figured I might as well get some use from my share now as later. If we should get a posting somewhere else, we'll have no trouble renting it."

"What about furnishing it?"

"Mom saw that was taken care of. If we don't want to use all our capital, she said we can go back to them for what we need." He looked at her cautiously. "The main thing is, did I buy the right house for you? This is the first time I've ever done anything without consulting you. But I heard this was for sale and I had to make up my mind at once, there was another buyer breathing down my neck——"

The children came rushing back to the car. "Hey, Mommy! There's nothing in the house but some old camping beds! We looked in the windows."

Jane looked at Matt, and he nodded. "That's right. I thought you'd like to start furnishing the house from scratch. You know what my taste is like."

"Your taste in houses is wonderful." She looked at the children. "Righto, buzz off. There's going to be a little bit of love stuff. I'm going to kiss your father for being such a nice man."

219

"Ah gosh!" said John, and looked at Stevie, his younger brother. "Come on, it's worse than those old movies on TV."

"Go ahead and kiss him," said Bunty, nine years old now and interested in everything her parents did. "I'll stay and watch."

"You'll do what you're told and buzz off," Jane said, but she gave Matt a quick peck on the cheek and got out of the car. "Righto, let's all start getting some of this luggage into the house. I can see the neighbours straining their eyes behind their curtains to see what sort of a gang of delinquents we are."

So Jane at last had a house of her own. Over the next few months she began to furnish it, taking her time about what she bought. The house was an old one, but it had been modernized inside by the previous owner without destroying its character. It was well suited to the American period furniture Jane loved, and so she spent her time driving out to small antique stores in neighbouring towns, looking for chairs and tables and beds that weren't tagged with what looked like the National Debt. She bought four-poster beds, Windsor chairs, Sandwich glass, hooked rugs; while down at Langley, where he stayed from Monday through Friday, Matt assisted in development of furniture for the future. He came home weekends, sometimes so worn out that all he wanted was to sit around the house. Jane didn't query him too much, but she knew that he was spending most of his time on runs on the spaceflight simulators.

Then early in January he and Duke were assigned to desk work at the Pentagon. At the end of January the United States put its first satellite, Explorer, into orbit.

National pride ran high, especially with Bob Crispin, who arrived that weekend with Nell and Anne to spend a couple of days with Matt, Jane and the children.

"I knew we could do it," Bob said. He had put on a lot of weight in the past couple of years and his hair was very thin now; he stared out at the world through his glasses like a plump owl complacently satisfied with its small stock of wisdom. With a manager now running the supermarket and with more time on his hands, he had begun to sound like a political pundit, an elementary school competitor of Lippmann and Alsop. "We've always prided ourselves on our know-how and it was only a matter of time before we came good. Forgive me, Jane, if I sound like a swollen-headed Yank, but believe me, this is a great thing for us today. We needed this fillip, eh, Matt?"

"Don't get too excited," Matt said. "It's still only a pretty small gadget alongside the Sputniks. The Russians still seem to have us licked for power thrust. Until we can equal them in that, more than likely they'll beat us in putting a man into space."

"Our fellers will solve the problem," Bob said confidently. "We make the most powerful auto engines in the world, we'll lick this other thing."

"Are we going to put a man into space?" Anne Crispin was now seventeen but looked older. Her silver blonde hair was cut short in the fashion of that year with high school and college girls, but that was the only concession to the fashion for her age. She did not wear saddle shoes nor sloppy sweaters; today she wore a plain blue wool dress and high-heeled shoes. There was a poise to her that had nothing to do with years or experience; it was as if when still a child she had come to an acceptance of life and its terms. She was not a melancholy girl, but when she laughed one felt that for the moment she had broken through the shell that she wore against frivolity: it was a full rich laugh, more like that of a mature woman than a girl in her last year at high school. Her mother was sometimes worried that other girls of her own age, and boys too, thought her stand-offish, but she had never been able to find any actual incidence of such feeling. In any case Anne was the sort of girl who would not have been upset, nor even noticed, such a reaction. But self-contained as she was for a girl of her age, there was still a look of fragility about her, the look of a girl who might be accident prone.

"We'll eventually put a man up there." Duke had come out from Washington for the day. He had an apartment there, but since his new rapport with Jane he had come to look forward to his visits to the Crispin home. He had been up to New York twice to see Cleo and Caroline since he had come East, at Thanksgiving, when the three of them had gone on to Cape Cod to spend the holiday with Phil Dalmead, and at Christmas. But he had not gone up each weekend as Caroline had asked him to: that would have looked too much like a surrender to Cleo. Though their relationship now was moderately free and easy, he was still cautious about complete reunion.

"Would you volunteer, Duke?" Anne no longer called him Uncle. It had been his suggestion that she drop the title. The Crispin children still called him Uncle, but he had felt a certain awkwardness over the past year when Anne had addressed him that way, an uncertainty as to whether she was mocking him or not.

He hesitated, looking across at Matt; he realized his mistake

221

at once, when he saw Jane intercept the look. He said lamely, "I haven't given it much thought."

"Didn't they ask you down at Langley if you'd be interested?" Anne persisted.

Jane was watching both him and Matt, like a woman waiting for a gate to open on a sight she had dreaded. *Christ,* he thought, *hasn't Matt even hinted to her that they've talked to us?* Suddenly he was angry at Anne for her stupid blundering questions: couldn't she sense the atmosphere? He looked at her, intending to put her off with some light sarcastic remark, and was surprised at the sudden perception that showed in her smooth oval face: she *was* aware that something was wrong.

"Of course, why should they?" she said. "It's probably all still top secret."

"Of course it is," Bob Crispin chimed in. "And over at the Pentagon, I was reading it in the *Monitor* only the other day, they're still arguing about how many planes a bomber wing should have. I'll bet the generals there aren't interested in a man in space. Not unless there are thousands of them, all of them flying neatly in formation and all of them part of the U.S. Air Force, eh, Duke? Right now the generals aren't happy about money for bombers being taken for missile and space research. No general wants to wind up commanding a force of unmanned missiles. He'd have no one to give orders to, eh, Duke?"

Duke grinned, glad that Bob Crispin had got the subject away from the sparks that might have flown. "I don't know that I'd want to be that sort of general myself."

"Be a space general then, Uncle Duke," said John. "General Duke Dalmead, First U.S. Interplanetary Air Force. How does that sound?"

"Crazy," said Jane, and Duke noticed her voice was not as light as she tried to make out. "Like all science fiction. Eat your broccoli."

"I wonder if they have broccoli on Mars?" John pondered. "Imagine going all that way to eat *this*——"

After lunch Anne said she was going for a walk and asked Duke to go with her. He looked around at the Crispins, senior and junior, and decided he was an intruder here, even if a welcome one. Bob wanted to talk space with Matt, and Nell wanted to talk furnishings with Jane; and he wanted to talk on neither subject. The children had gone off somewhere, and he and Anne had been on the fringes of the conversation that was now going on.

He and Anne put on their topcoats, Anne borrowed some walking shoes from Jane, and they headed for the woods behind the Crispin house.

The day looked colder than it actually was. Trees were laid like iron sculpture against the steel sky; a robin squeezed itself like a drop of blood from the black sac of a bush. Yet a mild wind blew from the south, hinting of the discoveries of spring down around the Gulf. There was a polished look to the air that Duke knew when he was flying in the upper atmosphere.

"I put my foot in my mouth, didn't I, when I asked if you and Matt had been approached about space flying."

"You sure did. Jane would like nothing better than have Matt give up flying."

"But that's selfish!"

"I would have thought so several years ago. But not now. She can't help it if she worries when he's flying. And if he volunteered for space flying——!"

"I'd let my husband do it if that was what he really wanted."

"Wait till you have a husband, Anne."

"Duke, I wish you'd come back to the Cape more often. I *never* see you."

He looked at her as she strode along beside him, swift, sure and graceful, her hair shining like a silver cap against the dark collar of her coat. Her mother had tried to talk her into wearing a hat, but Anne had been insistent that she did not need one. There had been a certain stubbornness in her refusal to wear a hat that Duke had not seen before; but Nell Crispin must have been familiar with it, because she had turned away with a resignation that had had the look of habit. Matt could be stubborn, as Duke well knew, but Anne seemed a girl who might even resent advice.

"I feel I can talk to you," she said, her lips parting a little as they began to climb a slope. "I can't talk to Dad and Mom."

He grinned, not unkindly. "I had the same trouble at your age."

"Don't talk like that, Duke! You were never my age. What my birthdays say, the number I've had, don't matter at all."

"You're ageless? Well, that's a good way to be, especially for a woman——"

"Oh Duke!" She had dropped a little behind him as the slope had increased; she stumbled in the mud underfoot and he put out a hand to help her. They continued climbing hand in hand. "Don't be flippant. Or are you being patronizing, being patient with my teenage prattlings? Because I tell you—I'm not a teenager! I never have been!"

He squeezed her hand. "Okay, Anne. Don't get excited. I'm not being patronizing. But what are you trying to say?"

They had reached the top of the slope. The trees thinned out here, and they stood in the open and looked down towards the distant Potomac, a rough broad sword buried in the hip of a hill. The wind blew Anne's hair across her face, a silver veil, but she seemed unaware of it.

"Do you ever wonder why you were put here on earth, Duke?"

Spoken aloud it was an adolescent question, but he knew that, in the secret chambers of their mind, men occupied themselves with its answer till they reached the grave. He had asked himself the same question at her age and had answered himself with nihilism: he was here purely for his own ends, unresolved though they still were, though he was now almost thirty-five. But lately the question had begun to recur: the answer he had carried for so many years had begun to prove unsatisfactory.

"Is that question rhetorical or do you want an answer?"

She shook her head and smiled. "Not really. I think we should all have some secrets from each other, don't you?"

"What's your secret?"

She smiled again, secretively. "I have several."

"Are you in love with some boy, Anne?"

She shook her head again, the smile gone. "No. Why? Does a girl's secrets always have to do with some boy?"

"It was a natural question. You're a lovely girl, Anne. *Some* boy, I'd bet a dozen or more, must be interested in you."

"Oh, they try," she said without conceit. "But most of them are so dull and gauche. They all have their mind on the same thing."

"Boys aren't interested in intellectual companions, Anne. Not when they are nineteen or twenty. Or even when they're older," he said, grinning inwardly at himself and his own recent interests. "I know a little about men, Anne."

"You really don't know much about women, do you, Duke?"

He laughed aloud at that, not so much amused as relieved: it was a change to meet a woman, no matter how young she was, who saw some innocence in him. "That's probably the truth."

She began to walk along the brow of the hill into the wind. "I'm leaving the Cape, Duke. I want to get away from New England. It's too smug and provincial. It looks on itself as so damned superior to the rest of America. That's the trouble with this country. Each section of it thinks it is so much better than the rest."

"That happens with all countries. Even in a tiny country like England. Ask Cleo."

She looked at him through the veil of her hair. "Do you still see much of Cleo?"

"Of course. She's still my wife."

"In name only."

He laughed again. "Anne, you're too intelligent to read *True Confessions*. That's what you *sound* like when you make a remark like that." She looked hurt, and he reached for her hand. She stopped and he looked down at her as she stood slightly below him on the slope of the hill. "Anne, I don't mean to be unkind. But don't form too many opinions at your age——" He held up his hand as she went to say something. "I *know*. Your age doesn't matter. But experience does. Wait till you've had a little more experience before you start forming opinions——"

"Does that mean you think persons *my age*——" her voice was thick with sarcasm "——shouldn't have opinions?"

"Not at all. Have as many as you like. I'm twice your age, Anne, but I'm still finding many of my opinions are wrong. I'm getting more cautious about voicing them. That's what I'm warning you against. Have your opinions, but don't be too vocal with them. Not to the people they concern. You might find that your opinions hurt them, something you might regret later on."

"Did that hurt you? That I said Cleo was your wife in name only?"

"Not me so much," he said slowly. "But it would hurt Cleo if ever she heard you say it."

She brushed the hair from her face. She stared at him, examining him as if he were a stranger; he stirred under her scrutiny, as if the wind had turned rough. Then she said gently, "You *are* kind, aren't you, Duke? But why do you hurt people so?"

He stared at her in turn. "How do you know I hurt people?"

"I've seen it, Duke." She was not accusing him; it was almost as if she were looking for evidence with which to defend him. "Oh, I hardly see you at all, except maybe two or three times a year. But I see the people you've hurt. I remember your mother——"

"I admit to that." He was angry at being interrogated by a seventeen-year-old girl, but he kept rein on his temper. In the past few years he had learned patience, something he had never had when he was *her* age.

"And you've hurt Cleo. And Caroline, too, I guess."

He had made enough admissions for the day. "I think we had better go back, Anne."

She put a hand on his arm as he turned to retrace their path. "Duke, would you ever hurt me?"

He glanced sideways at her, suddenly wary. The wind blew up the hill, wrapping them together; dead leaves whirled about them like silent birds about to attack. "No, Anne. Not wittingly. But as you say, I do hurt people. It seems to me that I can't help it. The safe thing is never to become involved with me. And that isn't likely to happen with us."

She said nothing, continuing to stare at him for a long moment, as if forming an opinion that she would never voice, at least not to him. Then she turned and began to walk back along the hill in front of him. He hesitated, then slowly he began to follow her. He could feel the beginning of cancer in him, the cancer of self-discovery. It meant nothing to his ego to know that Anne imagined herself in love with him. It was surely only infatuation, she was still young enough for that; but that did not mean she could not be hurt. And he had done nothing, absolutely nothing to set her on the way to such an experience. Without knowing that Jane had made the discovery before him, out in California at the Hoban house, he now suddenly was aware of the seeds of disaster that he carried within him.

4

Matt turned off Route 29 and headed out along the side road towards Chipp Falls. It was mid-afternoon and there was very little traffic on the road. The countryside was beginning to burst with the pressure of spring, and the air had a mildness to it that had prompted him to put down the top of the MGA. He had bought the car only two days ago from a fellow officer who had been posted to Germany. He had paid for it himself, but it had been Jane's birthday gift to him. He was thirty-five today —"old enough," Jane had said, "to have a car of your own." They had talked of buying a new car to replace the five-year-old Oldsmobile, but Jane had insisted on keeping it. Instead they had sold the fourteen-year-old Plymouth in which she did the shopping; she had taken over the Olds; and he had got the MG. His pleasure was unbounded; he was like Stevie with a new toy

226

spacecraft. All that clouded his day was the thought of what he had to tell Jane when he reached home.

Last December he and Duke had decided to apply for the team of men to be trained for space flights by the National Aeronautics and Space Administration. By then they had been working at desks in the Pentagon for twelve months; and both the work and its restrictions had begun to irritate them. They had occasional days of escape back to Langley Air Force Base, and periodically they took up planes to give themselves the minimum number of hours required for flight pay, but to all intents and purposes their full-time flying days were over. Unless there was a war, and neither of them wanted *that* as an excuse to go back to flying.

Their decision to apply as members in Project Mercury had not been a hasty one. When Congress, in the summer of 1958, had passed the act creating NASA, both men had known that they would be at least on the fringes of the project because of their long experience in upper atmosphere flight. Each had experienced moments of weightlessness, each had been subjected to a high number of G forces, each had enough engineering knowledge to be able to understand and explain the stresses on a machine at supersonic speeds. They knew they would be consulted and in time they had been called in for consultation. Nothing official had been announced that volunteers were needed for the project, but both men knew that eventually a call would be made. They talked about it, but neither committed himself other than in general terms.

"The thought of exploring space intrigues me," Duke said. "You know what I was like as a kid, always talking about another land being around the corner of a cloud." He grinned at the childhood fantasy. "Even now, you know, when I run into a big cumulus, I wonder what's on the other side."

"They're aiming a damned sight farther than the clouds, chum. I get the creeps sometimes when I think of where a man *might* finish up. Infinity's a pretty long road. What we know about it really adds up to fifty per cent guesswork."

"What those early explorers knew about our world was about ninety per cent guesswork. With some of the very early ones, it was all guesswork. Some of those peoples down in the South Pacific, they knew nothing of what lay over the horizon."

Matt nodded slowly. "Yeah, I know. But sometimes I just wonder how far we're intended to go. I feel Man *needs* his mysteries."

"You're talking like everyone with a sense of religion. You're afraid of disillusionment, afraid that heaven may not be out there after all."

Matt grinned. "The day we discover heaven, chum, we won't be in any space craft."

Then they were called before a board of the NASA and told that their names were on a final list of 69 pilots being considered for Project Mercury. They knew the moment of decision had come.

When they met after their interviews Duke said, "Well, what about it?"

"What about you?"

"I think I'll chance it. It'll be an escape from that goddamned desk."

"You think we stand any chance?"

"As good as the sixty-seven other guys. Some of them might be better theoretical engineers than us, but we could stand up to them in practical stuff." One of the requirements had been that a candidate should have an engineering degree or its equivalent. Neither Duke nor Matt had a degree, but Service schools and additional college studies had been accepted as being the equivalent of a degree. "But not many of them would have had as much test flight experience as we've had."

"What do you figure the risks are? I'm not scared, but like I told you once before, I prefer calculated risks to uncalculated ones."

"I don't know." Duke had already begun to see himself as a member of the project team; life had become a perpetual escape route. "I'm not interested if all they're going to do is put us in a rocket or whatever, fire it and just hope we come back. That's for dogs and monkeys. But I don't think they'll put a guy up there till they're almost one hundred per cent certain they can get him back alive. At that, I don't reckon the risk will be any more than the ones we took in the old US-XP."

Matt considered for a moment, then he said, "I'm inclined to give it a go, as Jane would say. But I'll have to talk it over with her first."

"That won't be easy."

"Are you telling *me*?"

"Look. I won't put in my acceptance till you've had it out with her. At least that way she can't say I'm putting pressure on you."

"You are, you know. If you go in, how the hell can I stay out? You think I want you coming to my house telling me all about your flights to the moon, while I'm still chained to a desk?"

"Who's going to the moon?"

"A figure of speech, chum. Has no real meaning, just like those crappy maxims you used to spout."

"I'll spout you a maxim now. Never quote your friend to your wife."

"Meaning?"

"Don't even give her a hint that I'm putting pressure on you, directly or otherwise. If she asks am I going in, tell her you haven't discussed it with me."

"You think she'll believe *that*?"

She hadn't believed it, not for one moment. He had gone home, driving through a storm that had whipped up in the late afternoon like a portent of things to come. He had waited till after dinner, till the children had gone to bed and he and Jane were alone in the living-room.

"You want to look at Perry Mason?" she said.

"Let's skip TV tonight. Anyway, I think I just heard the antenna go." Even as he spoke there was a crash outside, as if a heavy limb had been torn from a tree. "I've got something I want to talk to you about."

She picked up her knitting and settled herself in her favourite chair, a deep arm-chair with figured slipcovers. She still admired and collected antique pieces, but she had come to realize that many antique chairs were not as comfortable as more modern and less expensive ones. Duncan Phyfe was still one of her idols, but she admired him from the comfort of a Grand Rapids product. Her knitting was an old Australian habit that she had taken up again in the past year. When he had been in Australia during the war, Matt, travelling on buses and street-cars, had been fascinated by the number of women who occupied themselves with knitting. They would sit in the buses, placid faraway expressions on their faces, while their needles flew like berserk pistons. He had only learned that Jane knitted when socks began to arrive in parcels for him after he had returned to New Guinea. She had knitted for a while after they had come to the States, mainly things for the babies, then the needles had been put away and he had thought she had forgotten them. Then over the past year they had been brought out again. Somehow they have her a middle-aged look and he had begun to resent them, especially when she put on her glasses to examine closely what she had knitted.

"Don't knit," he said. "I can't talk to you when those damned needles are going. You remind me of Madame Desfarges."

She put the knitting back on the table beside her. "Go ahead."

"Well, don't say it like that!" He was nervous all of a sudden; there was another crack outside as another tree was stripped. "I'm wrong, you don't look like Madame Desfarges. You look like Madame President of the Tribunal."

She smiled patiently, and now he felt like a schoolboy before his headmistress. Goddamn it, why did women have to be so aggravating! "Get it off your chest, darling. You've been offered an overseas posting and you want to know if I'd like to go." She looked around the room which had taken her so long to furnish as she had wanted it, but which was now complete. Australian though she still was in temperament and sentiment, she had sunk her roots here; she had surrounded herself with old Americana, and this was home. "I'll hate to rent this to some stranger."

He wished it was as easy as all that. He felt the same unease he always felt when he had to put a proposition to her that he knew she would oppose. He knew how intractable she could be, how illogical in argument. He was not made to feel any easier on this occasion because he knew that logic would be on her side, that he should not even be thinking about what he was going to propose.

He felt like a man closing his eyes and being shot off into space: "I was offered the chance of joining Project Mercury today."

She knew what Project Mercury was. "You knocked it back, of course." She reached across and picked up her knitting, an almost automatic movement. He had heard that knitting steadied the nerves, that it was often prescribed as therapy. Had Madame Desfarges been a nervous case, sitting there day after day watching the guillotine lop off the heads of the French aristocrats? He had the feeling that the guillotine was on its way down towards his own neck. "Of course you didn't! You wouldn't want to talk about it if you'd knocked it back. I suppose you want to give it a go?"

"It's worth thinking about."

"Don't be bloody stupid! Nothing like that is worth thinking about when you're your age, with a wife and three kids. Leave it to the young chaps. There'll be plenty of them cracking their necks to have a go at it."

"There's less than you think. They don't *want* young guys.

They want fellers with my experience—and you can't have had that if you're only twenty-three or four."

She stopped her knitting for a moment, put on her glasses as if she were going to examine him closely, then took them off again. She had begun to wear glasses only over the past couple of years, for reading and close work; he resented them because they seemed a reminder that her youth was behind her, but he never said anything about them. She was still beautiful and would be for some years to come, still passionate in her loving and still enjoying life. But he regretted, as much for her sake as for his own, that the years were passing for her.

"Matt, why do you feel *you* have to volunteer for this?"

He looked at her helplessly. After all their time together she still did not understand why he had to fly. This time, however, there was something else urging him on—but he knew she would not understand *that* if he tried to explain it to her. She was not an American, never would be no matter how much she loved him, an American, and she could not be expected to understand.

"Honey, I haven't volunteered. Not yet, anyway. I've been *asked*, and that's a different thing. They wouldn't have asked me if they hadn't thought I had something they wanted."

"How many others have they asked?"

"Sixty-nine of us altogether."

"Righto, that still leaves them sixty-eight men to choose from. You won't be letting them down." She went back to her knitting.

"For Christ's sake, will you put that knitting down!"

She put the knitting down in her lap. "There's no need to swear at me. I'm the one who should be swearing. You tell me not to turn on the TV because you want to have a nice cosy chat——"

"Now don't start putting words in my mouth. I didn't mention anything about a nice cosy chat. One thing I knew for sure, it wasn't going to be any nice cosy chat."

She went off at a tangent, another of her distracting ways of conducting an argument. "Is Duke among the other sixty-eight men?"

"Leave him out of this. He's among them, but it's his business and has got nothing to do with this."

"You mean you and he haven't discussed this? You don't expect me to believe that, do you?"

He shook his head resignedly. "That's exactly what I told him. But leave him out of it. He hasn't tried to influence me one way or the other. Believe that, honey."

"I do believe you. Two or three years ago, I mightn't have. But I'm beginning to think now that sometimes Duke has more sense of responsibility than you have. Or anyway conscience."

He seized on the word. "That's why I feel I've got to volunteer for this thing. Conscience. Remember you once said patriotism was another name for conscience? You were telling me about that conversation you had with that producer, what was his name, Hoban, out in Hollywood. Well, that's the burr under my saddle, if you like. Conscience, patriotism, call it what you like. But it's what makes me want to say yes to this invitation."

"Don't go patriotic on me. You're trying to make me sound un-American."

"Well, that's partly it. I don't mean un-American. You're *not* American, that's the trouble. If this were Australia planning this project, you might feel differently."

The storm outside seemed to have increased as they talked, but not to the extent of the storm inside herself. He had taken her completely by surprise and now suddenly she was faced with the prospect of losing him. Space was a frightening mystery to her, an abyss from which there was no return. "I shouldn't care if the Catholic Church were planning it and they were going to excommunicate me for being against it. I'd still be against it. When it comes to the possibility, no, the probability, of losing you, patriotism doesn't enter into it. I'll tell you another thing that Mr. Hoban told me. He said I married you, not a country."

This was getting worse than he had imagined. She not only had him on the defensive; he was in retreat. "Honey, when you talk like that, how can I argue with you?"

She pressed after him: "I'll use any argument I can think of if it means I can talk you out of this suicide thing. Darling, don't you understand? I love you. You're my whole life. You and the kids, but mostly you. Do you think I can just sit quietly at home here, knitting, while you volunteer for suicide?"

"I wish I could get it through your head that this isn't suicide!" He got up and began to pace about the room. The wind had risen still more, beating against the windows like a demon that was on Jane's side. He remembered how frightened she was of storms, how even now they still suggested the wrath of God to her. The storms in space might be even worse than any that had ever been experienced here on earth, but he hoped she would not think of *that* argument. "They aren't going to put a man up there till they are absolutely sure they can get him back alive. Or as sure as they can possibly be."

232

"That's not sure enough for me."

"I could be run over crossing the street tomorrow, be killed in a pile-up on the parkway——"

"Are you trying to hurt me?"

He stopped beside her chair, leant down and took her face in the cup of his hand. He looked at her with a painful sadness that was like a foretaste of grief: he would feel like this if *she* were to die. And he understood then the depth of her own fear of loss. "Honey, that's the last thing in the world I want to do. I wouldn't volunteer for this if I thought it amounted to suicide. It is because I'm sure it doesn't that I want to be in it. Feel I *must* be in it.

She looked up at him and he noticed the first dullness of resignation in her eyes. It gave him no elation: perversely he wished now that he was not a flying man, that he had nothing to contribute to the space project. "You'll keep at me, won't you?"

"No," he said truthfully. "You know I don't harp."

"You'll harp inside, to yourself. You'll never forgive me if they put a man up there, or two or three or a dozen, and they all come back alive. You'll spend the rest of your life accusing me of not giving you the chance to be one of them."

"No," he said, lying.

"What is it you want, darling? To be famous, to be a hero? If I could understand why you want to do it——"

He knelt beside her chair. There were so many reasons why he wanted to belong to the project, but they could not all be contained in one statement of intention; at least not to Jane, who had all she wanted from life in him and the children. Despite what he had said to Duke this afternoon, infinity had its attraction for him. He had the urge to *know* that was there in every man: Man might need his mysteries, but that wouldn't stop him from trying to solve them. He had become curious about himself, wondering what mysteries he contained; there was surely more to Matthew Crispin than he or the world had so far uncovered. And from his reading he knew that every voyage of discovery was an exploration of man himself. Columbus, da Gama, Magellan had discovered more than strange lands: they had opened up another part of the human soul, even if only their own. But how to explain these reasons to Jane?

"Honey, there's just one reason. It's because they've asked me, because I feel I can contribute something. It's nothing more than that, unless you'd also like to quote patriotism." *And other abstracts,* he thought but didn't say. "I'm not a flag-waver, you know that. I always suspect flag-wavers—so few of them are sincere. They're waving the flag for themselves as much as for their country. Some of our Congressmen are prime examples of that. But in a way, I suppose this is a bit of flag-waving for me. I hadn't thought of it that way——"

Her fingers began to explore his cheek: she was still discovering him. "I know that, darling. I shouldn't have asked that question. You've never been a glory-chaser, not like Duke. No, I'm not criticizing him. That's the way he's made. He'd do this to be a hero, to be famous or even——" she hesitated "—even because he's suicide inclined. Remember what you told me about that incident with the Russian planes?"

"You may be right. But I think he's grown out of that now. But he's still a glory-chaser, you're right there. But I don't hold that against him. The world can stand a few like him. Columbus didn't head out of Palos because he liked going for a sail." He stood up, began to walk around the room again. He wasn't sure, but the storm outside seemed to be abating. Or was it that there now seemed to be more understanding in the room here? "Honey, let's strike a bargain. From what they told us today, there'll be a lot of combing out before they get down to the final team. I may not even make the last dozen or whatever they want. But at least I'll feel I've made myself available, that I didn't say no when they asked me to help."

"What's the bargain for me if you do make the final team?"

He gestured helplessly. "Then I'll bow out."

"Will that be fair to them?"

"I don't know. I guess not. But I'll bet this argument is going on in dozens of living-rooms or bedrooms tonight. It's a big decision, even for the single guys. The board must expect us to make some compromises at this stage."

"Then you do feel there's some danger in it?" Why was it women hadn't made a greater mark in law than they had? No man could equal them in the tenacity of their cross-examination.

"Honey, there's danger in all flying. I told you that years ago. But you remember you and I once talked about destiny and God?" That had been just before the birth of young Stevie, when it had looked for a time that it was going to be a difficult birth and the doctor had warned them both to be prepared for disappointment or worse. In the event the birth had not been a difficult one, but for weeks before it had been on the minds of both of them. "I believe in both of them, just as you do. I don't

234

go to church, but maybe that's just as well—that way we've saved any arguments about what church the kids should go to." There had never been any argument about religion between them. Matt, careless about his own church, had been quite content to see the children brought up as Catholics. Sometimes he privately objected to what he thought was the autocratic and selfish attitude of the Catholic Church, but he never said anything to Jane. He admired her devotion to her religion and sometimes regretted his own apathy. He had not become an atheist, despite his exposure to science; he had not found that the latter contradicted the former; the more he read of science, the more he was convinced there was a Creator. He was something of an agnostic, but it was more a mood than a belief. He was anti-royalist, too, but he would never do anything to depose the kings and queens of the world. "But I believe it's already in the cards when I'm to go. The only thing we have any control over is *where* we go—I'm like you in that respect, I believe in The Other Side, as my mother likes to call it. I don't think the NASA is interested in heaven or hell—eternity is a part of space that's beyond them, even if Congress would give them the money to explore it, which I doubt in view of the fact that dead men can't vote and no Congressman is interested in a dead voter."

She smiled, a little wearily. "Don't confuse me with American politics. Stick to your point, if there is one."

He grinned, feeling a little more sure of her now. "Well, getting back to the NASA board. I don't even know if the members of it are interested in destiny. There's a lot of talk about America's destiny, but that's bull I never believe because no one knows what destiny is in store for him, his country or anything at all. If I knew that, I could damn soon talk you into my joining the project. Or talk myself out of it. Whichever way the cards lay. But I don't know how they lie, and that's my point. I'm destined to die at a certain hour on a certain day, and I don't think it matters whether I'm in a space rocket or our car or in our bed. Like the man says, when you gotta go, you gotta go."

"I wish you wouldn't talk like that."

"Occasionally you have to, honey. Death doesn't go the other way because you turn your back on it." He straightened up. "But you're right. Why are we talking about death now? That wasn't our argument. Will you let me go ahead, volunteer for the project and see how far I go?"

She persisted. "But if you're chosen in the final team?"

235

He said nothing for a moment, then he shrugged. "Okay, I'll drop out. I'll be honest with you now. I won't feel the best, but at least I'll have gone half-way to proving to myself I made myself available. Sometimes that's as far as conscience will let us go anyway."

And so now, four months later, he was on his way home to tell her that he was in the final team of twelve. Seven men had already been announced: Shepard, Grissom, Glenn, Carpenter, Schirra, Cooper and Slayton. Then today another five men had been named: Matt, Duke, two Navy flyers, Blair and Meredith, and another Air Force pilot, Raccoli. He drove the MG as if it were a hearse, holding it back so much that on the hills its engine pinked and he had to change down. He was going to have to honour his promise to her, yet now the moment had come he knew he would try every way he knew to get out of it. He despised himself for his treachery, yet he knew he could not deny it. He wanted, *had* to remain in the team.

He drove the car into the garage beside the house, switched off the engine and sat for a moment. Then slowly he got out of the bucket seat, turned round and Jane was standing in the doorway of the garage, silhouetted against the thin sunlight.

"You're home early." He nodded. "You got word today?" He nodded again. "Me, Duke, and three other guys."

"They want you for the team." It was not a question and needed no answer. She stared at him for a long moment, and in the silence he was aware of the engine of the car cooling off behind him. Then she said quietly and flatly, "Righto. You can join the team. Happy birthday."

Then she turned and ran quickly towards the house, one hand to her mouth, like a woman rushing somewhere private to be sick. He felt sick himself, but he knew he was going to accept her release from his promise. It was her real birthday gift to him, one that might cost her her own happiness.

CHAPTER SEVEN

DUKE stood in the airport lounge gazing out at the glare of the Florida sun. August was not the best month for visiting Florida, but Cleo and Caroline were not just vacationers: Cleo had another reason for coming, one she had not stated in her letter. He had been in Florida, off and on, almost three years now and he had never invited Cleo and Caroline to visit him down here; Cape Canaveral did not offer much to visitors unless they were space flight buffs, and neither Cleo nor Caroline was one of those. Then a week ago Cleo had written asking if they could come visit him, saying she had something she wanted to discuss with him; it was the first time she had ever hinted that she should visit him, and he knew it must have been an important reason that had forced her to invite herself. Cleo's sense of independence worked in ways that he found hard to understand. They still slept together when he was in New York and she showed no independence there; but till this letter of last week she had never once made any demands nor asked any favours of him. He could guess at the torture she had gone through before she had sat down to write him.

He had phoned her at once, and after he had spoken to her, then Caroline had come on the line. "Daddy, I've been waiting years for you to ask us down to Florida." He had grunted something non-committal at that. A moment of telepathic perception told him that, for reasons of her own, Cleo must have told Caroline that the suggestion to visit Florida had come from him. "Can we go down to Miami for a day? I mean, it's so close———"

"It's nearly two hundred and fifty miles."

"What's that to an astronaut?"

"My personal transport still happens to be a car, not a space capsule. But look—tell your mother to book you through to Miami on the plane. I'll come down there and meet you, we can stay a day or two. Okay?"

So now he was waiting for the New York plane to come in. People sat listlessly about on chairs and benches, faces closed tight against the other faces that floated past them. Duke's own face was closed against the crowd; he was afraid of being recognized today. The Russian cosmonauts, Nikolayev and Popovich, had just completed their orbiting of the earth as a team; Nikolayev had been up there for an almost unbelievable 94 hours and Popovich for 71 hours. Every time the Russians outdid the Americans, there was always some crank who wanted to abuse the Project Mercury team for not being on the ball. It had happened to Matt after Titov's flight, and to Bruce Blair after Gagarin had been the first man into orbit. And Florida was full of cranks, although not so full as California. The sun seemed to attract them.

A mother and daughter, one fat, the other thin, ballooned by in mu-muus, looking like a couple of refugees from Hawaii, and he looked at them with distaste. Coming back from Australia in March, after he had been out there to Muchea to help track Rupe

237

Meredith on the latter's orbital flight, he had stopped in Honolulu for twenty-four hours. He had heard a lot about the beauty of Hawaiian women, but he had been turned off them by the baggy unflattering mu-muus they wore. Honolulu had looked like a huge maternity ward—— "even the virgins looked pregnant in those goddamned things," he had said to Matt, and had complimented Jane because she was sensible enough to wear dresses or slacks that showed off her figure.

The mother and daughter in their mu-muus, unaware of the sour reception they were receiving from the dark-haired handsome man who looked so vaguely familiar, wafted heavily away. A Cuban boy went past pushing a broom, his dark thin face dull with hopelessness: America was not the Promised Land to him. In the 1920's and 30's, Duke, mused, New York, Boston and Chicago had been the haven for refugees; but now Florida was the melting pot. Cubans fleeing Castro, elderly people fleeing the northern winters, gamblers and the jet set exchanging the sun for sun lamps. They were like locusts, a shifting crust on the state, and he wondered what the native Floridians thought of them. Did they resent them, as the Cape Codders resented the summer visitors there, or did they accept them as a necessary part of the economy of the state? Some time he would ask a native Floridian, if he could find one. On his four visits to Miami so far he had not met a man born south of the Mason and Dixon line. If the War between the States ever broke out again, the North would have its fifth column buried deep in the heart of the South.

Then the announcer, an invisible Floridian judging by her accent, broadcast that the New York plane was about to land. Ten minutes later he was escorting Cleo and Caroline across to his Corvette parked in the car park. He was pleased to see how smartly Cleo was dressed, in a dark blue silk suit that was perhaps a little tight for her but which she wore with style. But he was shocked at the slovenly casualness of Caroline: beside her mother she looked like another just-arrived refugee.

"I should have told you to go light on the luggage," he said as he struggled to find a place for their four suitcases on the car. "This isn't a family car."

"Well, you're not a family man, are you?" Caroline said.

Cleo spoke quickly, too quickly. "I'm getting no narrower in the beam, either. I'm sorry, Duke. Perhaps we should have driven my car down, instead of flying. Except that Caroline doesn't trust me driving and I don't trust her."

He saw the look that Caroline gave her mother, but he said nothing. He strapped the last suitcase on the rack, then got into the car and headed for the motel where he had booked them in. Caroline rode between Duke and Cleo, her head above the protection of the windscreen, her long untidy hair blowing in the wind.

"Are we going to a hotel, Daddy?"

"I didn't know you'd want to. This motel is just as luxurious, if that's what you're looking for, as any hotel. Excepting the hotels with hundred dollar a day suites, and we don't run to that."

"I just wanted to see how the other half lives."

"The parasites, she means," said Cleo, smiling at her daughter; smiling tentatively, Duke thought, as if she were afraid that whatever she said would bring some retort from Caroline.

Caroline did not smile back. There was a sullenness to her face that Duke could not remember having seen before. He had not seen her and Cleo since March, just before he had gone to Australia, and he was surprised at the change that seemed to have taken place in the girl since then. She was now sixteen (seventeen? He always had difficulty in remembering. It was a poor father who couldn't remember how old his daughter was. But then he was a poor father for lots of other reasons); and very soon she was going to be a beautiful woman. She had inherited the best of both her parents' features: Cleo's eyes and bone structure, Duke's teeth and skin; dark like her father, she had her mother's vitality and zest for living. Or had had. Something had happened to her in the past few months, and he knew now that this was why Cleo had invited herself and Caroline to Florida.

They drove through the sun-baked streets, past the houses that looked as if they were made of bleached bone, then on to the highway that led past the beaches. The motels beckoned them with garish invitations; neon palm trees were greener than the real thing; a giant painted girl raised a mountainous thigh into the sky. The heat pressed the landscape flat; the horizon was a watercolour in which sea and sky had run into each other. Then they had come to their motel.

"You go for a swim, darling," Cleo said to Caroline. "I'll unpack our things."

"Come in with me, Daddy?"

"I'll be down later. I haven't said hello to your mother yet."

"Oh, be sure to do that," Caroline said, and went out of their room and along to her own room.

239

Duke adjusted the venetian blinds against the glare outside, closed the door and turned to Cleo. "What's the matter with her?"

"Are you going to say hello to me?"

He crossed the room, put his hands on her shoulders and kissed her on the mouth. When they got to bed they were passionate lovers, but their first greetings were always as stiff, almost circumspect, as this, as if each were afraid that something might have happened to destroy the delicate fabric of their relationship while they had been parted. Cleo returned his kiss, then sat down on the bed and began to cry.

He was shocked: it was years since he had seen her weep. He sat down on the bed beside her. "What's the matter, honey?"

"I don't know whose fault it is, Duke, but we've let her down. I mean as parents." She dried her eyes and blew her nose into the handkerchief he handed her. "She resents us both. These past few months she's been going around with a lot of beatniks——"

"I thought she looked a bit careless of her appearance. She used to be so neat and clean. Like you."

"I was never neat, darling. Clean, yes, but never neat."

"Well, anyway, she looks neither. Where did she meet this crowd?"

"Down in the Village. She's never home, always down there."

After the Crispins had moved to California Cleo had remained on Long Island for a while. Then she had moved out of the apartment and taken herself and Caroline back to England for a summer. She had tried to persuade her mother to come back to the United States with them, but Mrs. Mulligan was now too tied to England. She had spent most of her early married life in far corners of the globe, always promising herself that she would spend her old age in the country where she had been born. She had been tempted to go to America with Cleo, but had finally decided against it when she learned she would have to live in an apartment; the old Quaker house was much too big for her but she loved its spaciousness and its garden. Cleo herself had been torn between love for her mother and love for Duke; if she stayed in England she knew she would have lost Duke forever. So she and Caroline had returned to the States and taken an apartment in one of the new blocks going up in lower Manhattan.

When Caroline had started high school, Cleo, bored with herself and the little she had to do, had got a job as a secretary at the United Nations. To her own and Duke's surprise she had made

240

a success of it; and it had contributed a good deal towards the philosophical acceptance of her relationship with Duke. She had never confessed it to him, but she knew that if she had continued to spend the long lonely days alone in the apartment she would have begun to crumble with frustration and self-pity. She was thirty-eight now, still a good-looking woman; but her looks had begun to fade around the edges and she had to watch her weight carefully. She did perfunctory exercises to keep her bosom from falling and to keep her legs firm—"I hate duchess thighs," she had once said to Jane. "You know, darling, thighs with lots of blue dimples in them"—but she was well aware of the horrible fact that her best days were behind her, that American men, unlike European men, worshipped only the young and firm. She knew that she could still interest some men in her, the United Nations was full of volunteers for love as well as peace, but she did not want them nor need them. So long as Duke continued to visit her four or five times a year, sleep with her and make a pretence of loving her, she was content. But lately, standing before her mirror after her bath, noticing the small rolls of fat thickening her waist and hips, regretting the breasts that were getting heavier and lower, examining the backs and insides of her thighs for the blue dimples, almost like a woman searching for lice, she had begun to worry that Duke would soon tire of her, would begin to look for someone younger. Although he was now thirty-nine he was in much better physical shape that many men in their early twenties: his job demanded that his condition should be as perfect as possible. She sat now with her hand on his arm, feeling the firm strength of it, glad of the comfort of him.

"Some of the types she goes around with—men with wispy little beards like pubic hair, girls who look like the women in those *New Yorker* cartoons—Did we carry on like that when we were young?"

"Well, you had a habit of taking your clothes off——"

"But that was healthy——"

He grinned, and pressed her hand. "Okay. But what's her trouble exactly? This beatnik business often isn't serious. It's a phase some of them pass through and grow out of in six months or so. You never see a beatnik in his thirties, except the failures."

"Then she must be going around with some of the failures. These aren't teenage kids, Duke. They're all older than her, in their twenties, some of them older than that. She brought one of them home with her one night, a boy about twenty-seven or -eight. He sat there and sneered at me all night through his beard, and she thought it was funny. I could have killed her and him! They believe in none of the things you and I believe in, darling."

He asked the question in all honesty, not meaning to be unkind to her: "What do you think I believe in, Cleo?"

She floundered. "Well, you must believe in *something*, darling, or you wouldn't be doing the job you're doing."

He didn't reply to that. He and the other members of the team had often discussed why they had volunteered. There were a few idealists, but he was not one of them. Raccoli was in it for the glory; Meredith was in it for the money; he was in it for both glory *and* money. So far he had made fifty thousand dollars above his service pay and there would be more to come. The glory as yet was only small, shared with the other pilots who had not yet made a flight; but the real glory was still to come, when he was chosen for the big flight that was rumoured for next year. He was confident he would be the pilot chosen, and sometimes he got heady with dreams of the reception he would get on his successful completion of the flight. But a striving for fame and fortune while working for a national project was not something you offered as an example to an erring daughter.

"I know you don't believe in God or anything like that," Cleo went on, not noticing his silence, "but you believe in certain conventions. In decency, for example. Respect for other people."

"I haven't been very decent towards you, have I?"

"Oh darling!" The tears welled in her eyes again. "Don't make it difficult for me, at least no more difficult than it is. I've come to you for help because there's no one else I can ask."

"I'm not meaning to make it difficult. And you should have come to me—after all, I'm her father and I should have been helping you with her long ago. But it is the truth—I haven't been very decent towards you. And that's going to make it hard for me to convince her. What do you want me to do?"

"Just have a talk with her. Find out why she is so rebellious. I think we're the reason, but I'd like to be sure. If we are, perhaps we can do something about it. If we're not, if there is some other reason——" She began to weep again, rocking gently back and forth on the edge of the bed. "I don't want to lose both of you!"

He kissed her softly on the hair and stood up. He walked to the window and looked out through the slats of the blind. "There she is now, going down on to the beach. I'll go down and talk to her now."

He changed into swimming trunks in the bathroom, then came out again into the bedroom. Cleo was standing by the window now, her eyes dry but still swollen, her hair disarranged by the nervous hand that had been running through it. He looked at her, saw her fully exposed to the erosion of age and worry, and felt an echo of the pity he had felt for her almost eighteen years ago. He determined he would do everything he could to save her further pain.

"Have a rest," he suggested. "I'll take you both out to dinner tonight, to one of those luxury hotels she wanted to stay at. Look your best, so we can put on a show for her."

"Do you think she'll be impressed?"

"I don't know. Kids of today are more sophisticated at least on the surface. But when I was sixteen, it was a very impressionable age. Has she got anything decent to wear?"

"I made her bring one good dress. I told her black sweaters weren't fashionable down here. That was the wrong thing to say, but when I also said they would be too hot in this climate, she gave in. I'll see she doesn't disgrace you, darling."

"I wasn't thinking of myself," he said truthfully.

He went out of the room, skirted the pool and walked down across the hot sands towards the daughter who was a stranger to him. The beach was deserted, only a few pompous gulls promenading along the long stretch of sand. Caroline looked up at him out of dark glasses as he approached. She had already been in the water and her black hair hung down like small snakes about her face.

He took his comb from the pocket of his trunks and offered it to her. "Do your hair. You look like Medusa, and she was never one of my favourite girls."

She hesitated, then took the comb and ran it carelessly through her hair. "Do you have many favourite girls?"

He sat down beside her, arranging himself on his towel against the burn of the sand. "Is that a question to ask your father?"

"Maybe not. But I have to keep reminding myself that you *are* my father." He remarked the only slightly veiled insolence in her voice, but he kept his temper under control. He had to keep reminding himself that she was at least half-right: he wondered if she thought of him as her father in name only. Anne came back into his mind for a moment, but he quickly dismissed her. *That* complication had to be forgotten right now.

"Touché," he said lightly, and was glad to note the slight doubt that crossed her face. He sensed now that she had expected him to play the heavy father, and he determined to play it the other way. "Your mother tells me you've met quite an interesting crowd in New York."

"*She* doesn't think they're interesting. I bet that wasn't the word she used."

"Well, no. She said they were beatniks. But *I* find them interesting. Not always convincing, but at least they're not dull."

She looked at him blank-eyed, but behind the dark glasses he could feel the suspicion. "Are you trying to be nice to me?"

"Naturally. But if you mean am I trying to flatter you, no. When I said I find beatniks interesting, I didn't mean I thought them admirable."

"I didn't expect you would. You're just like Mummy, really."

"Old and out-of-date, you mean? Square? Maybe, Caroline. I wouldn't deny that. But we're usually consistent. You wanted to stay at a fancy hotel to gaze on the parasites, I gather. Isn't there some inconsistency in a beatnik calling café society parasitical?"

"Beats are different. At least they don't worship money, status symbols, all that crap."

"Don't use that word when you're around me, honey," he said, still keeping his temper under control. "I have tender ears. I'm a square in that way—I respect women who are ladies."

"That's a laugh."

"I don't think I've ever once given you a hiding——" His voice rose a little.

"You were never around home long enough."

He put on his dark glasses: he needed some sort of protection against both the sun and her. "It's not too late to start now, Caroline."

"You wouldn't dare! This isn't the nineteenth century." But he noticed there was a slight edge of fear to her voice.

"No, you're right. If anyone should know that, I guess I should." He stared out to sea. Far out the white shark-fin of a sail was fixed in the haze; nothing was moving out there, not even the sea, it seemed. He could feel the sun biting into him even through the deep tan he had. He looked at her and her Greenwich Village paleness. "You got any sun-tan oil? You better put it on."

She took a bottle from the terry-cloth bag beside her and began to rub oil on her arms and legs. "I know why Mummy brought us down here. Because she wanted you to have a talk with me.

But frankly, Daddy, I don't think you have any right to interfere in my life. You've stayed out of it too long for that."

"Give me that oil. I'll rub some on your back." She turned her back towards him and he began to smother her in oil. The pale skin glistened, and he felt the ripple of the young backbone beneath his fingers; he felt a sudden deep sadness at the fragility of her, at her youth that could so easily be destroyed. He was glad she was turned away from him; even the dark glasses would not have hidden the crack in his defences. He loved her, but something told him she would only look on it as a weakness if he confessed it. Unlike her mother she was not looking for surrender. But what was she looking for? Security? Example? He could offer her neither. "Slim as it may be, Caroline, I still have some right. At least the law would hold me responsible if I didn't contribute towards your keep, didn't try to control you in some way. Legally, if no other way, I'm still your father."

The slim back tensed beneath his hand. "You mean you intend trying to play the heavy father?"

"I hope I shan't have to. Beats claim a certain intelligence, or so I gather. Intelligent people should be able to sit down and talk things out."

"What is there to talk about?" She turned to face him, taking the bottle from him as he handed it to her. "You and I belong to different worlds. Your generation has fouled up everything——"

"How did you come by all these opinions?"

"I had plenty of time, believe me. There was no home to come home to each afternoon after school. Mummy was at the office— Oh, I don't blame her for that. She needed something to take her mind off her own fouled-up world——"

"So it boils down to the fact that you think I'm to blame for everything?"

She hesitated, then she took off her glasses. She squinted her eyes, Cleo's eyes, against the glare from the sand. "Yes, Daddy. That's what I mean."

"Have you ever discussed this with your mother?"

"No."

"Why not?"

"Because she would only defend you. After all these years, all you've done to her, she's still stupidly in love with you. You come home half a dozen times a year, get into bed with her like some stud bull that's making the rounds——"

His hand struck at her mouth almost of its own volition. He was sick a split second after he felt it hit her; he dropped the hand, grabbing her wrist as she struggled to get to her feet. "Sit down! For Christ's sake, sit down, Caroline! I didn't mean to do that, can't you see?"

"I hate you!" She struggled to free herself, now on her knees and pulling away from him. He was glad now of the fierce heat that had kept other bathers from the beach. They were alone on the hot bare sands, from a distance they could have been playing a game. He wondered if Cleo was watching them, wondering what they were doing.

"Sit down!" There was command, not pleading, in his voice now; he couldn't remember ever having spoken to her like this before. She stared at him, her mouth open, the marks of his fingers still showing where he had struck her; then slowly she sank down, folding her legs under her, drawing her wrist out of the grasp of his hand. She began to massage the wrist, and he was surprised at how red it was.

He took a deep breath, tried to relax. "I'm sorry I hit you. I didn't mean to——"

"You don't like the truth, do you?" Her voice was flat, a little girl's voice but with a woman's perception.

"I've grown accustomed to it over the past few years. I didn't hit you because of what you said about me. It was what you said about your mother—it implied that she cheapened herself——"

"I think she does. She shows no pride at all where you're concerned." She had put on her dark glasses again, now sat calm and composed. One part of his mind had to admire her: he could not imagine himself showing this poise at sixteen when arguing with his mother.

"Caroline, I'm making no excuses for myself. I admit all you want to think about me. I'm not afraid of the truth, not so much as you seem to think. In fact I wish I knew more of the truth of myself. But I am not going to have you hurt your mother, not if I can prevent it."

"*You've* hurt her." She had her poise, but her youth showed in her arguments.

"I know. But do we have to make a family habit of it?"

Suddenly the poise cracked. "Oh Daddy, I don't want to hurt her!"

"Neither do I. Not any more."

"Are you going to come back to live with us?"

He stood up, taking off his glasses. "I can't give you an answer on that right now. I've been apart from your mother a long time——"

"She'd take you back like a shot." He remarked the English phrase: Cleo still had some influence on her.

"It's not as easy as all that. No, don't ask me for the reasons. But trust me."

She stood up beside him in her skimpy one-piece bathing suit. Her figure was that of a young woman, a younger Cleo, and he marvelled that he could be her father; he suddenly felt older, as if he had just crossed a threshold into another generation. He had to remind himself that she was only four years younger than Anne, and the thought hurt him. "I will trust you, Daddy. But don't let me down. Not the way you did Mummy."

He shook his head, making a promise he hoped he could keep. "I won't. Now how about a swim?"

They ran towards the water, plunged in. But it cooled only his body: his mind still ran hot with the trouble that lay ahead.

2

The three of them went to dinner that night at one of the big hotels. Despite the time of the year, the hotel restaurant was crowded. "There are no society columnists down here now," Duke said, "but these people here would never get in the society columns anyway. If they get their names in the Paddle Creek *Gazette* back home in Indiana, saying they spent their vacation in Miami, that's all they want."

"The whole country is taken up with status symbols," said Caroline.

"Don't some of your beat friends have status symbols?" Cleo asked good-humouredly. Duke had not told her all of what he and Caroline had said to each other, but he had told her he had made some progress with their daughter, and, optimistic as ever, she had begun to hope that her worries were over. "I mean, what's the beat uniform but a status symbol?"

"I'd have to let Jerry debate that with you." Caroline wore a bright pink silk sheath that Duke privately thought was too old for her, but which he had to admit did make her look more than ordinarily attractive.

"Jerry was her boy friend," Cleo explained. "The one who thought I was a middle-aged suburban square."

"Square was the last word I'd have used to describe you," Duke said.

Cleo blinked at him in puzzlement, then smiled. "Oh, you mean my curves?" She was dressed in what Duke had heard

247

described as a small black; it was small all right, and he grinned to himself at the memory of her trying to struggle into it as they had dressed. "I really shouldn't be eating this dessert. I'm getting much too copulent."

"Corpulent or opulent, Mummy, take your pick," said Caroline smiling at her father, reviving a mutual joke they had had for years at Cleo's expense. "Copulent sounds indecent."

"The interpreters at UN must have some trouble translating your letters," Duke said.

It was a gay, light-hearted evening. Duke danced with both Cleo and Caroline, and each time the other diners turned to look at the good-looking couple on the floor, the handsome Air Force colonel with his beautiful wife and equally beautiful daughter. When someone recognized Duke as one of the astronauts, a buzz went round the room. By now he had become accustomed to recognition and the stir it caused; he was glad that there were no cranks among the diners to ask him why he wasn't on the job tonight. He noticed that Caroline was pleased by the recognition of him, and the fact reassured him. She was not so far along the beat track that she could not feel pride in a father who was a public figure. He was her status symbol.

Later, lying in bed beside Cleo, he said, "She asked me today would I come back with you."

She did not actually stiffen in his arms, but it was as if everything in her body had stopped. "I didn't put her up to that, Duke."

"I know."

There was silence for a moment. Above the gentle hum of the air-conditioner he could hear the sea hitting the sand with the flat sound of lethargic gunfire. A car drew into the front of the motel bringing home some later revellers: a nasal Mid-West voice called to Susie to put on her shoes, and there was a burst of laughter from three or four other voices. In a room close by a child began to cry, lost in the quicksand of a strange bed.

"Would you come back, Duke?"

"Would you have me? I mean, if I still wasn't sure it would work out?"

"It would work out as far as I'm concerned." Optimism was part of her blood: a taste of love promised her a feast.

"I meant as far as myself. It's not all that simple."

"You mean about Anne?"

It was his turn to lie still; his arm stiffened round the soft plumpness of her body. "Who told you about her? Jane?"

248

"She wasn't gossiping, darling. I had to put the question to her last time I saw her, when she came through New York on her way to the Cape last month."

"How did you know I'd been seeing Anne?" For twelve months now Anne had been coming South every time she could get away from the college she was attending in Maryland. He had wondered at first why she had chosen such a college, not one of the better known ones; then he had thought it was because she wanted to be near Matt and Jane. It had been a shock to him to learn it was because she had wanted to be near him at Langley Air Force Base. Even when he had to come South to Cape Canaveral, she had tried to come down every weekend, arriving without warning and calling him from the motel in Cocoa Beach where she had booked in. At first he had welcomed her, but then he had begun to worry as the depth of her feeling became apparent. He had begun trying to dissuade her from coming to see him, but that had only resulted in scenes that reduced her to an emotional wreck and himself to a resigned acceptance of her that did not help the situation at all.

"Your sister told me when I went up to visit them."

"Christ, the world is full of chattering women!" He drew his arm out from beneath her and sat up straighter in the bed, propping the pillow behind him. He ran his hand over his stiff bristle of hair. He did not like it cut as short as this nor did Cleo, but the close-fitting helmet that was part of his space uniform necessitated it. There was glamour in being an astronaut, but no room for vanity.

"They weren't trying to start trouble, darling. I'm sure of that. Not your sister. Maria is a very innocent girl, despite the fact that she's married and has two children."

"Did you see Mr. and Mrs. Crispin while you were there? Did they say anything about Anne coming down here or to Langley?"

"They never mentioned her at all. That was what made me suspicious, as if they were afraid I'd find out something I shouldn't know. Duke, are you in love with her?"

He switched on the bedside lamp. "I did that so you won't think I'm using the darkness to hide any lies. I'm telling the truth, Cleo. I'm not in love with her, never have been. And we've never been to bed."

"Is she in love with you?" Her hand was clamped tight on his thigh. There was no pleading in her voice now, as there had been so often in the past: it was as if she had gained some strength, was going to fight for him now that he had assured her he did not love Anne.

"How can I answer that?" He remembered Jane's angry accusation of conceit when he had admitted what he had thought was the truth about Debbie Fairfax. He had learned now that women did not always want the truth; they had found the comfort in a lie or at least an equivocation.

"She's always idolized you. Even as a little girl I can remember how she thought the sun shone out of you. You shouldn't have encouraged her."

"You mean when she was a kid? How was I to know this crush would last all this time? She's almost twenty-one, old enough to be disillusioned about me. Christ, anyone who can't see my feet of clay after twenty-one years, she must have balls of clay for eyes. Like those ancient statues."

"Are you blaming her for the way she feels?" said Cleo, not mentioning her own eyes of clay. There was no longer any resentment in her voice towards Anne. She understood how the younger woman could feel.

"I'm not blaming anyone for the way they feel. Feelings are not something people should be blamed for—you can't blame someone for having a fever or a cold. Feelings are irrational things——"

She smiled, unable to control her mind that always went off on irrelevant paths. "I never expected to hear you defending something irrational."

He brushed the hair from her brow, ran his hand round the back of her neck and held her head. "I'm changing, Cleo. I'm going through the menopause of the mind. Christ knows what I'll be like when I come out on the other side. But it might even be an improvement."

"Have you told Anne you don't love her?"

"Not in so many words." He told the truth reluctantly. "I've given her enough hints, though. But I can't be brutal about it."

"You *have* changed." She pushed her head back against his hand, looked up at him. "No, I'm sorry, darling. You weren't always brutal. You could be kind, too. Too kind. If you hadn't been, you wouldn't have married me in the first place."

He knew that she had known for a long time that their marriage had not been started on love. Suddenly he wanted to tell her now that he loved her, but the old doubt was there again: would it be kindness or would it be true love? His emotions had the distortion of a cracked mirror: he could not believe even what

250

he felt. His defence of the irrationality of feeling had not been entirely for Anne's sake.

"If you came back to me," Cleo said with cold logic that seemed out of place in her, almost cruel, "you wouldn't have to tell Anne you don't love her. No matter how blind she is, she would get the message."

"You don't hate her because she is trying to come between us?"

"How can I? If we had been living together all these years, yes, I think I'd hate her. But not the way it's been between us———"

He switched off the lamp, slid down beside her. He put his arm under her and she opened herself to him like a giant fleshy flower. Her mouth found his: he tasted her hunger. It was his turn to surrender, defeated by a depth of love he could never hope to achieve. Caroline had been wrong: he was not the stud bull making the rounds. He finally admitted to himself that in no bed had he found the comfort, yes even the safety that Cleo offered him. Only here, wrapped by the soft warm flesh of her, could he forget himself, the self that at all other times was the burden on his back.

3

"You ready, Matt?" Oliver Shor asked.

Matt nodded, wishing the ride was over. Every three months the pilots of the team came here to Cleveland for their training rides on the Multiple Axis Space Test Inertia Facility—or MASTIF, as it was called with lack of respect and some relief. It was an essential part of their training and one that Matt liked least. MASTIF was a giant contraption mounted in an old wind tunnel, another of the weird devices designed to simulate any experience that the astronauts might encounter while in orbital flight. It consisted of three cages, each mounted on swivels, one set progressively within another, the smallest having a couch into which the pilot was strapped as he would be in a space capsule. The outer cage could tumble end over end; the middle cage spun round and round; the inside cage whirled round its own axis. Whirling, tumbling and spinning in all three directions at once, the pilot was expected to correct the countless variations of yaw, pitch and roll that MASTIF could produce.

Matt had already done the preliminary rides. He had been spun in the small cage at fifty revolutions per minute. Then he had been tumbled head over heels within the outside cage at thirty revolutions a minute. Finally he had spun like a human pinwheel at thirty r.p.m. in the middle cage. Now it was time to ride the MASTIF in all three directions at once.

Matt swallowed, trying to take the sick taste from his mouth. Only one thing allowed him to suffer this training: the assurance by the scientists that, once in space and if anything ever did go wrong, the gyrations of the Mercury capsule would be only one-tenth as bad as what he was about to go through now. Like King Mithridates, he was accustoming himself to the poison that for any normal man would be fatal. But he knew that if the strain were ever likely to be as bad as this in actual flight, and Glenn, Carpenter and the others had assured him it wasn't, he would have retired from the programme. He would not have trusted himself to be able to control the capsule. At least here he could always yell for help.

He focused his eyes on the dial on the panel two feet in front of him. There were three needles on the dial showing the degrees of yaw, roll and pitch. He grasped the control stick in his right hand, ready to move it in the right direction to correct whatever MASTIF did to him. He steadied himself as he began to feel the velocity building up.

The dial began to blur, then it was just a swirling catherine wheel before his eyes, and he knew that he must be whirling around at twenty r.p.m. He had slipped over the edge into what the doctors called "vestibular nystagmus", when his eyeballs, let loose by the disturbed mechanism of his body, became uncontrollable. It was as if he were about to faint, but the moment before unconsciousness was painfully prolonged.

The revolutions continued to build. His body was now a vessel in which his organs were a stew being slopped vigorously in all directions. His head and feet alternately boiled with an excess of blood; sweat broke on his face as if the blood were trying to force its way through his skin. His teeth ached, wanting to tear themselves from his gums. His ears roared with the surf of his blood and his tongue was trying to roll back down his throat. In a moment he would be ill, spewing his guts out in a wild explosion.

Then suddenly, as it always did, his balance mechanism adapted itself to the crazy motions of MASTIF. The nystagmus cleared from his eyes, the catherine wheel stopped spinning, became a dial again, and the needles were clear enough to be read. His hand began to work the control stick.

Then MASTIF began to decelerate. Once again the nystagmus affected him and his eyeballs began to roll. Slowly, still manipulating the stick to keep the needles at zero, he brought the machine to a halt. The test was over, the last he might have to make before an actual flight. He and Duke had been told that the choice lay between them to be the pilot on the next orbital flight.

Shor, as crumpled-looking as if he himself had just made the run, came into the tunnel as Matt eased himself out of the cages. "We'll take some blood and urine tests, Matt. Just routine."

"You'll have to wait a while," said Matt, grinning weakly. "Right now I think I'm full of a mixture of both."

His balance mechanism was already adjusting itself, but there was still a shakiness in his legs. He took off his helmet, wiped his face and slowly followed Shor out of the tunnel and across to the small office that served as the aeromedical adviser's consulting room. He stripped off his suit, Shor's assistant took a blood sample, gave him a bottle for a urine specimen; then Matt went into the nearby shower stall, showered and five minutes later was dressed in shirt and slacks and loafers. He sat down in Shor's office, put his feet up on a chair opposite and drank a lime squash.

"I think you're going to be the next man to go up," Shor said. "When's it to be?"

"Late January, early February, depending on the weather pattern."

"Why me and not Duke?"

Shor heaved himself round in his chair. His brows slid down like two caterpillars trying to crawl into the crevices of his eyes. His huge bottom lip came up and nibbled at his top lip. "Matt, is there anything worrying Duke? You're his closest friend——"

"There might be," Matt said, pondering a moment. He sipped his drink, gradually getting rid of the dry sick taste that was always in his mouth after a run on MASTIF. His eyeballs were sore, the muscles of them aching after the unaccustomed violent exercise. He had once read that jugglers rarely went blind because their eyes got so much exercise. With the exercise that his eyes got, his eyesight should be good enough for him even to see into the future. Not that he wanted that. He had developed a certain fatalism, but it was built on the shaky foundation of his ignorance of the future. He wondered if, now the next flight was close, Duke had begun to look too far into the future. "He's been pretty quiet the past month or so. Why do you ask?"

"Just wondering. It's probably nothing, but you know how I scrutinize you guys."

"Like a mother hen. I heard a guy down at the Cape the other day call us Mother Shor's Chickens."

Shor's big face folded in a grin. "I've been called a lot of things, but never maternal." He shuffled the papers on his desk, picked up a pen. Matt recognized that Shor wanted to get back to work, was going to talk no more about Duke. "You're not coming back to Canaveral tomorrow with us?"

Matt stood up. "No, Duke and I have got a couple of days off. We're going up to Cape Cod to see our folks. We'll be back Monday."

"How's Jane?"

"She's fine now I've at last brought her and the kids down to Florida. We've been talking about it for twelve months. She was not too happy about renting our house to strangers, you know what women are like, but in the end she gave in."

"You feel better having her and the kids down there with you?"

Matt nodded. "I think so. Back home in Virginia she got too much time to think, to imagine things. Down there at the Cape she can now see how much care and attention goes into each launch—I keep hoping it will convince her that the safety factor is as important as anything else in the project. She's still not a hundred per cent sold on this job of mine."

"I sometimes wonder how many of the wives are. But they've all done a wonderful job themselves, I mean putting on a face. But it must be hell on them. Sometimes I think we should have chosen all bachelor orphans, guys without anyone to worry about them."

"There's always someone to worry about you, Doc. Even the bums on Skid Row must have someone somewhere worrying about them."

He took his jacket and tie from the hanger behind the office door, said goodbye to Shor and went out into the mild September air. Duke was waiting for him in the rented car. "How'd it go?"

He slid in beside Duke. "Same as usual. How was it with you?"

"Seems I was a little slow this time. One time there I felt like Patterson is going to feel when Liston hits him."

"You still want to bet on Liston?"

"Son, I wouldn't take your money from you."

They drove into the city for lunch, called Shor to see if he needed them again, then caught the afternoon plane for Boston. The two hostesses fell over each other to usher them to their seats.

"Anything you'd like, Colonel Dalmead? Colonel Crispin?" Their smiles threatened to split their cheeks as much as their bodies threatened to split their uniforms; Matt, grinning to himself, tried to remember if he had ever seen a hostess whose uniform sagged. "Anything at all?"

Duke turned on the charm and the girls went away, convinced that though the astronauts wanted nothing now, in another time and another place— "When you flash that smile," Matt said, "those girls get nystagmus. Did you see their eyeballs roll?"

"It's nothing, son. You've either got it or you haven't."

"Nystagmus or a swollen head?"

Duke grinned, the smile showing considerable less wattage now. "It means nothing. Five or six years ago, a girl like that laid herself wide open to me, I'd have made a date with her right away. But not any more."

"You *have* slowed down."

The grin slipped away, his face clouded. "It's age, son," he said, but the lightness in his voice was forced. He pushed his seat back and stretched out, closing his eyes; the sideways light, striking in the window, threw into relief the line that now seemed to have become permanent between his brows. "I've even got that way I like an after-lunch nap. I can remember my old man used to say that was one of the luxuries of success in America. Back home in Portugal even the poor went to sleep after lunch. But here only the rich can afford it."

"We're not rich, chum. But I think I'll join you anyway."

Matt closed his eyes and lay back. They were not rich, as he had said; but they could afford a nap after lunch. *Life* magazine had signed the original seven astronauts to contracts for their stories; when the final five had been chosen, they in turn had been approached by several other magazines. The five of them had conferred, chosen a magazine and signed a contract for their stories. None of them would get rich on his share of the proceeds, but when all the returns were in each man expected to get about a hundred thousand dollars. Lately there had been some criticism of the astronauts making money out of a national project, and Matt had begun to feel uneasy. He had had doubts about signing

255

the contract at the very beginning, but he had not pressed his argument; Rupe Meredith, backed by Duke and Bruce Blair, had insisted that they were entitled to make everything they could out of their volunteering. Well, he was committed now, and it was a bit late to have pangs of conscience. He had the comforting thought that, if anything happened to him, Jane and the children were financially secure for life. And from what Shor had told him this morning, something *could* happen to him next January or February.

Jane and Cleo were waiting for them at Boston in Cleo's car. They drove out of the city, taking the coast road, heading for home. After all these years, Matt mused, he still thought of it as home. The old timers had been right: you might go away, but you left your footprints forever in the sands of the Cape.

"Where are the kids?" he asked.

"In swimming," Jane said.

"They must find it cold after the Florida water."

"Cleo and I went in this morning. We got goosepimples, but it put us in fine trim for tonight."

"What's on tonight?" he asked; but she smiled at him, putting her arm in his, and he shook his head in mock disgust. "These sex mad foreigners, Duke. How do they ever get into a clean-living country like this?"

Duke, who was driving, smiled in the rear-vision mirror, but it was an empty smile. For the past month he had seemed preoccupied, but Matt had not queried him on it. The astronauts had learned not to interfere too much with each other's moods; they all recognized that each was subject to strains that never faced the ordinary man. If a pilot had self-doubts, it was his business; he could be relied upon to confess them when he could not resolve them. They were like novices in a monastery: it was up to each man himself to decide if he had the vocation for the job ahead. The doctors and psychiatrists were constantly testing them, seeking the flaws in them, but in the end the decision lay with the man himself. Having got this far through the screening process, if he had any secret fears or doubts they were hidden too deep for alien discovery.

Matt and Jane were dropped at the Crispin house and Duke and Cleo drove on to the Dalmead home. When they were alone in their room Jane said to Matt, "What's the matter with Duke?"

"You noticed it, too? I don't know. He's got something on his mind."

"I think I know what it is. Cleo has asked him to come back

with her. She asked him when she came down to Florida last month."

"I guessed something must have been on. She and Caroline had never come down there before."

"Caroline was partly the reason. Cleo's been having trouble with her. She told me all about it on the way up to Boston today!"

"He's taking long enough to think it over. A month, for Pete's sake!"

"There's something else." He looked at her, and after a moment she said, "Anne."

"Anne? Oh, now cut it out——"

"You're like all brothers—or anyway, most of them. You never suspect your sister of anything. But she's been tipping her cap at Duke ever since I can remember."

"A schoolgirl crush. She called him Uncle till she was sixteen or seventeen."

"She doesn't call him Uncle now, hasn't for quite a while. Why do you think she spent so much time with us? Oh, I didn't mind having her—she helps around the house, she's good with the kids. But every time she went out, whom did she go with? That first time she came down to Florida, she had young fellows from Patrick always on the phone—she brushed them off like they were so many dead flies."

"Are you trying to tell me there's something serious between her and Duke?" He walked to the window, looked out across the bay where he and Duke, so many years ago, had spent so much time. The tide was out and he could see the wrecked hulk, now just a few grey bones protruding from the white skin of the beach. Did the local kids still play at Vikings? Was there a Leif Ericsson among them, setting foot again on Vinland? But the point and the beach were bare today: the kids of today had other things to discover. He had noticed it with John: America was a fact he took for granted, the past held no excitement for him at all.

Then as he watched he saw Cleo's car move slowly along the road towards the point. It stopped, and after a moment Duke got out. Matt watched the distant figure with a fascination he could not comprehend; it was as if he were looking at a stranger whom he knew as well as he knew himself. Or as well as any man can know himself, which he knew could never be completely. Duke walked to the end of the point and stood at the edge of the small cliff there, thirty or forty feet above the skeleton of the wreck.

"What's the matter?" Jane asked. Matt nodded, and she came to the window and stood beside him. "Who is it? I can't see that far, you know that."

"Duke."

"What's he doing?"

He shrugged. Duke could be out there on the point for a dozen reasons: looking for memories, for legends, for some sort of reassurance.

"Do you think he's going to jump?" Jane was straining her eyes, trying to bring the scene closer to her: her face puckered with the effort, making her look older. She was no longer a young woman and her beauty now was not a constant thing: an expression, a moment of reaching for something, could reduce her to the anonymity of plainness. Sometimes, without falling *out* of love with her, Matt looked at her and tried to remember the girl he had fallen *in* love with. She reached now with myopic eyes for something that would pain her if it happened, whether she could see it or not. "Is he thinking of suicide?"

"If he is, we're too far away to stop him." Matt was unworried. Whatever Duke did, he knew he would not commit suicide. Not in such an unspectacular way as jumping off a thirty-foot cliff. Already he could feel something like resentment of Duke building up: he was taking his sister Anne's side before he had heard either side. Again he felt the prick of conscience: he had neglected Anne for too long, had never really been a brother to her, only a long-distance relative.

Jane turned away from the window, her eyes pale with strain and the afternoon light. "Do you think you should talk to him, darling?"

"What about? Tell him to stay away from my sister or I'll flay his hide with a horse-whip? That's Dad's job, if it has to be done. If he can find a horse-whip in this day and age. It's difficult these days to play the stern parent unless you want to use a gun."

"I didn't mean for you to be stern with him. I meant you should try and help him."

"How?" He looked at her, aware once more that women never understood the relationship between some men. Men could never reach the depth of confidences that women could reach; on the surface women were always the more reticent, but not when it came to honest confession. Duke would never tell him the true extent of his doubt, he knew that.

Jane recognized that she was not going to get any help from

258

Matt, and neither was Duke. She turned away impatiently. "Oh, all right. Let him be. But you're his friend——"

"He knows that. If he wants my help, he'll come to me. Until then——" He looked out of the window again, at the figure standing against the steel sea. Suddenly he saw Duke as a lonely man, an image that had never occurred to him before. He cursed himself for his long stupidity, the disease of blindness to another's needs. Once before Duke had told him he needed him, but he had never fully accepted the admission. It flatters a man to know a woman needs him; it frightens him to know a man needs him. Because in the other man he can see the reflection of himself.

"I'll go and see him," he said abruptly.

But when he was outside the house, looking towards the point he saw that Duke and the car had already gone.

4

Anne was waiting for Duke where she had asked him to meet her, in front of the Episcopalian church. He drove the car slowly round the square, the one part of town that seemed unchanged. Every time he came back here to the Cape something seemed to have been altered on the face of the town; it was blotched with new buildings, the acne of development. But the square remained the same, a reminder of the past. The white clapboard church with its dogmatic steeple, the firehouse, the courthouse, the seats beneath the trees where the old men, all summer every summer, made the same checkers moves they had been making for what seemed like forever. The town had made no mark on history, but its own history was always there, now and again creeping into the consciousness of its citizens like the fogs that came in, like mists of the past, out of the Atlantic.

Duke pulled the car into the kerb and Anne got in. "I asked you to pick me up here because the loneliest place in town during the week is always outside the Episcopalian church."

"Are you trying to butter me up, make me feel smugly superior as a Catholic? I'm an ex-Catholic, remember. An ex-churchgoer. It's people like me make the Episcopalian Church a lonely place. Do you go to church?"

"That's the first time you've ever asked me that. No, I don't."

As he turned the car round he saw the big neon sign farther down the main street: Crispin's Supermarket; the sign stood

259

out against the grey sky like a laceration. Things were changing, all right: Bob Crispin had once been a man all for retaining the heritage of the past. But he had succumbed like everyone else to progress.

They drove out along the Cape, heading away from town and people who might recognize them. They passed the spot where the Conolly house and the old freezing plant had once stood; a motel now invited them to come in. When they caught glimpses of the sea they saw that a grey wind had begun to corrugate it; there might be rain before they turned for home. They passed through Hyannis-Port, and Duke glanced at the streets with a sardonic eye.

"I wonder if Republicans ever come here now for their vacations?"

"You mean because of the Kennedys coming here? They'd be stupid if they stopped just for that reason. Politics is like religion, it breeds too much prejudice."

"With some people politics is a religion."

"You're just beating about the bush, Duke. We didn't come out here to talk politics or religion. We came out here to talk about *us*. Find a place where we can park."

She spoke demandingly, and perversely he didn't obey her at once. He drove on in silence for some time, then at last turned off into a side road that led down to the sea. He pulled up the car, switched off the engine and sat looking out at Monomoy Island, like a dark cloud against the horizon.

"Matt and I used to come here to fish when we were kids. We were out here the day you were born. Going home we heard about Pearl Harbour on the radio. That was the beginning of my escape from the Cape." He looked at her, smiling without humour. "No play on words intended."

"I still have to find *my* escape."

He turned away from her, looking down at the rock shelf where he and Matt used to fish. He could not remember what had been said in those long hours there in the wind and the sea spray, but he would bet that the talk had been serious and full of doubts. Yet now those long-ago days had a serenity about them due not entirely to distance; the wounds to his spirit had been minor ones, requiring no stitches, repaired by the Band-Aid of a new enthusiasm for a new interest. But he was too old now for new interests, too tired for enthusiasm: today's wounds would never heal, like the bite from certain reptiles.

"You won't find any escape with me, Anne," he said bluntly:

bluntness, which he had avoided for so long, was the only course of action with her.

"I've got to find it with you!" She clutched at his shoulder, pulled him round to face her. "Duke, I love you! Ever since I was fourteen years old, I've built my life around you—some day I was going to ask you to marry me——"

"Anne," he said gently; the bluntness was already gone from his voice; as always he found it painful to hurt her. "I am already married. Was, even before you were fourteen."

"You're not married! You're only—you're not even just living with her!"

He smiled, again without humour. "I'm glad you didn't say I'm married in name only."

"Well, it's true, isn't it?"

He looked out to sea again. Gulls sketched hieroglyphics against the sky, a meaningless message that must have *some* meaning. Was he being rational in thinking there must be some meaning in such pointless natural acts as birds flying on the rising wind? But it was some time since he had given up trying to work things out on rational terms. He had tried to work out the human heart, only to find that reason did not apply to it.

"No, it's not true, Anne. I am going back to live with Cleo. Permanently."

He heard her draw in her breath. When he looked at her she had drawn away from him, was crumpled in the corner of the seat, her face almost as pale as her hair, her hands clasped in front of her and her teeth biting into her thumbs. It was as if she were trying not to scream, as if he had hit her, as he had hit Caroline that time, but much more brutally.

"Anne, please believe me, I don't want to hurt you." The words were an echo: he had said them to a dozen women, so many times that they had become almost empty of meaning; and yet he meant them with a truth that hurt himself. He pitied her, and feeling pity he also felt a love for her, since one is part of the other; but it was not the sort of love she craved and he was sensitive enough not to voice it. "But there wouldn't be any future for us. I've tried to tell you this a dozen times, but I couldn't come out with it—it seemed too brutal——"

"What are you being now?" She mumbled against her thumbs, not looking at him. She looked frighteningly young to him, her silver hair hanging down over her brows like that of a schoolgirl; there were no tears, but her eyes had darkened as though bruised. She reminded him of Caroline, and thinking of his daughter strengthened his resolve.

"To coin a cliché, I'm being brutal to be kind. For in the long run, five or ten years from now, or even less, a year, you will find that I *was* kind, that I did the right thing."

"You shouldn't have let me go on hoping!"

"Oh Christ!" He slumped back in his seat; he was too weary even to feel angry with her. "What hope did I ever give you? I've never once said I loved you, never tried to make love to you——"

"You wanted to often enough! I could feel you——"

"And I never did. That's the important fact, Anne. No matter what I felt when I was with you—and you're a beautiful girl, he'd be a cold man who wasn't attracted to you—no matter what I felt, I never did make love to you. I have a great deal of affection for you, but I don't love you."

"Why did you date me then? Why did you kiss me?" She was almost twenty-one, but she could have been fourteen: she had saved herself for one man and so she knew nothing about men at all.

"I shouldn't have done that. I know that now. But——" He had dated her, kissed her, because that was what she had wanted, and he had not wanted to hurt her. He had never approached her as he had approached Trudi, Debbie Fairfax, not even Cleo; he had been trapped by his own pity for her, although it was only now that he recognized that it had been pity. He sat up, switching on the engine. "I'm sorry, Anne. We're not going to get anywhere talking about it any more. I've made up my mind. I'm going back to Cleo."

"You don't love her."

He considered a moment, then he said with something like surprise, "I think I do love her."

"Why have you taken so long to find out then?" She was prosecuting him, charging him with the fraudulent use of love.

"That's something I'm asking myself. But I'm getting close to an answer. To the answer to a lot of things that have plagued me for years."

He turned the car round, drove back along the road and out on to the highway. There was rain out at sea now, clouds hanging from the sky like the beards of old disillusioned men; the wind keened through the trees, stripping them of the last of summer. Anne sat in her corner of the seat, silent all the way back to town.

"Shall I take you home?"

"No," she said sullenly. "Drop me where you picked me up."

He pulled the car in before the Episcopalian church. "We are coming over to your house tomorrow night for supper. Will you be there?"

"I wouldn't want to embarrass you." She got out of the car, closed the door quietly behind her. She looked composed now, but under the calm exterior he could feel the tenseness of her. "Good-bye, Duke."

She turned and walked away as the rain began to fall, seemingly oblivious of it, her silver hair turning grey as the rain darkened it. He watched her go, sick with the pity he felt for her, burdened by a guilt that reason told him was not deserved but which somehow he could not deny. He started up the car and drove towards home, so long forgotten and not thought of as such, and Cleo. As he passed the Crispin supermarket he noticed that the sign was flickering, as if about to go out. He would call up Bob Crispin and tell him.

5

Anne Crispin's body was washed up on the beach close to the wreck on the morning tide. It was found by John and Stevie, boys whose memories would be marked forever by someone else's unhappiness; they ran home to the Crispin house, and it was Matt who went down to the beach and carried his sister up from the water on to the dry sand. He knelt beside her, cold as she was, his mind number than it had ever been in any of the body-racking tests he had gone through as an astronaut, and tried to breathe life into a body that was beyond it.

"She's dead, Dad." John stood above him, all the electric energy gone from his young body, his face serious and pale and puzzled. "What happened to her?"

It was a question that would be repeated again and again over the next few days, but one which Matt would not answer truthfully. He looked up past John and saw his father, mother and Jane standing on the cliff above them. He stood up, stepped in front of the bloated ugly figure that had been his sister, and shouted, "Dad, bring down a blanket! Phone for the police! And don't let the women come down here."

He saw Jane put her arm round his mother, then the two women walked slowly away, one leaning on the other. His father had already disappeared, stumbling away like a half-blind old

263

man. Matt turned to John. "You better go up and look after Stevie and Bunty. And don't describe this to Bunty—she'll want to know all about it."

John nodded, then silently clambered up to the path and disappeared, his young shoulders bent with the sudden weight of an experience he had not even contemplated. Experience was an education that had no set curriculum.

Matt looked down at the silent figure at his feet, made terrible by its hours in the water. He felt as if he were in the presence of a stranger, not only because of the unfamiliarity of the bloated features; he had never really been close to Anne and he could not understand why she should have committed suicide. Because he had known at once, with no evidence at all, that it was suicide. Whatever else anyone might say, he knew that his sister had taken her own life.

Then his father was stumbling down the path by the cliff, bringing a blanket with him. He threw it at Matt as he approached, as if warding off a sight he did not want to view; then he stopped dead and stood like a man who had been hit a stunning blow but could not fall over, his red face now white and his eyes blinking behind his glasses. All his life he had been inventing crises, but his invention had never run to anything as tragic as this.

Matt covered Anne with the blanket. "You better go back to the house, Dad. I'll stay here till the police come. Phone Duke and Cleo, would you? Tell Duke I want to see him."

Bob Crispin nodded, unable to say anything. He opened his mouth, groping for words, but it was as if his own tongue were dead; he could not manage even a strangled murmur of grief. He turned and walked stiff-legged back up the path, suffering as apparent as a cross laid across his bent back.

Then Matt heard the wailing of the police car's siren. It died away to a moan, like that of a beast in pain; then the two policemen had appeared at the top of the cliff, were scrambling down the path. In a moment they had taken over, trained for such tragedies but still unable to hide the shock on their faces. Then Matt was climbing the path, his ears pierced by the needle mewing of the gulls nailed in the sky like white carrion birds.

When Duke, Cleo and Caroline arrived at the house, Matt was sitting out on the porch on the swing seat, wrapped in a mackinaw against the wind that now blew in from the sea. "Go on in," he said to Cleo and Caroline. "Jane is upstairs with Mom. They had to put her to bed."

Cleo looked as if she were about to say something, then she changed her mind and ushered Caroline ahead of her into the house. Duke stood irresolute, hands dug deep into the pockets of the jacket he wore over his pyjama top. "You think I should go in and say something to your pop?"

"There's nothing you can say to him. He wouldn't hear you anyway." Matt held up a small leather-covered book. "I found this up in Anne's room."

"What is it?"

"Her diary. The last entry was last night. You want me to read it to you?"

Duke hesitated, then he put out a hand. "I'll read it myself." Matt gave him the book and he leafed through it. He stopped and read one or two passages, then he read the last entry. There was no expression on his face; he could have been reading a map. *But it is a map*, he thought. It was a map to the last year of Anne's life, landmarked with his own name; yet the grid references were all wrong, it was a map based on a wrong bearing. He had never even hinted at the future she had promised herself in these pages. He closed the book and gave it back to Matt. "The last entry. It isn't true. And neither are the others. Not completely true."

"I could kill you," Matt said quietly, still sitting in the porch seat. His face was white and strained, like that of a man suddenly sober after a long heavy drinking bout. Had he been drunk to have trusted Duke for so long? "Not only for what you've done to Anne. Part of the blame must be hers, I can see that from the diary. But for what you've done to Mom and Dad."

Duke seemed to shatter all at once, his face, his whole body. He collapsed on the seat beside Matt; it swung beneath his weight, dragging Matt's feet along the floor of the porch. "Christ, Matt, I did nothing! That diary isn't *true*! I made her no promises—Look!" He snatched at the book, riffled through it. "This entry here—*He made love to me tonight. But when in our own bed?* Matt, we were never in *any* bed. I never touched her——"

"Why did she commit suicide then? Last night's entry makes it pretty clear what she was going to do."

Duke fell back in the seat; they rocked back and forth like old men. He felt as he had felt the first time he had ridden The Wheel, the large centrifuge that whirled them round at terrifying speed to test their reaction to high G forces. He had been crushed by the G forces of shock and emotion. "She committed suicide

265

because she was Anne. I had no idea yesterday she would do such a thing—but now I know she must have had it in mind all the time. Matt, she wanted me to marry her. And I told her no. I'd never even thought of it——"

Matt tapped the book he had taken back from Duke. He could not remember ever having felt like this before; even in Germany, after the buzzing by the Russian planes, he had made some attempt to understand Duke. But not now. "You gave her plenty of encouragement for her to think so."

Duke slapped his hand in frustration on his knee. "How can I convince you that all that——" he waved a hand at the diary "—it's all romanticising?"

Matt stood up, putting the diary into the pocket of his mackinaw. "I'll burn this. No one need know it was ever found."

"Thanks," Duke said, but there was no time for relief to ease the strain in his face: Matt went on:

"I'm not doing it for you. I'm doing it for Mom and Dad. And for Anne, too. There's no evidence, as far as I can see, other than this, that she committed suicide. If you and I keep our mouths shut, they'll have to record it as death by misadventure or whatever they call it. They'll have nothing more to go on."

"I'll keep quiet."

"You'd better, you crud!" Matt leaned forward, his voice still low. "All your life you've done nothing but ruin other people. You're a leper, and everyone who's touched you has been afflicted by you. I've been fortunate—I saw through you years ago and I was able to take precautions. But if Cleo does take you back, then Christ help her. The world would be better off if it had been you I'd fished out of the water this morning. I wish to Christ it had been!"

Then he turned and went into the house, closing the door gently behind him, his anger more terrible because of his quietness. Duke sat and stared out at the sea, not seeing it, his dark eyes dull and black as two bruises in the yellow mask of his face. He felt empty, as if he had been scoured by a sharp knife; there was no feeling deep inside him, but his outer shell stung with pain. It was as if all emotion in him had drained to the ends of his nerves, was there just beneath the skin, waiting to burst out of him in an eruption that would shatter him forever.

Then the door opened and Cleo came out on to the porch. He looked up at her, having to blink to bring her into focus. She sat down beside him on the seat and took his hand.

"You had nothing to do with it, did you, darling?"

266

He shook his head slowly. "I don't know. Maybe I did. Matt thinks I did."

"Did you see her yesterday?"

He told her quietly and without any feeling in his voice what had happened yesterday afternoon. He recited it as he might have into a tape recorder, going back in his mind over everything that had been said, looking for guilt on his part. He was not looking for total exoneration; but he did not believe he was a murderer. At last he looked at her. "That's all that happened, Cleo." He did not mention the diary: the fewer people knew about that, the fewer would be called upon to hide the truth. But was it the truth? What Anne had written in the diary was not the truth: it was only an expression of hope, and hope was only another dream of the truth. "If I had anything to do with her death, it was unwitting."

"Do you think she committed suicide?"

He hesitated: the lying might as well begin now. "I don't know. Maybe it was an accident. I think for Mr. and Mrs. Crispin's sake it would be best if that was the verdict."

"Well, let's hope they find no suicide note. For your sake as well." She put her hand against his lips as he went to speak. "No, I don't blame you, darling. I believe you when you say you had nothing wittingly to do with it. But I know how a woman can go on hoping even without encouragement. I've done it for over ten years. Except that last night my hopes came true." She looked away from him towards the grey sea streaked with bars of pale gold from the early morning sun trying to break through the clouds. "I'm sorry Anne was the one who had to pay the price for them."

He leaned forward, turning her face towards his with a gentle hand. "She paid nothing for anything between you and me. Don't ever think that, or ever let me know you're thinking it—I couldn't live with you if that's the way you felt. Whatever happiness you and I have together from now on, we don't owe it to Anne. I'm sorry for what—" Again the momentary hesitation: the lie was not yet easy on his tongue "—for what happened to her and maybe I was to blame. But *you* owe her nothing. Promise me you'll never think that way again."

There was a hint of tears in her eyes. She wore no make-up and her mouth was still bruised from last night's kisses. There had been no love-making, for fear that they would be heard by the Dalmeads in the other rooms of the house. But when he had told her that he was coming back to live with her and Caroline, she had devoured him with the kisses of a woman suffering from a ten-year hunger. They had slept together in the one bed in the room that had been his so long ago; physically it had been uncomfortable, but mentally she had not known such comfort for years. It had been a brutal shock to be woken this morning with the news of Anne's death.

"I promise, darling." She leaned forward and kissed him, softly this morning, not with hunger but with compassion; she saw now, not with pride but with wonder, that he needed her, that he would never leave her again. "And we'll be happy. I promise you that, too."

6

Anne's death was recorded as an accident. Several people, including her parents, came forward to testify that it was a habit of hers to go for walks alone along the shore at night. No one but Matt and Jane, Duke and Cleo, queried the verdict; and they did so only in their own minds, not raising the question again even to each other. Matt drove out along the Cape, found a lonely spot in the scrub and burned the diary and buried the ashes there; he never told Jane of it nor did she ever guess that such a book existed. But when Jane asked him if he thought Anne had committed suicide, he did not deny the possibility. All he asked was that she never mention it again to anyone they knew.

"I'm not stupid," she said, wondering if there had been some premonition at the back of her mind that had prompted her to bring her dark topcoat instead of her mustard one. They were in their room, dressing for the funeral; Matt was fitting the black armband on the sleeve of his uniform. "That would only hurt your mother and father. But what about Duke? You haven't spoken to him in the last two days. Does he know something? Have you had a row?"

"Whether Anne committed suicide or whether she died by accident, I think he was responsible for her death. I'm finished with him."

"There will be reporters and photographers at the funeral." She was always practical. "You had better say *something* to him. The reporters will soon make a story out of it if you stand on opposite sides of the grave glaring at each other." She put on her coat, put on the small black hat she had gone into Falmouth and bought yesterday. The black hat and the dark coat made the grey in her hair more apparent, but she did not look at herself with wounded vanity. "Keep up some sort of pretence till you get back to Florida. But if you want my opinion——" She turned away from the mirror and faced him. "I don't think Duke should be blamed for this at all."

"I don't want your opinion, honey," he said quietly, looking past her at the reflection of himself in the mirror; a stranger looked at him, a middle-aged man whose face was set against the world. "I've got one of my own."

Matt, Jane and the children stayed on for an extra day after the funeral. Duke, Cleo and Caroline left immediately for New York. As he put their bags in the back of Cleo's car, Duke was joined by his father and Pete, who had come down from Boston for the funeral.

"Cleo told me she and Caroline are going down to Florida with you," Phil Dalmead said. He was an old man now, retired from fishing, moving with slow reluctant steps towards his grave. Arthritis had begun to cripple him and his eyes now were dull with constant pain. But this morning there was a glow of happiness in the dark gullied face. "I'm pleased, Duke. It makes me real happy."

Duke nodded. "I'm sorry you had to wait so long, Pop." He looked at his brother. "How's the parish coming along, Pete?"

Pete grinned. He had put on weight, but Duke was glad to see he had not become complacent as so many priests did in their middle age: their struggles were over and they had become civil servants of Heaven. Pete was not like that, was still working at his job, worried as much by his parishioners' temporal needs as their spiritual needs. "I think maybe I should have volunteered for the missions. Ministering to the natives in Africa could not be tougher than looking after the Boston Irish. Especially now that Kennedy's President. With God and the President both Catholics and on their side, they think they're entitled to every dispensation in the book. If ever we have a Boston Irish Pope, I *am* going to Africa."

Duke grinned in reply, suddenly feeling an affection for both his father and his brother that he could not remember ever having felt before. He was being ploughed by suffering, opened up for the seed of love. "Next time I'm in Boston I'll drop in. You know I've never heard you say Mass, except at Mom's funeral."

"I've never seen you fly a plane or a space capsule, so we are square. But you'll be welcome any time, Duke."

"You gonna be the next man they blast off, Duke?" Phil said. "It's out of you and Matt, ain't it?"

"I think it'll be Matt, Pop." Cleo and Caroline were coming out of the house, and Duke was glad of the interruption. He was half-way to a decision that he did not yet want to discuss. "They are saving me for the moon."

"The moon?" Then Phil's face cracked as he laughed. "Oh, a joke, eh? Well, tell 'em not to keep you too long. I want to be still here when you make your orbit. Maybe then I'll write home to the old branch of the family, the de Almeidas, tell them the American branch has raised a famous man, too."

Duke smiled indulgently at his father: the old man now firmly believed what had once been only a wishful fancy. Then Cleo and Caroline were kissing Phil good-bye; they shook hands with Pete. "Even though you're my brother-in-law, Pete, I'd feel very self-conscious about kissing a priest good-bye," said Cleo.

Pete smiled, leaned forward and kissed both Cleo and Caroline on the cheek. "You've heard the Vatican joke, haven't you? It's all right for priests and nuns to kiss each other good-bye so long as they don't get into the habit."

Cleo looked shocked for a moment, then she split the morning with a peal of laughter. "Oh Pete, you're human!"

Pete was not offended. "Did you ever doubt it?"

"You've always scared me. Priests and ministers always have."

Pete, still smiling, looked at Duke. "I think Duke is scared of me, too. Or of what I represent."

It was too late now to take up the challenge, even if he had wanted to. "No proselytizing, Pete. Some other time."

A few minutes later they were headed south towards New York. They passed the cemetery where Anne had been laid to rest a couple of hours before, but no one said anything. There had been a crowd at the funeral, people who had come not so much out of respect for Anne as for her parents. Anne, who was born on the Cape, who had lived there all her life, was more a stranger than many of the summer visitors. But Bob and Nell Crispin, blank-faced and stiff like puppets of grief, had always been part of the town: the townsfolk shared their grief if not their loss. Duke had stood by the grave, aware of the silent brooding figure of Matt deliberately avoiding his gaze, and had looked across at the Crispins, trying to pierce the sad masks they wore, looking for hatred of him as a murderer might look for suspicion of himself. Once Nell Crispin had looked up and directly across at him, but there had been nothing in her dull eyes: she had been looking at the past, not seeking a reason why Anne had died, only searching for memories to make the future easier to bear.

The Dalmeads stopped for lunch just outside Providence, then drove on again.

"When do we come to Florida, Daddy?" Caroline was dressed in the suit she had worn to the funeral; she looked smart, nothing like the embryo beatnik of a month ago.

"As soon as I can get us a house."

"Jane will help you look for a place," Cleo said, and looked at Duke as he shot her a quick glance. "I told her at the funeral we'd be coming down there."

He went to say something, but changed his mind, aware of Caroline in the seat behind them. His image was brighter for her this morning than it had ever been; he did not want to tarnish it by raising queries in her mind. If Matt persisted in his attitude, the split between them must eventually come out into the open. Till the moment was inevitable, however, he wanted to keep the break a secret between himself and Matt.

They arrived in New York in mid-afternoon, and Duke caught the Air Transport plane bound for Patrick Air Force Base. There were other officers on board who recognized him and wanted to talk to him, but he avoided their glances and found a seat by himself at the rear of the plane. He took some papers from his briefcase and made a pretence of studying them. But he saw nothing of what was on the papers and all the way south he slowly, carefully, painfully, searched his mind as a surgeon might search a body for some growth that, if not detected in time, would kill it. He was riddled now with the cancer of self-doubt, the companion disease to self-discovery but more malignant. All his old confidence had gone: he was like a mountain climber whose rope had broken at the moment the storm clouds swept up the cliff-face. As a rationalist he had sought definition. Doubt had been his starting point, but the ending was also doubt; and doubt, he knew now, could never be defined. It could be replaced by truth, but the truth of himself was a discovery he had yet to make. And only he could make the discovery, for no man has ever fully explored another nor ever can.

It was dark when the plane reached Patrick Air Force Base. He picked up the Corvette from the parking lot and drove north along Route A1A towards Cape Canaveral. He passed through Cocoa Beach and made a mental note to come back here to-morrow and see the local realty men about getting him a cottage.

Motels, with their space age names, lined each side of the highway: a neon rocket looked ready to shoot down a neon satellite. The motels, bars and diners were crowded: this once almost-deserted stretch of coast had now become the dress circle for the greatest show on earth. And he was one of the stars of the cast.

He drove past the end of the harbour, noticing that all the shrimp boats were out tonight; past the huge citrus-processing plant, the reminder that there were still other things in Florida besides rockets; then he had passed through the security gate and was on the Cape itself. Above the hum of the Corvette's engine he heard the loud hiss coming from the liquid oxygen plant over to his left: somehow for him the hiss of escaping lox had become the sound of the Cape, more so even than the roar of rockets blasting off the pad. It was a sinister sound, hinting at the mysteries of space. The roar of a rocket was only an echo of war, an earthly event that held no mystery at all.

He parked the car in front of the building where Oliver Shor had his office. He went into the building and, as he had hoped, found the big doctor seated behind his untidy desk. Shor looked up, put down the paperback detective novel he was reading, and waved a hand towards the chair opposite him.

"Matt come back with you?"

"No, he's stayed on another day or so. His mother took Anne's death pretty hard."

"I only met her once or twice, but I liked her. Bit quiet, but that's a change these days. Pity to see an attractive girl like her go so early. There's enough elderly shrews we could do without. Coffee?"

"I'd like something stronger if you've got it."

Shor opened a drawer in his desk, produced a bottle. "Haig and Haig. A wonderful medicine. You want this for medicinal purposes, of course?"

Duke grinned, but he was really too weary for jokes. "A little Scotch courage, that's the main reason." He took the glass Shor handed him, sipped the drink and sat savouring it for a moment. Then he said, "Doc, I want to resign from the team."

There was a tinkling sound as the bottle in Shor's hand knocked against the top of his glass. He finished pouring his drink, put the stopper back in the bottle, picked up his drink and tasted it, then put the glass back on the desk among the snowdrift of papers there. He kneaded his face with a huge hand, his dark eyes gleaming like molluscs above the crawling crab-legs of his fingers.

At last he spoke, hesitantly, as if he had searched for words and not found the ones he wanted. "I'm not the one to decide, Duke, you know that. It's much more formal than just dropping in here and handing in your verbal notice."

"I know that." Duke drank again from his glass. "Maybe I just wanted you to talk me out of it." Then he shook his head. "No, that's not what I want. I've got to get out. I can't be talked out of it."

"Why do you have to leave the team, Duke?"

"I'd have to tell you the story of my life to explain that, Doc. And even then it mightn't be clear."

"NASA will want clear reasons. It's spent a lot of time and money training you. It's not going to let you go just like that." He made a throwaway motion with his hand.

Duke put down his drink; he didn't need the extra courage after all. "Doc, I haven't got what it takes to be an astronaut. There are cracks in myself that I wasn't aware of till just a month or so ago. But they're serious cracks, ones that maybe I can patch over, but which could always break open again."

"I've been watching you for some time now, I'll admit that. *Something* seemed to be wrong with you." He pulled on his ear. He could be as relaxed as any man on the Cape for most of the time, but when something serious began to worry him his hand was constantly pulling and pushing at his face and head, like a man checking the strength of his own edifice. "I only ask you this because I'm trying to help you—but has Anne Crispin's death got anything to do with your decision? I know you had several dates with her when she came down here."

They hadn't missed much, Duke thought; they were the FBI of medicine. Then he dismissed the sour thought from his mind: they were working for him as much as for the project.

"No, it's got nothing to do with her." Anne's death was only a part of the whole complexity that clouded his life; he could not name her without naming a dozen others.

"Your wife?"

He pondered for a moment. "In a way, yes. But then there's a contradiction there—we're going to live together again. I'm in love with her, something I wasn't sure of before. People are usually disturbed by a break-up in their relations, not by a reunion."

Shor nodded. "True enough. So there must be another reason."

"There are dozens, Doc. A whole life full of them. But in the

273

end I guess it boils down to one thing—I've lost confidence in myself."

"You're scared, you mean?"

"Not in the usual way. I think I could—I *know* I could take up a plane and put it through all its tests and not be scared. But that would all be over in thirty or forty minutes. No, Doc, it's another kind of scaredness. I don't know who is slated for the next flight, me or Matt. I know it's to be one of us. Whoever goes, he goes for three or four days, maybe more. He'll be up there longer than any man ever before, he'll be exposed to solitude longer than we know for sure that a man can endure. Nikolayev was up there for almost four days, but he had Popovich with him for the last three days. Not with him in the capsule, but there in orbit with him—a guy's not really lonely who can see another man, who has someone else with whom he can identify himself. But Matt or myself, we're going to be exposed to real solitude, not the solitude of a cell or a hermit's cave. You know what I mean—the sort of solitude where you lose all points of reference, where you have no identification at all. We've been trained for it, but who knows how long we can stand it? And *that's* what I'm scared of, Doc. Because I don't think I could stand it. I think the cracks I've found in myself would split wide open before I'd been in orbit even a couple of days."

Shor recognized the possibility of what Duke had said. He himself had supervised some tests in the endurance of solitude. The degree of disorientation suffered by some men had been startling: in a matter of hours some of them had even lost memory contact with the world they had known. Others had experienced hallucinations such as had never happened to them before. Scientists, from their observations of the tests, had come to the conclusion that the utter solitude of a long space flight could reduce a man to no more than a vegetable. The only defence was the man's own moral strength, and now here was Duke telling him that there were already flaws in *his* defences.

Shor sighed, heaved himself about in his chair. "I wish you'd found these cracks in yourself three years ago, Duke."

"I don't know if they were there then. I guess they were. But you and the other doctors didn't find them, and you tried hard enough." Duke remembered the examinations, mental and physical, that he and the other astronauts had been subjected to. The six hundred questions on the personality inventory test: those had peeled him as a fruit might be peeled, till only the core

274

of him remained: the doctors had not been able to get inside *that*, and maybe that was where the flaws had been all the time. He remembered the so-called *Who Am I?* paper: twenty times they had had to complete the sentence, *I am . . .* I am a man. I am John Dalmead, American. I am a lieutenant-colonel in the US Air Force. I am a husband and father. (He had hesitated about that sentence at the time; and he wondered if the doctors had been able to read his hesitation?) The first ten or twelve sentences had been easy to complete. By the time he had reached the last four sentences, he had been struggling to identify himself, like a man whose memory was fading even as he tried to remember. Those tests had been conducted before the final selection of the team had been made, and ever since the doctors had been probing and watching, trying to find the flaws that still remained uncovered.

"Duke, would you like to think about it for another twenty-four hours?"

"I've been thinking about it for a month, Doc." Who knew if he was fitted for a job? Did a man himself know it better than others or did they know it better than he did? Who could measure capacities and aptitudes; what scale was there to weigh a man as a man? But *someone had* to decide. "I've reached a decision. I want to resign from the team."

Shor poured himself another drink. He looked at Duke's glass, still with some whisky in it, then he put the bottle away in the desk drawer. "I don't think we need any more of that tonight. It's not going to help—not you, anyway." He drank, then sat cupping his glass in his hands. "Duke, it isn't going to be easy for you to resign. Or more exactly, it isn't going to be easy for NASA to accept your resignation."

"They'll have to——"

"Oh, they'll accept it if you want to fly off the handle, kick up a storm that might get into the newspapers——"

"You know I wouldn't do that."

Shor nodded. "I know you wouldn't, Duke. But if you do resign, what's to stop the newspapers hazarding guesses? By and large most American newspapers have a sense of responsibility, but there are some of them who think the only news is bad news, who think that the only thing that boosts a newspaper's circulation is controversy. The Russians, too, they wouldn't miss the propaganda value of it. It would look good in *Pravda*, wouldn't it, to read that one of America's astronauts, one of the twelve top men in the country if we think in terms of physical, mental and personality perfection—and that's what you guys are. There may be better physical specimens on the beaches here in Florida, there are certainly brainier men walking around this base, there are undoubtedly men somewhere in the country better co-ordinated personalities, and there are possibly better flyers loose somewhere in the skies. But there are very few men in this country—and if there are, I don't know how we missed them—who have all the things you guys have, who are, if you like, the perfect men for the technological age. I won't say the space age, because actually that still has to come. The perfect man for the space age may turn out to be another mutation of the human form altogether different from you and the other guys." He took another drink. "The prospect frightens me. Where the hell was I?"

Duke grinned. "Reading *Pravda*."

"So I was. A dull newspaper, hate to have it thrown on my stoop every morning. But it wouldn't be a dull newspaper, not to a Russian reader, the day it ran the story on the American astronaut who couldn't take it."

Duke flushed and said angrily, "I'll bet one or two of their men have cracked."

"Sure," said Shor, unruffled. "But who knows about it? We have an institution in this country known as freedom of the press. Unfortunately at times we suffer from a surfeit of such freedom. I know I am un-American in thinking so, but I can never see what benefits the American people gain by being told everything that goes on here, including what goes wrong. And a lot has gone wrong here. It's part of the contradiction of the American character. There are more secret societies, most of them harmless, I'll admit, in this country than in any other country on earth. But no true, red-blooded American wants his government to have even the smallest secret." He took another drink, looked as if he were about to spit it in the face of every true, red-blooded American. "Things have gone wrong here, but that was to be expected in a place of experiment, which is what this is. The public expects to be told every little thing, yet when things do go wrong they blame us for letting down the American image abroad. We're pretty sure the Russians have made just as many mistakes as we have, we think they've even lost a man or two in space, but their image has never suffered. They've kept their mistakes to themselves, let only their successes be broadcast."

"I don't know if I still don't prefer our system."

"That's because you suffer from the naïve honesty that is another part of the imagined American image. In our own minds, that is. I don't know that foreigners think of us as naïvely honest. If they think of us as being honest at all, they think of us as being stupid, too. Oh, I'm just as American as you and everybody else. Maybe not as much as the John Birchers, but who is?" He took another drink. Duke had never seen him so disturbed. "But I believe in discretion when it comes to publicizing mistakes. In the cold war honesty isn't admired—it's the propaganda that counts."

"So it would be bad propaganda if I resigned?"

"I think it would be disastrous. Don't get me wrong. I'm only offering advice on this, I'm not *telling* you what to do. I think you should ask for an interview with the board, explain to them how you feel, and ask their opinion. You may not be able to fly the capsule, but you could still help in lots of ways. Deke Slayton has been just as important to this project as anyone else, even though we had to rule him out of a flight because of that heart murmur we picked up. He was disappointed, naturally, but he's got over it and he's still a member of the team. You can be, too, Duke. You're too valuable for us to let you go."

"But how do I get out of making a flight? There's nothing physically wrong with me. You checked me only last week before I had my spin on MASTIF."

"We might find something." Shor drained his glass. "How are your eyes?"

"Good enough to see what you're getting at. But how does a man pull a trick like that? Someone is sure to find out. And you can't expect all the fellers examining me to keep their mouths shut that there's nothing wrong with me physically, that it's just a cover-up."

"You're right about letting as few people as possible know about this. It would be ideal if it could be kept down to the members of the board and myself. We might even be able to do that. If we can, leave it to me to think up a way to have you scrubbed on physical grounds. It could still be your eyes. A sudden lack of co-ordination. How did you feel on MASTIF last week?"

"A hundred per cent."

"You're really making it hard, aren't you?"

"No, Doc," said Duke slowly, "but I'm trying to make this as foolproof as possible. I see your point about how bad it would look, from the national prestige angle, if I did just bow out

277

because I couldn't take it. It is a bit late for that, I guess. But whatever reasons you find for me, it's got to be one that no one will suspect."

"It will be, Duke. And I'm sorry for your sake that you find you can't go through with it. I know how much it has meant to you."

"Strangely, I'm not as disappointed as I thought I'd be." When he had come in here he had worn his mother's frown; now it had begun to smooth out. "I may be later on, but not right now. Now I'm just pleased that I was able to look into myself and admit something of the truth."

CHAPTER EIGHT

MATT felt the surge as the rocket lifted off the pad. The spacecraft, *Columbia Twelve*, vibrated, building gradually, like an animal trembling towards a fit of anger; then abruptly the vibrations smoothed out, but not completely. He could feel the G forces building up against his body, but it was as he had been told by those who had already made flights: the real thing was nowhere near as bad as what they had been subjected to in training. He had felt worse than this once or twice while flying test planes out in California.

"Starting to bump a little now," he reported.

"Is it getting worse?" asked his Capsule Communicator, George Raccoli, in the Control Centre, below him and swiftly getting farther away from him.

"Easing out now." He gave the fuel, oxygen and amp. readings as the drill required at this stage.

"Flight path is good, sixty-nine degrees."

Now that he was on his way all his fear seemed suddenly to have disappeared, as if it were something left behind among the smoke and dust and debris on the launching pad. The doctors had told him that one of the best antidotes to fear was occupation of the mind; and he certainly had enough to occupy him now. He could still feel the bumping, and he knew he was passing through what was called the Maximum Q area, at around 35,000 feet, where the capsule and booster encountered the highest aerodynamic forces. One flight with an empty capsule had blown up at this point. He knew that since that accident the engineers had improved the rocket, and the abort system was as near perfect as they could make it; nonetheless he felt a momentary sweat of fear and knew then that the mind could never be so occupied that there was no room for fear. Only the totally blank mind was the one that could not be afraid. And a totally blank mind could be one of the results of too much solitude. But that possibility lay ahead of him, an ambush still to be reached.

He felt the bumping beginning to build and knew at once that something had gone wrong. "Bumping getting worse."

Down in the Control Centre in the main blockhouse Raccoli, tense and strangely taciturn, all his loquacity gone, stared at the console in front of him. All round the room other men were seated before banks of instruments, but Raccoli was unaware of them: he was aware of only one man, Matt Crispin, riding the capsule along the edge of an invisible hurricane that might blow him to smithereens before the flight had really got under way.

"How is it now, Matt?" His voice had become thick with accent: one almost expected him to break into Italian.

"Still bad." Matt's voice came into the silent room, sharp, irritable sounding, as if he were unconsciously accusing the engineers for exposing him to this unexpected danger.

Raccoli watched the instruments before him; they stared back at him like banks of cold eyes. Only seconds were passing, but to Raccoli it was as if he were living through an eternity. Every instinct told him to order Matt to press the abort button; it was what he would have expected of Matt if their positions had been reversed. But when he opened his mouth to give the order, no words came: he had been too long conditioned to the aims of the project. He almost wept with anger at himself, at this betrayal of a friend; he half-raised a fist to smash it against the cold-eyed board before him.

Over on the small beach behind their bungalow Jane stood with John, Bunty and Stevie. All three children were unnaturally quiet and their quietness only added a sharper edge to her own tension. She had not slept at all last night, her ears ringing all night with Matt's last words to her on the phone. *I love you*: They would be small consolation if they proved to be his last words of all time to her. She had got up this morning hating him as much as loving him, feeling abandoned and desolate, only partly comforted by the presence of the children.

"Whoosh!" Stevie had expelled the sound more like a wet sigh than an excited shout; across on the Cape they had seen the huge rocket climbing against the morning sun like a giant fish rising to a line. "It looks like a Go!"

Jane twisted the rosary beads tightly round her hand, as if strangling herself with prayer: you couldn't pray quickly enough, the rocket rose too fast.

"Geez, it's a wonderful sight!" John stood with feet wide apart, turned full to the glare of the morning, his face a small sun of pride and excitement. "Go, Dad, go!"

Jane looked at Bunty, saw the reflection of her own fear and tension: neither of the Crispin women had time for pride at a time like this. Jane moved closer to Bunty, took her daughter's hand, and they stood stiffly, their sandaled feet buried deep in the sand, staring at the rocket now disappearing into the glittering blue of the morning. *Oh God, bring him safely back to us!*

In the blockhouse Raccoli's nerves were stretched tight, drawn out like taut fine wire that was being pulled out by the soaring rocket. Only a split second more. . . .

Then: "Getting no worse."

Raccoli looked at the instruments, licked his dry lips. "You're through Max Q."

In the capsule Matt had felt the bumping beginning to ease. "Smoothing out now. Cabin pressure beginning to drop."

He looked out and saw that the sky had now begun to darken, the first sign that he was on his way into space. His hand was still on the abort handle, had remained there as if it had a mind of its own and was prepared for any emergency. There was no time at this stage for flights of imagination; the real flight demanded all his attention. But later he would marvel at how his body reacted to all the required exercises; all the months, years, of training were paying off in smooth reflex actions. The hours spent in the procedure trainers had now made him one with this capsule. It had been impressed on all the astronauts that the capsule was an absolutely literal machine, that it was not capable in itself of an illogical manoeuvre. Ten thousand parts, seven miles of wire, every major system carrying its own alternate in case of failure: every item built into a machine as nearly foolproof as man could make it. The one percentage of possible error was the man who rode in it, the human fool always capable of making mistakes.

"Two minutes coming up." He reported again on the fuel and oxygen. "The G's are building. Now at 6."

The G forces were pressing on him, but he had experienced this so many times now over the past few years that he felt no discomfort at all. The human body was a flexible instrument whose limits still had to be found: with proper training it could be pushed to extremes that earlier generations had never dreamed of: the four-minute mile, the seven-foot jump, this absorption of high G forces. What would the bodies of John and Stevie be capable of twenty years from now?

"Stand by," said Raccoli.

This was the third hurdle, the insertion of the capsule into the orbit pattern as one might fit a lever into a slot. If it did not go in at the right angle, he could be shot out into the infinity of space. He tensed in his couch, trying not to think of any error that might have been caused by the excessive bumping. There was no way back now: the invisible slot in the sky waited for him, his only escape.

The two booster engines were shut down and fell away. "G's decreasing. Down to one and a half." He wondered how his voice sounded to them below: in his own ears it had the sound of a man hoarse with terror.

"Roger." Raccoli's voice told him nothing. *Goddamn you all* he thought irrationally, *aren't you worried for me?* But he knew they were, just as he had been for Shepard, Glenn and the others.

Then he felt the slight bump as the escape tower was jettisoned. He saw flame and smoke whip past his window, then he saw the tower fly away from him at tremendous speed, gone like a stone hurled into a bottomless sea. "Jettison tower green."

"Roger. Flight path still looks good." Raccoli's voice sounded less strained now, ready to burst into its old loquacity. "Stand by for Sustainer Engine Cut Off."

"All systems are Go." He waited, then he felt the small explosions: the posigrade rockets had fired, pushing the capsule away from the booster. "Zero G's."

He was on his way, in orbit, the journey really begun.

He was one hundred and twenty miles up, travelling at 18,000 miles an hour, weightless as an idea. He had left the influence of the earth: eternity lay ahead of him like an open road. True, he was still under the influence of the Control Centre; but if the urge took him he could break all contact with that authority. He could deliberately play the fool, succumb to the suicide urge that, he knew now, was there in every man.

Now for the first time he looked out the window. He remembered the excitement of those who had already made flights when they caught their first glimpse of the earth from such a height; all the sophistication born of their long training had disappeared in the simple entrancement of what they had seen. Now he felt exactly as they had felt. Beauty was in the eye of the beholder, but here in space all eyes must hold beauty: only the blind could not appreciate this. The world curved away beneath a blue-black sky of such richness as no painter could ever match, a stretch of horizon long enough to encompass the dreams of a lifetime. Florida lay below and behind him like a green empty glove flung on a blue-green table; at this height the sea was not sun-flecked, but was coloured only by its channels and currents. Streaks of cloud covered the earthscape like patches of wind-blown snow farther below him than he had ever seen cloud before; he remembered the fantasies of Duke's cloudland, but at this height cloud held no mystery at all. Far to the south he saw the darker cloud of Cuba poised on the edge of the world as if about to fall off; from here it, too, held no mystery or threat; Castro was only another man among the billions of tiny men who meant nothing to a man here in the throne of the sky. The air was indescribably clear: he felt that if it were not for the world curving away from him he could have seen as far west as California and even beyond, as far south as the gaping wound in the shoulder of South America that was the Amazon. All his studies had not really prepared him for this; for the first time he was seeing the world with the eye of a stranger. He felt exhilarated and at the same time humbled.

"You have a Go." Raccoli, a hundred and twenty miles below him, suddenly spoke in his ear. "A Go for at least seventy-five orbits. Godspeed."

"Roger. Understand Go for at least seventy-five orbits."

So now the journey and the test had begun; he had passed the point of no return. For the next four days he would be exposed to the dread of absolute nothingness, his only insulation the voices in his ear from the tracking stations far below. He had read of Arctic hunters who, psychologically haunted, had died of aloneness; of shipwrecked sailors who had surrendered to death from solitude days before death from thirst or hunger would have claimed them. This was his greatest fear, something that had occupied him more than the fear of disaster at the take-off or when the moment for re-entry into the earth's atmosphere would come. From now it was he, and not the capsule, that carried the flag.

He was out of contact with Cape Canaveral, had passed the Bermuda station and was well out over the Atlantic. He had loosened his chest strap and now had more ease of movement than during the actual launching. He was scheduled to test all the systems before he was too far on his journey, and he began to go through the flight plan. It was important, too, that the ground stations should establish an exact pattern of radar tracking, so he kept in constant communication with each station as he passed through its range of contact. For the first orbit there would be little time for silence: he would be talking his way round the world, a lecturer on an 18,000 mile an hour platform.

He could see the booster drifting along behind him like a dog reluctant to be left behind by its master. Eleven minutes and fifteen seconds after launching he came into contact with the tracking station in the Canary Islands. Eighteen minutes after launching he had crossed the Atlantic; somewhere the ghost of Columbus stirred. The African coast slid by below, appearing from beneath the capsule like a giant brown carpet being unrolled behind him. Facing rearwards as he was, there was a certain pleasant surprise when clouds, islands, the African mainland came suddenly into view. A quick memory came back of a boyhood journey to Vermont: riding backwards in the train the fall countryside, red and rusted, had fallen like iron splinters into his vision. But the scene below him today was so remote that there was no clash when he looked at it. The world at this height was painted in muted colours.

He crossed Africa, communicating with the Kano station in Nigeria, then he was in contact with Zanzibar. A flight surgeon now came on the air.

"*Columbia Twelve*. Would you go through the 30-minute check?"

This meant, among other things, doing some exercises on a cord attached beneath the instrument panel, taking a special sugar pill, reading from the small eye-test chart set up in front of him, and moving his head slowly to see if any disorientation was brought on. All these exercises were designed to see what effect weightlessness was having on him. So far he had found weightlessness a comfortable and agreeable experience, but the doctors had suspected there were hidden dangers in it if it went on too long. Nikolayev and Popovich appeared to have suffered no ill effects in their long flights, but it was known that Titov, another Russian, had suffered nausea and dizziness after six orbits.

Zanzibar reported that he had responded normally to the tests, then he was over the Indian Ocean, had checked in with the ship stationed there, and now he began to prepare for darkness. Night would last for forty minutes before he hurtled into another day. Too short for love-making, Jane had remarked when he had told her; all time for her was marked in terms of her own pleasures and practices. He grinned at the thought, and wondered how she and the children were sweating out this experience of his. He had a momentary twinge of conscience, then he put it out of his mind. It was too late for conscience now: the only way to compensate Jane, and then it would only be part payment, was to ensure his safe return and never to make the trip again.

He placed red covers over the lights in the cockpit and turned on the tiny lights at his finger-tips. Darkness began to slide in above, below and around him: it was as if he were hurtling backwards into a huge tunnel. All the colours of the universe suddenly seemed to be concentrated on the western horizon; the day was disappearing as a blazing cluster of gems. The sun was the centrepiece, a bluish-white perfectly round jewel that blazed with the blinding brilliance of God; now he understood why man, even in his most primitive myths, had always seen God as the source of light. The scientists could think in terms of measurable incandescence, but no one, believer or atheist, could measure this light. He had thought the lights illuminating the pad at Canaveral had been bright; they were only flickering candles compared to this. He picked up a photo filter and held it before his eyes to protect them from the brilliance.

The sun went down, the colours contracting into bright bands under the black press of night coming down from above. A black tide of shadow raced across the surface of the earth; day was squeezed out, pressed flat like molten metal on the anvil of the world. For a moment he was looking into blackness such as he had never experienced; the devil of fear raced through his blood again. Then suddenly the moon came into view and once more he had some perspective, some grasp of reality.

It was coming up time for him to contact the tracking station at Muchea in West Australia. The voice from the ship in the Indian Ocean had faded out and for a moment he again had the numbing feeling of being utterly alone in a void. Then a voice, a familiar voice, spoke to him.

"*Columbia Twelve*, this is Muchea Com Tech. Do you read us?"

"Read you loud and clear, Muchea. How are things down there, Duke?"

"Fine, Matt. You sound fine. A cobber here wants to speak to you."

"Cobber?"

"That's what he calls himself. Don't ask me what it means. I'm in a foreign land."

Another voice, vaguely familiar, came in. "This is Murrumbidgee, Matt. Good luck."

Then he remembered. Murrumbidgee, now an air commodore, was the senior Royal Australian Air Force liaison officer, in charge of the rescue team that would be standing by every time he crossed Australia during the next four days. He felt a flow of warm affection for Murrumbidgee, as if this were a moment of reunion after a long parting: indeed, it was a reunion, but he was surprised at the emotion it aroused in him. Were all emotions heightened in this environment, did weightlessness also apply to the heart?"

Then Duke was back on the air. "Check your markings. Can you sight Pleiades? And Orion?"

Duke's voice was mechanical, that of a man doing his job and only that: a stranger one hundred and sixty miles below in the pit of the night. Matt remarked the irony of the fact that the capsule should reach its apogee just as he passed over Muchea: he was farther away from Duke than he would be from any other communicator along the whole track of his flight.

When he had arrived back at Canaveral from Cape Cod last September, Oliver Shor had told him that Duke had gone up to Washington. Shor had not offered any reason for Duke's trip north, and something in the doctor's manner had warned him not to ask. He was still feeling the effect of Anne's sudden and tragic death, and in a way he had been glad of Duke's absence. He had come to regret a few of the remarks he had made to Duke, realizing now that he had spoken out of a feeling of his own guilt that he had neglected Anne, but in general he still blamed Duke for Anne's death.

Duke had been four days in Washington. The day he arrived back at Canaveral it was announced that, owing to defects that had developed in his vision which it was thought might hinder his co-ordination during an emergency, he was being withdrawn as a flight member of Project Mercury. He would remain a member of the team, however, and would act as a Capsule Communicator on all subsequent flights. The same day it was announced that Matt would be the next astronaut to make an orbital flight.

Matt drove home to the cottage he had rented for Jane and the children just north of Cocoa Beach. As he got out of the car John and Stevie plunged from the doorway like two misdirected rockets.

"It's just come over the radio!" John for some time now had been doing his best to act like a responsible teenager. His seriousness had become even a little pompous, but Matt had said nothing: as he had told Jane, they could have had a delinquent for a son. John was in his last year at high school, the brightest boy in his class, and like his father before him, had his sights on M.I.T. But today he was no more than a boy who was intensely proud of his father. "You're next, Dad!"

"Can I have your autograph, mister?" Stevie was twelve now, a boy who took nothing nor anyone, not even himself, seriously. The world was to be enjoyed, even gently poked fun at: the world would always need one or two like him.

The boys each grabbed an arm and pulled him towards the house. Their pride in him was heart-warming. At first he had been worried that they might have become superior and swollen-headed about him ("What's your father? *Mine's* an astronaut."); but Jane had put a stop to that very early in the piece. Her firmness towards the boys in this respect had brought on a second worry: was she deliberately stamping on the boys' enthusiasm to show her displeasure at his being a member of the team? She had never mentioned again her opposition to his joining the team, but over the past 18 months, since Alan Shepard's first flight and through all the subsequent flights, he had noticed that when a launching was due she was invariably quieter than even the wife of the astronaut involved. She did not approve of his belonging to the team and he knew now that she never would. But he had been relieved to find that her attitude towards the boys was not born of spite against him. It was her innate good sense coming to the fore again.

She was waiting in the living-room for him with Bunty. She was wearing a new green linen dress, one he hadn't seen before, and Bunty was in new yellow slacks and a tan shirt. Bunty had missed her mother's beauty, but she was still an attractive girl, ambitious to be a woman, bored by her father's job: romance for her had nothing to do with machines and space. "Are the photographers with you, Daddy?"

"I told you." Stevie kicked off the rubber scuffs he had been wearing, prowled barefoot about the room, doing his imitation of Enos, the chimpanzee that had made an orbital flight. There

286

were only two photos tacked on the wall above his bed: one of Matt in space uniform and one of Enos. "Mom gets us all dressed up like it was a christening or something. All for nothing."

"The day I take you and John to a christening in just a pair of clean shorts and a T-shirt, may the Pope put a black mark against my name." Jane looked at Matt. "If you did bring home some photographers with you, I didn't want us looking like a family on relief. That was all."

He noticed the tenseness in her, but did not comment on it. He smiled, trying to be casual, as if this were just another day. "They'll be here tomorrow. I told them you were suffering from an Australian virus called didjeridoo."

"You might as well go back to your homework," Jane said to Bunty, who looked disappointed now she had been told she was not going to be besieged by photographers. When Bunty and the boys had gone, Jane turned back to Matt. "When you start cracking your corny jokes about Australia, I know you've got something on your mind. What is it?"

"I thought you had something on yours." He poured himself a beer and a dry sherry for Jane. Her taste for sherry amused their friends on the base, some of whom had thought it was only a flavouring for soups and desserts. She rarely had more than one glass each evening, but he noticed now that the bottle's contents seemed to have shrunk considerably since last night. He walked across to her with the drink, kissed her on the mouth and smelled the sherry on her breath. He wondered how many she had had since she had heard the news on the radio of his selection to make the next flight.

"I thought you might have phoned to let me know you had been chosen."

"I wanted to come home and tell you. I didn't think they'd have it on the air so soon. I got held up."

"It came over an hour ago."

He sat down beside her on the cane couch, propping some cushions behind him. The living-room faced out across the Banana River; the westering sun streamed in in a yellow blaze. He got up, adjusted the venetian blinds against the glare, then returned to sit beside her. The room had suddenly become dark and cool, lit only by bands of yellow light reflected from the ceiling. He composed himself, determined not to argue with her, to offer her all the comfort he could without being hypocritical about it.

287

"I'm sorry, honey."

"For being chosen?" She drank almost half her sherry at one gulp. To his knowledge she had never been drunk in her life, but it looked as if she might be this evening.

"For not calling you," he said evenly, ignoring the knife in her voice. "Something else held me up, besides. Did you hear the news about Duke?"

She looked at him sharply. "What news? I turned the radio off as soon as I heard the piece about you."

"He's been scrubbed from the team as a pilot. Bad eyes or something."

"I don't believe it."

"Don't believe he's been scrubbed or the bad eyes?"

She put down her glass on the table beside the couch, turned her back on it as she twisted to face him. The gesture, even if it was only temporary, pleased him. "Did you speak to him?"

"No. I didn't go looking for him, if that's what you mean."

"I think we ought to drive over and see him right now."

"Are you more concerned about him than you are about me?" He regretted the words as soon as he said them: they had a cruelty he had not intended.

She turned round, picked up her drink and sipped it, then held the glass against her breast. "If you want to know the truth, I'm trying not to think about you. If I have someone else to worry about, I'll feel better. Or rather I shan't feel so bad."

He took her free hand in his and was surprised at its coldness. "Some time in February it will all be over."

"That's what worries me," she said, deliberately misconstruing his words.

"The others have come back. We haven't lost one man."

"The Russians have."

"That's only rumour. We don't know for sure."

"You're going up for longer than anyone else ever has. Four days. You haven't talked about it, but I've read about it. What solitude can do to you."

"Do you think I'm the type who's likely to crack in those circumstances?"

She scanned his face, looking deep into the man she knew better than anyone else in the world. She was still bitter about his decision to join the team. She had done her best to scour the bitterness from herself, but there had remained a sediment of which she could not rid herself: there was a possessiveness about her love of which she was secretly ashamed but about which she

288

could do nothing. The fact that so much of her married life had been spent apart from Matt only increased her possessiveness towards him. But however bitter she felt, she could never be less than honest with him.

"No," she said, and her voice softened for a moment. "If anyone can stand it, you can. I know Duke couldn't have."

"And you think that's the reason he's drawn out?"

"It could be. But I don't blame him."

"Neither do I. All of us in the team have had that understanding. No man goes down in the others' estimation if he feels he wants to drop out. I think we understand the reasons for it better than anyone else ever could. I don't believe this about his eyesight, but I guess there's a reason for that. Maybe someone else suggested it."

"I wish they'd suggest it for you."

He put down his glass. He opened his arms and after a moment's hesitation she moved closer to him, laid her head on his shoulder. "Honey, I'm committed. Not just to the project, but to myself. Mostly to myself, I think. I admit, as far as you and the kids are concerned, I'm selfish, maybe even cruel. I don't know. About being cruel, I mean. I don't mean to be, and cruelty always implies a certain amount of intention. I'm selfish, but I've reached a stage where I can't do much about that. All I can do is go through with the flight, get it out of my system, if you like. Then, as they say in the movies, everything is gonna be all right."

That last had been an old joke between them for years, especially since old movies on television: they had tossed the tired old clichés between them as if they were *bon mots*. He smiled now, but she didn't smile back: her own joke was a bitter one: "You mean it's bigger than both of us."

He stopped smiling. "I didn't say that."

"That was what you meant."

"Honey, why can't you accept this like the other wives have?"

She had her own cliché, which was also a truth: "I love you."

"The other wives love their husbands."

"I know that. And I wish I could be like them. No, honestly. But I can't. I just don't have their capacity for sacrifice." She lifted her face, stared at him for a moment, then kissed him with a sort of desperate resignation. "I'll try, darling. We're both selfish, and I guess we'll both be that way till this thing is over." She kissed him again, lightly this time, then stood up, straightening the creases in her dress. "Now I think we should drive over and see Duke."

"You can go if you like. But not me." He got up, opened the blinds again; the room glowed in the blood-red glare from beyond the river. "I feel sorry for him, that he's dropped out. Being in the team meant as much to him as it does to me. Maybe more."

"I think he might need you now."

"I've got nothing to offer him. He killed Anne just as surely as if he had thrown her into the sea himself." He spoke with too much emphasis: again there was the feeling of guilt.

She shook her head. "I don't believe that."

"Why not?"

"Well, why do you believe he was responsible for her death?"

He hedged: he could not tell her about the diary. "I've seen more of Duke than you have. I know how he thinks. How he feels about women."

"I doubt that."

"Why are you all of a sudden on his side?"

"Because I'm beginning to understand him. I've learned things about him. About his mother, for instance. She was a real tyrant, a narrow-minded bigoted old Tartar."

"You're blaming her for what he is? You amateur psychiatrists. What about Pete, the others in the family? Mrs. Dalmead didn't ruin them."

"You don't know them as well as you know Duke. Perhaps they've got their problems, too. But I'll bet Duke gave up his religion, has been running away from Cleo all this time, all because he was running away from his mother."

"Well, you think what you like. I appreciate that psychiatry has its uses—I've experienced some of it myself in training—but I also think it often provides good excuses for people who won't face up to the fact that they, and only they, are to blame for what they've done with their lives. Duke's made a mess of his life and those of half a dozen others and I don't think his mother can be blamed for all of it. I never liked her and maybe she was what you said, but Duke's got to take some of the blame. He's ambitious, selfish——"

"Who isn't?" She turned the knife against him, but she did not drive it in; she did not want to get into any bitter argument with him. "Perhaps Mrs. Dalmead wasn't responsible for all he's done. But she helped, I'm convinced of that."

"You're getting to be more American every day. Blaming

290

everything on Mom." She laughed ironically, but he went on: "That's one of the troubles with this country today. We have so much money we can go to a psychiatrist or analyst and have *him* tell us what's wrong with us. Pretty soon everyone will have his own analyst, a *de facto* member of the family. That'll be a new status symbol, be a two- or three-analyst family. When I was a kid we solved our own problems, took the blame ourselves for whatever mistakes we made. America wasn't built by men suffering from mother domination——" He argued on, edging away from the suggestion that he should go with Jane to visit Duke. Deep within him he knew that his attitude had a mixture of bases, something more than just anger at what he sincerely believed Duke had done to Anne. For one thing, there was a rejection of Duke: he had taken advantage of Anne's death to rebel against Duke's domination of *him*. That would be one for the psychiatrists and analysts; but he would never confess it to Jane.

"It's hard to believe you're a product of the mid-twentieth century in America," she said. "You're talking like someone out of a 1925 Western. Who's your hero? Jack Hoxie? Tom Mix? I agree with you that too many people rush to analysts, but that doesn't say *some* of them haven't deep-rooted troubles they can't solve. And I think Duke is one of them. I'll bet after this news today, especially on top of your being chosen for the next flight, he's got a problem that's threatening to blow his head off. And I think it would be a decent gesture if you went to see him."

"He'd misunderstand. Especially after what I said to him up at Cape Cod."

"You never did tell me what you said there."

"And I'm not going to. But if I went to him now, he'd think I'd just come to crow over him."

"Do you mind if I go over and see him?" She noticed his hesitation. "I wouldn't suggest this if Cleo was already down here. But she's not—he's over there on his own——"

"Okay." He moved to her and kissed her on the cheek. "I'd be a heel if I said no. I think he's past deserving anyone's help or sympathy, but I can't stop you from throwing him a rope if you feel you should. You might put a loop in it, though, as a suggestion."

"At a time like this," she said coldly, "when you've got what you want, you might have a little charity for someone else who didn't get what he wanted."

And now, five months later and half a world away, he remembered the disappointment in her voice, the way she had looked at him, as if he had revealed a meanness in himself that she had never suspected. He had not really meant to say what he had said: the words had slipped from him, let loose by the treacherous tongue always ready to betray in a man the weaknesses, the vices, that were all in all men: was it coincidental that most saints were silent men? But she had turned and gone out of the room before he could speak again. He had tried again later to retract the words, but the time had never seemed opportune and in the end he had decided it was best to forget it and hope that she had done the same.

Duke's voice came in over the headphones: "The doctors want a blood pressure reading."

"I am sending it."

"Blood pressure received. In good shape. You'll be picking up Woomera in a minute or two. Good luck, Matt. See you next time around."

There was no envy in the voice, but he knew that had their positions been reversed, *he* would have felt envious. He felt a spark of sympathy for Duke, the first he had felt in months. He moved on through the southern night, a slow moving star that was an intruder in the heavens, man's tiny bleating challenge to the mystery of infinity.

2

Duke took off the headphones and handed them to Briggs, one of the officers from the Australian Weapons Research Establishment. "I'll get a breath of air."

"There's some coffee," said Briggs, a black-haired man with a broken nose who looked more like a broken-down boxer than a top class radio engineer. "I've been experimenting, trying to make *American* coffee."

Duke grinned. "Will you be offended if I have tea? *That* you do know how to make."

Briggs grinned in reply, made a gesture with his thumb and sat down at the Flight Controller's console. Duke patted him on the shoulder, then crossed the room and went out through the door that Murrumbidgee Finn held open for him. As they stepped out of the air-conditioned building the hot night air fell on them like a blanket.

"Phew! What's the temperature out here?"

"Don't know right now." Murrumbidgee offered Duke a cigarette. "It was a hundred and five this afternoon."

"What happened to the Fremantle Doctor today?" This was the southerly breeze that usually came in late in the day here in south-west West Australia, to bring down the temperature and make the night bearable.

"It got side-tracked, I guess." Murrumbidgee squinted up past the smoke of his cigarette at the night sky. "He's in the best place tonight."

"Yeah," said Duke, and did not miss the quick glance that Murrumbidgee gave him. They had met for the first time when Duke had come out here to Australia last March. Murrumbidgee was now almost fifty, still a big dynamic man, still as outspoken as a rebel aircraftsman, even though he was now an air commodore. Duke had been welcomed like an old friend, and the two of them had now reached a personal understanding that made their working partnership an easy one. Duke had not discussed his break with Matt with Murrumbidgee, but the latter obviously suspected, or had been told by Jane, that something was wrong. But no matter how outspoken the big man might be, he knew when to mind his own business.

Above them the telemetry towers turned slowly against the sky like giant angular flowers seeking the energy that kept them alive. The scrub stretched away behind the Control building, in the darkness a reminder of how vast and lonely this land was. Duke could not remember when he had felt so far away from home.

"You hear from Cleo today? How is she?" Murrumbidgee remembered the big foolish girl who had too much sympathy and love for her own good. He was always circumspect when asking about her, but he was convinced now that Duke never even suspected that he knew Cleo better than as a passing acquaintance.

"Oh, she's fine," Duke said, and felt some of his restlessness go as he thought of Cleo.

She and Caroline had arrived in Florida two weeks after he had returned from Cape Cod and Anne's funeral. Cleo had resigned from her job at the United Nations, had somehow or other got out of her lease on her apartment, had arranged for the furniture to be stored, then had piled herself and Caroline into the car and driven south at a speed that had earned her a ticket in every State through which she had passed. It was as if, now that Duke wanted them to set up home together again, she had to be with him quickly before he changed his mind. He had been amused, flattered and finally deeply warmed by her rush to rejoin him.

When she and Caroline had arrived he had been surprised at how pleased and relieved he was to have them with him.

The pleasure and relief had gone on through the succeeding weeks. Then he had begun to feel contentment, a certain peace such as he could not remember ever having felt before. He and Cleo had not slipped easily into the renewal of their married life; nor had he and Caroline found their new relationship one that did not have its awkward moments. They had lived too long apart to accept at once the everyday idiosyncrasies of each other; they cautiously explored each other and made allowances. Duke found it easier with Cleo than he did with Caroline. With his daughter he was not sure where to draw the line of authority; yet he knew if he did not establish some authority with her, no matter how indirect, it would be no time at all before she came to despise him as much as she had before. He had never really been a parent, but some instinct told him that a child (and Caroline was his child, no matter how old she might think she was) needed someone to look up to, respected authority more than doting spoiling kindness. He recognized however the dangers of too much authority, of trying to impose the pattern of his thinking on Caroline. He had begun at last to escape from the shadow of his own mother, and he did not want to throw his own shadow over his own child.

He had found a house for them south of Cocoa Beach. "It's lovely, darling," Cleo had said as he had brought them into it. It was a modest cottage built with all the loving care and pride in his work of a speculative builder; but Cleo would have been happy to hang *Chez Nous* on a Bedouin tent. "Are we close to Matt and Jane?"

"They're on the other side of town."

"We must have them over." Caroline had gone through into another room, already sensing that her mother and father would need their moments alone to get to know each other again. Cleo smiled and kissed him on the cheek. "But not tonight."

"No, not tonight."

She had another of her moments of perception. "Is there something wrong?"

"Matt and I don't talk to each other any more," he said slowly.

She opened her eyes wide: incapable of lasting bitterness herself, she could not imagine why other people could not solve their quarrels by concession and understanding. "Does he not want to talk to you, or is it the other way round?"

"He just walks right by me. So far we've managed to cover it up from the others over at Canaveral. They think he's become a bit withdrawn since he was nominated for the next flight. That's happened with one or two of the others."

"What do they think about you? I mean do they think you've become withdrawn, too, since you were taken off the flight team?"

"I don't know. Maybe they do. It's no use trying to kid myself or them. I was disappointed."

He carried her bags into the main bedroom and she followed him. "I was terribly shocked, darling, when we read the news. I mean, you look so all right. I just can't believe there's anything physically wrong with you."

So far he, Shor and the members of the board had managed to conceal the real reason for his withdrawal from the flight team. He was still adapting himself to the frame of mind necessary to accept and to hide the lie; his disappointment did not have to be hidden, for everyone would understand that, no matter why he had been scrubbed. "For all practical purposes, I'm still a hundred per cent. In orbit, though, you need to be about a hundred and twenty-five per cent. I'm just not that good, that's all."

"In a way I'm glad," she said. "My worries are over. Jane's aren't."

Caroline had come to the door of the bedroom. "Are you terribly disappointed, Daddy?"

He stood between them, directly in the current of their sympathy. "Yes," he said, and something went out from him to establish contact with each of them: he felt the pain of love, something he had forgotten. Or, he told himself with brutal candour, had perhaps never experienced. "But I could feel worse than I do. Being on my own I might not have been able to bear it."

The next morning Jane had driven over to welcome Cleo and Caroline. He was just getting into his car to drive to the base when she pulled in off the road. "You look like a new man," she said as she got out of her car. "Perhaps I'm being un-diplomatic saying that, but I've been hoping for years that this would happen. And now it has, I think you look better for it."

He grinned, even pleased to concede defeat. "I feel better, too. How does that sound to you?"

"Wonderful." She leaned on the windshield of the Corvette, looking down at him as he sat behind the wheel. "How bad is it between you and Matt?"

"Pretty bad."

She made a masculine motion of spitting in disgust. "I've been praying for years for you and Cleo to get together again—no, really," she said when she saw him raise an eyebrow, "I'm a firm believer in the efficacy of prayer. It's been answered, hasn't it?" She gestured towards the house: from the kitchen came the sound of Cleo and Caroline singing as they washed up the breakfast dishes: neither of them had tuneful voices and "Moon River" had broken its banks, but they were enjoying the sound they made.

"You'll wear your knees out trying to get Matt to change his attitude."

"Does all the blame lie with him, Duke?"

He considered a moment. A jet whistled overhead, its sound scoring the glassy stillness of the morning. "Not all, maybe. But my part of the blame goes back a long way. He's the one who's slammed the door shut now."

She straightened up. "I'll talk to him," she said determinedly.

"No, Jane," he said quietly. "Let him work it out himself. Don't push him into it. I *know*." He nodded towards the house; the singing had stopped, lost in laughter. "Nobody pushed me into going back with Cleo. It was my own idea. And that's why I think it will last." He started up the car. "If you want to do anything, go back to your prayers."

"I thought you didn't believe in them?"

"I'm revising a lot of my beliefs."

And the revision of his beliefs was still going on. He was not like Saul: he had not suddenly seen the light on the road to Damascus. Rather it was as if the truth were only a faint glimmer, a distant star in a galaxy of other, misleading stars. His training for an orbital flight had been more than physical and mechanical. There had been mental training, a probing into fields that had never really concerned him before. Now space was the Unknown; but the Unknown had come to have a double meaning for him. The more he had read, the more mysteries he had discovered; wisdom could not keep pace with wonder. He knew of the arguments that went on among the scientists and engineers working on the project; their beliefs went right through the religious spectrum from dogmatic atheism through humanism, rationalism, agnosticism to dogmatic Catholicism. Atheists, agnostics, Jews, Christians, they were all represented among the project workers; the tower of Babel was a gantry on a launching pad. It was impossible to explore the possibilities of space and

296

not come to have opinions about the origins of what it contained. He had found with himself that the farther he probed into the mysteries of space, the farther he delved into the mysteries of himself. He had begun to believe in God again, something he had never expected nor sought; and the stronger his belief, the stronger was his recognition that he had never really lost his belief. It had been hidden behind clouds of self-delusion. But now the clouds were being dispelled, he was being guided by a faith which, though still shaky, did at least give him a lead. He had not yet reached the stage of praying nor had he gone to Mass yet; but he no longer turned his back on the thought of such practices. He was taking things gradually, realizing that experience suggests truths more than it imposes them. He had discovered very late the value of caution, but he knew that in the end it would repay him its use of it. Truth was never tarnished because one approached it with prudence.

In the weeks before this flight there had been occasions when Matt had *had* to speak to him. But all their old intimacy had gone. He had allowed Matt to set the tone of their discussions, always on matters relating to the coming flight, and Matt had chosen to speak to him as he spoke to dozens of others on the team: impersonally, almost as if he had already embarked on the flight, was already preoccupied with its exigencies and dangers.

On the day he was scheduled to leave Canaveral for Australia, he came home to find that Jane had arrived there with Bob and Nell Crispin. He had not seen the elder Crispins since Anne's funeral, and as he walked in the door to face them he had a moment of panic. Had they come to accuse him of something, had Matt changed his mind and told them of the diary? But a moment later the smiles on their faces held no accusation against him: they were pleased to see him. He shook hands with Bob and kissed the cheek of Nell, suddenly feeling an almost filial affection for them.

"My, look at the grey in his hair!" Nell exclaimed. Since his retirement as a pilot in the team he had, humouring Cleo and his own vanity, begun to grow his hair longer; since he would not any more be required to wear the close-fitting helmet, he did not have to wear his hair closely crew-cut. The longer hair along his temples now emphasized the grey there. "You make me feel old, Duke. It seems only yesterday you and Matt were teenagers like Caroline——"

"Careful, Mum," said Jane. "Caroline is a very adult teenager. She mightn't like your reference."

297

Caroline smiled. In the past couple of months all the sullenness had gone from her face and she had become much more like her mother, sparked by a zest for living in which self-sympathy had shrivelled and died. "I'm not offended, Mrs. Crispin."

"Anne used to get angry when anyone called her a teenager." Duke looked at Nell Crispin as she spoke, but there was no hint of tears in her voice; she had adjusted herself to the loss of her daughter, was not going to spend the rest of her life wearing her grief like a membership badge of the bereft. "Even from the time she was thirteen."

"I think it's a horrible term anyway," said Cleo.

Bob Crispin winked at Duke, jerked his head towards the door and the two men escaped from the room. They went out through the kitchen and Duke took a couple of cans of beer from the refrigerator as they passed through. They sat out on the small patio, looking out across the beach towards the ocean. Half a dozen shrimp boats beat their way south a long way out, retracing the faded line of the horizon. Some children played on the sands, nibbling at the early afternoon quiet with their fragile shouts. Far down the beach a figure walked alone, its tiny shape trembling in the afternoon haze like a distant memory that would at any moment slip from the mind.

"I didn't know whether we should come," Bob said, taking the beer Duke offered him. "But Nell insisted. She wanted to be with Jane and the children."

"Why did you have doubts about coming?"

Bob shrugged. "I don't know. Since Anne's death, I guess I've come to half-expect the worst all the time——" Duke remembered all the small crises of Bob's early life, his diet of emergencies. But he had never been morbid. "It's wrong, I know. But——" He nodded up towards the Cape. "There's so much can go wrong with these launchings."

"I hope you haven't mentioned any of them in front of Jane."

"Oh no! Heck, Nell would never forgive me if I did anything like that. We both know how Jane feels. That's one of the reasons Nell wanted to come down here." Then he grimaced and waved a hand in front of his face, as if brushing away a cobweb of embarrassment. "I understand you and Matt aren't hitting it off these days."

Duke could understand the pain in the older man and he lied to assuage it. "The women think it's worse than it is. Matt's a bit keyed up, that's all. I'd be the same if I were making the flight."

Bob Crispin looked down towards the children on the beach. Now that Matt's flight was close, he was filled with a mixture of pride and fear. He felt no envy for the latter's having become a hero; all his life he had aspired to the same status, but he was content now to bask in the reflection of his son's glory. At the same time, however, his old sense of impending disaster had come back: you had to prepare for the worst, be prepared for death and its stain, grief, before they happened. He was only half-convinced that Matt would return alive from this mission. But he could not confess his fear: that would imply a certain cowardice, something he had always tried to avoid. Something, he was secretly glad, in which he had never really been tested.

"You and Matt have come a long way together. It 'ud be a pity if something spoiled it all just now."

"Everything will be all right when the flight is over," Duke said, and hoped he sounded more confident than he felt.

Late in the afternoon Cleo and Caroline drove him down to Patrick Air Force Base to pick up the transport plane that was taking him to San Francisco. Caroline kissed him goodbye, then walked away to leave her mother and father alone.

Cleo looked after her. "She's very discreet and understanding!"

"She gets the second quality from you. I don't know where she gets her discretion from. Neither of us have it."

During the long years of their separation they had had these goodbyes often: always stiff and constrained, each afraid of committing himself or herself too far. But this time, their first farewell since their reunion, there was no strain at all. Cleo almost welcomed the chance to say goodbye, as if it were some proof to her of the permanence of their reunion. The lover who never left your side was the one whose love had never been tested. And she was certain now that Duke would survive any test.

"Jane tells me her brother will be at Muchea." She remembered the only time she had tested her own love, when her unfaithfulness had only proved her faithfulness. "Remember me to him."

Duke looked at her in surprise. "I didn't know you knew Murrumbidgee."

"I met him once when he came to New York, oh, ages ago." She had come to learn, almost too late, that love was a contention:

total surrender, including telling the truth, brought no lasting joy.

"Did you like him?"

She had been to bed with him and now she couldn't remember him. "I've forgotten. He's terribly large and hearty, that's about all I remember."

"That's Murrumbidgee," said Duke, remembering the welcoming slap that had almost broken his back when he had first met Murrumbidgee last March.

Then Caroline came back and it was time for him to go. He kissed Cleo, then kissed Caroline again. "Look after her, Caroline. I'll be back late next week."

"Daddy." A breeze came across the airfield, blew Caroline's hair across her face. She looked frighteningly young and vulnerable, and suddenly he saw her as the dark twin of Anne. What dreams of love did she have, what man lay in ambush for her? "Daddy, I'm glad you're not the one who's making the orbital flight. Do you mind my saying that?"

He looked at her, at Cleo, then back at Caroline. "No, honey, I don't mind in the least. Once I was eager for the glory of it, but not any more."

And now he stood here in the West Australian scrub, sweating in the hot night, standing sentinel to Matt, who was getting all the glory. He had told Caroline a lie. He regretted bitterly that he was not the one making the flight. He felt a moment of envy, of furious antagonism towards Matt, and he was glad of the darkness. He had come to know, even on short acquaintance, that Murrumbidgee, for all his extrovert behaviour, was a man of remarkable perception. It would not do to have him know that one member of the Project Mercury team envied and resented another. As much as did Matt, Duke also carried the image of national prestige. He wore the face of America and found it a stifling mask.

"Let's go in." Murrumbidgee threw away his cigarette. "I think I'd rather catch cold from the air-conditioning than stifle in this."

Duke, bogged in his thoughts, caught only one word. "Stifle?"

"What's the matter with you, Duke?"

"Nothing." Duke recovered himself. He looked up at the night sky, the domain that he had once hoped would be his. Trying to cover up, he threw out a phrase he had read in the morning paper. "I was thinking of myself as a spectator to history in the making."

"I read that editorial, too. I don't like that sort of mullarkey.

300

There are too many people who always suspect history in the making—oh, not for the event itself, but whether it really will be history some day. They have little faith in the intelligence of posterity. Have you ever wondered what happened to Archimedes' bath water? His wife, a sceptic, probably pulled the plug out—as far as she was concerned, history was something for the plughole. A lot of Aussies are like that."

"You bloody Australians," said Duke. "Don't you ever get worked up about *anything*?"

Murrumbidgee grinned. "Only unimportant things. It's bad for national progress, but good for the individual's ulcers. This country doesn't have a national temper. There were some dandy tempers here when we were a bunch of colonies, but once we became a nation—" He shrugged. "We'll wake up one day. I just hope the day isn't too late."

Duke didn't want to agree with him for fear that Murrumbidgee, perversely, would then argue with him. Matt had once told him that Australians invited criticism, then took umbrage because you accepted the invitation. He changed the subject, looking up at the sky once more. "Matt must be over the Pacific now."

"I remember once," said Murrumbidgee as he opened the door to the Control building, "I flew a Canberra west to east across Australia, Perth to Sydney. Got a push from a tail-wind and did it in just under three and a half hours. I thought that was moving!" He stopped for a moment and looked back up at the sky. "I know it's progress and all that, but I don't think I'd want to be hurtling round the globe at 18,000 miles an hour. I miss the horse and buggy days of flying. I flew an old Gladiator in Greece——"

"Shut that bloody door!" yelled someone from inside, then saw whom they were addressing. "Sir."

"Up you," said the air commodore, and winked at Duke. "There has been no progress in politeness. They may be scientists, but they're still the grandsons of bullock drivers."

3

"*Columbia Twelve*, this is Hawaii Com Tech. Do you consider yourself Go for the next orbit?"

"That is affirmative. I am Go for the next orbit. Check my number. This will be orbit eighteen, correct?"

"Eighteen it will be. One up on Titov."

Matt did not reply to the last comment, but checked out. He was not up here to break records, to prove he was any better than the Russians or even the Americans who had gone before him. He had been set a mission of seventy-five orbits; that was what he had to achieve, no more and no less. He had come to know that progress in science was not achieved by trying to be better than the other man; no true scientist was ever a competitor. In bull sessions with the scientists at Canaveral and Langley, they had impressed this on him—"Once you become a competitor, you're working for someone else," one of them had said. "For a government department, for a private outfit, it doesn't matter which. You're working for someone else, not for the advancement of science."

"Is that the end in itself?" Matt had asked. "I thought the idea was to be working for the advancement of man?"

The other man had shrugged. His name was Dan Israel, and he was a mild inoffensive little man, who looked as if even butterflies might attack him. "One follows the other. Emotion never solved any scientific problems. Take the guys who are looking for a cure for cancer. They aren't helped by the thought of the millions who die from cancer. Writers like to make a lot of how such things spur the guys on, but it just ain't so. Ask these fellers here—" Israel nodded around at the five or six other men in the room. "We were all working on this project when the Russians put Gagarin into orbit. Sure, we were all upset by the news. But it didn't help us any. We were useless for the next two or three days. Then we settled down, got the thought of the Russians out of our heads, stopped reading all the editorials and the speeches by Congressmen telling us to get off our asses and get cracking, and we just went on working the way we'd been going. We *knew* we were on the right track. Oh sure, the manufacturing end of it picked up a bit. But research doesn't happen any quicker for someone standing there cracking a whip. So un-American as it may sound, Matt, we do better when we forget about the Russians. We're scientists and engineers, not Olympic high jumpers."

He had done his best to agree with Dan Israel. It had not been easy. Israel was one of many scientists on the project: any blame for any of their errors sank in the swamp of their anonymity. But *he*, he was the flag-carrier; the army of the project all marched in the shadows, but not he. No one ever gave a flight its official name: it was never known as MA-1, MA-10 or whatever. It was known as Shepard's flight, or Glenn's or Carpenter's or

Meredith's. This would be known as Crispin's flight, whether it was successful or not, and he had no more claim to anonymity than he had to immortality. Nonetheless he agreed whole-heartedly with one point in Israel's argument: he worked better when he forgot the Russians. A dedicated pilot was of more use to the project than a dedicated American. To paraphrase Israel, one followed the other.

California was now in contact with him. "The aeromeds are ready for another check."

"I am just about to have supper. A ham sandwich with dessert of apple sauce and one xylose tablet. Who dreamed up this menu anyway?"

He finished the sandwich, then put the end of the apple sauce container, no more than a toothpaste tube, into his mouth and squirted. He let the container float in the air while he took his sugar tablet from its phial, then he put both containers away. He had already become accustomed to the convenience of weightless objects. He remembered the old vaudeville gag of the comedian who hung his coat on a nail in the air: the gag wouldn't get a laugh in the weightlessness of space.

"What reaction?" That was one of the aeromedics in California.

He considered a moment before he replied. "There's some squeamishness."

"Are you going to be sick? Any desire to vomit?"

"Not as bad as that."

"This squeamishness checks with Titov's reaction. Report at end of next orbit."

But by the finish of the next orbit the squeamishness had gone. He had been in flight for twenty-four hours, had not slept for thirty hours. It had been expected that he would try to sleep after twelve hours in orbit, but he had not felt like it and the aeromedics had given him permission to stay awake as long as he felt like it. Apart from the natural thrill of being in orbit, there had been continual diversions that had stalled off sleep. He had watched thunderstorms *below* him, the sky *beneath* him boiling with clouds that looked like blue-black mud; for the first time he had felt he was a *real* spectator of the elements, beyond their threat. He had watched dust storms, sunsets, sunrises, falling stars that had made him feel as if he were standing still despite his tremendous speed; his mind had been kept awake by wonder, and had he slept he would have been as restless as a boy waiting to begin his first vacation in a foreign land.

303

California slid by below him for the umpteenth time, the sun-faded fringe of America. He looked down, remembering Muroc and the flights in the old US-XP over the desert, remembering the day he had guided Duke down when the latter had blacked out from anoxia, when Duke had been headed for *here*, the land beyond the clouds. That was all so long ago, in another century.

He dragged his eyes back from the scene outside and below, aware again, as he always was, of the constricting interior of the capsule. The instrument panel, two feet in front of him, seemed to press in on him; even the suit he wore was constricting, wrapping him like a shroud. But it took only a moment to adjust himself: this constricting environment guaranteed his safety. Space had its temptations, but they were all fatal.

He was weary now, physically and mentally; he did not need the aeromedics to tell him his reactions were slowing up. "This is *Columbia Twelve*. I am going to try and sleep now. Eight hours if possible. Now I lay me down to sleep——"

"*Columbia Twelve*, this is your guardian angel. Sleep tight."

Matt made himself as comfortable as possible for sleeping in the contour couch. He settled down, glad that he had waited so long: as tired as he was, sleep would come more easily. There was no fear now, or if there was it was dormant: the rats were no longer gnawing at him. This, of course, was another danger: it was possible to become so confident as to become careless. He had seen it happen to other pilots during the two wars he had fought in, on the day-to-day flights on peacetime commercial runs; he had seen it happen to Duke. So before he fell asleep he thought of fear for a moment, the guardian angel of those who might become too confident.

The world spun beneath *Columbia Twelve*. The capsule had now flown half a million miles, the distance to the moon and back; romance and fantasy were gradually being reduced to mathematical sums. While Matt slept the ambitions of his youth were diminished; the mysterious world of those years was wrapped securely in the tracking pattern of his flight. He did not dream while he slept, which was a pity; because old dreams, like old houses, were being demolished by his achievement. His dreams of Paris and London, Duke's dreams of Samarkand and Tashkent, were nothing now; romance now lay in the names of faraway stars. Man would always need his dreams, but it was his tragedy that as he achieved them he also destroyed them.

Matt was over Africa when he woke. It was coincidental that

he woke at dawn; day and night had flickered by a dozen times while he slept. Light streamed by the capsule; day came at him backwards. Coming awake he sat up suddenly, felt a moment of dizziness that he put down to his weightlessness. He checked in with the tracking station at Zanzibar, was medically checked as he passed over Muchea, and began to eat breakfast as he saw the Pacific begin to slide below him. There was no squeamishness after this meal, and he settled down to another routine period of wakefulness. Day and night no longer held any meaning as measurements of time. He grinned at a small joke: he was both a day and night worker, a moonlighter of express speed.

Time passed, and now he was bored. He had been warned that this was one of the dangers of solitude; man could crack as much from doing nothing as he could from overwork. He had given up taking pictures: even space had its limits of photographic interest: he did not want to be tagged as a man who had brought back hundreds of boring pictures of his vacation. He did his exercises on the bungee cord, but even that had now become a bore; the treacherous thought insinuated itself into his mind that he was in such excellent physical condition that it was ridiculous to go on exercising. He tried to read the books he had brought with him: *A Stillness at Appomattox*; a volume of Mark Twain; a volume of Thurber. He had deliberately chosen not to bring with him any books that dealt with the immediate present; his reading was to be an escape as far as possible from here and now. He had even considered bringing a volume on ancient Greece or Frazer's *The Golden Bough*; in the end he had decided that his escapism must also provide him with something that really interested him. But now the War between the States and the War between the Sexes did not interest him at all; he stuck a little longer with Mark Twain, but then he, too, began to pall. Boredom had become part of the atmosphere of the capsule.

He was on his forty-fifth or sixth orbit, he had lost count and did not care any more, when he passed over Muchea in daylight.

"This is *Columbia Twelve*. I am on fly-by-wire at present."

Duke's voice came in: "How do you feel?"

There was less restraint between them now. Matt had become so bored that any voice was welcome. Up here, too, personal conflicts seemed to have become academic. How could you argue with a man from another world?

"Okay. No worse than on the Berlin airlift." He hadn't meant to say that. There was malice there that he hadn't intended. He shook his head in his helmet, angry at himself; then felt a moment of panic, felt the sweat break quickly on him. That was one of the symptoms of cracking under the strain of solitude, saying things which had not been in your mind the instant before you opened your mouth. That had once been Duke's failing, having a tongue that had its own treacherous words.

Duke's voice came back cool, impersonal, just tinged with more good humour than Matt felt he deserved. "Watch out for buzzing Russians."

"I'll do that," he said, and forced a laugh, hoping it would not sound too hollow and sarcastic over the distance between them. He changed the subject. "One thing that would break up the monotony up here would be some Burma Shave signs. Any sort of billboard at all."

"Billboards in the sky?" That was Murrumbidgee. "God forbid!"

"How's the beard?" Duke asked.

"Itchy. That's going to be a problem for any guys up here for any long periods."

He passed on over Australia and the Pacific, having the same inconsequential chats with the communicators at Woomera, Canton, Hawaii. He had grown tired of looking at the world below him; the globe had become no more than a familiar road. He had passed over the USSR with the negligent curiosity of a man speeding through dull countryside to a definite destination. From this height Russia and Siberia had no political colour; the clouds below him threw the same shadows as the clouds above America, Africa, Australia. He saw the tundra of Siberia merging into the white cap of the North Pole that merged into the tundra of North America; boundaries were buried beneath miles of ice. He looked down, drowsy with boredom, his mind rocking aimlessly on a tide of ennui. *I am the universal man,* he thought. *The world is me and I am the world. Russia is me, and America, and Europe, Africa, Australia, and all the oceans.* He was compounded of nations and continents; the seas were his blood. He drifted above the symbol of himself, a native only of the country of Man.

He slept again and still again; the capsule had now become no more than a hammock slung between the Poles. He dreamed, of Jane and the children; and woke with a sense of having lost them. The world and reality were gradually slipping from his grasp; there was one horrifying moment, realized only later, when he found himself without any desire to return to earth. For the next hour he talked almost feverishly to the ground stations, clutching at sanity like a man trying to cling to a slippery rope. Something of his emotional disturbance must have got through to those in communication with him.

Duke spoke to him as he came in over the Indian Ocean. "Matt, could we have a medical check?"

He knew that his own voice had given him away. Each pilot, before his flight, had had tape recordings made of his voice so that all communicators might become familiar with his normal way of speaking. His voice was not normal now; and perversely he resented the fact that they should have noticed it. He strained to sound calm and composed; he felt certain none of the physiological checks would give him away. One part of his mind told him he was on the verge of danger, but he couldn't bring himself to call for help. Was pride a reflex action?

He went through the necessary checking procedure. "Have gone through head movements and no effect at all. Reach test, no problem there. My orientation is good. So is my vision——" Ah, his vision was wonderful! What man had ever had such vision? He remembered a poem Jane, trying to teach the children something of Australia, had once recited: *I saw the vision splendid, of the sunlit plains extended, and at night the wondrous glory of the everlasting stars*. He was seeing the world extended, was himself one of the everlasting stars——

"*Columbia Twelve*, this is the surgeon. Have you switched to secondary oxygen?"

"Negative." But then he had passed out of communication with Muchea. Something in the surgeon's voice came through to him, a chill, as if the sub-zero cold of space had got through some chink in the capsule. He checked the secondary oxygen tank and was surprised to find that the supply had declined. The shock sobered him and he came back to earth—He grinned at the old metaphor. He was practical once more, began again to do the job for which he had been sent up here.

The report of the malfunctioning secondary oxygen tank had gone ahead of him. As he passed over Hawaii, the question was asked: "Canaveral wants to know if you want to go through with the re-entry sequence on this orbit?"

"What orbit am I on now?"

"You are completing your seventieth."

"I feel okay to complete full mission. The secondary oxygen tank is down, but the main system seems to be functioning okay. Tell Canaveral I want Go for another five orbits."

When he passed over Canaveral they asked him to check again

with the stations in the Canaries and at Kano, in Nigeria. "Everything is okay," he replied irritably.

"*Columbia Twelve*, everything is not okay. Repeat not okay. We are getting different readings here on your oxygen supply from what you are giving us. Matt—" Raccoli's voice was worried. "Matt, can you feel any of the symptoms of anoxia?"

Anoxia? What was that? All he could feel was a sense of euphoria. Now there was a word. A disease that required no cure. "Euphoria, that's what I feel. Over and out."

Reception was faint, but that did not worry him; rather, he welcomed it. The less he had to do with the people below, the better; he was headed for aloneness such as no man had ever experienced before. He looked up and away from the earth, now dark beneath him, to the heavens, seeking the lodestar that would lead him to eternity. He had said good-bye to everyone, to Jane, the children, his parents, to all the world without regret. He had found what every man sought: peace.

Another voice came at him, worrying him like a snapping dog (why wouldn't they leave him alone? Did they resent his escape to peace? Was envy part of the regret men felt for another man's death?): ". . . *Twelve* . . . Jolson . . ." The voice was faint and gargled. "Jolson . . . oxygen. . . ."

Jolson? Who was Jolson? The name stirred in the sediment of memory. He felt a rub of conscience, that he owed the people below *something*; he made a weary effort to remember the name and what it meant. He carried the name with him across the face of Africa, out of night into breaking dawn; but it meant nothing, the urge to escape only grew stronger. Then another voice was barking at the edge of his mind: "This is Kano . . . *Columbia* . . . Check oxygen . . . Jolson . . . oxygen . . . Jolson. . . ."

The name was suddenly a red light in his brain. He struggled to rise up out of the invisible quicksands that had almost buried him; his body was weightless, but his mind was rooted by the gravity of resignation. His weightless hand, as if by its own volition, moved towards the switch on the secondary oxygen tank. He watched it, detached from it, hating it; did the body, apart from the mind, have its own urge for survival? The hand settled on the switch, and a moment later he heard the hiss as the oxygen entered his helmet. His recovery was almost immediate; now his mind, too, wanted to survive. He checked the main oxygen system and found it was hardly functioning at all; there must be a leak somewhere, but there was no time to find it. The secondary supply tank was also depleted; it, too, must be leaking.

He controlled the flow, allowing the oxygen to enter only his suit and helmet and not chance its being dissipated in the cabin. He could feel the sweat on himself, and he checked to make sure that the temperature of the cockpit had not risen. No, it was normal. He was feeling the sweat of fear.

Kano was still on the air, still faint and barely coherent: "*Columbia* . . . you read . . . .?"

"*Columbia Twelve* to Kano. Can barely read you. You are faint and garbled. Am now on secondary oxygen tank. Am considering re-entry. Warn Muchea. Over."

But he got no reply from Kano, and the next voice he heard was from Zanzibar, also faint: ". . . your batteries . . .?"

"Batteries appear to be dying. Oxygen low. Have decided to re-enter. Inform Muchea."

He was now fully awake, the effects of the anoxia thrown off. He was working swiftly, but without panic. He had been trained for this as much as he had been trained for the successful launching and re-entry; experiments in this field were not based solely upon the prospect of success. At no time in the project's planning had a pilot ever been considered expendable. And he was glad for such a philosophy.

There was no voice coming through to him, which meant almost certainly that his voice in turn was not getting through to Zanzibar or the tracking ship in the Indian Ocean. Nor would it get through to Muchea, upon whom he now had to depend. He began to click out his message on the telegraphic key set, the ultimate back-up for the several radio systems which the capsule carried.

"Am preparing for retro-sequence. Attitude is correct. Zero yaw, 34 degree nosedown." The Indian Ocean was below him now. He had to time the firing of the retro-rockets so that he would not land in the sea. From the moment of firing the capsule would travel 3,000 miles before it landed; it might travel considerably more than 3,000 miles, but never less. It was better to land in the sea than on land—but only if recovery vessels were close at hand. Australia was his target. He went through the pre-retro check list, said a quick prayer, then clicked out his message. "I am about to begin firing."

He put the capsule under manual as well as automatic control, then pressed the switches for the rockets. He felt them fire at the right five-second intervals. As each rocket went off there was a surge, as if the capsule had run into a giant wave in the sky; he had the feeling that he was being hurled backwards, but he knew from the experience of previous pilots that this was illusionary. Deceleration began to increase, and at the same time he felt the G forces beginning to increase. After over a hundred hours of weightlessness, this sudden reversal had its effect on him. It was as if his whole body were being pulped, but from the back and not the front as had happened during launching. He closed his eyes, waiting for the sensation that he and the other pilots called "eyeballs out". His eyeballs pressed against his lids; he could feel the muscles that held the eyes in their sockets being stretched. Then the deceleration began to decrease; at once so did the G forces. And now the heat began to build up.

A bright orange light began to glow outside the capsule window; it was as if he were sitting inside a meteor. The sweat was pouring from him, both from the heat and from fear: this was the worst moment of the whole flight. He tried to steady himself with the thought that if he was going to die it would be all over in a split second; but fatalism did not help at all in a moment like this. All that he had tried to tell Jane that evening long ago when he had first told her of his desire to join the project meant nothing now; only the man without hope, or the saint whose faith was so great it was almost a perversion, admired the reflection in the polished wood of his own coffin. And he was neither the hopeless man nor the faithful saint. He was only one of the millions who clung to life no matter how imperfect it might be.

The heat was still building: he knew that the temperature of the capsule's heat shield would now be 3,000 degrees Fahrenheit. If he did die, there would not even be ashes of him left to mark his passing. He was sweating profusely; it was as if the pressure suit had an inner lining of his own liquid. His mouth, conversely, was dry and rough; his tongue rubbed like sandpaper against his palate. His palate itself was dead; unless fear was really a taste. He made no attempt to communicate with Muchea: even if the batteries had been working, all communications would have been blacked out as he had come through the ionosphere. He had to ride this out alone; sweat it out, literally. He looked out the window, saw that the sky had turned black beyond the glow of the heated capsule. He was startled, puzzled by this sudden darkness; then he saw a flash of light and instantly recognized that he was coming down through a violent high-level storm. With the glow from the capsule and the wild blazes of lightning beyond, it was as if he were re-entering a world that was already doomed: he was the fifth horseman of the Apocalypse, hurtling towards the sound of the last trumpet blown on the field of Armageddon.

Then the capsule began to rock and sway. The heat began to diminish, and now he knew the worst was over. Suddenly he shot out of the storm into a blaze of sunlight that, coming so unexpectedly, almost blinded him. He looked down at the instrument board: time for the drogue parachute to go. His hand went towards the hand switch, when he felt the thump of the automatic mortar that released the drogue 'chute. The swaying of the capsule stopped almost at once. He pumped up the periscope by hand; a moment later the snorkels opened up to let in outside air. Then the main 'chute went out behind him, a long brightly coloured streamer trailing stiffly against the starched blue sky. Everything was working perfectly now. The main 'chute opened, a huge orange and white flower; the capsule slowed with a jolt but the bump was a pleasant one this time. All that lay ahead of him now was the final impact on landing.

He tried to communicate with Muchea, but the radio was dead. He rapped out his call signal on the telegraph key, but there was no time to send more. Rapidly he went through the check list of landing procedure. He unsnapped the plug that connected the biomedical sensors to his suit and body: there was no further need for them now. He disconnected the blood pressure equipment, unhooked the respiratory sensor; from now on the doctors, if they found him alive, could look at him again as a human being, not as a compound of chemical reactions. He broke the oxygen exhaust hose from his helmet and shot a quick glance at the dial on the secondary tank: it was almost empty. He checked the green light that showed his landing bag was ready to take up the shock of the capsule's landing. He knew his batteries were dead, but, because it was part of the landing procedure that he had been learning for months, he pushed the button which was supposed to start the flashing light on top of the capsule and the Sarah beacon on which the recovery force could home in on his position.

Then he said another prayer and sat waiting to come back to earth.

4

"We've lost him," Duke said. "There's no contact at all."

Murrumbidgee swore, but somehow the word did not seem obscene; his mixture of anger and worry seemed to purify it. "Try skin tracking him."

Duke was already doing that: bouncing a radar beam off the surface of the capsule and receiving a reflected signal. That was the theory; in practice now he got no signal at all. He looked up at Murrumbidgee hovering over him like a too-solid dark cloud, almost as if threatening him for having lost contact with Matt. "We've lost him," he repeated. "We don't even know if he got through the heat passage."

"Snap out of it, Duke. We've got to keep thinking optimistically. Let's check the ground track."

Briggs and two other men, Saxe and de Burgh, were already at the plot board with the tracks of the orbits traced on it. "He's kept a steady course up till now." Saxe, a short thin man with a pendulous bottom lip that looked as if it were about to fall off his face, took off his glasses. Duke had noticed he always did this in moments of excitement, as if his eyesight became more acute as the adrenalin increased in his body. "He was on course when he passed Zanzibar. They got enough of a check there to know that."

Duke was abstracted, removed from the hatch of lines that covered the chart like a drawing of rolls of wire. He was *in* the capsule with Matt: he knew what it would be like, much more than the others could know. He looked up as Murrumbidgee spoke sharply to him. "Duke!"

"Sorry. What were you saying?"

Murrumbidgee had a pistol barrel of a finger on the chart. "If he fired the retro rockets here, as that Morse message said he was going to do, we reckon he'd finish up about here——" The finger moved across the Indian Ocean, came to rest at a spot in the western half of Australia. "The Gibson Desert."

"What's it like there?"

"Pretty bloody," said Briggs, pulling at his hair as if trying to remove a wig.

"Worse than that," said Murrumbidgee. "I was looking at the met. reports this evening. Marble Bar, Meekatharra and Kootapatamba, they're the three closest towns to the desert, they were each a hundred and twelve today. It's been over the hundred at Kootapatamba for the past two months."

"What's there in the desert?" Duke asked. "Any cattle or sheep ranches?"

"————" Murrumbidgee's speech was even more obscene than usual, yet strangely it was still unoffensive. At this moment, Duke thought, words meant nothing anyway. Even prayers would be as meaningless as obscenities. He had no faith that Matt had survived. He remembered the effect on himself of anoxia when he had almost died in the US-XP; it had been he who had suggested to Kano and Zanzibar that they try to get through to Matt by mentioning the word Jolson. But there was no guarantee that Matt had been fully conscious when he had begun his re-entry procedure. So Matt could be dead. And he was filled with a sense of blame, clouded but nonetheless hardly bearable. Matt was dead because of him: the chain of blame ran back through the years, its starting point no longer memorable: it was like a long anchor chain whose anchor was buried at the deepest point in a constantly changing sea. He tried to concentrate as Murrumbidgee went on speaking: "We've got to move quick. I'll get on to Pearce——" Pearce was the nearest RAAF station. "Get them to have aircraft standing by for immediate take-off. Les—" He turned to Briggs. "Give me as definite a plot as you can get. I'll have the aircraft in the air in half an hour."

He moved to a nearby phone, while Duke, throwing off his depression under the influence of Murrumbidgee's practical and constructive actions, moved to the huge map of Australia hung on one wall of the control room. "These lakes, do they hold any water?"

De Burgh came across the room. He was a young Dutchman, already balding in his twenties, and he had a look of shock on his face now, as if somehow he had been tricked: his contract hadn't called for the possibility of anyone's death. "Hard to tell. This is the Wet season up there, but there's been no rain for a month inland. These lakes most of the year are just dry clay pans. Then in a good Wet they can look like an inland sea. But they dry up so damned quick—" He shrugged, still looking bewildered. "I'm just glad it's not me that is out there, that is all."

"You think he's out there?"

"Don't you?" De Burgh looked almost imploringly at Duke, and the latter realized he needed reassuring.

He searched for a grain of hope in himself: the search was as hopeless as seeking Matt in the vast expanse of the desert. But he had always been an actor: he put on the mask of optimism, trusting that De Burgh was not too perceptive a critic. "Yes, I think the chances are pretty good that he's made a landing."

Murrumbidgee came back from the phone. "Righto, it's all set. The C.O., he knows that area backwards, he's recommended we use Kootapatamba as a base." He looked at the map. "There. It's a settlement of half a dozen houses and a pub. Mostly well-sinkers and telegraph linesmen live there, plus one or two oldtimers. The airstrip is the main street. We'll fly in extra fuel and stores and operate from there. I'll have them report in to you every half hour. There's a phone line through to there."

"I'm coming with you," Duke said suddenly. "There's nothing I can do here to help—Les and the others can handle it if anything does happen——"

Murrumbidgee hesitated, then shrugged. "Righto, I know how you feel. I don't think I'd want to sit here on my arse if my mate was out there."

As they moved towards the door, Duke suddenly stopped. "How many phones are there in—what's its name?"

"Kootapatamba. One, at the pub. Why?"

Duke turned back to Briggs. "Get them to put a call through to Mrs. Crispin at——" He gave the Crispin number at Cocoa Beach. "Get priority if you can. I'll take the call at the pub in Kootapatamba in—" He looked at Murrumbidgee. "When will we be there?"

Murrumbidgee looked at his watch. "Book the call for 1330. If we're late, tell them to hold it." He and Duke went out of the air-conditioned building into the eye-cracking glare of the day. They put on their dark glasses, like men laying black bandages on bruises. "You're a thoughtful bastard, Duke. I should have put in that call to my sister, and yet it didn't even cross my mind. But she'll appreciate some word from us."

"I wish we could give her more comfort than we're going to."

As they were about to enter the RAAF staff car that waited for them, Murrumbidgee stopped and looked up at the sky: it wrapped the world like a tight faded blue shroud. For a moment his huge shoulders slumped and a bitter agony worked his mouth. "Nobody wishes that more than I do. Jane's happiness means a great deal to me." He got into the car and spoke to the driver. "You have my permission to break the speed limit, Jenkins. You'll be on a charge sheet if you don't."

Twenty minutes later they were airborne out of Pearce in a Canberra bomber. "There are helicopters already on their way," Murrumbidgee said. "I worked out our plan weeks ago. Never thought I'd have to bloody well use it." The bitterness in his voice seemed to be increasing, as if the closer they got to where Matt might be, his hope was lessening. "The Canberras will make quick sweeps over the area along the line of the track. I've got six slower aircraft, they'll criss-cross the track. The choppers I'll use to fill in the spaces between."

Duke had to admire the efficiency with which Murrumbidgee had mapped his search pattern. Matt had often told him of the RAAF's practical skill during the New Guinea operations of World War Two; their standards of navigation, for instance, had surprised the Americans. It was an American boast that American know-how was the world's best; but sometimes Duke doubted it. He knew what the Germans could do when everything went according to plan; their efficiency only fell down when they had to depend upon improvised ingenuity. The French, when they stopped squabbling among themselves and got down to business, could set an example of proficiency that the rest of the world had to admire: there were many pilots, Americans among them, who believed that the Caravelle was the world's best airliner; and if you wanted to be macabre, no better execution machine had been devised than the guillotine. The British had their moments when their inventions still showed the way; the jet engine showed that they had lost none of their old skill when they wanted to shake off the lethargy that seemed to have affected them over the past generation or two. The Italians, the Japanese, and certainly the Russians: they, too, had their practical skills. On his first visit to Australia, last year during Rupe Meredith's flight, Duke had not been too impressed by Australians in general. The men at Muchea had done their job competently enough, but it had been routine and there had been no emergency to test their mettle. They had gone about their job almost casually; Duke had resented their casualness. Now he knew that this was their general demeanour; they did not wear their enthusiasm for a job on their sleeves. He wondered if that would have meant a concession to the boss, whoever he was: something that Murrumbidgee had told him every Australian was congenitally opposed to. Whatever the reason for their casualness, it was no longer apparent. Once this emergency had occurred, they had sprung into action like a well-oiled machine only waiting for the right button to be pushed.

The Canberra put down at Kootapatamba just after one o'clock in the afternoon. Duke had been staring out at the vast glaring landscape stretching away to the edges of the world; every minute he could feel the hopelessness growing in him till he felt ready to burst with it. If Matt had survived a landing here, how could they hope to find him? The deserts Duke had known in the States were nothing compared to this. In every American desert across which he had flown there had always been *some* sign of man: a shack, a paved highway, a wayside gas station, even billboards put up by optimistic real estate developers. As they came in over the tiny town Duke looked north-east, the direction in which they would have to search. The landscape stretched away as barren as the moon, the air dancing above it as if vibrating under the thrust of heat.

Kootapatamba ("It's aboriginal for Waters Where the Eagles Drink," Murrumbidgee explained. "A dry joke, eh?") was no more than as Murrumbidgee had described it. A wide main street of red dirt ran down between a low rambling iron-roofed building that was the pub and half a dozen small cottages that stood lined up like thirsty alcoholics waiting for opening time. Several aircraft stood just on the edge of town; in such a desolate area they reminded Duke of huge buzzards waiting for death to happen. The pilot of the Canberra made a dummy run in over the main street, banked and came back in. When he brought the plane to a halt it was right opposite the pub.

"Precision parking," said Murrumbidgee. "We'll have a beer, then we'll get started."

"I'll see about that call for Jane first."

As he crossed from the plane to the pub Duke was aware of the sun pressing him into the dry dusty anvil of the earth. Though this was the Wet season there was little humidity in the air; the sun scorched his face and arms like the blast from a furnace. A group of RAAF aircrew and some aboriginal stockmen in wide-brimmed hats and scuffed riding boots stood in the shade of the pub's veranda; two women, faded and motionless as two anthills, and several children stood apart from the men. All of them nodded to Duke and Murrumbidgee as the two men walked into the relatively cool cave of the pub's bar.

The pub owner, a thin elderly man with a sun-bleached drooping moustache in a face that looked like a patch of eroded earth, had two glasses of beer waiting on the counter for them. "There's a phone call from America waiting for some bloke named Dalmead." He had a voice like a wind sighing down a dry gully, soft and dusty. Later Duke was to learn the pub owner had lived here in the north-west for fifty years, always in the desert or on the edge of it. "Is that you, mate? Don't forget to ask 'em the charges. America! Stone the bloody crows, I never even ring up Perth, except when we run outa beer."

Duke crossed to the old wall phone, taking his beer with him; his throat was so dry that he doubted if his voice would be any more than a croak over the phone. "Duke?" He was surprised at how clearly Jane's voice came through. "They've given me the news. Have you sighted Matt yet?"

"Not yet." He took a sip of the beer and swallowed. Then he realized the dryness of his throat was not due solely to the heat and dust. He had been afraid of talking to Jane. But there seemed to be no hint of hysterics at the other end of the line, and that made it easier. Only later would he wonder why he had expected hysterics from Jane. "We're just about to begin the search in the area where we think he might be—" He corrected himself, hoping his voice was not as clear to her as hers was to him. "He is. We'll find him within the hour, Jane."

"Don't tell me lies, Duke," she said matter-of-factly. "What are the *real* chances of finding him alive?"

Murrumbidgee was standing beside him, and he handed his beer to the big man: it had suddenly become tasteless. "Jane, we've got this organized as well as it's humanly possible. Murrumbidgee is in charge of the search, so you know he has a personal interest in this. So have I——"

"You still haven't told me what are the chances of finding Matt alive."

He was lost for an answer, and Murrumbidgee abruptly took the receiver from him and pushed him aside. "Jane? This is Tony. Look, we're taking off in ten minutes. I'm not going to say don't worry, because that's bloody silly—it's natural for you to worry. But listen to me—no, *listen*—when they put Matt up there, they designed everything so that we could assume he'd come back safely. Something's gone wrong now, but I'm working on the assumption that he's got back safely. All we have to do is find him. And we'll do that. As soon as we find him we'll bring him back here and put him on the phone to you. Hooroo now. Give my love to the kids." He hung up and turned round. "Righto, let's get cracking. Everyone's got their orders. You and I will stay here and run the search. The choppers should be here within the next hour. We'll go out in one of them if the other aircraft sight the capsule."

Five minutes later the first of the search planes took off down the main street, drawing a long red drogue of dust after it. Duke stood on the rough boardwalk of the veranda watching the plane as it climbed into the cloudless sky. He took off his dark glasses and closed his eyes. The fierce glare of the sun glimmered even through his closed lids, like a film of blood staining his eyes.

"Poor bastard," he heard one of the men nearby say. "I wouldn't give a brass razoo for his chances out there."

Matt lay beneath the rough canopy of the parachute, looking out at the aborigines crouched among the rocks a hundred yards away. There were four of them and they had been there two hours now, ever since he had first crawled out of the capsule.

The impact when he had landed had been much more severe than he had expected. The capsule had landed on the side of a steep boulder-strewn hill. It had bounced and rolled like a giant cotton-reel down the long slope to come at last to rest among a rout of rocks at the bottom of the hill. He had lain on his side in his couch, aware of his ribs hurting as they pressed against his straps. His left forearm was dead and his left hand useless; and he could see the blood running from his knee through the gash in his suit. For a moment he thought that something had happened to his eyes, then he realized that the visor of his helmet had been cracked. He had been vaguely aware of something hurtling about the cockpit as the capsule tumbled down the hill. He saw now that it must have been the camera, which had come loose from its holder; it lay between his feet, smashed wide open, its film snaked out like entrails. Water dripped on his cracked visor from the smashed water container. He was alive, but he was in a mess.

He undid his straps with his right hand and tried to stand up to push against the hatch. He gasped with pain as something bit into his side; he knew then that he had cracked at least one rib. He pushed against the hatch, but it wouldn't budge. All this time he had been working in a daze; he must have sustained a bump on the head during the rough landing. Then abruptly his mind cleared. He sat back awkwardly in the couch, conscious now of the heat inside the capsule; he would have to get out of here soon or he would suffocate. There was no hiss of oxygen coming into his helmet, so that meant the tanks had at last run dry. But air must be getting into the capsule somehow, probably through the snorkels; he realized he was having little difficulty in breathing other than from the pain of his broken rib. He sat back, looked for the plunger that would detonate the primer cord running round the inside of the hatch, found it and pressed it. The hatch blew off, the smoke cleared and he was looking straight up into the fiercest sun he had ever experienced. Its light seemed even brighter than when he had looked at it in space; its heat drove down through the open hatch like a giant piston. He flinched, and for a moment had a wild desire to stay here in the capsule: he was safe here, he did not want to emerge from this womb into a world he did not know. Then abruptly he reached up with his right hand, grasped the hot metal of the capsule, and painfully, with great difficulty, screaming once as the broken bone in his left arm stabbed into the flesh, he clambered out of the capsule and fell down among the rocks.

He lay against the blackened side of the capsule, waves of pain rushing over him. He looked away across the rocks down towards the great plain that stretched away into the haze; the landscape quivered as if some huge explosion had taken place far underground and the shock waves had only just reached the crust of the earth. The metal of the capsule was creaking behind his back, but the tiny sound only heightened the silence that covered this lonely world like a great glass bowl. He turned his head and saw the parachute draped over some rocks. It was ripped, but there was enough of it left intact to make a serviceable canopy.

It took him almost half an hour to make a rough shelter of the 'chute; in all his life he had never experienced such difficulty in moving. At last he had something to break the onslaught of the sun. Then, sick with the pain of his arm and ribs, he crawled back into the capsule, tried the radio and telegraph key, got no answer, and knew then he could offer no help at all to the search parties in finding him. The Sarah beacon was useless and so was the flashing light on top of the capsule. All he had was the mirror from the recovery kit and his flashlight; but the search planes would have to come within visual distance of him before they would be effective. He crawled back under the torn orange bloom of the parachute and sat down to wait, to be rescued or to die.

Then he saw the aborigines. For a moment he thought his eyes were playing him tricks. The dark shapes appeared one by one from behind rocks, not all at once and not close together. He saw a man stand up from behind a large red rock, and even while he was looking at the dark figure ten feet tall silhouetted against the quivering haze behind it, it disappeared. At once another figure, looking even taller, appeared from behind another rock some thirty yards to the right; it stood for a moment, then it too disappeared. Another figure rose up, and another; each in turn disappeared, leaving him staring at the rocks that, in the dancing light, seemed as large and no more substantial than the dark ghosts that had just visited him. *I'm going nuts*, he thought; and felt a moment of terror. Heat madness was not supposed to strike as swiftly as this.

He stood up and stepped out into the full blaze of the sun. The glare from the ground and from the bright exterior of his suit dazzled him; his dark glasses had been smashed to smithereens before the capsule had come to rest. He squinted, peering at the rocks with the concentration of a man trying to prove to himself that he was not going mad. His concentration was repaid: he saw a shadow move behind one of the rocks. He shouted, but got no answer. He shouted again, then began to stagger over the rough ground towards where he had seen the dark shapes.

At once the aborigines materialized, coming up from behind the rocks and instantly moving away from him, swiftly and silently as wraiths. They stopped when he stopped, standing alertly and looking back at him, ready to flee as soon as he moved again. He shouted at them once more. The shout was no more than "Hey!"; he was aware of the ridiculousness of trying to make such a word sound friendly. The shout bounced off the rocks amongst which he stood, splintered and was gone before he was certain that it had reached the natives only fifty yards away. They did not move, but just stood staring back at him. All four of them carried spears, and two of them also carried long boomerangs. They were completely naked, primitive as the original man.

Matt watched them for a moment, then he turned and retreated to the shelter of the parachute canopy. He was sweating profusely, but he could not take off his pressure suit. He had tried to do so once and had almost fainted as he had twisted and the cracked rib had cut into him. He was afraid that if he contorted his body too far, the broken rib might puncture one of his lungs; one result of the training of the past three years was that he knew the geography and working of his body as well as any doctor. He debated whether to cut the suit from himself with his knife, but decided against it; he did not know how cold the nights got here in this desert and in a few hours he might be glad of the suit's warmth. He looked at his watch, but it had been smashed in the collision that had broken his arm; and he knew that the clock in the capsule had also been broken. He glanced out at the sun and guessed it was just past noon.

He lay there beneath the canopy the rest of the afternoon, shifting to stay in shadow as the sun moved down the bowl of the sky. He ate some of the food from the food container he had brought out of the capsule, but his throat was so dry there was no taste to the food. The aborigines had now come out into the open and squatted in front of some rocks fifty yards away. Two or three times he hailed them, trying to make friendly gestures with his good arm, but they did not respond. At this distance through the afternoon glare, it was impossible to tell if the expressions changed on their black bearded faces. He was certain that they did not speak to each other.

Every so often he stepped out from beneath the shelter and scanned the naked sky. Once he thought he heard the distant hum of a plane; he jumped up and at once reeled with dizziness as pain shot up like a blast of flame from his rib. He leaned against the searing hot capsule, hardly aware of its burning him, gasping and wanting to be sick; but there was nothing inside him to come out. He stood on trembling legs, trying to regain control of himself, then he gingerly stepped out into the open and once more looked at the blazing sky. Nothing.

Then almost at his feet he saw the bee hovering over the small clump of withered wildflowers. Its hum came up to him; and he grinned crazily. He raised a boot and stamped on the wild-flowers; the bee shot angrily away. He retreated to the shelter once more, biting the lips that felt like dried paper beneath his teeth. He lay down and stared out at the watching aborigines, hating them for their ability to survive in this bone-arid wilderness.

I'm going to die, he thought; and tasted a bitterness that dried his mouth even more. He was the ultimate symbol so far of man's progress through the ages, he represented Man's achievement as far as it had gone; yet the aborigines out there, the most primitive men on earth, could survive here where he could not. He guessed now why they would not come near him; to them he was some god or spirit or whatever they believed in. But he was *not* a god: like Phaëton he had tried to match the gods and, as Murrumbidgee would say (he grinned at the thought), he had come a gutser. He had driven his chariot across the skies and had come plunging back to earth. Maybe that was why the aborigines would not come near him, they thought he was a fallen god. He looked out at them, waved to them and shouted again through cracking lips, trying to convince them he was as human and fallible as they were. But they did not move, just sat and waited for him to die.

In the late afternoon he saw the plane in the western sky, moving north to south. He did not even try to stand; the plane was too far away for its crew to sight him or even catch a flash from his mirror. He watched it move slowly across the sky, a black moth against the flame of the dying day. He watched it with the detachment of a man watching a moving star that could not in any way influence his life or death.

Dusk moved in over the desert; the aborigines became part of it. The moon came up, grinning sardonically; the stars had the look of the cold eyes of strangers. An army of shadows congregated around him; he looked for the aborigines among its ranks but couldn't find them. Both his arm and his ribs were numb now; only when he moved sharply was there any pain. He lay flat on his back on the hard ground, careless of discomfort; comfort was a luxury that no longer had any meaning. His head was propped on his helmet and he lay staring out across the desert to where it met the star-perforated sky. He was weak from dehydration, and his tongue and throat felt swollen from lack of water. Each time he opened his mouth his lips rubbed against each other like dried leaves.

As the fluid had evaporated from his body, so had hope. Thirst was the taste of defeat: he waited for death to raise its banner. There was no bitterness now that he could not see the aborigines; their ability to survive no longer mocked him; everyone died for a while in the night. They were only a reminder to him of how far Man had come; yet they were also a reminder that Man could never forget his beginnings. He had travelled among the stars, but his boots were still caked with some of the mud from the swamp where he had begun. Yet, he told himself with faint rebellion, that did not mean Man was destined for defeat. The angels would always be there to remind him that he was not immortal; but they wept for him, never laughed at him. He personally had failed in this voyage of discovery (*Columbia Twelve* creaked as the heat left it; he put out a hand and touched it, as if it were a living thing dying like himself); but he was not the end of the line of volunteers for progress. Eternity, infinite space and infinite time, needed meaning; and everything that Man did must help towards that meaning. In the end that meaning could be God Himself, but he was not sure of this: his faith was the faith of the sceptic, that the answer would only come with his own death. But whatever the meaning, Man was the means to it, he was sure of that. He put out a hand and touched the rocks amongst which he and the capsule lay: out of these a cathedral could be built, but it was Man who would give it dedication. Columbus had not turned back because of storms; the exploration of space would not be halted because of what had happened to him. He looked out from beneath the canopy at the stars blinking at him with cold indifference. They were not meant to remain a mystery.

He looked at his watch, forgetting that it was broken. He had no idea of the time; it seemed that it had been dark for hours. Whatever the hour here, it would be tomorrow in Florida. Would Jane and the children have slept this night? The kids perhaps; but not Jane. He felt a sense of guilt as he thought of her, which was why he had tried not to think of her before. Now it was both a pleasure and a punishment to think of her and the children: memory and guilt were twin lashes across the masochist's back. His throat thickened still more: grief was even worse than thirst. He closed his eyes, trying to sleep, but the past was a bright light in his mind: he was being third-degreed by memory. Incidents he had forgotten came back like splinters driven under the finger-nails of his mind; who was it had said that even the sweetest memory was mixed with pain because it was already past? Forgive me, darling, he said; but the cracked dry lips made a mockery of the words: all that came was a hiss, the sound of deceit. How could he ask forgiveness when he was going to die and she had to live on, fighting day after day to stop her love from turning to hatred for what he had done to her? He was no better than the hit-run driver who murmurs Sorry and drives on, leaving his victim crippled in the gutter. He owed Jane more than a confession of guilt; but what was there to offer her? The human heart was too limited.

He slept fitfully, hurtling through a succession of days and nights as the capsule had done. When he woke it was dawn, and the aborigines stood above him against the rising sun. He tried to sit up, but he was too weak. *If they're going to kill me, let it be quick!*

One of the men knelt down beside him and put a small wooden bowl against his lips. The water was cold and sweet; Matt had never tasted anything as good. He looked up inquiringly at the black bearded face above him, and the man smiled and pointed. The metal surface of the capsule glistened with dew; there were smear marks where hands had scooped off the moisture. He nodded to show that he understood, then he slowly eased himself up into a sitting position. His left arm was dead, the numbness now reaching as far as his shoulder. He must have lain on his side some time during the night, because he could now feel the broken rib cutting into his flesh. He unzipped one of the openings in the suit and put his hand inside and felt the warm stickiness on the cotton undersuit; that meant he was bleeding externally and he felt a measure of relief if not of comfort. He wiped his bloodied hand on his suit, and shook his head reassuringly at the aborigines as he saw the look of concern crease their faces. He reached for the food container and took out the five biscuits that remained, glad that there were not less. He took one of the biscuits himself and handed the others to the natives. They hesitated, then as they saw him bite on the biscuit they followed his example. They sat there, the four naked black men and the white man in his now-useless pressure suit, and ate breakfast while the sun climbed up the sky and began to dry out the night-moistened landscape.

When they had finished eating, the man who had given Matt the water stood up. He appeared to be the eldest of the four natives and was evidently their leader. His body was covered in dust and dirt through which scars and sores showed, yet there was an air of pride and dignity about him. This desert was his domain and he had the confidence of a man who would not allow it to defeat him. He said something to the other men in a soft deep voice, then he reached up and began to pull the parachute away from above Matt.

"Hey, cut that out!" The words were a croak that turned into a moan of pain as Matt sat up straighter and the rib cut into him again.

The aborigine smiled down at him, shook his head, then pointed towards the west. He pulled down the 'chute, folded it till it formed a bed about ten feet by six, then laid it beside Matt and motioned for the latter to ease himself on to it.

Matt sat for a moment before moving. He had no idea where they intended carrying him. He knew that the Australian aborigines never built villages as other natives did; they were the complete nomads and there was no word for home in their dialects. So they would not be taking him home, at least not to their home. He was convinced that when the capsule had made its re-entry it must have been off-course; somewhere or other he had made an error in yaw. He could be a hundred or even two or three hundred miles off course either side of the ground track; the search planes might spend days searching for him. Yet the capsule was his best marker; it was what they would look for first. If he left it he might never be found.

Then he looked up at the four aborigines waiting patiently for him to let them carry him to safety. There was concern for him written on their dark faces; but there was no concern for themselves and that finally made up his mind. They did not expect to die nor did they expect him to die. He eased himself on to the parachute and lay back, committing himself to their care. He motioned with his good arm, and one of the aborigines handed him the food container, the mirror and the flashlight. Then another of them, a boy of eighteen or twenty, picked up the helmet. He looked at it curiously, and Matt gestured that it was meant to cover the head. The boy lifted it high, looked up inside it suspiciously, then solemnly and carefully, as if it were a crown, placed it on his own head. At once the other three men broke into uproarious laughter, throwing back their heads so that their teeth flashed like bone knives, beating their sides till the dust rose from their bodies in explosive puffs. Matt, weak, still thirsty, already a little delirious, began to laugh, too, coughing with pain as the rib bit into him.

The four aborigines had laid their spears and boomerangs on top of Matt; he was like a warrior king about to be buried with his weapons. The men bent now and each took a corner of the parachute; gently they lifted him till he hung in the nylon hammock between the pair in front and the pair behind. Then, with the boy still wearing the helmet, all four of them giggling like young girls, Matt moaning softly with something close to hysteria, the small party headed away from *Columbia Twelve*, down the hill and towards the west, out into the vast parched plain that stretched away into the vague shimmering distance like the wild and unexplored shores of space itself.

6

"You look buggered, mate," said the pub owner pulling on the weed of his moustache and peering at Duke with deep concern. "I think a good strong cuppa brew would be the shot. You like it black or white? It's goat milk we put in it, and it ain't homogenized."

"Black," said Duke, and the pub owner went away, calling to one of the black gins out in the kitchen at the back of the pub to bring in some tea. Duke went out on to the veranda and sat down in one of the tattered canvas chairs, putting on his dark glasses against the glare of the street.

"Go easy," said Murrumbidgee, seated on a rough wooden bench against the wall of the pub. "Those chairs won't take any rough handling."

"I'm the same way," Duke said, easing himself gently back

in the chair's threadbare seat. "The last twenty-four hours have been as rough as I ever want."

He had tried to sleep last night after the search had been called off because of darkness. He had been provided with a reasonably comfortable stretcher, but it might just as well have been a bed of nails; in the odd moments when he had slept it had been like lapsing into a feverish coma. Headquarters for the search had been set up in the pub bar, the only room in town big enough to accommodate the radio equipment and the men operating it. Maps had been tacked on the walls beside signs recommending beer as a man's drink—a recommendation that Murrumbidgee had allowed the men to take: "Nobody's going to get drunk in this heat," he told Duke, "and beer's the best thing for replacing the sweat they'll get rid of." The bar's customers had been moved out on to the veranda. "Most customers I've had in here since I took over the pub back in 1920," said the pub owner. "No, it ain't no inconvenience, mate. Glad to do it. I'd be a crook sorta bastard if I said no, wouldn't I? No, let 'em drink out there on the veranda. Do 'em good. Do me good, too, my oath it will. They'll drink more grog out there in that heat than in here in the bar. Have a drink on me, mate."

It seemed that the town had decided to stay awake for the night. Duke had been surprised at the number of people who had congregated around the pub: he would have estimated the town's population at no more than twenty or thirty people. Then the pub owner, a garrulous man who seemed to welcome this opportunity to talk to strangers, told him that stockmen, well sinkers, road maintenance men and one or two gold fossickers ("the old jokers you'll always find out around here") had come into town as soon as they had noticed the movement of aircraft in the district. The men had sat up all night yarning on the veranda; while Duke had tossed on his stretcher their talk had come in to him like the murmur of a slowly trickling stream. He had rolled on his back and listened to them for a while, their flat drawling voices barely understandable at first to his unaccustomed ear. Then gradually he had become used to the flattened vowels, the stretching of one syllable into two, the slang that had a flavour all its own ("a real no-hoper, always going walkabout on me"). As he had listened he had become aware of the fact that for all their casualness, they were concerned for the fate of Matt; they were not just bystanders come in here for some relief from the monotony of their existence here in the desert country. He listened to their yarns of past tragedies and came to understand

326

their philosophy. Death did not disturb them unduly, but they treasured life; their fatalism did not prevent them from enjoying the moment. Enjoyment: the word had an ironic ring; but who was he to pass judgment on another man's way of life? "You wouldn't get me up there in one of them space things," he heard one of the men say. "A bloke wants his bloody head read, taking on a job like that."

The talk had gone on. Occasionally a glass tinkled as the neck of a bottle rested against it; drinking hours in this town went right round the clock. The man on radio duty had dozed in his chair, now and again sitting up to take messages coming in from Muchea, which was relaying them from Canaveral. Once a newspaperman, several of whom had arrived by chartered plane in the late afternoon, came in to phone the story through to his paper in Perth. But the mood of the town was one of quiet patience: nothing more could be done till the sun came up. Murrumbidgee and Duke had discussed whether the search should go on through the night, but had decided against it.

"Sure, he's got a flashlight," Murrumbidgee had said. "But that's all he's got to guide us to him in the dark. I think we can rule out the Sarah beacon and the capsule light—if his batteries were working at all, we'd have picked up some sort of signal. So that leaves the flashlight—and we aren't even sure he's able to work it. He could be still in the capsule, unable to get out. I've got to think of the crews, Duke. They've been flying now for eight hours, and they'll be out again tomorrow at sun-up, flying all day if necessary. Daylight offers the best chance of finding him, so that's when I've got to concentrate what planes I've got."

So the search had been called off at dark and the crews had bedded down beside their planes for the night. And the town had settled down to wait. Duke, listening to the lazy mutter of the voices on the veranda, had been struck by the difference in atmosphere between here and Canaveral. He had been at Canaveral when John Glenn had been launched into orbit; he knew the atmosphere would have been the same there for the beginning of Matt's flight. There would have been an air of suppressed excitement, time measured in minutes and seconds ("T minus ten minutes"; "5-4-3-2-1-zero!"); here, there was an air of resigned patience, time was not even measured in days ("the last time I saw old Ocker was the beginning of the Wet"). If Matt had survived, he would have done more than have circled the earth seventy times; it would be as if he had also travelled back in time, at 18,000 miles an hour, to an earlier, simpler day. He had come back from the frontiers of space to a frontier that no longer existed in many parts of the world. History was laced together by irony.

Now in the glare of the early morning Duke said to Murrumbidgee, "Are you altering the search pattern?"

Murrumbidgee was looking down towards the end of the street where a plane was lining up for its take-off. "I've widened the pattern either side of the ground track. We'll find him today or else."

"Or else what?"

"Or else he didn't make it through the heat passage."

Behind his dark glasses Duke closed his eyes against the thought of Matt's being burned up as he re-entered the atmosphere. He opened them again as the pub owner, followed by an aboriginal gin, came out on to the veranda. Duke took the cup of tea the girl handed him, then moved his chair as the pub owner sat down on another of the rickety chairs. The gin gave Murrumbidgee a cup of tea, then shyly and mutely turned and padded back into the pub.

The pub owner nodded after her. "I've sent for her old man. He lives out in the mulga, but he used to do some tracking for the police. When we had a police station here. He might come in handy."

The plane came roaring down the street, its sound pushing them back against the wall of the pub. Dust fell in on them like a brown breaking wave; when it cleared they saw that the plane was airborne. Another plane was now taxi-ing into line at the end of the street.

"This black tracker," Murrumbidgee explained to Duke. "It mightn't be a bad idea if we took him along in one of the choppers. They're uncanny, these fellers. They'll leave a dog for dead when it comes to following a trail."

The second plane came bursting down the street, and a third and a fourth. Each plane waited till the dust raised by the previous one had settled; but in less than fifteen minutes all the planes were airborne. Duke watched them disappear into what seemed to him the biggest sky he had ever seen; tiny dark insects that disappeared in the vast glare even as he watched them. Their numbers seemed so inadequate for the job that faced them; he would have filled the sky with planes. Now the helicopters were taking off from the end of the street.

"I'm keeping one chopper standing by," Murrumbidgee said. "In case you and I have to go out."

The morning wore on. Duke went back inside and listened to the reports from the planes as they came in over the radio. Muchea was constantly on the air, asking for progress reports that could be relayed to Canaveral; but there was nothing to report. Once Duke passed the phone and hesitated for a moment, wondering if he should put in another call to Jane. He looked across the bar and Murrumbidgee came towards him.

"Leave it, Duke," the big man said, guessing his thoughts. "If they call her to tell her there's a call coming through from Australia, she'll expect it to be either good news or the worst. Either way it will be a disappointment, or anyway a let down, if it's just you telling her there's been no change. We'll call her when we know something." He turned and led the way out on to the veranda. "Come and meet Right Hand Plonk."

An old grey-bearded aborigine stood in the shade of the veranda. He wore a torn and battered stockman's hat, a faded red shirt and a pair of moleskin trousers through which his knees showed like the dark heads of a pair of snakes. His bare feet splayed out beneath the tattered ends of his trouser-legs, his broken toes looking like encrustations growing on two black rocks. His left hand was missing, cut off at the wrist, but the right hand that he put out to Duke had the strength of a young man in it.

"G'day, boss." His voice was the deepest and roughest Duke had ever heard, as if the man were imitating a rock slide he had once heard.

Duke acknowledged the greeting, then went back into the bar with Murrumbidgee. "Right Hand Plonk?"

"Plonk is the Aussie name for cheap wine. Evidently Right Hand had a liking for it once. So did his brother. He was known as Left Hand Plonk. People give the abos all sorts of queer names up here. I remember——"

"Commodore Finn!" An RAAF sergeant standing by the radio turned excitedly and called across the room. "They've sighted the capsule!"

Murrumbidgee and Duke hurried across the bar, stood by the sergeant as the operator ordered the air to be cleared. "Okay, C for Charlie. Go ahead."

The voice came in clearly, as if the man were standing just outside the door: "We've sighted the capsule. No sign of life anywhere near it. The navigator is working out the position—here it is——"

The sergeant jotted it down, then crossed quickly to the map between the beer signs. "There, sir." He made measurements, then turned back to Murrumbidgee. "About ninety minutes' flying time in a chopper, sir."

"Righto," Murrumbidgee said. "Zero the other choppers in on it. Tell C for Charlie to hang around till we get there. Righto, Duke, let's get the finger out." As they came out of the pub door he snapped his fingers at the old aborigine leaning against one of the veranda posts. "Come on, Right Hand. We might need you."

They were airborne in less than five minutes. Murrumbidgee sat beside the pilot, and Duke sat in the back with Right Hand Plonk. Duke had expected the old aborigine to be frightened, but Right Hand was beaming through his beard.

"Bloody good, boss," he croaked. "Better 'an walkin'."

They came in over the wrecked capsule in the full blaze of noon. The helicopter put down at the bottom of the hill and Duke and Murrumbidgee jumped out. They raced up the hill and by the time they reached the capsule they were covered in sweat. Murrumbidgee, out of condition and carrying too much weight, leaned against the side of the capsule, wiping the sweat from his face and panting.

"Well, we know he got down alive." He gasped for breath, then straightened up. "Depends on how far he's gone now."

"I can't understand why he left the capsule," Duke said.

Murrumbidgee glanced up, squinting against the fierce glare of the sun. "You and I haven't been out here, Duke, for a whole day. He might be off his head by now. I wouldn't bet on remaining sane too long in this heat." He looked down the hill, put finger and thumb between his teeth and let out a piercing whistle. "Now we'll see how good Right Hand Plonk is."

The old aborigine came clambering up through the rocks. He listened to Murrumbidgee for a moment, then he began to search around amongst the rocks. He went down the hill, walked out a little way on to the plain, then came back up the hill to where the two white men still waited by the capsule.

"They bin gone that way, boss." He pointed out into the desert. "Four black fellers. They bin walkin' pretty heavy. Maybe carryin' somethin'."

"Can you follow their tracks?"

"Too right, boss." The old man didn't look hurt; he didn't have to prove himself to these white men. "Easy."

"Get going then." Murrumbidgee turned back to Duke as the old aborigine went down the hill. "He can get started. We'll

330

catch him up in the chopper. Anything you want to get out of this thing?"

This thing: to Murrumbidgee it was no more than another vehicle: the important thing was the man who had been in it. *And he's right*, Duke thought. No matter how much progress was made, Man would always be more important than the machines he invented. "We'll take the whole capsule back to Muchea with us. Here come the other choppers." He nodded towards the north where three helicopters were bearing in on them. "These guys can take it back to Kootapatamba, put it aboard a plane there."

"You want to stay, make sure they do the job properly?" Duke was looking down towards the plain, out at the small dark figure of the old black plodding away into the haze. Murrumbidgee followed his gaze. "Righto, I'll stay here. Give my regards to Matt. Tell him I'll buy him a beer if he's in a fit condition to swallow it."

Duke nodded, then ran down the hill to the helicopter. The pilot, a cheerful young man whose nose was a white cherry of zinc ointment in the brown plate of his face, started up the engine.

"Brings you back to earth, doesn't it?" The blades started rotating, the helicopter climbed and began to head slowly out over the desert after the ambling figure of Right Hand Plonk. "We've got to employ an old blackfeller to find for us a man who's just been half-way to the moon. It's a nice lesson in humility. But then they never give a Nobel Prize for humility, do they?"

They put down twice to give the old man a drink and a chance to rest for a few minutes in the shade of the helicopter. Each time Duke got out and looked at the hard baked ground, unable to discern even a heelprint. "You sure you're on the right trail, Right Hand?"

"Too right, boss," the old man croaked. "They bin goin' this way all the time."

"Well, why not get back into the chopper with us and we'll just follow this line? We could make better time."

The old aborigine pondered for a moment, making sure he had got what Duke had said. Then he shook his head. "Better not, boss. I dunno this part of the country too much. Maybe black-fellers——" He made a gesture with his hand, indicating that the men he was trailing might have decided to strike off at a tangent. "We'll find 'em, boss. Don't worry."

His confidence was not false optimism. They found the four aborigines and Matt in mid-afternoon, resting in a dry gully by a clump of huge red rocks. The aborigines had stretched the parachute out to form a shelter, and the five men lay in its shade. The natives ran out as the helicopter, sweeping ahead of the old black tracker, came down the gully. They stood for a moment staring up at the strange bird with its whirling wings, then they fled in terror up the gully. The helicopter settled down and Duke leapt from it and raced towards the parachute shelter.

Matt lifted a bearded and blistered face in which the smile looked like a grimace of pain. "What kept you, chum?"

Duke nodded, grinning idiotically, choked with an emotion that he had never experienced before. All through the last twenty-four hours he had been wondering what sensations would pass through him when they found Matt, either dead or alive. He was not prepared for the flood that churned up in him now. It was as if he had stepped through a thick wall and found the other half of himself that had been missing all his life. He said a prayer of thanks, speaking silently to a God whom he had so long ignored, and reached out a hand to Matt, the bright companion of his life.

CHAPTER NINE

"DADDY, may I borrow your car tonight?" Caroline said. "John and I are going to a party over in Hyannis-Port."

Duke looked at the two of them. "Who's taking whom?"

"She's meeting her date at the party," John said. "He doesn't have a car."

"What about your date?" said Matt. "Does she have a car?"

"A TR-4. She lets me drive it. She's a beauty."

"The girl or the car?" Jane asked.

John grinned. "Oh, the girl's all right, too."

As the boy and the girl ran back towards the water, Matt called after John, "Watch out for dryads in the wood tonight!" But John didn't hear him, and Matt lay back on the sand beside Jane, Cleo and Duke. "Those two would be a nice pair if they ever got together."

"They never will," Jane said. "Caroline is already too old for John. You ought to know that a girl is a woman at eighteen. I was only a year older than Caroline when I trapped you. I'm supposed to have trapped you, aren't I?"

"That was how it was," said Matt, loving her even more now than he had loved when she was nineteen. There was no gulf between them now; only now, when he had virtually retired from the astronaut team, had she come to realize what had driven him to join it. She did not condone his ambition, but at least now she understood it. Or said she did; and he did not know nor did he care if that were no more than feminine diplomacy. Whatever secret doubts she still held, they were no longer expressed. They had reached a stage where their love was impregnated against the rot of doubt, where each lived his or her life for the other. He knew it had always been that way with her, but the balance would be his way from now on. He owed her that for the days of her life she had lost while he had been in orbit and then missing in the Australian desert. When he had returned to the States it had been as if she were welcoming someone back whom she had already given up for dead. It was the one and only time he had seen her break down into hysterical sobbing, and it had been an experience he had sworn then that neither of them would have to go through again.

"I thought I was going to the movies with you," he said. "Instead, I found myself at St. Mary's Cathedral. I remember thinking as we walked up the steps, Boy, what a movie house! We must be going to see one of those Biblical epics——"

"Righto," said Jane, smiling at him, saying a silent prayer behind the smile for what God had given her. "Enough of your dirty anti-Catholic propaganda."

Beside them, Duke looked down the beach at his daughter, the woman of eighteen. Then he turned to Cleo, who lay beside him, lazy as a great blonde cat in the sun. "How do you feel, having a fully grown woman for a daughter?"

Cleo smiled, gently snapping her teeth at him as if she would like to bite him. "Darling, I'll never feel old. Some day I may look old, absolutely *senile*, but I'll never *feel* it." She sat up, stretching her arms, then slowly stood up, brushing the sand from herself. She was almost forty and plump, but, Duke thought with pride and love, she could still wear a swimsuit without risk of being charged with indecent exposure. The duchess thighs hadn't developed and her bosom was still reasonably firm; her jawline had begun to soften, but her eyes and mouth were still young. She was in the middle of her life, still enjoying it, still expectant of the future. "Time to be getting back to help your ma-in-law with the lunch, Jane. The men can bring the children up later."

The two women gathered up their towels and went up the beach towards the Crispin house. It was August and both families had come up here to Cape Cod for the month. Matt had recovered from his ordeal in the Australian desert; his broken bones had knitted without any after-effects. Despite the inglorious ending to the orbital flight, *Columbia Twelve's* mission had been successful. The plan had been no more than a further progression of the original objective of Project Mercury: To determine man's capabilities in a space environment. Matt had proved that, on the properly trained man, prolonged weightlessness need have no effect; the Russians had already proved the same before him, but there was no experiment that did not benefit from further evidence. He had proved, too, as no one had before him, that utter solitude, if not prolonged indefinitely, need not make a vegetable of a man. The fibres of his mind had held, and he could, if he wished, take pride in the fact that he had come through a test that other men had yet to face.

Both men were now stationed back at Langley, in Virginia. They were still members of Project Mercury, but eventually they expected to be transferred back to normal Air Force duty. They were both full colonels, old men as far as flying men went, and soon they would have to make way for younger men. Already Project Mercury was routine, and already the team for Project Gemini, the two-man capsule plan, was in training. They in turn would be succeeded by the men of Project Apollo: the moon was no more than a few years away. The world was reaching out towards the rest of the universe, taking its place in the neighbourhood of stars. But the same tide rolled in on this tiny Massachusetts beach as had come in here for centuries and, come Moon, come Mars, the Crispins and the Dalmeads would keep coming back here, looking for yesterday's footprints on the tide-washed sands.

"I'll retire here," Matt said, looking down across the beach to where his children and Duke's child swam in the apple-green water. "It's still home to me."

"Cleo and I have already begun looking for a place." Duke looked along the beach at all that remained of the wreck. Only a few broken ribs now showed above the sands: the worms of time and storm were slowly eating it away. "I'd liked to have seen my grandkids playing on that old wreck. But it won't last that long."

"Nobody wants to play Leif Ericsson any more. I was listening to two young kids down here yesterday. One of them had on a space helmet, he was yelling that he wanted to be *me*. I'm Colonel Crispin, he kept shouting, just like you used to yell you were Leif Ericsson. I was flattered at first, then, I don't know why, I got annoyed. Finally, I was sorry for the kid. Don't ask me why.

But somehow it just seemed to me that there had been more romance in our lives. Maybe the kids of today don't want the romance of the past. But I'm sorry for them that they're missing it. The fantasy of the future is all right, I guess, but we can't learn anything from it."

"You reckon we learned anything from Leif Ericsson, all those other explorers we used to play at when we were kids?"

"Don't you think we did?"

Duke stared out at the sea, trembling under the summer haze, saw the mirage of Europe beyond the horizon, whence the old explorers had come. "Sure we did. But don't write yourself off, son. There'll come a day when some kid, reading about you, will learn a thing or two. Murrumbidgee once said something to me, that too many people suspected the intelligence of posterity. I shouldn't fall into the same trap, son. Posterity isn't going to be made up of dopes. And despite what you think of today's kids —and I don't know that they're to be blamed, history has never moved as fast as it is right now—I think posterity will always have a yen for the romance of the past. And some day you'll be part of that romance."

Matt looked sideways at him, diffident about putting the question in his mind. The last few months had been everything Duke had always wished for: a reception by the President, an appearance before Congress, a ticker-tape parade up Broadway, cover stories in magazines, interviews on television, recognition every time he walked down a street. But it had all happened to *him*, not to Duke. "Duke, are you sorry you missed it all?"

Duke continued to stare out to sea, then slowly he nodded. "I'd be a liar if I said no. But not the glory, I'm not regretting I missed that. Somehow that doesn't matter any more. But I'd like to have been a part of history. Not to be remembered by some kid in the future. But for what I'd have felt in here while I was doing it—" He tapped his breast. "You remember your Browning from English Lit.? *Aye, but a man's reach should exceed his grasp; Or what's a heaven for?* I'd liked to have reached, that's all."

There was nothing to say. *I was one of the lucky ones*, Matt thought; and wondered why. History was studded with accidents: accidents of time, of geography, of human nature. History was made by heroes, by cowards, by fools, by ordinary men like himself. And in the end history was the autobiography of Man, of him and by him. It was the record of lives as numerous as the stars, of hope not yet strangled by despair, of faith entangled

335

by doubt but still alive, of hearts vexed by misery but still not admitting defeat. He and Duke had written their own paragraphs, and if his should have more lustre than Duke's, it did not matter, at least not to him. They had flown their chariots into the face of the sun, and advanced Man another step out of the darkness. He looked down the beach, saw Caroline, John, Bunty and Stevie running up out of the water, part of the unwritten chapters of the future.

And he knew then that there were more ways of reaching for heaven than making history. And Duke, whether he knew it or was not confessing it, had also reached for heaven. Caroline, coming up the beach, glistening with water in the bright sun, full of life and promise, smiling at her father with love, was not a symbol of failure.

"You've had your moments, chum," he said.

Clareville Beach, N.S.W.
August 1962-March 1963